The Oyster
Volumes V and VI

ANONYMOUS

BLUE MOON BOOKS
NEW YORK

The Oyster, Volumes V and VI

Copyright © 1990, 2006.(Vol. V) by Glenthorne Historical Associates
Copyright © 1991, 2006 (Vol. IV) by Potiphar Productions

Published by
Blue Moon Books
An imprint of Avalon Publishing Group, Inc.
245 West 17th Street, 11th floor
New York, NY 10011

First Blue Moon Books Edition 2006

ISBN: 1-56201-508-7
ISBN-13: 978-1-56201-508-4

9 8 7 6 5 4 3 2 1

Printed in Canada
Distributed by Publishers Group West

THE OYSTER
VOLUME V

INTRODUCTION

This salacious, entertaining selection of material from *The Oyster* well illustrates the decadent, *fin de siecle* image we have of upper class society in the late Victorian era. In spite of the stifling morality of the times there were days (and nights!) of endless sauciness, a long round of gaiety for the privileged few. These were years of high jinks and low necklines and at the centre of it all was HRH the Prince of Wales.

As Godfrey Smith has commented: 'What made the Nineties naughty was a small coterie of rich, idle and sexy men and women whose life revolved around Albert Edward, Prince of Wales . . . his entourage widened over the years to admit some cosmopolitan and raffish figures: adventurers, bounders, philanderers, mistresses, courtesans and actresses.'

Yet hand in hand with the fun-loving frolics of the very highest came the gospel of smug, often aggressive puritanism. A doctrine was preached of sexual abstinence and of celibacy as a desired state. Even within marriage only the minimum sexual activity was allowable and then solely for the purpose of procreation and in no way was the activity to be enjoyed simply for its own sake!

Naturally, this suppressive attitude found a mirror image in the forthright celebration of sexuality that was reflected in the growth of underground magazines such as *The Oyster* or *Cremorne Gardens* that flourished during the last two decades of Queen Victoria's reign.

Many of the authors who contributed to these journals were journalists working on the fledgling popular newspapers that were burgeoning around this time.

Interestingly enough, the letters section of *The Oyster* were edited by Jenny Everleigh, whose own risqué diaries have recently been republished and Doctor Jonathan Arkley, who was called in privately by the Prince of Wales in 1892 to treat some unknown ailment that must have baffled the Royal Family's own physician Sir James Reid.

Doctor Arkley's 'Ask Doctor Jonathan' advice column was perhaps the most popular regular feature in the magazine. As Professor Alan Haley noted in his preface to *The Oyster 4* (New English Library, London 1989): 'Ignorance of even basic knowledge about sexuality was far more widespread than today and the agony column of Doctor Arkley provided a valuable conduit of information.'

The handsome young doctor was a leading light in the fast South Hampstead set whose members included Sir Ronnie Dunn, Sir Lionel Trapes and Colonel Cripps of the West Kents. But even his connections with the highest in the land could not save him from the consequences of seducing almost every pretty feminine patient who entered his surgery in Harley Street. After a cuckolded husband threatened to report him to the authorities, the randy doctor ceased practising and spent several years working in medical research in Europe and in the United States of America.

The letters to the editor of *The Oyster* (some written to Doctor Arkley and some simply penned for the delight of the writer and his or her reader) were often sent with instructions for a *nom de plume* to be printed, although several correspondents were happy to allow their full names and addresses to be published.

Perhaps, as Professor Cuthbertson of Glasgow suggests, the devotees of *The Oyster* believed themselves to be members of a loosely organised club and that members of the general public were excluded from this close, private circle. For so limited and exclusive was the circulation of this illicitly published magazine that the use of real names became a daring indulgence, a kind of curious private joke amongst the cognoscenti. And it is true that 'London Society' consisted of a very small group indeed. In his seminal work on horse racing in the latter half of the nineteenth century, Dr Loring Sayers estimates that all the people who 'mattered' in London could have fitted into the Prince of Wales' luxurious ballroom at his Marlborough House residence. And in the country as a whole, most of the political and social influence as well as wealth was concentrated in the hands of six or seven hundred land-owning families, many of which were closely interlinked through timely semi-arranged marriages.

It was a proud boast of *The Oyster* that all letters printed in its pages were uncensored and their contents are indeed explicit. This is bawdy writing without inhibition even by today's more liberal standards. Sexual adventure presses hard on the heels of sexual adventure and the sheer energy and variety of these frolics could become exhausting were it not for the high-spirited imagination and — more often perhaps in the case of the female scribes — frank and occasionally amusing wit displayed by the authors. This selection of letters shows that beneath those swelling but high-buttoned bodices, under that waistcoated, upright worthiness, there was an eager and inventive appetite for sexual pleasure, even in the most unlikely places.

For the social historian the letters pages of *The Oyster* show that the magazine provided a platform of resistance to the suffocating, guilt-ridden climate in which they first appeared. In the words of Antoinette Hillman-Strauss: 'They set themselves firmly against the notion that sexuality was an area over which the Establishment should exercise a stringent, rigid control and this led to a more sceptical questioning attitude which in turn brought about the more relaxed and liberal philosophy that by and large exists today.

'Copies have fortunately survived to delight and amuse us as well as to provide an unusual and unconventional insight into the manners and mores of a vanished world, the reverse side to the coin of iron-clad respectability which appeared to characterise British society one hundred years ago.'

Godfrey Fulham
Nairobi
November, 1990

He who loves not wine, woman and song
Remains a fool his whole life long.

Attributed to Martin Luther

LETTERS TO THE EDITOR

From Colonel Leon Standlake

Sir,

Being a shareholder in the Mersey Railway Company, last week I accepted an invitation from the joint contractors of the Mersey Tunnel, Major Isaac of London and Waddells of Edinburgh, to descend the shafts of the tunnel and inspect the works beneath the river now that they have been practically completed. Readers may care to note that the excavations have amounted to more than twenty thousand cubic yards, all got out by hand.

The project was first mooted twenty-five years ago but the excavations have been dogged by many difficulties. However, since Professor William Bucknall's famous boring machine got to work three years ago, progress has been swift and very shortly the tunnel will be opened to the public.

Afterwards, along with a group of other major shareholders, I was invited to dine with the Lord Mayor of Liverpool at the Adelphi Hotel and stay the night at that august establishment as a guest of the Company. Naturally, after descending into the bowels of the earth, so to speak, I decided to run myself a bath before dinner. I began to undress but whilst pulling out my bathrobe from my valise I noticed that a handsomely bound book had been placed at the bottom of the bag. This was most curious as I had not instructed my valet, Stanley, to pack any reading material for me. I picked up the book and opened it to find that a card had been clipped onto the first pages.

11

Who could have sent this to me? I unclipped the plain white card which read: 'Leon, in case you get bored in Liverpool, I thought you may care to see the latest selection of French photographs just published by Monsieur Pierre Breslau of Paris. All best wishes — Rodney.' Now all was clear! You see, just a few days beforehand I had invited Sir Rodney Burbeck and his current amorata to spend a few days in London as my house guests, and the wealthy baronet must have surreptitiously smuggled this much-sought-after new book over from France. How kind of Rodney to give me a copy, I mused, as Monsieur Breslau's books are highly prized by the cognoscenti.

I sat down on the bed and browsed through the pages which were full of coloured photographs of the most lascivious evolutions of *l'arte de faire l'amour*. There were naked youths and girls with their cocks, pussies and bottoms displayed as they frigged, sucked and fucked in all kinds of varied positions. Perhaps my favourite was one of a most beautiful dark-skinned girl seated on the lap of her lover. Between her voluptuous thighs her cunt is seen delightedly engorged with his thick standing prick. Her arms are round his neck and her face is turned up, beaming with the satisfaction she is experiencing in her well-filled cunney.

Another showed a handsome couple dancing together, the boy pressing the soft bum cheeks of his partner who is holding his stiff prick in a tender, loving grasp. In the next plate the buxom beauty is shown lying nude on a bed, her legs apart with her splendid cunney protruding its full rounded lips from the midst of a covering of crisp curly hair, whilst the crimson crack between gives promise of a warm reception to his stiff standing prick which she has in her hand.

'I wouldn't mind taking his place for an hour or two,' I murmured to myself. And then I almost jumped out in shock! For a sweet feminine voice chimed out: 'And I wouldn't mind changing places with the girl either.'

I swivelled round to see who had entered my room unannounced and unbidden. No, it was not one of the sneak thieves who make a speciality of breaking into hotel bedrooms, but simply a very pretty young chambermaid, a slim young girl of no more than eighteen years of age, I judged, who sported a mane of long black hair, a pair of large blue eyes and a pretty retroussé nose.

She brushed back her hair sensuously as she said: 'Oh, I am so sorry to have startled you, Sir. I came in to turn down the bed but you failed to hear me.

'That must be a very absorbing book, Sir. May I have a look at it?' I nodded and the little minx sat down on the bed next to me and reached over to take the book. As she did so, her hand brushed against the bulge in my undershorts. 'She is a lucky girl,' said the maid softly. 'Just look at her aroused nipples, her luscious lips, she is just ready and waiting to be fucked.'

'I like the look of her too,' I said hoarsely and, before I could say anything more, this sweet girl pulled out my cock from my drawers and started pulling the swollen shaft up and down. Nothing loath, I unbuttoned her blouse and found that she was wearing nothing underneath! I began massaging her beautifully rounded breasts and then I pulled her skirt up with my other hand and soon we were locked in a passionate embrace.

'I've time for a quick one if you have,' she said softly, so lifting her in my arms I placed her on top of the bed. Soon we were fully nude and I started by sucking her breasts and massaging her clitty and pussey lips with my long fingers. I raised her legs and rested them on my shoulders as she directed my cock to her juicy pussey. I fucked her in my most favoured fashion, alternating slow and fast rhythms, responding to her thrusts. We were voyagers on a journey to the seventh heaven of fucking as I kissed her luscious lips and sucked her long, hard nipples. She exploded with multiple orgasms and my own pleasure was heightened by her moans and sighs. I pounded home the strokes faster and faster as we rocked together, climbing to almost unimaginable heights as my raging prick slid now uncontrollably in and out of her sopping love channel.

She moved excitedly under me as my prick jerked inside her and I could see by her wriggles of delight how much

13

she was enjoying this glorious surprise fuck and she panted: 'Oh Sir, how nice, how lovely, oh, how I am spending! I can feel my juices gushing. A-h-r-e, now, now, spunk into me!' I prolonged the pleasure for as long as possible, slowing down my thrusts to feel the delicious throbbings of cock and cunney in their perfect conjunction, but nature was not to be denied and I soon shot a copious stream of creamy white sperm inside her cunney as we swam in a mutual emission, both of us being so overcome by our feelings that we almost swooned in our ecstasy.

We would both have preferred to stay in bed for a repeat performance, but such a desire could not be granted as Sally (for we exchanged names after the fuck) had work to do and I could not excuse myself from attending the Lord Mayor's Dinner as I had accepted the invitation to propose the loyal toast.

I must note here what splendid fare we were offered at dinner. After a delicious thick vegetable soup I relished some excellent poached turbot followed by a selection of roasts: beef, mutton and fowl. But the highlight was a dessert of a succulent array of peaches, plums, apricots, nectarines, raspberries, strawberries, pears and grapes all grouped in generous pyramids among the flowers that adorned the buffet table.

So I was quite tired by the time I climbed into bed later that evening. I fell asleep almost immediately and I dreamed about fucking Sally again, sliding my cock into her wet pussey as I fondled her full breasts, and kissed her neck and shoulders from behind. Then I lay back and let the dear girl suck my cock to full erection before she mounted me.

Amazingly, awakening from my slumber, I realised that this was no dream! I was lying on my back and I could see and feel a girl bouncing up and down on my prick! I tried to speak and reached for the lamp but my lips were sealed with soft hands and a sweet little voice murmured: 'It's all right, it's only Sally. Everything is just fine.' Then she kissed me as she rode my cock and I fondled her stalky nipples, rubbing them to stiffness against the palms of my hands. Faster and faster she rode and as she cried out with joy, she spent and I felt her warm love juices trickle down my shaft.

She started to gyrate her hips round and round and I grabbed her bum cheeks as I jerked upwards to meet her downward thrusts. Her lithe young body slipped up and down on my throbbing length, taking every last millimetre of my shaft deep into her pussey and the continuous nipping and contractions of her cunt soon brought me to a climax. I tried at first to hold back but I could feel the hot spunk boiling up in my balls and I crashed powerful jets of love juice up into her womb as she moved her hips faster and faster. The feel of her beautiful body rocking to and fro kept my cock hard even though I jetted spurt after spurt of spunk, filling her cunney with my cream. Gad! What an Elysian spend!

Yet still this highly sexed girl remained unsatisfied! She lay panting next to me, her long dark tresses shimmering in the moonlight that poured in through the window. She stretched and arched her back, caressing her pert young breasts and moving her legs suggestively as I placed my hand on her crisp, damp bush. I licked my lips and moved over to kiss her white belly and then ran my tongue lower, through the tickly pubic moss. My hands circled around her glorious bum cheeks as I buried my head between her thighs and drew her against me. My tongue found her glistening crack and she gasped and shivered as I found her clitty immediately and began to roll my tongue around the erectile piece of flesh.

'Oh! Oh! Leon, you suck clitty marvellously. That's gorgeous, gorgeous!' she cried out. 'Now let's try something else!' And with those words she wriggled herself onto her belly and twitched her rounded bum cheeks provocatively at me. Despite our previous exertions, my cock swelled up again at the sight of this lovely naked girl and I gave my shaft a little rub to bring it to its fullest stiffness.

Yet I hesitated for a moment as she pushed her bum upwards and opened her legs to give me a good view of her bum-hole. I looked at it for a moment and then placed my knob, which was still wet from our spendings, to the entrance of the puckered little rosette. 'Yes, yes, Leon,' she panted. 'Go on, go on, I want a nice thick length of cock up my bum. Go carefully though and we'll have a lovely bottom fuck.'

I angled her legs a little further apart to afford a better view of her little wrinkled nether orifice and gently eased my knob between her cheeks. At first I encountered a difficulty but then her sphincter muscle relaxed and I slid my cock in and out of the tight sheath, plunging in and out of the now widened rim as she reached back and spread her cheeks even further, jerking her bum in time to my rhythm as I wrapped one arm around her titties, frigging each of them in turn, and snaking my other arm round her waist I was able to finger-fuck her pussey to afford her a double pleasure.

Her bottom responded gaily to every shove as I drove home, my balls bouncing against her smooth rounded cheeks. I worked my proud prick in as far as it would go and I enjoyed a delicious tingling as I corked her to the very limit. I moved in and out as she worked her bum to bring me off in a flood of gushing spunk that both warmed and lubricated her delicious backside. As I spurted into her I continued to work my prick back and forth so that it remained stiffly hard until, with an audible plop, I withdrew from her well-lathered sheath.

'That was very nice indeed, Sally,' I said with genuine solicitude. 'I always worry a little about suggesting a bottom fuck myself as unless performed with care it can be painful for the lady.'

'Thank you for being so thoughtful, my dear. I wouldn't like to be cornholed every day but it makes a pleasant change now and then,' she smiled. 'Do you know something, I am rather thirsty. Now I hope you will excuse the impertinence but I took the liberty of ordering a bottle of iced champagne to be sent to your room. I brought it up myself and I hope you don't mind too much.'

'Of course not, Sally! So long as it's a good vintage,' I laughed.

Now the champagne (a Moet and Chandon '82)

invigorated me to a further bout which began with a lovely kiss and cuddle. We lay in a comfortable *soixante neuf* with Sally's thighs clasped round my head and her spunk-coated pussey lips pressed firmly against my mouth. As I licked up the morsels of our previous repast, she sucked my cock up to yet another fine erection and licked around that ultra-sensitive area between my arsehole and my balls. Then she moved her wicked little tongue up my cockshaft to my helmet, flicking at it with the very tip so expertly that I could feel my balls tightening and my prick swelling up to a rock-like hardness.

I slowly entered her until my prick was in to the hilt and I stayed still a moment, savouring to the full the delicious little contractions of her cunt as it welcomed my cock into its portals. I don't think I have ever experienced a more soothing, moist, warm home for my throbbing prick.

We started moving together and Sally treated me to a long, slow fuck as I glided my shaft in and out of her pulsating pussey. Then we raised the tempo and our lips meshed together as our bottoms began to work in unison. How tightly her cunt enclasped and sucked upon my prick! We gloried in each giant thrust as her juices dripped onto my balls as they banged against her bum. She implored me to drive deeper by twirling her tongue in my mouth and, cupped now in my broad palms, her bum cheeks rotated eagerly as my trusty tool rammed in and out and she cried out with joy at the stinging excitement of my thick prick driving furiously into her soft depths. I felt the white froth spurt upwards and Sally gave a little yelp of pleasure as the hot creamy spunk flooded and I felt her shudder as she drained me of every last drop of love juice.

She let my now limp tool slide out of her before covering me with kisses and we fell exhausted into a deep sleep. Luckily Sally was not on duty until two o'clock the next day for we did not wake up until half past eight in the morning. In order to keep our assignment secret from the hotel management, we shared the large breakfast that I ordered to be sent up to my room and Sally hid in the bathroom when it was brought in.

Although she asked for nothing (except the use of my cock!), I insisted on leaving her a present of ten guineas in gratitude for making my stay in Liverpool so pleasant, which after first demurring to take, she accepted, thanking me heartily for my generosity.

Now, Sir, my old friend Sir Robert Dixon has chided me for leaving 'such a trifling sum' whilst Mr Peter Stockman of Sevenoaks insists I was wrong to even offer any money at all! I would be most interested to read your comments upon this matter.

I am, Sir, Your Obedient Servant

Colonel Leon Standlake
Goldstone House
Cramley
Near Stafford
March, 1885

The Editor replies: The general consensus in our office is that your behaviour was beyond reproach. It is easy for Mr Stockman to criticise for it is well known that certain ladies pay him large amounts of cash for their weekly fuckings. But then, is there a man in Britain who can equal the length and girth of Mr Stockman's extraordinary organ? He occasionally is guilty of forgetting his good fortune.

From Miss Anna Curkin-Nayland

Sir,

Like the poet I too best enjoy the 'season of mists and
mellow fruitfulness' and I trust your readers will find to their
liking this completely true tale of autumnal lechery in which
I must confess my involvement. Well now, perhaps 'confess'
is the wrong word to use for I am not in the least ashamed
at what took place. In the words of Mr Sheridan, 'certainly
nothing is unnatural that is not physically impossible' and
I would be happy to submit to your judgement of my
admittedly lewd behaviour.

Last Wednesday I decided to take a post-prandial
constitutional stroll through Hyde Park. It was a fine if
slightly chilly afternoon but I enjoyed my unhurried walk,
listening to the first thrushes singing and watching a group
of starlings swarming around a clump of crab apple trees,
pecking wastefully at the ripe fruit. Leaves were still to be
found lingering in some trees — deep, shiny yellow on the
birches, pale green and golden on the elms.

I was so engrossed by the beauties of nature that I failed
to notice that a girl who was walking in front of me had
stopped to deposit an unwanted newspaper in a litter bin
and a slight collision ensued.

'Oh, I do beg your pardon,' I gasped. 'How very foolish
of me, I was simply not looking where I was going.'

'That's alright, Anna, no damage done,' said the girl
cheerfully. 'It's just as well though that you were not at the
wheel of one of these new horseless carriages or a really nasty
accident could have ensued.'

How did she know my name? I looked at her closely and

19

although I recognised the voice, I could not quite place the face of this extremely attractive blonde-haired blue-eyed creature who giggled and said: 'I do believe that you have forgotten who I am. Mind, it must be four or five months ago since we dined together at my cousin Jenny Everleigh's house in South Audley Street, Mayfair, a few days before I sailed to New York.'

Suddenly my memory returned. 'Of course I remember you! Your name is Molly Farquhar, Jenny's cousin from Cockfosters in Hertfordshire. What a nice surprise to meet you again. Yes, I recall your telling me that you spend a great deal of time in America. When did you come back home, Molly?'

'I returned last week as my Mama insists that it is time for me to "settle down" and look for a suitable husband. As she says, *ad nauseum*, you are now twenty-two Molly and we don't want you left on the shelf! Aren't parents difficult!'

'Well, mine are away in France until November. But tell me, Molly, have you any beaux in England? I have just ended a friendship with Benjamin, Sir Ronnie Dunn's son, as although we enjoyed each other's company very much, neither of us wishes to make a commitment in respect of a permanent relationship. So I suppose I am on the look-out myself for male friendship.

'Ah, you poor love. Have you been saddened by the ending of the affair? I hear from my cousin Jenny that Sir Ronnie wields a good stiff prick but I don't know whether his son is as good a cocksman as his father.'

I was somewhat shocked at her forthright speech but I was determined not to appear unsophisticated and replied: 'Oh, Ben could fuck very passably. He was a most gentle and considerate lover and his prick was always up to the mark.'

'That's good to know for a hard man is good to find. One so often comes across those who after just one spend can no longer raise any further interest, which can be most unsatisfactory, particularly if one has not yet spent oneself,' commented Molly as we continued our stroll together. 'Tell

20

me, though, Anna, have you ever experienced the joys of female-only fucking? I can thoroughly recommend it as it makes a very pleasant change which I know from my own personal experience.'

'Not since some horseplay in the sixth form dormitory of Lady Bracknell's Academy for Young Ladies,' I said doubtfully. 'I think it would take a lot to persuade me that it could rival the benefits of a hot, stiff cock in my cunney, a joy that surely cannot be bettered.'

Molly laughed and said 'I used to think like that but since I joined Lady Slapbum's Ting Tong Club in Redcliffe Gardens, I have changed my mind about tribadism. Look, if you have no appointments this afternoon, let's hail a hansom and I'll show you round the place for as a country member I am entitled to sign in up to three guests per month. In any case, they serve a delicious tea at the Ting Tong which you will enjoy whatever you think of the goings-on at the club. I always try and smuggle out a slice of Mrs Bickler's sponge for my current beau and pretend that I made it.'

[*The Ting Tong Club flourished between 1888 and 1899 when its flourishing membership was threatened by exposure following a police raid. Although lesbianism was not, per se, illegal the Club's owners were charged with keeping a disorderly house. However, as its members included those from amongst the highest ranks of Society, the matter was swiftly hushed up. Nevertheless, the Club was forced to close and the house was bought by Professor Taylor Cuthbertson, a close friend of the Prince of Wales — Editor.*]

My diary was free of engagements so I accepted her kind invitation. We were fortunate enough to find a cab almost immediately and within ten minutes we were at the entrance of the club. Molly insisted on paying the driver and we climbed the stairs to the front door. An attractive young girl dressed in a rather scanty maid's uniform opened the door and took our coats as I signed my name in the visitors' book.

'Are there no footmen?' I asked Molly quietly. 'An establishment such as this should really boast a butler or some other male flunkey.'

21

'Are you joking?' whispered Molly. 'Why, they wouldn't even let a eunuch or a nancy-boy darken its doors. They say that even Lady Slapbum's Pekinese is a bitch! Anyhow, let me show you round the club.'

It certainly was a luxuriously appointed house with rich fittings in every room. All amenities one would expect to find were provided – a lounge, card-room, dining room etc., although smoking was not permitted except in the billiards room as a majority of the members disliked the smell of tobacco.

'There are a number of bedrooms upstairs for the use of members,' said Molly brightly. 'Shall we take a look?'

I somehow guessed that we would be staying a while upstairs, but I allowed myself to be shepherded aloft and Molly pushed open the door of the room on the right at the top of the stairs. 'Take a look at this bedroom, Anna,' said Molly, inviting me inside. 'See, through there is the bathroom and Lady Slapbum has installed these new showers which I find most invigorating.'

'Really,' I said with interest. 'Do you prefer using them as opposed to taking a bath?'

'Well, I always enjoy a nice soak in a warm tub but these new showers do tone one up as well as cleansing the grime of the city from the skin. One can adjust the hot and cold taps so that the water comes through at just the right temperature. Look, I will call down and see if we can try it out here and now.'

Her call on the internal telephone system was quickly answered and she gaily informed me that the room was ours for the next two hours. We undressed in an unhurried manner and I followed Molly into the bathroom where she switched on this new-fangled equipment, and after putting on special caps for our hair, we splashed around together underneath the warm water that cascaded down on top of us. Afterwards we dried ourselves on the large soft towels provided and Molly curled herself up sensuously on the bed.

I must admit that I had already noticed her superb figure and I envied her golden blonde locks of hair as I have always been firmly of the opinion that gentlemen prefer blondes.

Nevertheless, although her firm uptilted breasts were well proportioned, I judged that mine were larger and my legs were perhaps slightly longer than hers. At the base of her flat tummy there was conclusive evidence that Molly was indeed a genuine blonde for her silky pussey hair was also that fine shade of gold which I so envied, although my own black bush has been the object of admiration from not only young Benjamin Dunn but by such well-known cocksmen as Gordon McChesney, David Haines and Colonel Philip Pelham of the Lancashire Fusiliers.

Molly was leafing through a copy of *Cremorne Gardens* and I leaned over to see if there was anything worth reading in this naughty publication. 'Come and lie down with me and read out one of these stories. I do love listening to lewd tales,' said Molly invitingly, patting the snowy white sheet with her hand.

I obediently lay down beside her, snuggling my head inside the welcoming crook of her arm, and began to read from a story by Madame Estelle de Quentonne, the famous French courtesan who is reputed often to entertain the Prince of Wales when he makes one of his frequent visits to Paris. However, in the tale from which I read, she was writing of an enjoyable little joust with Claude, the sixteen-year-old nephew of Eduard Raspis, the industrial magnate. I began: 'My lips were drawn as if by an invisible magnet to the mushroom dome of Claude's lovely young cock. I kissed the smooth, hot head and thoroughly wet the top as I opened my mouth and took in the glistening knob, lashing my tongue around the succulent sweetmeat. Ah, it tasted so masculine, with a fresh salty tang that I closed my lips around it as tightly as possible and worked on the tip with my tongue, easing my lips forward to take more of the shaft. In his eagerness he pushed my head down to take in more of his throbbing tool but I almost choked in doing so.

'He retracted slightly so that it lay motionless though pulsating inside my mouth. I closed my lips around this monster and moved my tongue across its width. I sucked greedily on his youthful cock and twisted his head down so that his face was pushed into my own sopping groin and

23

my body shook with delight as the clever lad realised what he had to do and began to circle his tongue around my dripping slit.'

It may have been inappropriate to read such a tale inside the Ting Tong Club but it certainly aroused myself and Molly who was by now idly running her cool hands up and down my thighs and, combined with the stimulating story I was reading, we were both soon squirming around on the bed. She took the magazine from me and threw it on the carpet and leaning over me, she kissed me fully on the lips before transferring her tongue to my ear which set shivers all through my body, especially when she started to press my titties between her fingers which intensified the tingling sensations tremendously.

By now my whole body was shaking with lust and when Molly began stroking my pussey I grasped her hand and pushed it firmly between my legs which I squeezed together, crushing her hand between them. She understood my urgent need for she let her head slide down from my ear to my tummy and into my black thatch of pussey hair. She parted my lips with her fingers and slipped her tongue into my wet cunney, licking all round the edge with the tip before thrusting it all the way in. She was teasing my pussey to unbelievable heights, using tongue and fingers to spread my wetness all round my cunt. I just closed my eyes and let myself dissolve into a glorious sea of lubricity as her teeth now nibbled along my cunney lips whilst her pink little tongue teased my clitty with long, rasping licks. Up and down, in and out her long tongue lapped up my slippery juices as, by now totally abandoned, I threw my legs high up upon her shoulders.

Now I could feel myself begin to experience the first sensations of a spend build up inside me. 'Oh, Anna, your juices taste so delicious. I love sucking your juicy cunney,' gasped Molly, diving back again to give me the final *coup de grace*. She lashed her tongue against my clitty, rubbing it until it stuck out between my lips. Then she wrenched her mouth from my sopping muff and replaced it with her fingers, finding my swollen clitty which she tugged only for

24

a few seconds before I was away! My body thrashed wildly about in a frenzied ecstasy as her finger slid into my bumhole. I exploded into uncontrollable spasms of excitement and my juices flowed freely as I reached a gigantic peak of orgasmic lust.

Molly and I writhed about in each others arms, our breasts crushed together, our tawny titties rubbing against each other as we kissed feverishly until a second eruption made me arch back again, almost crying with joy as the raging storm of my spend coursed through me.

Now it was my turn to make Molly spend and she laid back expectantly as I kissed her stalky red nipples with their saucer like brown aureoles, drawing circles with my tongue, flicking the nipples up to a ripe hardness. Then I kissed her belly all the way down to that soft, golden nest . . .

Dipping my face close so that I could nuzzle into that silky blonde pussey, I licked my fingers and separated her folds, inhaling the tangy feminine odour of her dripping slit. Spreading her lips with my tongue, I explored her sopping pussey, gauging her responses, then sliding my arms around her thighs I adjusted my position and relaxed into flowing movements with my head, my tongue nudging her clitty, pushing against the hood. Her pelvis set the tempo, coming to meet me faster and faster as I increased the speed, pressing down with my teeth as she began to toss from side to side.

'Oh, Anna, that's marvellous. Oh yes, oh yes! Now darling, finger me,' she panted. 'Finish me off with your fingers.' She put her hands on her inner thighs and pulled her legs apart, revealing her fleshy pink outer lips. She was so swollen and wet that she hardly noticed three of my fingers slide into her sopping cunney. But she certainly did when I started to work up a pacey rhythm, working my fingers in and out, slowly at first, then faster and faster as she got wetter and wetter. She now frigged her clitty at the same time, working the little rosebud around with her thumb and forefinger. I straddled her and whilst I jerked one hand in and out of her pussey I roughly tweaked her titties with the other, making her moan with pleasure as she spent profusely, shrieking so loudly with delight that I was afraid we might be disturbed.

Well, dear readers, we were indeed disturbed — but not by any outraged members of the Ting Tong Club. What we had failed to hear in our haste to enjoy each other's bodies was the sound of a ladder being placed against the window and the thwack of the window cleaner's shoes as he climbed up the rungs to undertake his duties. It was Molly who first discovered that we had been performing in front of an audience. She suddenly shot out of bed and grabbed a towel to cover herself as she padded towards the window.

'Anna, look outside, we have an unannounced guest!' said Molly fiercely, opening the window to drag in a young man of about twenty-three who was still clutching his washleather. 'Shall I call Lady Slapbum and tell her that we have a Peeping Tom or —'

'Oh please don't do that,' said the young man who spoke in a far more educated voice than one would have expected from a London workman. 'I'm only doing the job because the regular window cleaner is ill and my aunt, Mrs Norma Swaige, who lives next door told me to offer my services to Lady Slapbum with whom she plays bridge every Wednesday afternoon. I had no idea this room was occupied but I must admit that when I saw what was going on, I was transfixed and just could not bring myself to move away.'

'Yes, I thought you were a member of the leisured classes as your face is quite familiar,' I mused, quite forgetting that I was sitting up in bed stark naked in front of this handsome young man who was now engaged in the most fulsome of apologies for looking in on our love-making.

'My name is Richard Gewirtz,' said the handsome youth with a slight bow. 'My father is Count Gewirtz of Galicia and though he never married my mother he immediately settled ten thousand a year and a London house upon her when I was born and he has kindly allowed me to bear his name.'

'I know your father,' said Molly promptly. 'He is a very kind gentleman as you rightly say. Why, after fucking my cousin Jenny Everleigh he insisted upon sending her first class tickets for herself and a friend to travel to New York upon the Dutch liner *S. S. Rotterdam*.'

'Well, it wasn't all that kind,' admitted Richard with a short laugh. 'After all, he does own sixty per cent of the Trans Europe Shipping Line and he gets more free tickets than he knows what to do with.'

'Still, he need not have offered them to Jenny,' smiled Molly who was now mollified by Richard's forthright explanation and apology.

'Meanwhile, I have an excellent idea. You can make up for your intrusion by lending us your cock for the next thirty minutes. I have a great fancy for a fuck whilst I am sure that Anna would also be interested in seeing what you have to offer and whether you can use your tool half as well as your dear Papa,' she added.

He blushed shyly and said: 'Nothing would please me more but I feel so nervous that I don't know whether I will be able to — '

'Oh don't worry about all that, we'll get you in the mood, have no fear. Now you go and undress and take a quick shower. When you come back we will be ready for you,' commanded Molly.

Richard stripped off and I stole a quick look at his hairy, muscular torso, his well-made legs and tight little bottom as he made his way to the bathroom.

Meanwhile Molly clambered back onto the bed, but this time she leaned over and took out a wooden box standing upon the bedside table before wrapping an arm around me. 'This is a Ting Tong dildo box,' she explained. 'Let's hunt around and find something to play with whilst Richard gets ready.' It didn't take long for us to discover a superbly fashioned ivory double-ended godamiche which we put into immediate use. Molly lay back and pushed one end into her soft, sticky pussey. I lay with my legs through hers and positioned myself on the other end of the dildo. What a great feeling it was, cunt-to-cunt with a dear friend and with a nice thick staff inside me. We rocked back and forth together, enjoying the wonderful feeling of rigidity inside us. I love that sensation of having something hard and stiff

27

pushing up inside me, filling me up whilst my cunney juices flow all around it. It was extremely stimulating although of course it could not really rival the hot, throbbing hardness of a genuine cock.

Richard came back into the room as we finished our spree. Neither of us had actually come but our pussies were now well juiced up and ready for a male intruder. 'Come and join us, there's no need to be shy,' I said, as the young man still held back. He smiled and dropping the towel which was draped around his waist, he walked towards us. He certainly was blessed with a thick stalk between his legs, but though it was swinging heavily, it was far from being ready for business but as I judged at the time, he only needed a little encouragement to light the fire.

For how quickly things changed when we got Richard onto the bed between us. We rolled him over on to his back and I sat across his knees while Molly sat perched on his chest. I took hold of his prick in my hand and it immediately swelled up under my soft touch. I knelt down and rubbed my breasts and nipples over his stiff shaft and then took the gleaming helmet into my mouth and began sucking noisily upon it as Molly moved up to place her pussey over his mouth so that he could tongue her cunney. Molly was making throaty noises as his tongue probed inside her cunney lips. His now huge prick was more than a mouthful for me as I sucked away on his knob, caressing his shaft until it was as stiff as iron. Then I shifted myself and lowered my lubricated cunt over his pulsating penis. I sank down gratefully, feeling the ivory column penetrate deeper and deeper inside me. Molly and I bounced up and down on poor Richard in unison and together we wriggled atop our young stud and I could feel waves of arousal taking me over.

After a minute or two of this treatment he removed his face from Molly's pussey and let out a loud growl. I felt his cock throb wildly and shoot out a rivulet of frothy white spunk as he spent copiously, the hot love juice filling my cunney and running down my thighs. A considerate and thoughtful man, Richard recovered himself enough to keep

28

stimulating Molly's pussey with his tongue while his fingers now sought my clitty to finish me off. Molly came quite quickly and he lapped up her love juices as she spent copiously over his face.

'I can't get there without a cock in my cunt,' I said regretfully as I did not believe that Richard was capable of raising any interest for a while. But happily he proved me wrong as the young sportsman simply gave his cock a swift shake and I was amazed to see it swell up to its former flagpole-like state. I took hold of it in my hand and found that such was the girth that I needed two hands to grasp the thick pole. Molly made way for me to lie on my back and Richard threw himself across me. He took his monster cock in one hand and drove home. I could feel it stretching my muscles beyond any previous capacity and I experienced a fulfilment that was simply divine and the thought flashed through my mind that as nice as the little tribadistic episode had been with Molly, nothing could beat the sensation of a big fat prick up one's cunney. Ah, what bliss! Every millimetre of my nook tingled to the pumping of his surging shaft as his wrinkled hairy ballsack bounced against my bum.

'Oh, you big-cocked boy! Fuck my juicy cunt with your thick prick!' I panted as he thrust home, sliding his shaft in and out of my squelchy wetness.

Several times I thought he was on the point of spunking yet somehow he held back until I was ready for him. Again and again, faster and faster he pounded in and out of my crack until my lips emitted one long, hoarse wail as I climaxed again and again in a seemingly multiple orgasm.

Then suddenly he pulled out and reared over me. He gripped his prick hard, giving it two or three convulsive jerks until a huge squirt of salty sperm spouted out, arcing towards my breasts, splashing my nipples, streaming down my belly and into my curly bush.

'Oh, how lewd!' gasped Molly who was watching avidly, frigging herself unashamedly with her hand as she watched me rub the spunk around my erect nipples and all over my belly.

29

'I haven't finished yet, Anna,' grunted this son of Count Gewirtz, one of the most famous fuckers in Europe. 'Let me show you how I earned my soubriquet of "the gobbling Galician".'

For yes, dear readers, young Richard Gewirtz's cock was still standing stiff as he knelt back between my legs and slipped his rigid rod back into my soaking slit. Frankly, I just could not keep up and whispered that my pussey could not take too much more cock without a rest. Being a gentleman he replaced his thick prick with his soft, caressing tongue which soothed my sore pussey. He moved round so that his cock was dangling over my face and I took it immediately into my mouth, sucking hard on it. I flicked my tongue against the ridge of his helmet, moving my lips from balls to tip and back again, faster and faster, intoxicated perhaps by the rhythm we had set up.

Suddenly I felt that warm ripple begin in my womb and at the same time his tight buttocks jerked and his great cock shoved hard against the back of my throat. Then his hot frothy flood was released and I felt it spurting out as I greedily swallowed all his love juice, milking that lovely prick until the last drops had been drained from him.

When we had recovered we discussed a plan for Richard to visit us when he was next in Mayfair (for the lad was currently living in Islington) and he exited from the room through the window and down the ladder to the ground.

'Lucky for us that Lady Slapbum will never get to hear of what happened here this afternoon,' commented Molly, 'or I would be expelled from the Club.'

We talked about our three-in-a-bed frolic over tea and I maintained that despite my enjoyment of being finger-fucked by Molly, I still preferred boys as, shall we say, the main course as compared to the girls who could provide a dessert. If a choice were imposed, I would happily live on the meat and easily forgo the pudding — especially if all the cocks measured up to that of Richard Gewirtz.

So ended a grand afternoon's fucking, Mr Editor, but now I must ask you — was I too forward in accepting Molly's invitation to take part in lesbian love and should we perhaps have simply ignored our randy young window cleaner who may have only fucked us both out of politeness?

Your humble scribe,

Anna Curkin-Nayland
69 Laurie Mansions
Kensington Gore
London, W.
July, 1891

The Editor replies: I am sure that all our readers agree that you deserved your enjoyment. One must experience as many of the joys placed before us by a beneficient Creator as possible or we could be accused of scorning his gifts.

As Mr Coleridge has it:
All thoughts, all passions, all delights.
Whatever stirs this mortal frame,
All are but minister of Love,
And feed his sacred flame.

I do hope that you continue to enjoy an active and varied love-life.

From Mr Stanley Wright

Sir,

One of the most stringent areas of control exercised by our so-called 'betters' has been that of human sexuality. It is drummed into us that all sexual expression, other than the minimum required for the purposes of procreation, are 'bad' and we ourselves are somehow sinful if we 'pander' to those normal deep-seated biological drives.

Of course, there must be rules and regulations for the conduct of civilised sexual relations. Men who force themselves upon unwilling partners — both inside and outside marriage — are worth little more than the beasts of the field and deserve the harshest of punishments.

However, there can surely be no harm in fantasising about fucking and I must admit that if, for example, I were fortunate enough to be dining with Miss Jenny Everleigh, the scenario would unfold in the following fashion . . .

After a sumptuous repast in my London *pied à terre* in Dyott Street, Bloomsbury, I would slip under the table and gently kiss her knees until she relaxed. I would lift her skirt and continue kissing her legs, gradually working higher and higher, my tongue making wet tracks on her soft inner thighs.

When I reached the edge of her brief knickers I would breathe deeply to inhale her pungent feminine odour and then I would place my lips on the crotch of her knickers and blow gently, my warm breath causing Jenny's pussey to become damper and even more fragrant. She would then wriggle her delicious bottom to assist me in pulling down her knickers so that I could nuzzle my face into her silky pubic bush. I would then kiss those pouting pussey lips and, spreading them apart I would alternately drive my tongue deep into her cunney and then pull out to tickle her clitty with small flicks of the tip of my tongue. Finally, I would suck upon that hard button until she gasped with pleasure and flooded my mouth with her tangy love juice.

We would then move to the bed where we would undress each other and she would lay down on the sheet, her eyes gleaming with anticipation as I fondle her breasts and suck the nipples up to a delightful erection. Then I would slip first one finger and then several into her cunt, playfully rubbing her engorged clitty. Occasionally, I would slip my sopping fingers out and let her lick off the salty wetness.

My cock would now be throbbing as Jenny stroked it and gently squeezed my balls. She would smile at the way my hot, hard prick would leap around in her hand and then she would slip down and lap at the fiery red helmet before tonguing my shaft and giving each of my balls a little suck. She would then transfer her attention back to my knob, lapping her wet tongue around the 'eye' before taking my prick into her soft mouth, her wet lips straining to encircle it, finally sliding juicily up and down my pulsating prick until she sucked it deep into her throat, all the way up to my balls.

Somehow, I would manage to turn round into a 'sixty-nine' so that my face was level with her pussey and I would lap up and down her lips, pulling them apart with my fingers so that I could concentrate on her erect little clitty. She gasps with joy and cries out: 'Yes, yes! You're so good. Keep sucking! Eat my pussey! Oh, how I adore it!' and I flick her clitty harder until she spends, her hips bucking as her juices soak my lips.

It is all that I can do not to spend myself, but I manage to maintain my composure as we separate and she would raise her knees and spread them, inviting me to implant my cock into her warm, private love hole. I move up and place her legs on top of my shoulders as I bend down to kiss her. I rub the head of my cock against her soaking crack and slowly I sink into her gorgeous cunt. I pull out and re-enter; each stroke brings me slightly deeper and she whispers fiercely: 'Fuck me, Stanley! Fuck me! What a huge cock you have and how divinely you use it!' Thrusting deep into her dripping pussey I feel her cunney grasping my cock as I slide into the hilt. Her slick channel clasps my shaft lovingly with each long, slow stroke. My hands are roving around her fabulous breasts and she cries: 'Tit-fuck me, darling! There's a good boy! Squirt your spunk on my lovely nips!'

As always, I am ready to please a lady so I pull out of her cunt and she wraps her big breasts around my cock. I thrust between the jiggling flesh and with every stroke she kisses the crown of my cock . . .

It is too much and I finally erupt with wads of white sperm shooting out of my cock and she opens her mouth and catches some to swallow. She takes hold of my throbbing shaft and sucks it feverishly, milking my prick of every last drop of frothy juice.

Time is closing in on us so once my cock has hardened up again (with a little help from Jenny's friendly tongue), I am ready to fuck her pussey and she turns on her hands and knees and, raising her tight little rounded bottom cheeks, begs me to fuck her doggy-style. I guide it into her sopping slit from behind, my knob sliding easily between her cunney lips and she thrusts her bottom out as I pump forward, locking us into a sensuous rhythm as my thick, stiff shaft rams in and out of her soaking crack. But all too soon I can feel the hot sperm bubble up in my balls and up through my prick which is now thrusting at speed in and out of Jenny's delightful passion pit. I let out a cry of warning and then wham! I plunge my trusty tool as far into her cunney as possible and my balls bang against her bum cheeks as the gorgeous girl thrusts back her bum to receive the spurts of spunk that shoot out from my cock.

Alas, she cannot stay the night and we bathe and dress for she must return home before midnight or risk the wrath of her Mama. Ah, if only I could but translate a fond fantasy

34

into a glorious reality, at the end of my days I would enter the fields of Elysium.

Yours sincerely,

Stanley Wright
Stamford Bridge
York
September, 1892

The Editor replies: I have taken the liberty of sending your billet doux to Miss Everleigh who is spending the summer in the Lake District with Lord Goulthorpe. She asks me to convey her sincere regards but regrets that she is currently being fucked by Sir Graham Giddens and cannot entertain any further pricks until further notice. Nevertheless, she was most flattered that she was the object of desire in your spellbinding fantasy. She is in possession of your name and address, and if the occasion ever arises that she finds herself in Yorkshire, be assured that she will contact you.

From The Honourable Lawrence Judd-Hughes

Sir,

This cautionary tale will demonstrate the necessity of keeping an accurate appointments diary.

Last Thursday evening I invited three friends from my Club round to my apartments for a few rubbers of bridge. For the record, these gentlemen are probably known to many readers of *The Oyster*; Sir Lionel Trapes, the *bon viveur* and Permanent Financial Secretary at The Treasury; Captain Jock Gibson of Edinburgh and Mr John Walsh, the noted author and critic.

As I shepherded my guests into the lounge, I instructed my man, Bacon, to put a magnum of champagne on ice and bring it in when the bottle had chilled.

'Very good, Sir,' said Bacon who then, instead of retiring with our hats and coats, laid his hand on my arm and hissed: 'Sir, I hope you will not mind my reminding you that you have a *rendez-vous* tonight with Lady Paula Platts-Lane. I could not help but overhear your telephone conversation with her the other morning.'

'By Gad, Bacon, it had completely slipped my mind. I was going to take her to some wretched concert this evening at the Wigmore Hall. Damn, damn, damn! I can't even contact her as she's spending the afternoon with friends out of town.'

'What shall I do, Sir?'

'Well, she said she would take a Prestoncrest carriage and meet me here at eight o'clock, but if she was delayed she would simply come round here as soon as possible and we would spend the evening quietly together.'

36

'Let's hope she is so engrossed with her friends that she decides to forgo the pleasures of the concert,' said Bacon hopefully. 'After all it is only a charity affair tonight put on by Lady Valerie Fitzcockie of Finchley, and so long as you have bought the seats it hardly matters whether or not they are occupied.'

'That's true enough,' I said. 'Nevertheless, at best I shall still have to explain to Paula that we will be unable to dine *à deux* as I promised. She will be very angry, to say the least.'

'But so long as you fuck her, Sir, I am sure that she will be satisfied,' murmured Bacon.

I smiled briefly and ordered him to announce Lady Paula and to show her into the lounge whenever she made an appearance. I then followed my guests inside, mixed them some hearty drinks and we sat down to enjoy our game, though I warned them that I had forgotten my previous arrangement with my current *amorata*.

As it so happens, Paula did not arrive until nearly nine o'clock so that in any case we would have been unable to attend Lady Fitzcockie's concert.

Bacon brought in some sandwiches and champagne, which went down perhaps a little too well as between us we managed to finish the best part of two bottles of my best Scotch whisky even before we began to eat. I freely admit that I was having a slight problem distinguishing spades from clubs and diamonds from hearts for frankly, I have never been a great imbiber and am unable to consume the vast amounts of alcohol that Messrs Walsh and Gibson, for example, can enjoy without any apparent ill-effects.

I well remember, however, that I was dealing out the cards when Bacon threw open the door and announced the arrival of Lady Paula Platts-Lane. I rose somewhat unsteadily to greet her along with the other three gentlemen and I apologised most profusely for having double-booked the evening.

'Oh, don't worry, Larry,' said Paula brightly. 'We would never have been able to go to the concert and I'm quite tired with all the talking this afternoon. You see, some of us girls are going to start up a ladies' club in Belgravia to rival some of your wretched men-only institutions.'

'I trust you do not plan to exclude men from this new establishment,' commented John Walsh, his eyes roving over Paula's wavy brown hair, her attractive face, slim figure, well rounded, firm breasts and long, shapely legs. 'Alas, our club committee will not countenance a lady being introduced into the place.'

'No, we are not so blinkered as the members of the Rawalpindi,' smiled Paula. 'Men will be allowed inside our club, but strictly by invitation only.'

I finished dealing the cards but none of us made to pick any up. Like my three friends I was staring unashamedly at Paula's cream-coloured blouse which was made of such a flimsy material that it was quite transparent and we could easily make out the outline of her large, heavy breasts for she was wearing nothing underneath it, and despite my somewhat dazed state, my prick began to stir as I gazed upon her dark, swollen nipples that pressed against their thin covering.

Paula knew full well what we were staring at but she said nothing except to tell us to finish our game. Slowly and unwillingly we picked up our cards and tried hard to concentrate upon bridge and to banish the sight of Paula's titties from our brains. It was a most difficult feat to accomplish and Sir Lionel, who is generally considered to be amongst the best players in London, unnecessarily trumped John Walsh's winning ten of diamonds whilst I foolishly neglected to cover Jock Gibson's queen of hearts with the king. In normal circumstances such plays would have brought forth cries of rage from the wronged partners, but our minds were no longer on the game.

Indeed, play slowed to a complete halt when Paula said: 'Hasn't it been a warm day, gentlemen? Larry, you do keep this room far too warm. I do declare that you must have also forgotten to instruct Bacon not to light a fire in the hearth.'

With a gleam in his eye Sir Lionel suggested that perhaps she might like to take off some clothes. '*Some* clothes,

Lionel?' echoed Jock Gibson. 'All of them, more like. How about it, Paula?'

She said nothing but looked the gallant Scottish soldier straight in the eye as she undid the buttons on her blouse and slowly peeled it off. If Bacon was listening at the keyhole (a habit which is endemic in many servants) he must have heard the collective intake of breath as we were given full view of her nude breasts that jutted out proudly, the large titties pouting lasciviously as she caressed her delicious globes, rubbing the nipples up to a stalky firmness.

Then she quickly undid her ankle-length skirt and we gasped as she let it fall to the floor. She was wearing only the briefest of frilly lace knickers and after she stepped out of the skirt which lay on my Persian carpet, she sidled up to Jock and in a tantalising whisper said to him: 'Well, Jock, do you like what you see? Is your Caledonian cock rising in your drawers? If you'll pull down my knickers I'll show you that even an empty whisky bottle has its uses for a clever girl.'

'This promises to be interesting if my guess at what Paula has in mind is correct,' grinned Sir Lionel lewdly.

'Wait and see,' she replied throatily. 'Larry, be an angel and play a little light music on the piano to get me in the mood.'

You are already in the mood, Paula, I thought to myself as I acceded to her request. What should I play? Brahms, perhaps, or maybe Lizst? No, let it be Beethoven, I decided as I knew how fond she was of his music. I struck up the chords of the beautiful Appassionata and this certainly set Paula off. She danced sensuously around the room before sitting on the sofa with the empty bottle in her hand. Then she slowly leaned backwards, her legs pressed tightly together and she caressed the neck of the bottle with her lips and tongue. Then she moved it lower, running it over her breasts and snow-white tummy before moving it even lower to cut a path through her thick brown bush of curly hair at the base of her belly.

Then she moaned and opened her legs so that we saw her

pouting pink pussey lips appear and she moved the bottle between them, pressing the neck gently into her pussey, frigging herself off with it, sliding it in and out of her dampening cunney. This stimulating sight sent Jock Gibson's blood boiling and in a trice he had stripped naked, and holding his stiff shaft in his hand he padded over to the couch. He leaned over Paula to massage her lovely big breasts and she lifted her head to press her mouth over the bulging uncapped knob of his thick prick.

The sight of the beautiful girl holding Jock's cock while she lustily sucked his balls drove us wild and my hands left the keyboard to tear wildly at my trouser buttons so that I could release my huge erection that was threatening to burst through the crotch of my trousers. Sir Lionel was the first however to divest himself fully of his clothes and he sunk to his knees between Paula's legs and firmly removed the bottle that had been sliding in and out of her pussey and replaced it with his tongue as he licked and lapped at her juicy quim, his nose buried in her mossy mount.

'Now, Lionel, that's enough of your tongue – stick that thick prick up my cunt, there's a dear fellow,' cried Paula, her lips temporarily leaving the glistening shaft of Jock Gibson's meaty cock. 'I want it all. Oh, Lionel, please fuck me!'

As befitted a gentleman and a scholar, Sir Lionel raised his head to her titties and lapped at them in turn as the excited girl took hold of his throbbing tool and guided it herself, inserting the uncapped knob into the welcoming folds of her cunney. At the same time, Paula resumed sucking Jock's veiny staff, noisily slurping away as he fucked her mouth, his slippery shaft almost fully between her red lips, so that his knob must have been almost touching her tonsils.

She wriggled merrily as Lionel pumped his raging shaft in and out of her sodden cunney. Paula bucked and twisted, all the while urging the randy baronet to thrust deeper, deeper as she raised her elegant legs and wrapped them behind his broad shoulders. Cupped now in his palms, her tight little bum cheeks rotated savagely as he pushed in,

40

pushed out and pushed back again, his balls slapping against her bottom.

John Walsh reached this lewd trio just seconds before me and Paula grasped his erect penis with her right hand leaving me to stand alongside Jock Gibson so that she could clasp her fourth cock, which was standing high against my belly, with her left hand. 'This is better than bridge,' declared John and we all chorused our agreement except for Paula, whose mouth was still engorged with Jock's huge cock, but she managed to nod her head slightly in agreement.

What a tableau greeted Bacon as he wheeled in a trolley of assorted sandwiches! There in front of his astonished eyes were Lady Paula naked on the Chesterfield being fucked by Sir Lionel as she fellated Jock Gibson whilst frigging John Walsh and myself with her hands.

The old valet stood transfixed as with a yell Jock shouted: 'Hoots! Here it comes!' as he ejaculated a veritable flood of spunk into her mouth. She swallowed as much as she could but the juice ran out over her lips and down her chin as with a grunt Lionel expelled his essence into her cunney, the white froth filling her love channel to trickle down her thighs. John and I were the next to spend which we did simultaneously, our fountains of spunk jetting upwards to rain down on Paula's large titties and we rubbed in the white love juice around her nipples as she herself shuddered with a most delightful series of climaxes.

We lay panting in an exhausted heap as Bacon cleared his throat and said: 'I have taken the liberty of running a bath, Sir, and perhaps you and your friends might like to allow Lady Platts-Lane to avail herself of the facilities.'

'What a splendid idea, Bacon,' I said and after Paula had finished in the bathroom we four men took showers before assembling back in the lounge where we refreshed ourselves with smoked salmon, caviare and champagne.

After we had quaffed our fill, Paula giggled and said: 'Larry, I have a confession to make to you.'

'Really, darling, and what might that be?' I asked.

'Well, I did not actually spend this afternoon quietly

discussing the formation of a new club with my friends Carolyn and Melanie,' she began.

'Ha, ha, ha,' laughed Sir Lionel. 'I'll wager a thousand pounds there is a man involved somewhere. Come on, Paula, don't be shy — who was the lucky fellow? Anyone I know? Jonathan Arkley, perhaps, or young Harry Price? Or is there some dashing new young man about town?'

'Oh, Lionel, I can never keep anything from your sharp brain. Well, if you must know, there were two boys involved,' admitted Paula. 'But I don't think I should really tell you exactly what went on.'

'You'll do much better if you make a clean breast of it,' suggested Jock Gibson firmly and John Walsh nodded his agreement.

'You won't be angry though, will you, Larry?' asked Paula anxiously. 'Promise me you won't be cross.'

'Of course I will, my sweet,' I reassured her, kissing her on the lips. 'After all, anything you did will pay me back for forgetting our arrangement tonight, though truth to tell I am well satisfied with the outcome so far this evening.'

Paula downed the rest of her champagne and said: 'Very well, then, I will tell all. I did take tea with Carolyn and Melanie and we did talk about the possibilities of starting up a new ladies club — but at five o'clock who should walk in but Carolyn's fiancé, young Antony Jammond, with his friend Fred Noolan. We chatted gaily to the boys about this and that but I noticed that poor Antony looked somewhat miserable and far from his usual bright, cheery self.

'"Is anything the matter, Antony?" I asked him. "Oh, don't worry about him, Paula," said Fred. "He is agitated over a personal matter and although I and several other friends have assured him there is no cause for concern, he cannot rid his mind of a foolish and unrewarding notion."

'"This sounds serious," said Carolyn. "Darling, do tell us what is worrying you. Perhaps we will be able to take the weight of whatever is troubling you off your mind."

'At first Antony was bashful but in the end he admitted what was causing him such anxiety — "It's the small size

42

of my prick," he said. "I have noticed in the bath after cricket that all my friends are far better endowed than me. I am sure that Fred here, for example, can give the ladies far more pleasure with his huge chopper than I can with my relatively tiny little instrument."

'Melanie frowned and said: "It never ceases to amaze me that so many men are obsessed with the size of their pricks."

'"Yes, but we girls worry in the same silly way about the size of our titties," said Carolyn.

'"We're as bad as each other," I summed up, "for as everyone knows, it is quality not quantity that counts. As Jenny Everleigh puts it, what counts is not the size of the wave but the motion of the ocean!"

'"All very well," said Antony. "But ask any one hundred young men if they would like another three inches of cock, and if they answer honestly, you would find that the huge majority would reply in the affirmative."

'"I agree," said Carolyn. "And if you asked one hundred girls if they would like extra inches added to their busts, you'd get a similar result, I'll be bound."

'"Let's face it," added Antony, "we are not created equal. Carolyn would like a bigger bust and I would willingly give anything to be able to boast a nine-and-a-half-inch prick like Fred here."

'I gave Fred's crotch an admiring glance, for though I stoutly maintain that size is not all-important, I must admit that the sight of a big thick prick does cause my knickers to moisten! However, I turned my mind back to the problem of how best to show Antony and Carolyn the error of their ways.

'I decided that only a physical demonstration would show how misguided they were about this whole matter. So I asked if they would be prepared in a practical fashion to help me prove my point that size is immaterial so long as both partners are in receptive mood. They readily agreed and so, very sportingly, did Fred and Melanie who needed no persuasion to take my point of view but were eager to assist their misguided friends.

'To cut this story short, I began by instructing the two

43

men to leave the room, and to take off all their clothes upstairs in the main bedroom where we would shortly join them. After they left us, I explained to the other girls what they had to do and they laughed heartily when I explained my plan.

'We three also stripped naked but before we went upstairs, I borrowed three of Carolyn's silk scarves which I took up with me. When we entered the bedroom the two boys looked goggle-eyed at the three pretty naked girls and their shafts stiffened up nicely as we fondled their cocks and balls and let them play with our titties and cunnies. Then I blindfolded the two girls before guiding them over to a small table and telling them to bend over it. They obeyed, giggling, and the boys licked their lips at the sight of this pair of rounded bums thrust out towards them. It was time now to explain to Antony that he was to be blindfolded and I bound Melanie's scarf around his head until he assured me upon his word of honour that he could see nothing. At the same time I called for complete silence and for all conversation to cease.'

'What a splendid story, I can't think what you had in mind. I am sure we are about to hear of a most *récherché* happening,' said John Walsh enthusiastically offering Paula a fresh glass of ice-cold champagne.

'Hold on and all will be revealed,' laughed Paula, accepting the glass from the handsome literateur and *bon viveur*. 'Despite his blindfold, Antony's cock was still stiff as a poker as I grasped it and brought his sturdy shaft (which was admittedly only of average proportion) to the vale between Carolyn's well-rounded contours. "Listen, Antony," I said to him. "I am now placing the crown of your cock between the cheeks of this delightful girl's bum. Can you feel your knob sliding into her juicy grotto? Now gently thrust your shaft all the way in until your balls bang against her inner thighs whilst at the same time you take hold of her breasts in your hands and flick her titties up to stand hard and proud against your fingers. Let your prick throb its pleasure inside that juicy cunt but let it stay immobile until I tell you to begin fucking. And please

44

remember, everybody, if this experiment is to work there must be no talking."'

'I then turned to Fred Noolan and stretched out a hand to caress his huge prick which was at least two inches longer than Antony's instrument and whose girth was appreciably thicker. I rather fancied being fucked by Fred myself but my experiment had to take precedence. I inserted his cock into Melanie's cunney from behind and then said: "Very well, begin fucking but remember, not a word from anyone!"

'The lack of conversation did not inhibit in the slightest and the only sounds to be heard were the smacking of bellies to bottoms and the squelchy sound of pulsating pricks sliding juicily in and out of clinging cunnies. I frigged my own sopping pussey at the lascivious sight but I wanted a cock in my crack so I squeezed Fred's big ballsack and then Antony's smaller little bag to make them spend quicker. The touch of my soft fingers worked its magic and both boys squirted out copious emissions of love juice into their partners' pussies.

'Fred moved away and I was delighted to see that his glistening shaft was still semi-stiff. I took hold of Antony's hand and led him to the centre of the room where I took off his blindfold and at my bidding we all sat down as I began to question him. "Now, I know you will all promise to answer my questions truthfully," I said. "First, let me begin with Carolyn. Now, who do you think was fucking you just now? But before you answer, was the thick cock sliding in and out of your pussey big enough to satisfy you?"

' "I think it must have been Fred fucking me, Paula, for in answer to your last question, yes, indeed, the owner of the cock concerned can be justly proud of its length and girth. What a whopper! It stretched my cunney muscles delightfully."

'I said nothing but turned to Antony and said: "And which girl do you think had her love channel filled by your charger? I noticed that you had your hands around her breasts whilst you were pumping your spunk inside the lucky lady's pussey. Can they provide a clue?"

45

'Antony thought the matter over for a moment and said: "I really cannot be positive but as the girl concerned possessed ample bosoms and the most delightfully stalky nipples, I will plump for Melanie. Yes, I am sure that I was fucking her and not Carolyn."

'I bowed and said: "I rest my case. Both of you, Carolyn and Antony, wrongly judged the identity of your erstwhile partners and without any prompting from me you both stated how satisfied you were with the equipment a beneficent Creator has provided!"

' "A rock solid case," chimed in Fred. "I think they both owe you a debt of gratitude for neither should worry any longer about the intimate side of their future life together."

'To their credit, both Carolyn and Antony showered praise upon me but more than anything, I preferred to be rewarded by being fucked by Fred. The happy engaged couple left the room and left us to it. It was quite stimulating to see us both nude in the dress mirror and I pushed Fred down on the bed and kissed him passionately on the lips whilst my hand stole up and down his thick staff whilst his hands roamed freely all over my curvaceous body. Then shaking clear a fringe of hair from my face I leaned downwards to kiss the uncapped helmet of his cock and I opened my lips to take it in my mouth. I sucked slowly, tickling and working round the little "eye" on the top of the bulbous dome whilst Fred parted my unresisting thighs and inserted two fingers into my moist, longing cunt.

'I could feel a delicious sensation spread from my cunney to all over my body as he moved carefully across me. I was able to keep sucking his great cock as he managed to wriggle over and nuzzle my pussey lips so that we found ourselves in a perfect *soixante neuf*. He nipped lightly at my lips, running his tongue along the edge of my crack which fairly turned my insides to liquid. Oh, Fred was a marvellous artiste with his tongue and I tossed and turned as his wicked lapping in and out of my cunney brought me off to a spend. I sucked a little harder on his cockshaft and massaged his balls as I sucked away with relish. Soon I felt his balls tremble inside their sack and I judged that he was about to spend. In a moment a stream of hot cream spurted into my mouth and his prick bucked as I held his knob between my teeth. Again, I enjoyed the supreme pleasure as I swallowed the copious rivulet of spunk that poured from Fred's magnificent cock. Then, as the last drops had been gathered up by my flickering tongue, I felt the spongy textured tool soften as I rolled my lips around it.

'But I mightily desired this magnificent cock in my cunney — and the question which had to be faced was whether Fred could build up another head of steam. I gently drew him over my body and directed his semi-stiff prick between my pussey lips. He was hardly fully ready for business but the instincts of nature triumphed as he helped shove his shaft inside my willing love channel. At first we lay motionless, billing and cooing with out lips, till I began a slight motion with my bum to which he eagerly responded. Ah, what ecstacy as I felt his thick prick swell inside my luscious sheath which received it so lovingly.

'How I enjoyed that delicious fuck! Fred opened the lips of my splendid cunney gently with his fingers and he cunningly frigged me with the mushroom helmet of his cock until I got so excited that I began thrashing around and shouted out: "Oh! Ah! Shove it in, Fred! Do push it in further, Fred darling! I must have it! Oh! Oh! Ah-h! Ah-h-re!" and I wantonly heaved my bottom upwards to each of his lustful thrusts.

'This was such a delightful engagement that I tried to keep Fred from spending for as long as possible. Once every last inch of his magnificent tool was inside me and our pubic hairs were mashed together, I closed my thighs, making this handsome young chap open his own legs and lie astride me with his cock sweetly trapped inside my cunt. Fred could not really move his shaft forwards or backwards as the muscles of my cunney were gripping his staff so tightly, but then I ground my hips round, massaging his shaft as it throbbed powerfully inside my juicy love-channel which was dribbling juices all down my thighs. He grasped my bum cheeks (something that I absolutely adore whilst being fucked) so I eased the pressure round his prick very slightly and he began to drive wildly in and out, fucking me at high speed which was most exciting.

'My pussey clamped down in a final burst of joy as his stiff, jerking prick gave a final throb before jetting out a torrent of hot cream deep inside me. I pushed my pussey up against him, burying his pulsating cock even deeper and let all that wonderful white froth bathe my inner walls as my whole body glowed with lust. Fred pumped away until his cock was milked of every last drain of juice and he slowed his thrusts to a halt. Panting heavily, he rolled off me and we lay gasping for breath as we gradually recovered our senses. What a magnificent cock! But even more important, as I gently reminded Antony, was that Fred was a passionate and considerate lover who would make any girl happy even if he had not had the good fortune to have been blessed with such a large instrument of pleasure. However, the thought did cross my mind that a big, big prick like Fred's did wet the appetite more than Antony's relatively puny little penis.

'We dressed ourselves after a refreshing warm bath and enjoyed our tea. Don't you all find how hungry one feels after a good fuck? We wolfed down sandwiches, cake and later toasted each other with a farewell glass of brandy.

'And that,' concluded Paula brightly, 'is how I spent this afternoon. It was a most energetic affair, but do you know, gentlemen, the recounting of these lewd happenings has made me terribly randy again. Perhaps I could prevail upon you, John, to fuck me as I have a great desire for it just now.'

Well, as readers of *The Oyster* will know, John Walsh does not have to be asked twice! In a trice the pair were thrashing around naked on the sofa and John was moving his hands around her gorgeous body with practised ease. He squeezed her firm breasts, rubbing the big dark nipples against his palms, making them rise up into little red stalks. He then began to kiss her entire body from her forehead downwards until he arrived at her open pussey and I could smell Paula's tangy feminine aroma as she guided the good-looking young critic's thick prick into her yearning wet cunney.

She wrapped her arms and legs around his well-built frame and urged him to make it 'hard and fast, John — let me feel every inch of your big tool.' 'As you wish, my love,' replied the literary cocksman politely as he slowly moved on top of her and Paula responded excitedly, opening her legs wide and clamping her feet round his back as he guided his throbbing shaft into her soaking little nookie. She took up the rhythm of his thrusts and I could see her legs shake and tremble and from my own encounters with Paula, I knew that she would soon be spending.

This erotic spectacle was too much for me to bear and I grabbed hold of my own swelling shaft and pulled my fist up and down, frigging it to its highest erection. 'Join in, Lawrence, join in!' cried Paula so I approached them, my cock in my hand as I knelt down to insert my knob into Paula's willing mouth. She grabbed hold of my cock and pulled three inches or so into her mouth, lashing my pole with her tongue as she sucked noisily away upon it.

Sir Lionel Trapes now approached us, his great aristocratic cock twitching uncontrollably in his hand, but just before Paula could grasp it he cried out: 'I'm spunking!' and he pumped out spurt after spurt of hot sticky cream over the entwined Paula and John, who, oblivious to their coating of jism were still panting and thrusting. The end was nigh, however, and I felt the sperm boiling up in my balls as with a gasp I shot a fierce jet of juice into Paula's mouth as John gave a powerful surging stroke and drenched Paula's eager cunney with a flood of frothy sperm as her hands grabbed his bum cheeks, pushing him deeper and deeper inside her until they collapsed, utterly exhausted, in a tangle of limbs on the cushions, and I must confess that the somewhat uncharitable thought flashed through my mind that I would have to instruct Bacon to sponge the sofa as soon as possible with Lady Gaffney's special stain remover as love juices can be the very devil to remove.

Well, Mr Editor, so ended the evening for me as Paula decided to spend the night with John Walsh and I was left to spend the night quite alone. As I wrote in the foreword to this missive, it certainly does pay to keep an accurate appointments diary, and I commend the diligent keeping of such records to all readers of *The Oyster*.

I am always, Sir, Your Obedient Servant,

(The Hon.) Lawrence Judd-Hughes
Dunton House
Albemarle Street
London, W
September, 1889

The Editor replies: Readers need not shed too many tears for Mr Judd-Hughes who must surely be one of the most famed cocksmen in Old London Town. We know for certain that in the last six weeks he has plugged the cunnies of Lady Emily Aldegonde, the ravishing young redheaded ingenue at the Drury Lane Theatre, Miss Beatrice Buxley and the lovely Lucy Lockette, the seventeen-year-old daughter of Lady Clare, after first having his way with her dear Mama the previous evening!

If these memories of past glories fail to mollify our correspondent let him remember the verse he himself penned in a previous issue of this magazine two years ago:

When wishes first enter a maiden's breast,
She longs by her lover to be caressed;
She longs for her lover to do the trick,
But in secret she longs for a taste of his prick!
Her cunney is itching from morning to night,
The stiff cock of her boy will yield her delight;
She longs to be fucked, and for that does deplore,
For what can a young maiden wish for more?
She'd like very well to be laid on the grass,
To have two ample bollocks sent bang 'gainst her arse,
If fever or sickness her spirits doth shock,
Why, we know what she needs, 'tis a stiff standing cock!

From Miss Deborah Davenport

Sir,

It is with pride that I pen this epistle to you for I believe that I can justly claim to be the first girl to be fucked by Mr Jeffrey Longbottom M.P. inside the portals of the House of Commons. Of course, I do not claim to be the first feminine recipient of Jeffrey Longbottom's cock in my cunney – his many conquests have been the subject of gossip in London Society for several years. However, I do claim the distinction of being the first to enjoy the pleasant sensation of lodging this clever politician's prick in my pussey during a Parliamentary debate, and at the suggestion of my old friend Sir Lionel Trapes (*see the previous letter from The Hon. Lawrence Judd-Hughes – Editor*) I now set down the circumstances of this historic coupling, which I trust your readers will enjoy as much as I delighted in partaking of this lewd experience.

I had met Jeffrey at a dinner party hosted by Doctor Le Baigue in aid of the Society For The Dissemination Of Useful Knowledge Amongst The Deserving Poor and I was pleased to find that I was sitting next to him during our meal. During the small talk that accompanies introductions, we discovered we had friends in common in Scotland and we had indeed met before (though we had not actually been introduced as such) at Colonel David Taylor's summer ball at his country seat just south of Glasgow. Anyhow, Jeffrey and I chatted about this and that and I asked him about the newspaper reports on rowdy scenes in Parliament – were they as bad as had been detailed in the newspapers?

'Not really, m'dear,' he replied. 'It is quite true that in the House of Commons we have nowadays occasional scenes of disorder which are not very creditable to us. And amongst the Radicals there appear to be a few ill-mannered individuals who seem unaware of their responsibility and who bring contempt upon the body of which they ought to be proud. But I am sure that this is by no means a new state of things and that in former times similar scenes occurred.

'After all, we live in a sensational age,' he continued. 'The popular papers take up a little *contretemps* and blow it up out of all proportion. So readers are told about scenes in the Commons and think that the country is going to the dogs. They forget, though, how smoothly and on the whole satisfactorily the Government of this world-wide Empire with its three hundred million subjects is being carried on.'

'That is good to hear, Mr Longbottom. However, I do hope that not all the business carried on is conducted in a terribly serious and formal way as I had planned to visit the House tomorrow as part of my studies for my entrance examinations to university.'

'Good heavens, you are not going to study Political Economy are you?' he gasped. 'Is a pretty young girl like you about to turn into one of these wild women who are demanding the vote?'

'I'm afraid that I am, but don't let's argue. After all, we won't convince each other of the correctness of our positions. And as I am sure that women will gain the vote in the end — for the tide of history cannot be turned back — there is little point in engaging in a debate.'

He laughed and said: 'By George, that's a fine way to win your points! I must use that trick in the House! But to reply to your original query, no, not all the business is conducted with great solemnity.

'It is a very curious thing but the House of Commons always seems to contain one amusing fellow. Mr Joseph Chamberlain told me only last week that there is always one wit in the House and when he dies or ceases to be elected, another springs up immediately to take his place.'

'Is he usually a Liberal or a Conservative?' I enquired.

'Oh, he could belong to either party for along with his predilection for buffoonery he has a hatred for which ever Government happens to be in office.'

Now it was just at this point, when the lobster bisque was being spooned into the tureens of Doctor Le Baigue's famous and indeed almost priceless seventeenth-century French china dinner service, that I felt a foot insinuate itself between my own and rub gently up and down my leg. Surely it could not be Jeffrey Longbottom for the Honourable Member had given no indication of amatory intent whilst he was speaking to me. I glared at the gentleman on my left but he was busily engaged in conversation with the lady on his own left flank . . .

The intruding foot continued its journey, rubbing sinuously against my leg, getting higher and higher and almost reaching my knee as Jeffrey concluded: 'Oh yes, m'dear, there will always be a place in the House for one chap who is a little cracked. He is there today, he was there fifty years ago and will doubtless be there fifty years hence.'

Yet still I could feel this mysterious foot which had insinuated itself between my feet and was now moving between my legs up to my knees. I glanced at Jeffrey and I could see that strange as it might be, it was indeed this handsome MP who, being a supple athlete, was moving his right leg in time to the movement I could feel underneath the table. I said nothing and he stopped caressing me with his foot until the ladies retired. I went straightaway to the powder room and when I emerged, he was standing in the hallway having taken his leave of Doctor Le Baigue and the other male guests in the dining room.

'I am bored by all the masculine talk in there,' he said lightly, pointing behind him. 'Why not join me upstairs for *tête a tête* coffee and liqueurs in Doctor Le Baigue's inner sanctum?'

'Will we not be missed?' I asked anxiously. 'Won't people start searching for us?'

'Unlikely, but even if they did, no guest would venture into Denis's little private room,' said Jeffrey cheerfully. 'It is so private that he fucks Kitty the chambermaid on Tuesday evenings and Betty Morgan the actress on Thursday afternoons here.'

'You are remarkably well-informed,' I said, trying to sound sophisticated rather than shocked at his frankness.

'Well, we are old friends and he often confides in me,' he replied simply, opening the door of the aforesaid room for me. Obviously, the rogue had prepared everything whilst I had been in the powder-room for there was a pot of steaming coffee on a gas burner and a fine selection of liqueurs arranged on a small table.

'Do you fuck, Debbie?' asked the rascally politician. 'I hope the question does not offend.'

I suppose I should have at least credited him with posing a question in a straightforward fashion but I was rather cross at the crudity of his approach. 'Yes, of course I do not refuse myself the pleasures of the flesh,' I replied. 'But I find your bluntness unappealing. Like the vast majority of women I prefer to be wooed.'

He begged my forgiveness and then insisted that it was my beauty that had captivated him; that the sight of my breasts bulging out of the admittedly low neckline of my evening gown had given him a huge hard-on which was still troubling him almost an hour later; and that he desperately needed to relieve his feelings.

I looked down and sure enough there was a meaty bulge in the area of his crotch. I leaned forward and stroked it and he groaned as I felt his staff pulse through the material of his black evening trousers. 'Oh, do take it out, Debbie, or I will spunk inside my drawers,' he whispered fiercely. I was now aroused and I could feel my pussey dampening as I unbuttoned his fly and drew out his cock. It was a fine specimen with a large ruby head and I took hold of the sturdy shaft and gave the ivory column a preliminary little tug. He smiled and placed his arms round me and I made not even a show of resistance as he raised my head upwards and closer to his own and our lips closed upon each other's and we melted away into a most arduous kiss.

I felt myself being borne back and we fell together, Jeffrey taking extreme care however that I would come to no harm in doing so. As our lips remained glued, he carefully unbuttoned my dress and somehow I managed to wriggle out of it. He pulled down my drawers and with a certain roughness that I did not find displeasing he thrust my legs apart, raising himself a little above me on one hand whilst with the other he pulled down his own clothing as the large knob of his cock pressed down upon my cunney lips.

'M'mm, that's nice,' I murmured as his knob continued to press into my wetness. For a moment our eyes locked together and then, with a heartfelt sigh, he inserted an inch or so of his thick prick and was full upon me. Our lips meshed and I wriggled my arse to obtain more of this meaty morsel. Jeffrey understood my need and clutching my naked bum cheeks, embedded his throbbing cock down to the root and in some magical way my cunney expanded to receive it . . .

'Would you enjoy a thick prick sliding in and out of your juicy love-channel, m'dear?' panted the randy rascal.

'A-h-r-e!'

I could not speak. I was filled by him. His big balls hung in their hairy sack beneath the bulge of my bum as his lips savaged my own. With a passionate jolt of his loins, he inserted the full length of his hard, smooth shaft inside my cunney. Then the rotter took out all but the very tip of his knob which made me beg for its immediate return! I know that some measure of modesty should be present at all times even in the first few moments of erotic bliss but I cried out unashamedly for his cock to be thrust back into my ever-dampening cunt.

We began to fuck in joyful unison, our bottoms heaving together as he worked his staff in and out of my luscious crack. 'Oh, what a delicious pussey you have,' he gasped. 'How tightly it clasps and sucks upon my cock! That's it, Debbie, work your arse! Ah, now not too much or I shall spunk before you are fully ready to receive my juice!'

55

Fortunately no-one entered the room during our joust, though in truth we were lost in that sensual world where fulfilment is all. Jeffrey's cock slewed in and out of my slit, pistoning back and forth and I gloried in each powerful stroke as my own juices sprinkled his balls. Cupped now upon his broad palms, the tight cheeks of my bum rotated savagely as his lusty tool continued to ram in and out of me at an increasing pace. I was now ready for his libation and I cried out: 'I'm almost there! Empty your balls, you big-cocked boy!' And with his face buried in my neck and his hot breath on my shoulder I could feel that he too was passing the point of no return. Though we both may have wanted it to last, we were very soon lost in the throes of orgasm and I felt my cunney awash with spunk as my pussey exploded around his throbbing cock. We were enveloped in the delight of a beautifully judged simultaneous climax as we collapsed in a rather undignified heap of limbs.

'That is a truly fine member you have there, Jeffrey,' I said, complimenting him upon his prowess, for I always believe in praising a good lover. Especially in London, I rarely fail to lavish affection when due, as unlike back home in Scotland, down South a hard man is good to find. Perhaps I lack the necessary information for a scientific appraisal, but my own empiric research shows that Scots possess thicker pricks than Englishmen — Jeffrey Longbottom, of course, is an exception to this rule.

We dressed hastily, for we did not exactly care to explain where we had been, and fortune was with us as we were not missed by the other guests. Jeffrey offered to escort me home but I explained that I had already booked a Prestoncrest carriage for the short journey to Brown's Hotel, Mayfair.

[An interesting aside here — Prestoncrest Carriages was a coach (and later motor car) hire service used by a select band of people who knew that their drivers were sworn to secrecy about who was being transported to whatever address. Many illicit liaisons were consummated thanks to Prestoncrest vehicles. Amongst well-known men-about-town

who were regular users of this semi-secret service were Sir Ronnie Dunn, Colonel Nettleton and the Society painter Ian Orpington – Editor]

However, we arranged to take tea together the next day at the House of Commons and I hardly slept that night as I was so excited at the idea of being escorted round the grand Parliament Buildings.

Jeffrey had informed the attendant at the gate of the visitors' entrance that I was expected and a messenger was dispatched to find him. 'What constituency does Mr Longbottom represent?' I asked the gatekeeper.

'He represents Cockermouth in the Liberal interest,' said the liveried flunkey. How appropriate, I thought to myself, as Jeffrey's tall figure came into view.

'Hello, Debbie, how nice to see you,' he said as we shook hands. 'Look, if you're quick we could nip into the Lords and you could see Black Rod.'

'I saw enough of "White Rod" last night,' I said gaily.

'Ha, ha, yes indeed, and I trust you enjoyed the view. But as I am sure you know, the Black Rod to which I allude refers not to the colour of the King of Cameroon's cock but to the officer of the House of Lords and Order of the Garter whose job it is to summon the Commons at the Opening of Parliament.'

We didn't see Black Rod as a matter of fact but Jeffrey escorted me into the Distinguished Strangers Gallery of the Commons chamber where a debate on agricultural matters was taking place. The speaker, Mr Derek Tong, MP for West Kent, was droning on about the high incidence of poaching. He was railing about the pathetic pictures which are frequently painted of the game laws and the constant and pitiless persecution of the poor poacher.

'It is really quite laughable,' added Mr Tong, 'to all who know that during the last thirty years, poaching has been steadily followed as a "trade" by men who will not work even when work is plentiful and easily found. We can all sympathise with the occasional starving labourer whom some overzealous keeper has found with a couple of rabbits in his pocket which he had knocked over for his wife's pot;

but to bestow words of sympathy on the lazy scoundrels who shoot hares and net the partridge preserves must be left to the friends of humanity who become sentimental at the expense of sound old-fashioned common-sense.'

The debate continued and Jeffrey whispered to me how interesting it was to compare the colours of dress favoured by the honourable members. 'My friend Professor Trower says that to look our best, we should wear colours suited to our personalities.

'Strong, solid types like Arbuthnut Powell, the Under Secretary for Home Affairs, should dress conservatively in medium tones such as brown. Bright sparks like the Financial Secretary, Harry Price, look best in navy and in summer should forget any muted colours and go for striking shades.'

'An interesting theory,' I murmured over the drone of Mr Tong's voice. 'But not so interesting as that bulge between your legs, Jeffrey Longbottom.'

He grinned and sidled round behind me, looking around to check that there were no other visitors in the Gallery. When he was satisfied that the coast was clear he cheekily slid his hands under my dress and proceeded to pull down my drawers! I looked behind to see him unbutton his trousers and take out his swelling shaft, slipping the skin down to bare his purple-domed helmet. I licked my lips as I took his erect prick in my two hands and dropped down on my knees.

My hair tumbled over my face as I moistened my lips and let his knob slide into my mouth. I could feel his cock gliding in till it was at the back of my throat − I gulped and it slid down and down. He withdrew slowly and began to slide my lips slowly over his fat crown and then I was sliding my mouth faster and faster up and down that hot shaft. He bucked his cock in and out of my mouth and I could feel his balls slapping my chin. My climax was building quickly inside me as I felt Jeffrey's fingers in my hair and suddenly he grunted as his body went rigid and then his prick was bursting in my mouth and jet after jet of his thick salty spunk was hitting the back of my throat. I swallowed and swallowed, gulping down the tangy juice as I milked his cock of every drop of his jism.

Slowly his cock slid from my mouth and now it was my turn to gasp for air. But silently, the honourable member for Cockermouth laid me down on the padded bench and, throwing up my skirt, began to kiss and lick at my dampening pussey. He wiggled his tongue all around my crack. My senses reeled and I started moaning and panting as his tongue flicked against my clitty. I pulled his face tightly against my cunt as his lips slipped inside, his warm tongue prodding through my wet cleft to lead me to a little series of tingling peaks.

This was nice but I fancied a proper fuck, so I whispered to Jeffrey to lie on his back on the bench which he did with his noble cock waving like a flagpole, and then I sat astride him, pressing the lips of my aching slit down upon the glistening knob.

I spread my cunney lips apart and directed the tip of this glowing cock to the entrance as I slowly eased myself on top of him, spitting myself beautifully on his rigid rod. His hands slid round to clasp my bum as I wriggled around to work the hard staff as far up inside me as possible.

I bounced merrily away as I leaned down to Jeffrey and chuckled: 'Keep your cock up! Oooh! That's marvellous, you're giving my clitty a good rub as well!' Somehow we stayed silent as I worked my bum from side to side as Jeffrey jerked his hips up and down in rhythm to my own movements. But whilst I enjoy the so-called female superior position as a variant in one's pattern of fucking, it can be quite exhausting when your legs are in a cramped position as mine were on that bench. So I let the rhythm slow down as Jeffrey continued to thrust upwards to meet my own downward pushes.

Meanwhile, on the floor of the House, Mr Tong was still on his feet. 'From what is called "game",' he said sternly, 'the national commissariat derives an annual contribution of twenty-seven million pounds weight of wholesome and palatable food. Abundant evidence exists to show that sport wrongs no-one and benefits many. Those who rail against all forms of sport should bear in mind that the pastimes of country gentlemen help thousands of the lower classes earn their daily bread.'

'Do you want to come now, Jeffrey?' I asked just as Mr Tong was building up to a rhetorical point. 'Is there anyone here who dares disagree?' he thundered.

'Yes! Yes! Yes!' growled Jeffrey, oblivious to everything except the boiling sperm that was building up in his balls.

Mr Tong looked up angrily at the Gallery where fortunately only my face could be seen over the rail. Luckily he could not see his fellow member's hands running freely across my breasts, tweaking the stiffly standing little nipples under the thin silk of my blouse. I smiled sweetly at Mr Tong who looked angrily at me but who, after a brief interlude, decided to return to his speech.

As he continued, with a fierce little groan Jeffrey worked his cock up inside me and commenced pumping his spunk in a copious emission until all was done and I lifted myself off the sodden shaft, still quite thick and long, as it dribbled its tribute in a snail's trail of white froth along his thigh. I had come several times and had also splashed Jeffrey's trousers with my spendings. 'Goodness me, I hope you are not needed to vote in a division,' I giggled softly.

'It's just as well that I'm not needed,' he murmured. 'It would take a far cleverer politician than me to explain away these spunky stains. Not even my friend Professor Trower could help me here!'

Coincidentally, the Speaker then called on the members to vote. 'All those in favour say "Aye"' he shouted. I joined in the chorus for though I am not and probably never will be a Parliamentarian, I think my conjoining with an honourable member entitles me to at least a footnote in Hansard!

A final word to feminine connoisseurs: Mr Longbottom's spunk is tangy enough but though plentiful, cannot compare in smoothness of flavour to that of the Duke of Hampstead or of the Laird of Midlothian.

I am concerned, though, Mr Editor, that my making love

in a chamber other than that of the bed will not upset the sensibilities of your many readers.

I am, Sir, Your humble servant,

Deborah Davenport
Castle Abroch
Loch Hayim
Scotland
October 1890

The Editor replies: It is to be hoped that Miss Davenport feels no worry about her enjoyment of this erotic encounter in the Mother of Parliaments. Again, let me use Lawrence Judd-Hughes' verse to illustrate my feelings upon the matter:

'Let maidens of a tim'rous mind
Refuse what most they're wanting;
Since we for fucking were designed,
We surely should be granting.
So when your lover feels your cunt,
Do not be coy, nor grieve him;
But spread your thighs and heave your front,
For fucking is like heaven.'

From Mr Henry

Sir,

I know it is the policy of your publication to print only letters which give the name of the writer. But I must beg your indulgence and pen this epistle under the cloak of anonymity for if my identity were to be established I would almost certainly lose my position as a private tutor.

I must explain that whilst the majority of my students are of a mature age and drawn from the very *crème de la crème* of our best families, very occasionally I am called upon to coach younger persons for school or university entrance examinations.

Perhaps I should add that I myself am the second son of a most respected clergyman whose parish is not a thousand miles from the parishes of St James and St George (*Mayfair* — Editor) and many parents entrust their sons and daughters to my unchaperoned care. Until last week, none of my students have distracted my attention from the work to be performed but as the old saw has it, there is always the first time . . .

Let me set the scene for you; picture if you will the study in my apartment near Baker Street. I await the arrival of Miss Tilly Diddlecombe and her younger twin sisters, Lottie and Eugenie. Tilly needed extra preparation for her final examinations at Bedford College where she is taking a degree in Modern Languages whilst her Papa, the Reverend Mark Diddlecombe, had informed me that he would be grateful if I could also assist Tilly's twin sisters who needed help with their French as they wished to gain proficiency in that tongue before setting off on a grand tour with Sir Timothy and Lady

Heather Shackleton, who as many of your readers know, take young people every summer on a cultural tour of the Continent.

It was last Thursday afternoon when I first set eyes upon my new pupils. My maidservant, Minnie, ushered the girls into my study and I must admit that my eyes fairly goggled as three of the most beautiful creatures I have ever seen walked demurely into my room. Tilly was twenty-one years old, somewhat tall and slender of build with shoulder-length reddish-brown hair that seemed to shine in the bright sunlight that was pouring through the bay windows.

As for Lottie and Eugenie, they were only just eighteen and both were as pretty, nay prettier than the girls whose faces adorn the boxes of expensive confectionery. They had come straight to their lesson from riding in Rotten Row with their boyfriends and were attired in white blouses which well accentuated their firm, well-shaped breasts, and tight riding trousers that moulded the contours of their tight little arses to perfection. Each had the face of an angel and a twinkle in their eyes as they apologised for not changing before coming to see me. I sat in my chair, fighting back an erection that was threatening to push my prick through the thin material of my flannels.

I passed round the syllabus for the first French lesson and caught sight of Tilly's tongue running over her raspberry-red lips, adding a glisten to her sensuous mouth which did nothing to bring down the bulge in my crotch. Then, still reeling, I spied Eugenie's hand slipping up Lottie's smooth thigh, rubbing sinuously up between her legs. Lottie moved her head back slowly, suppressing a sigh of delight whilst her sister's hand gyrated intricately above her crack.

'Excuse me one moment,' I said in a small choking voice. 'I will just check my own books before we start our French lesson.'

The girls giggled and Tilly said: 'Oh, Mr − −, never mind work for the moment. Perhaps you will appreciate another kind of French exercise at which my sisters and I are most proficient. Yes, I am certain you will prefer it to those boring old books. I know that we do, don't we, girls?'

'Very much so,' chorused the sisters as they joined Tilly in crowding round my chair. The elder girl smiled as she placed her soft hand on my raging hard-on that stood out like a sore thumb between my legs. She rubbed my crotch ever so gently as she turned her head to the twins and winked. I saw the outline of Lottie's nipples rigid under the straining cloth of her blouse as her twin sister caressed her breasts with one hand whilst she rubbed her own pussey with the other.

'You don't object if we call you Henry, do you, Sir?' cooed Eugenie.

I silently nodded my consent and then my attention was distracted as I felt my fly buttons being opened by Tilly's delicate hands and, in a trice, my eight-inch shaft was bared in her grasp. She slid her fingers up and down my truncheon, capping and uncapping my knob until she swooped down and sucked in at least half my eight-inch column into her saliva-filled mouth, lashing my cock with her tongue.

The twins now undressed each other and stood naked in front of me, their proud breasts jutting out defiantly as they moved their hands across to play with each other's auburn-haired pussies. Tilly realised that the sight of these two thrilling young bodies would speed the passage of sperm through my prick. So she alternated her lusty sucking with a nibble on the underside of my cock as she cupped my ballsack in her hand.

'As the eldest, I claim the right of having the first fuck with Henry,' said Tilly calmly. 'I think I would prefer to be taken from behind, if that is alright with you?'

I was only too happy to oblige as the sweet girl tore off her clothes with reckless abandon. Just the sight of her rosebud-tipped breasts was enough to cause some pre-come juice to dribble from the 'eye' of my helmet. Add to that the sight of her gorgeous, undulating bottom cheeks to those golden globes and you may well imagine the frenzy to be found in my loins. I raced over to the delightful girl who was now leaning over the mahogany table, waggling her bum in a most sensuous fashion. Holding my shaft in my hand, I entered her juicy cunney immediately and the warmth and smoothness of her velvet channel sent me into a delirium of delight. An added bonus was that there was a mirror on the wall facing us and it was an unbelievable stimulation to watch myself fucking this beautiful girl.

She squealed in ecstasy as I pumped in and out and she screamed out: 'Yes, yes, yes! More, more! Make me come!' It was easy to oblige and in seconds she was yelling and shaking as I brought her to a full climax as my own explosion burst through my staff, flooding her cunt with hot, creamy froth and she shuddered blissfully as she drained me of every last drop of love juice, as I pumped my fluids into her dark, secret warmth.

Now the twins clamoured for a taste of my cock and as I withdrew my still semi-stiff shaft from their sister's cunney, they handled my cock so cleverly that within a moment or two it was again as hard as steel. The twins dropped to their knees and took turns to suck my throbbing stalk as they played with themselves. This was too much to ask of any man — I just had to fuck them both and I gasped out the instruction that they should both lie down on the carpet with their legs spread wide to receive the gift of my throbbing truncheon.

Then I too dropped to the ground and rolled first onto Lottie, who returned my burning kiss with equal ardour as she took hold of my cock and guided it immediately between her pussey lips. After a few thrusts I leaned back and withdrew my glistening length. After all, how unfair it would be to leave Eugenie out in the cold. The sweet girl was rubbing her cunney in eager anticipation as I leaned over her and let her first kiss and gobble my knob for a few moments before I tit-fucked her, rubbing the crown of my cock on each of her nipples before finally sheathing my ecstatic column into her juicy cunt. I reached over to slide my hand between Lottie's legs and I massaged her pussey as I fucked Eugenie, ramming my cock in and out of her dripping cunney. Shrieks of delight left their breathless mouths and my own thrusts increased in tempo as a second spend fast approached. I flexed myself and with a hoarse cry poured out a luscious flood of creamy sperm into

Eugenie's cunney, which like her sister's was already awash with her own juices.

But, Mr Editor, now I was faced with a problem of how to satisfy poor old Lottie as both her sisters had reached the pinnacle of delight but my cock was in no state for a third game. Hard as the pretty girl tried, rubbing and sucking my limp penis produced no resultant erection.

I kissed the sweet girl passionately on the lips and laid her down on the carpet. Then I draped her long legs over my shoulders and dived down headfirst into her yearning love box. Her pungent pussey was already wet as I lovingly began to eat her, forcing my tongue deeper and deeper into the warm, juicy slit, sliding up and down the crack as I savoured her tangy aroma. Lottie gasped with joy as I probed between her cunney lips and thrust deep, finding her clitty which I rolled and sucked between my lips as she writhed around, rubbing herself off against my mouth. As I let the tip of my tongue dart in and out of her snatch she grabbed my head and pressed my face deep into her minge as she felt the first stirrings of a gigantic spend. Her juices dribbled like honey from her parted labia and her erect little clitty swelled even more as I flicked gently at it with the tip of my tongue. So I moved my hand up to my face and Lottie opened her legs even wider as I frigged her slippery clitty with my thumb. Her body was now jerking up and down which made the affair even more exciting as my face rubbed against her silky red bush. 'A-h-r-e!' she yelled as I worked my tongue around until my jaw ached, but I was rewarded by the lovely young girl achieving a tremendous orgasm, splashing my mouth and nose with her juices as her cunney spurted love juice all over the place until, as it subsided, she gently pushed my face away from her.

Well, the hour of tuition was nearly up and we dressed ourselves quickly, only just finishing in time before Minnie knocked on the door to announce the arrival of young Harry Barr whom I am tutoring for his entrance examinations to Oxford University.

The girls are due back tomorrow for a further French lesson and I will endeavour not to repeat last week's performance but actually instruct the delicious ladies in the French language. Whether I will be able to resist temptation is a matter upon which this pedagogue must ponder. Perhaps you, Mr Editor, with your vast experience of human behaviour, can advise me.

I, am, Sir, anxiously, ever Your Obedient Servant,

Henry 'X'
Marylebone,
London W.
April 1892

The Editor replies: I see no reason why you cannot teach these delightful girls the intricacies of irregular verbs whilst tickling their titties and playing with their cunnies. There is nothing wrong in combining work and pleasure. Are the girls cognisant of the important French words for pricks, pussies, etc?

I have taken the liberty of showing your letter to Mr Peter Stockman, the proud possessor of the biggest prick in London, and he assures me that his mighty penis is at your disposal should you need another stiff tool at your disposal during the next French lesson. Indeed, should you require a third, I understand Herr David Zwaig is in town and his continental cock is also available at no cost whatsoever should you require it. Both gentlemen may be contacted through my office.

From Miss Norma Radlett

Sir,

The merry month of May has always been known for its propitious influence over the voluptuous senses. It will give me the greatest of pleasure to share with your readers a little incident of such matter that occurred the day before yesterday when I went to visit my family's country seat in the heart of the Sussex countryside.

The house is a large enough residence, standing in spacious grounds of its own and surrounded by small fields of arable and pasture land, interspersed with numerous interesting copses through which run footpaths and shady walks where one is unlikely to meet anyone in a month of Sundays, even during the summer season.

Sheltered in many of the hollows in the hills you may find a Downland 'dewpond'. These are shallow depressions half-filled with water that may be seen on some of the highest hills of the Sussex range. The curious have often exclaimed on beholding these watering-pans which are well supplied with water yet with no apparent sign as to its source. In even a hot, dry season such as we have at present they very rarely fail the passing shepherd.

So when on a very warm afternoon I decided to cool myself by bathing naked in such a pond, I believed the chances of anyone else being in the area were slim. I had no idea that I was about to meet a rugged blond farmer's boy.

Jeremy was a real Adonis, tall and well-muscled but with the slender grace of a true athlete. I did not hear him approach as I splashed cool water round my dark pubic bush

68

and at first I almost believed that he was part of a heat-induced fantasy. When I realised that he was in fact real, I jumped out of the pool and wrapped myself in a bath-towel that I had brought with me.

'I must apologise for disturbing you, Miss Norma,' he said with an engaging smile and not a hint of embarrassment.

'The fault was mine,' I said. 'But how on earth do you know my name?'

'We were introduced at Christmas at your parents' annual party for their tenants,' he replied. 'My father, Martin Lawbress, farms forty acres near Old Payning to the west of your fine mansion, and I had the pleasure of escorting you into the ballroom after dinner. But as I recall, you were suffering from a bad headache and you left the party before the dancing which was a disappointment, may I say, to me and every young man in the hall!'

I laughed. 'How kind of you to say so! I do remember you now, Jeremy Lawbress, and if my memory is correct you are attached to the purchasing office of Count Gewirtz of Galicia in London. I haven't seen the Count for some months now. Is he planning to visit England this year?'

'I doubt it as he has an invitation to spend the autumn in the United States with the President and he will probably go on to visit his Australian sheep farms,' said Jeremy.

'Really,' I said. 'He must be an extremely wealthy man. But is he a generous employer?'

'Oh yes, he is a surprisingly kind gentleman. When he was informed that I had suffered a severe bout of influenza, he telegraphed that I must take a long, fully paid leave at my parents' place in the country out of the poisonous London air, and that I should not return until I had fully recovered.'

Jeremy's handsome face attracted me and I invited the youthful lad to join me for an *al fresco* luncheon. As we sat there admiring the beauty of the surrounding countryside I could barely keep my mind on our conversation. I have not been involved with a man since last February and it was driving me insane to see this good-looking boy sitting across from me, the sun turning his blond hair into gold, and the

69

smooth muscles rippling under his bronze skin when he took off his shirt to lie in the shimmering heat. I could feel my excitement growing and my love tunnel getting damper all the time.

It was hardly difficult to attract his interest. I shifted position, sitting so that my long legs were in full view and he was afforded just a hint of my pubic bush. This had the desired effect as Jeremy stopped in mid-sentence about the latest acquisition of Count Gewirtz, and had to swallow hard a couple of times before he could continue. His gaze travelled up and down the length of my legs and he now shifted somewhat uncomfortably as I noted with delight a bulge swelling up in his lap.

'It is so warm that I suggest we go in the water for a quick dip,' I suggested shamelessly, throwing off my towel and exposing my nude body to his glowing eyes. I stroked my large breasts suggestively before walking sinuously down to the water's edge and splashing my way in.

'Come on in, it's not cold at all,' I called out as Jeremy hesitated for a moment before shucking off his clothes and following me in. I noticed with satisfaction that he was blessed with a thick penis, already almost erect as he joined me in the pool, which was so small that we could scarcely help but bump into each other. As his hand brushed my hip I moved closer and stroked my fingers through the soft golden hairs on his chest. Jeremy took a deep breath and then decided to take what I was obviously offering to the lusty lad.

His strong arms wrapped themselves around me as our lips came together in a passionate kiss. I squeezed one of his tight little bum cheeks and brought his hips hard against mine. The throb of his rock-hard cock rubbing against my belly afforded me the greatest satisfaction and I was dying to find out what this huge sausage would feel like inside me . . .

Jeremy began by kissing my neck and shoulders and stroking my breasts until I was moaning and begging him to touch me. We climbed out of the pool and onto our piled-up clothes to continue our love-making. Jeremy sucked and licked my nipples while his magic fingers played around my pussey, before moving down and letting his lips and tongue take over.

I adore having my pussey eaten and Jeremy's cunnilingal technique was quite superb, especially for a relatively inexperienced young fellow. He first knelt between my open legs and deftly parted my wet cunney lips with his fingers. Ah, how I shuddered as he smoothly massaged the inside of my pussey with his tongue, an arousing prelude rarely practised, alas, in this country although our continental cousins are adept at this arousing art. (Afterwards, Jeremy told me that Count Gewirtz himself had coached him in this valuable skill with ladies from Madame D'Arcy's salon in Brighton.) But now he moved from my inner lips to my clitty and began to suck on it very lightly as his hands moved up to my distended nipples which he rubbed in small, precise circles. I always find this produces a delicious sensation that courses throughout my body and already by now I was floating, my orgasm building up inexorably inside me. My love juices were flowing wildly as the tension grew and I could wait no longer to feel his bulging prick inside my raging love channel.

I let my right hand grasp his magnificent cock and, my God, was his penis big and stiff! There must have been at least nine good inches of it, hard as steel and panting with hot lust. Its thickness too was almost extraordinary and I could not fully wrap my hand around the throbbing shaft.

'What a whopper!' I exclaimed with undisguised admiration.

'Thank you, Miss Norma, it is very kind of you to so comment,' he replied modestly as I smoothed my fingers up and down this enormous pole.

At first he just teased me with this wonderful weapon, only inserting an inch at a time until I was crazy with lustful excitement. I rolled him onto his back and took his full length into my sopping crack, sliding up and down on my glistening charger as we thrust hard at each other, our cries of passion echoing around the empty hills until we spent together in a burst of ecstatic glory.

We lay together quietly for a time and then we went back to the pool to wash. To be certain that Jeremy's cock was really clean I began to lick and suck it until it was soon swollen up to full erection, standing stiffly up against his flat belly. This way and that I played with his cock in my mouth, now sucking deep, now licking only the very tip with the softest tongue of velvet. Jeremy sighed his delight, whispering to me how incredibly good my kisses felt and I was getting so turned on that I rubbed my nipples with one hand as I held his twitching tool in the other. Such high peaks of pleasure could not be long contained and all too soon his body tensed and he spurted a fountain of hot, creamy spunk down my throat. Not till his lovely cock had quite shrunk down did I withdraw my lips.

We returned to the bank to dry off and Jeremy finger-fucked me to another orgasm before we finished the afternoon with a final *soixante neuf*. It was time now to dress and return to our respective homes. Jeremy and I plan to spend further afternoons at the dewpond, but I shall have to journey to Doctor Nettleton's in Cocking for a jar of his famous cunney lotion for my poor pussey will need refreshing if Jeremy's mighty prick again batters her waiting portals.

I trust, Sir, that the loyal devotees of *The Oyster* will have enjoyed reading this true account of my unashamed lewdness as much as I have taken pleasure in recounting this tale.

Your humble (and happy) scribe,

Norma Radlett
Grove House
Lower Charlton
West Sussex
July, 1893

The Editor replies: Miss Radlett may be interested to hear of Professor Allendale's new idea for the easy insertion of big cocks into tight cunnies. He recommends the placing of the half skin of a peach, turned inside out upon the tip of the man's prick before he begins fucking.

Alternatively, a thorough sucking of the prick usually suffices. Lessons in this exquisite art may be obtained from Lady Margaret T —, Mrs Tessa P — and any of the inhabitants of a certain well-known house in Great Portland Street. Or again, readers may be safely recommended to purchase a bowl of cold cream from any reputable chemist.

From Mr Harry Wharton

Sir,

Undoubtedly one of the most remarkable evolutions of recent years has been that of the athletic girl. Against a hurricane of protest she has come surely and by deliberate intent into her own until, as the well-known (and aptly named) medical authority Professor Herbert Balls recently declared at a meeting of the Royal Society: 'the girl who has played games and entered into the spirit of games is not only the best made for any man who respects his comfort and happiness but is mentally and physically best suited to acquire a clearer and franker relationship with the opposite sex.'

My own observations upon this matter would seem to bear out the truth of the good doctor's remarks. For since taking up the sport of lawn tennis, my dear lady wife Helene has been a different woman who now is completely forthright about what she expects and enjoys in the bedroom. We have only been wed for six months and until now we have both been somewhat shy in telling each other what we most enjoy in the marriage bed.

Perhaps I should explain that as an Old Nottsgrovian (*See The Oyster Books 1 and 2, New English Library – Editor*) I have always been wary of being too forceful in *l'arte de faire l'amour*. It was rightly drummed into us by Doctor Simon White, our revered old headmaster, that no girl should ever be asked to do anything against her will. This excellent maxim still holds good, of course, but perhaps I have taken it a little too far and consequently been somewhat inhibited in even questioning whether we have experienced the full range of sexual delights of fucking and sucking and we have never been totally open in admitting our fantasies to each other.

Since Helene has taken up tennis, however, all this has changed. The first barrier we surmounted was the uninhibited use of language to stimulate our love-making. One night last week, after a particularly randy session, I was unable to restrain myself any longer and told my sweet wife how much I loved to fuck her dear little cunt. Rather than be angered by my use of strong language, Helene sighed that she loved my big strong cock above all and could not think of anything nicer in the whole wide world than being fucked by her powerful husband!

This lewd talk sent our blood boiling and during the next few days we hardly spoke of anything else. She would whisper about how she wanted to kiss and suck my hot, throbbing cock whilst I murmured my desire to lick and lap at her warm, wet cunney. Both of us would then hug and grab and grope before settling down into a delightful *soixante neuf*, my wife gobbling greedily on my helmet whilst I thrust my tongue in and out between her full cunney lips, nipping her erect little clitty playfully with my teeth, and you may well imagine that it took but a little while before my face was drenched in her juices whilst her mouth was filled with my tangy sperm which she swallowed with evident enjoyment.

Last Wednesday night came a real surprise of which I had not the slightest hint. We were lying naked on the bed and Helene was idly fondling my cock, rubbing my shaft up to peak erection and playfully capping and uncapping my knob as she pulled at my foreskin. Then suddenly she exclaimed: 'Harry, I must be totally honest and ask if you will take part in a very special little intimacy that I know will excite us both.'

'What exactly are you thinking of, my love?' I enquired, caressing the insides of her soft thighs.

'I want you to shave my pussey!' she whispered firmly in my ear.

Sir, I could hardly conceal my astonishment at this brazen

suggestion! At first I was speechless but then I thought to myself how interesting a shaved mound would be and Helene's wispy dark pubic bush would be easy enough to remove.

'Your wish is my command,' I said with a smile, and within a few minutes I had organised a bowl of hot water, scissors, shaving cream and a safety razor. First, I just clipped her bush but then I spread the cream all over her pubic hair and carefully proceeded to shave the lot away! I shaved around her thick, red outer cunney lips until all that could be seen, clear and true, was her bald pussey. I handed Helene a small mirror and she squealed with delight as she took a good look.

After cleaning her up with a warm washcloth I rubbed a light oil over her now even more voluptuous cunt. By this time we were both feeling extremely randy and my cock stood up like a flagpole as Helene lay down and spread her legs invitingly. I needed no further encouragement and went down on her without pausing. I chewed and lapped at her cunney lips and let my tongue dart between them to find her erect little clitty. After rhythmically circling it with the tip of my tongue, I nibbled and sucked on the dear morsel and indeed she tasted even better than before. She spent passionately over my face before I withdrew and substituted my knob in place of my lips. Helene eagerly thrust up her hips as my cock slid into her sopping crack. She threw her legs over my back and heaved up and down in time with me as we commenced a most excellent fuck. Despite her own libations, her cunt was exquisitely tight, holding me in the sweetest vice imaginable, so much so in fact that I could feel my foreskin being drawn backwards and forwards with every shove.

But her juices were now flowing so freely, oiling her cunney walls so well that my further thrusts were made easier as my trusty tool buried itself within the luscious folds of her shaven slit.

'Harry, Harry!' she yelled. 'Now, my dear husband, fuck me hard! Push in, push in, there's a love. Oooh! How marvellous, how gorgeous, how you make me spend!'

I made one last lunge forward, my balls banging against her bum cheeks as with a hoarse cry of triumph I shot a stream of hot spunk into her pulsating pussey. I wriggled my shaft around inside her as the sperm continued to gush out of my prick in great jets as we writhed around together, enjoying this great fuck to the full.

On Sunday night we discovered a further bedroom delight and I do not believe it to be merely coincidental that it arose after Helene had taken part in a hard-hitting game of tennis with Mrs Fitzcockie, the Northern Area champion.

Let me note here that neither of us were ignorant of the practice of masturbation but we had not imagined it to be part of our sexual relationship. Last Sunday evening proved how wrong we were!

Often, before and during a fuck, I would bring Helene to orgasm by playing with her clitty. Occasionally, I would bring her hand to play with her pussey but before now she was reluctant to do so. On this night, however, I simply asked her to finger-fuck herself and she took off as one obsessed! Whilst I was inserting my cock in her cunney from behind as she bent over the bed, she reached down and grabbed her clitty and manipulated it superbly. She soon reached a tremendous orgasm moments before I spunked my stream of juice into her cunt from between her bottom cheeks.

Since then she has been doing this whenever I ask her — and occasionally even when I don't — and she even finger-fucked herself in our carriage on the way to Sir Andrew Stuck's literary soirée in Bloomsbury the other evening.

Helene is a most stunning creature and it is a beautiful sight to see her writhing in ecstasy as she masturbates, her shaved pussey arching upwards as she approached her spend, her head thrust back and her tits straining against the thin material of a summer blouse.

Indeed, yesterday afternoon Mr Colin Ramsay, the well-known photographer, came round to our house to take some portraits of Helene in the nude and she put on a special performance for the great man; and there is one shot (for

Mr Ramsay was so excited that he worked all night to be able to show us some sample proofs early this morning) of Helene, one hand caressing her nipples and the other fingering her cunney, that deserves publication in your esteemed journal.

I must add that after Mr Ramsay left this morning Helene insisted that I join in the fun and toss myself off in front of her, an idea that had indeed crossed my mind. At first I was hesitant, not having wanked in front of anyone since our circle jerks in the third form at Nottsgrove. However, after swallowing a large whisky and soda, I pulled off my clothes and took my penis in my hand. My initial shyness prevented me from really letting go but then I gradually got into the swing of things and my hand sped faster and faster along my shaft until with a gasp I shot a stream of semen all over Helene's waiting titties and she rubbed in the white juice over her stalky strawberry-coloured nips.

Incidentally, my wife's tennis has much improved too and tomorrow afternoon she is playing in the London and Middlesex Championships at Hendon. Those knowledgeable in the game confidently expect her to reach the final rounds and if Helene plants her drives and volleys with as much grace and enthusiasm as she now shows in her fucking, I do believe that I will soon be the proud husband of an international player. So I have a great deal of which to be thankful to the game of lawn-tennis, which is why I have today donated two thousand pounds to the organisers of women's tennis so that more young ladies will be encouraged to take up this most edifying of all sports.

I believe that all patriotic men should follow my example for in conclusion I quote again from the lecture given by Professor Balls: 'The husband of an athletic girl may find his friends wondering why he does not sigh for the "foolish little thing" of other days. But in place of the fragile young flower, prone to swoon at every turn, we now have a growing number of well-built young women of amazing cheerfulness and vigour with a grip on life and upon themselves.' And indeed, if I may be so permitted to add, upon their husbands' cocks!

Yours faithfully,

Harry S. Wharton
Watford Lodge
Rondunn Road
Hampstead
London, N.W.
August, 1894

The Editor replies: My sincere congratulations to the gallant gentleman and his lady wife on discovering that all forms of fucking tend towards achieving the acme of felicity.
  Captain John Gibson of Edinburgh, who happened to be in my office when your letter arrived, suggests there is a further avenue which you may care to follow, best expressed in the following verse:

There was a young lady of Glasgow,
And fondly her lover did ask: 'Oh,
  Pray allow me a fuck,
  But she said: 'No, my duck,
Though you may, if you please, up my bum go!'

From Miss Fiona Bunter-Dunne

Sir,

I am happy to share with readers of *The Oyster* the ecstatic experiences of some fine fucking I was recently privileged to enjoy on a railway journey to Bonnie Scotland.

As a demure (sic) young girl of just nineteen, normally I would have been chaperoned on the night sleeper to Edinburgh. But my mother's companion, Miss Harrow, had turned her ankle quite badly that very morning, after tripping up over Rex, our pet corgi, so to my great joy it was decided that I could travel alone as Cripps the butler would escort me to Kings Cross Station and I would be met at Waverley, Edinburgh by Colonel McGraw's personal carriage.

I was travelling to Edinburgh to attend the coming-out ball of one of my oldest friends, Susey McGraw, in whose company I spent not only my schooldays at St Hilda's Academy in South Devon but also a year at Fraulein Metternich's Finishing School For Young Ladies in Zurich, Switzerland. Susey and I both lost our virginities during the first term at Fraulein Metternich's to the same handsome young mountaineer, Konrad Kochanski, but that is another story which, Mr Editor, I will relate at a later time if you so desire.

Be that as it may, when I boarded the train five minutes before we were due to depart, the first class lounge was almost empty, and by half past eleven all the other passengers had retired except for two young men who invited me over to their table for a nightcap. This sounds terribly forward but I must hasten to add that Kevin Durie (of the

Argyll Duries) was known to most of the best families in London and had been a guest only the previous month at one of my mother's musical evenings where we had been introduced. The older of the two – previously unknown to me – was none other than that infamous man about town Sir Andrew Stuck, whose reputation was of course known to me although I had not had the pleasure of being introduced to the handsome young baronet before this unexpected meeting.

'I did enjoy your mother's concert, Miss Bunter-Dunne,' said Kevin politely. 'I am particularly fond of Mendelsohn's string Octet which I thought the little orchestra played with great brio.'

'Yes, it is a fine piece of music,' I agreed. 'The piece has astonishing instrumental and contrapuntal skill that serves an original conception of delightful freshness. It is quite extraordinary to think that Mendelssohn was only sixteen years old when he composed it.

'Are you fond of music, Sir Andrew?' I asked.

'Not overmuch, to be honest,' he grinned. 'I prefer the theatre to the concert hall and a rousing chorus of a Gilbert and Sullivan show to the boring dirges of many of the so-called classical composers.'

'Not only are you a Sassenach but you are also a barbarian,' grinned Kevin, but we chatted amicably enough, polishing off an alarming proportion of the bottle of malt whisky Kevin had brought with him to while away the journey.

Then the door opened and who should come through but Clare Corisande, another alumni of Fraulein Metternich's establishment (and who had also been deprived of her maidenhood by Konrad Kochanski, by the by) and who was also bound for Edinburgh and Susey McGraw's dance. Her Aunt Maud, who was accompanying her, was fast asleep in the lounge. She knew Sir Andrew very well and I was pleased to introduce her to Mr Durie. In honour of this pretty girl, whose blonde tresses I had much admired, we finished Kevin's bottle and then prepared to make our way to the sleeping compartments.

81

But as we rose, Sir Andrew said: 'Tell me, ladies, are either of you familiar with Scottish dress?'

'Not really,' said Clare. 'Indeed, this will be the first time I have been North of the Border.'

'Well, they have some curious customs in Scotland,' grinned Sir Andrew. 'For instance, let me show you a photograph of Kevin here in his kilt at Lord Bourne's ball.'

Clare and I looked at the photograph of Kevin in what appeared to be a tartan petticoat which left his knees naked to the elements.

'Did you waltz in your kilt?' asked Clare mischievously.

'Aye, I did, right enough,' said Kevin. 'And why not?'

'Oh it is just that I would have thought that the whirling motion of dancing would have caused your kilt to fly up and expose your . . . ' and she stopped suddenly and giggled.

'Arse, you were going to say, Clare,' chipped in Sir Andrew gaily. 'Well, what would have been the harm in that? Girls like to get a glimpse at a man's firm bum cheeks sometimes.'

'Andrew, hold your tongue,' scolded Kevin, colouring as we looked again at his photograph.

'I have a far better one taken from the front,' leered the randy baronet, taking another photograph out of his wallet.

'Don't you dare!' panted Kevin, trying without success to grab the offending picture, but Sir Andrew laughed and passed it across to me. My eyes widened as I looked at it for there was Kevin, holding up his kilt to show that nothing was worn underneath that garment. His prick looked of a fair proportion, a thought that crossed Clare's mind as she told me afterwards, and we both noticed how Kevin's heavy balls hung low in their hairy sack.

'Kevin,' said Andrew. 'I do not believe that the girls think the sight of your Caledonian cock is more beautiful than the view of your bottom.'

'Well, that proves that our education has not been neglected,' said Clare boldly. 'For as the catechism puts it: "What is the chief end of man?"'

'My dear girls, we are all quite private here as the guard has gone to his compartment. Would this not be a fine opportunity for you to view the genuine article? Come on, Kevin, be a sport and show the girls your prick in the flesh,' said Sir Andrew. 'Meanwhile, you must excuse me for a minute whilst I answer a call of nature.'

Kevin blushed but I said: 'Now then, don't be shy. Both Clare and I are familiar with the sight of a naked prick. We will give you our honest judgement upon the dimensions and general look of your staff of life.'

'If you insist, then,' he said, unbuttoning his fly and baring his erect cock. 'I am always ready to please the ladies.'

Clare and I inspected his tool and we told him fairly and squarely that it was as big as he had any reason to expect and was well-fitted for all but the most cavernous cunt.

'I would be more than happy to entertain this cock in my cunney,' said Clare, moistening her lips with her tongue.

'So would I,' I agreed and I took hold of Kevin's rock-hard shaft and gave it an encouraging little rub. A few moments later the three of us were in his compartment, all quite naked and kissing and cuddling up together. I found myself on my back with Clare lying on top of me, our tummies and breasts pressed together with her legs stretched out between mine. Kevin moved between her legs and, after he had pulled her up to him, pushed his prick deep into her bum-hole. As he fucked her wrinkled little rosette she moaned and sucked upon my own rosy titties and when he spunked into her arse she almost achieved a climax herself as she grabbed my hands and held them very hard.

Clare then pulled one leg over mine and pushed her thigh up against my cunney. We were both wet with love juice as she began rubbing her lithe body up against me. Kevin moved his head towards my face and we kissed, our tongues inside each other's mouths as Clare continued to rub sensuously against me. He now climbed up on top of us and placed his twitching tool against my lips. I opened my lips to suck in his helmet and I lashed the succulent shaft with my tongue before taking in another three inches of his delicious cock in my mouth.

Meanwhile Clare was now kissing my erect little titties and

83

I could see the shadowy figure of Sir Andrew Stuck in the background, undressing as fast as he could. In a trice, the randy baronet had his cock in his hand and was sliding in beside Clare, guiding his mighty rod towards my waiting cunney lips, which opened as if by magic to enclasp the crown of his thick tool.

All three were now fucking me in perfect rhythm and it was the most exciting sensation I have ever experienced. I came simultaneously both with Sir Andrew who spurted a copious emission of spunk splashing against the walls of my juicy cunt, and Kevin who filled my mouth with his frothy white jism so wonderfully well that I could not gulp it all down and some of the juice ran down my chin.

After a short intermission we paired off and I lay down with Kevin as I had not yet had the pleasure of having his cock in my cunney. We embraced in a kiss of blazing ardour and then his tongue moved downwards from my mouth, circling one nipple and then the other as they hardened under his tongue. I purred with pleasure as I ran my fingers down the length of his shaft, and then delved underneath to tickle his unusually heavy balls.

He must have read my mind for he said softly: 'They're overflowing with spunk and it's all for you, Fiona,' as he slipped his arm around my waist and pulled my bum up so that my dripping cunney lips were brushing against the tip of his knob. For a few moments he continued to tease my sopping crack as he rubbed his knob all along my slit, but then at last he slid the bulbous mushroom head into my welcoming cunt and began fucking me with long, gentle thrusts.

I could feel his lovely staff getting even larger inside my cunney and he groaned, reaching up to tweak my titties with one hand and fondle my clitty with the other. My juices were now simply seeping out of me as he flicked that little button backwards and forwards as he continued to move his shaft slowly in and out of my pulsating pussey. His hips were thrusting that hard rod further and further up me and the walls of my love channel were opening and closing around it. And then whoosh! with a great shudder he creamed my cunt with a huge flow of hot sperm.

After that I reckoned he would need some time to recover, but as he removed his sticky shaft from my pussey I could see that it was still stiff and would need only a little help to regain all its former glory. I slid down his chest to crouch over his knees, leaving a trail of love juice all the way down to his belly. Whilst his cock was still wet I clamped my lips round it and tasted our combined juices. They were quite deliciously tangy and I could not resist a lusty suck of Kevin's big balls before tonguing his shaft up to its full height and hardness.

I lay back to receive a second shafting from this majestic prick, but as he inserted his cock as far in as possible so that our pubic hairs matted together, I decided to change positions. Still holding his staff firmly inside me by contracting my cunney muscles, I rolled over on top of him and sat astride his broad chest to ride him in what turned out to be a magnificent St George. I bounced happily up and down, pivoting gracefully on this throbbing column as we spent almost together, our juices mingling in a further flood of mutual jism.

As we lay recovering from our exertions, I glanced over to see that Sir Andrew was being given the full treatment by his delightful partner. He was lying flat on his back whilst the gorgeous girl was holding his erect prick in her hands. She wet her lips and knelt between his long, muscular legs and then took the finely formed crown of his cock between her lips, clamping them around his not inconsiderable shaft, her blonde tresses spreading along his thighs as he jerked his hips upwards to stuff as much of his shaft as he could inside her soft mouth.

But when he tried to establish a rhythm, she lifted her head and giggled. 'No, Andrew, I would rather have your big cock inside me, if you please,' she said, and straddling his body she pushed herself down upon his sturdy truncheon, squeezing his thighs with her knees and riding him like an American rodeo rider, pushing him harder and harder until he spent with a husky groan.

At once, Clare rolled off and propped herself on one elbow, watching Sir Andrew's face as she traced delicate patterns along his limp prick. 'Are you all done so soon?' she teased. 'Let me see if there is any more spunk that I can milk from your lovely cock.' The handsome baronet sighed and said: 'I fear that what you see is all you will get.'

'I think you are capable of better things,' said Clare, and before Sir Andrew could reply she began licking the perspiration from his body — first his chest, then along his arms and legs. Her hands cupped his bum cheeks, probing and massaging and lo and behold his prick began to stir again and with a smug smile Clare said: 'Just one little suck should do the trick.'

She rolled his stiffening white column between the palms of her hands and sucked his helmet into her mouth. Her prognosis was absolutely accurate for it took only a few seconds before she withdrew her lips a second time from his now rock-hard prick and smiling smugly, she knelt on all fours in front of him, thrusting her firm white buttocks into his face. 'Now give me a firm pressing of juice up my bum!'

Nothing loath, Sir Andrew scrambled up to mount her, his left hand prising open a channel between the cheeks of her splendid arse, the other holding his massive blue-veined tool that had risen rigid from its nest of dark curly hair. He forced his knob to the rim of her wrinkled little brown bum-hole and Clare cried out at first as he slowly forced his huge knob inside after wetting it with some spittle. But then her sphincter muscle gradually relaxed as he entered the tightened orifice and she told him to sink in all of his shaft up to the hilt.

Sir Andrew leaned forward to fondle her breasts, his eyes bright with excitement as he pounded his shining, slippery shaft into her lithe young body. His prick rose in and out of its narrow sheath, plunging in and out of the now widened rim, pumping and sucking like the thrust of a steam engine.

'Ah, Clare, what an arse, what warmth, what tightness!' groaned the lucky young rascal, patting her flanks and savouring no doubt the plump rondeurs of her bottom cheeks against his belly. A gentle movement of Clare's hips sufficed to show the pleasure she was evidently sustaining.

'Do not move your cock for a moment! Oh, Andrew Stuck, fuck my bum, you big-cocked boy!'

And with those lewd words, the pretty blonde reached back to spread her cheeks even further, jerking her delicious bum to and fro until, with a tremendous shout which I feared would wake the sleeping passengers, Sir Andrew shot a jet of frothy sperm inside her as they spent together in perfect accord.

He withdrew his still semi-hard prick with an audible little plop and we all lay together in a sweaty tangle of arms and legs.

I have always wondered, Mr Editor, why the male of the species is known as the stronger sex for both Clare and I were ready and willing to continue this sensuous joust, but both Kevin and Sir Andrew were now deep in the arms of Morpheus and we girls were forced to play with each other for the next hour or so — not that I minded too much, for Clare managed to bring me to a truly superb spend. I just about have enough time left to tell you about how she did it . . .

She began by licking her finger and placing it at the base of my throat. And then slowly, very slowly she traced a line down the middle of my body. She kept licking her finger so that it was always wet as it slid down my body, between my breasts, over my belly and down into the silky dark curls of my pussey hair. Then she insinuated the other between us and manipulated my firm breasts, tweaking my rosy nipples up to a peak of hardness and I gasped and twisted for the caress was even more enervating than I had judged and my aroused globes seemed to swell to her touch.

The tips of our tongues met and then we were exchanging the most burning, the most devouring of kisses as my own arms wrapped themselves around the sweet girl. I gasped again as Clare carefully slid her knuckles around my oily cunney lips and at this first ardent rubbing of my pussey I was on my way to Elysium. My legs parted, enabling her to slip full length upon me. Withdrawing her urging finger, her furry blonde mound now nestled moistly against my own. My whole body tingled as I felt the rubbing of our cunt lips, the tingling merging of our pubic hair as, coiling her arms under my knees and raising and thrusting my legs back, she caused our cunnies to meet and rub fully together. I clasped her shoulders as our bottoms squirmed in mutual delight. Very soon, a violent shuddering racked my body as I achieved an enormous spend and my cunney spattered out its juices all over Clare's blonde bush.

With a sigh, the gorgeous girl rolled off me and I kissed her sweet lips saying that I would now ensure that she too achieved the delight that I had just had the pleasure of experiencing.

How could I best have my way with the beautiful blonde girl who languidly stretched naked before me, purring like a kitten, her legs wide open and her hand playing around the silky hairs of her golden pubic bush?

Without hesitation I rolled on top of her and licked her titties up to a fine state of hardness, letting my eyes feast on her delicious pussey. The blonde hairs were silky and the lips looked oily with the excitement of our previous encounter. Oh, how she wriggled and writhed as I worked my tongue first into the whorl of her navel and then my lips slithered down to her hairy mound until they were directly over her eager quim and I could inhale the unique feminine aroma from the rich cunney juices which were already flowing freely from her. I parted her thighs to ease my head down into a comfortable position and then plunged my pointed tongue back and forth inside her pussey. Clare squirmed under my ministrations, pressing her mound up against my nose and almost threatening to choke me with her hairy muff.

'Oh, Fiona darling, don't stop now!' she pleaded as I paused for breath.

She need not have been concerned as I had no intention of ceasing to suck that delicious cunt. My tongue slid through her smooth passageway and outlined the mound of her erect little clitty which rose up to greet me. I licked and lapped all around it, sending Clare into a delirium of delight as her legs waved this way and that as my tongue continued remorselessly to slurp around it. Then I took the pulsating morsel in my mouth, rolling my tongue around it and nipping it ever so gently with my teeth. She squealed with joy as I continued to work my tongue until she heaved violently, arched her back and then came in a fierce spurting. My hand slipped under her comely bottom and as her love juice flowed out, I worked my forefinger in and out of her bum in a most exciting way.

I continued to suck her cunney until her orgasm finally faded and we lay happily together as the last drains of our juices were released, oiling our thighs as we too now fell into a deep welcoming sleep.

By the time we reached York the boys had woken up again although Sir Andrew was still a little groggy. However, I sucked his balls which had the desired effect and we formed a nice little fucking chain that lasted almost until we passed Tyneside. I lay on my tummy, thrusting my bum cheeks out towards Kevin who fucked my pussey from behind as I gobbled Sir Andrew's thick prick. Meanwhile, Kevin had his hand working in and out of Clare's cunney as she kissed Sir Andrew, whose hands roved along her bosom, his hands squeezing and caressing her jutting young breasts. Clare and I changed over and after she rummaged in her travelling bag for a 'ladies travelling companion', or dildo as the common vernacular has it, we were able to vary our positions.

Perhaps my particular favourite 'wholesome foursome' was fucking Clare's lovely bottom with the dildo as she sucked away on Kevin's smooth shaft whilst the dear lad was lapping at my pussey. At the same time I used my other hand to toss off Sir Andrew as he tongued Clare's cunney in rhythm with her bottom fuck afforded by my thrusting of the dildo (which was bound in soft leather) in and out of her arse.

As you may imagine, we were all quite exhausted by the time we reached Edinburgh, but it did not stop us enjoying a grand holiday in the Athens of the North. Susey McGraw's dance was a great success and she has just sent me a photograph from the Scottish Tatler which shows me in conversation with her cousin, Jack Webster of Aberdeen, a most good-looking young man whose cock was to enter my love channel some three hours after the photograph in question was taken!

Alas, *tempus fugit*, Mr Editor, and I must now close for I am already late for my appointment with Monsieur Josef, the new French hairdresser in Bond Street much favoured by Society since Princess Alexandra became a regular patron earlier this year.

However, I must not forget to add a footnote from dear Clare — she is presently spending the summer in Italy with her Papa and Mama at Lord Horn's villa and would be grateful to hear from any gentleman of good family between twenty and thirty-five who might be visiting that country from now until September. She may be contacted by telephone (Florence 1189) or by post at Via Cavour 69, Florence, Italy.

Yours in haste,

Fiona Bunter-Dunne
21 Belgrave Square
London S.W.
June, 1894

The Editor replies: A splendid letter, Fiona, and reading your adventure sent my pego standing stiffly to attention. Fortunately, Miss Reddie, my faithful secretary was on hand to suck me off or I would have been forced to indulge in a five knuckle shuffle.

Do accept, with my compliments, the gift of a magnum of champagne and feel free to come round to my office at any time. And do give the young rogue Sir Andrew Stuck my kindest regards when next you see that randy baronet.

From Mr Clive Kinison-Jones

Sir,

After our final examinations at Trinity College, Cambridge this summer, members of the Epicurean Society at this august seat of scholarship decided to hold a ball — and I was lucky enough to find a girl who was prepared to take this invitation literally!

There must have been some forty of us crammed into the supper rooms at Mr Burbeck's famous hotel (and there being only ten or so girls from the neighbouring college for schoolteachers, I was hardly optimistic about the chance of a kiss let alone a fuck). Anyway, our senior tutor Dr Tagholm began the proceedings with a spirited rendition of an old Sussex drinking ditty sung at harvest suppers in that rustic county. It goes like this:

'The miller's old dog
Lay on the mill floor,
And Bango was his name, O!
B-A and N-G-O
And Bango was his name, O!'

Then he instructed us on how the company should join in. Now the method of singing this song was as follows: the leader would sing the verse, repeating the fourth line thrice and then turning to his right-hand neighbour, would say 'B', the next man would say 'A', the third 'N' the fourth 'G' and the fifth 'O' whereupon we all had to roar out the chorus — but if any singer missed his proper letter he had to drink a glass of champagne — hardly an onerous forfeit!

91

Well, an inexperienced group such as ours made quite a few mistakes and within a short space of time we were all very merry indeed! To cut a long story short, after half an hour or so I got up and answered a call of nature. As I washed my hands, however, I noticed in the mirror that the door was open and leaning against the wall in the hallway was a perky little blonde girl whom I had noticed sitting with her friends in front of me. I smiled at her as I came out and we exchanged some small talk and later our forenames.

'I was looking for the ladies' room but I fear that I have been misdirected,' she said, a delicious dimple appearing on her right cheek as she smiled.

'It is just down here on the left,' I said, motioning the way with my arm. 'I will wait here and escort you back when you have finished.'

'Thank you, Clive, how nice of you,' she said and, well, again, to be brief, when she returned we agreed that it was too noisy a party for our liking and she accepted my suggestion to see my rooms which were only over the way in my college.

It was easy to smuggle her past the doorkeeper and once in my room Lizzie herself closed the door and locked it. As soon as I turned round this little vixen was all over me. 'Ah, you dear boy, I fancy you,' she whispered in my ear as she grabbed my bum and pulled me towards her. 'It is the champagne which always has this effect on me.'

'Gosh, Lizzie,' I stammered as her finger stole round to rub against my swelling penis. 'Does this mean you want, to, um, I mean, would you like to, er — '

'Oh very well, you persuasive young man,' she laughed. 'You've talked me into letting you fuck me.'

With those words she stuck her tongue in my mouth and, showing commendable dexterity, unbuttoned my fly to release my erect prick which was straining against the confines of my trousers. She pulled me down upon the bed and took as much of my cock in her mouth as she could, stroking my staff with one hand and teasing my testicles with the other. Somehow we managed to strip off all our clothes and we rolled over as she spread her creamy thighs. I buried my lips in her buttery bush and as I licked her, I ran my thumb into her cunney and this drove her absolutely wild. She grabbed my hair and pushed my head back into her curly motte. 'Eat me!' she commanded and a few moments later her cunney was grinding down on me as her juices soaked my face.

By now my balls were aching and I needed to spend. Lizzie anointed my thick young flagpole with her wonderfully wet tongue and then climbed aboard for a ride. Guiding my cock into her cunt, she leaned over so that her big, stalky red nipples brushed my chest. I have a mirror on the wall opposite my bed and it was unbelievably erotic watching us fuck. All too quickly I spurted a huge flood of spunk inside her as she bucked to and fro on my sturdy pole, reaching, as the first jets of spunk hit her cunney walls, a truly shattering orgasm.

My cock was still hard so Lizzie took hold of my wiggling prick which was sticking high in the air and rubbed my knob in the vale between her large titties with their deep red nipples. Then, kneeling before me, she slung my legs over her shoulders and taking my stalk in her hands, began to tongue my hairy ballsack. Then she moved up to embrace my knob with her lips. She opened her mouth and sucked in my shaft until it touched her throat. Oh, how I loved being sucked off! Up and down, up and down bobbed her head, until, with a low growl, she changed the steady movements into an erotic circling pattern until I could stand it no longer. I bent forward until I was almost doubled-up and shouted: 'I'm going to shoot, Lizzie! Do you want it in your mouth or in your cunt?'

She pushed me back and before I could spend, she sprung back and laid herself on the bed, encouraging me to throw myself upon her in the most ardent terms. She threw her legs over my back and we commenced a short sharp bout of the most enjoyable fucking. The muscles of her cunney tightened gloriously around my shaft as, with a gigantic whoosh, the white froth burst out from me, hot and seething, into her eager nook. Gush after gush spurted uncontrollably deep inside her as Lizzie happily screamed out that her own climax was upon her and our cum juices mingled as we came together in a glorious mutual spend.

We could both have wished to continue but, alas, Lizzie had promised to rejoin her friends on the charabanc back to their hall of learning. But we have arranged to see each other again during the summer. She lives eighty or so miles from my home but it is a journey I would happily make by foot if necessary for another hour with Lizzie, an honours graduate in *l'arte de faire l'amour*.

I have the honour to be, Sir,
Your Humble Servant,

Clive Kiniston-Jones
Belsize House
The Grove
Norwich
June, 1890

The Editor replies: You do not say whether the young lady has completed her studies. If she has not and requires employment during the long summer vacation, do not hesitate to pass my address to her.

THE REMARKABLE ADVENTURES OF PORLOCK HOLMES

'Unless I am very much mistaken,' said the great detective, 'we are about to have a visitor. A woman of some standing in society who has just enjoyed a prolonged and vigorous bout of sexual congress.'

'How on earth do you know that?' I asked, amazed at his powers of prediction.

He beckoned me over to the drawing room window. 'Note the carriage standing at the kerb outside the house,' he said. 'It drew up some three quarters of an hour ago. Since then, no one has emerged. You will observe also that it is a private equipage, well maintained and with a discreet monogram on the door. The blinds are down and it has been swaying rhythmically on its springs ever since it first arrived. In my experience that is a sure sign that the occupants are engrossed in the noble sport of fucking.

'Had they been involved in a fight, the movements would not have been nearly so regular and had the parties not been mutually eager for their encounter the duration of their activities would have been considerably shorter. Only a willing couple could have kept up the engagement for such a period of time.'

'Good God, Holmes,' I said. 'You continue to surprise me.'

'Simple observation,' he said. 'You are not, I take it, of a musical disposition? The tempo of their movements, as far as I could judge by the bouncing of the carriage, moved from *lento* to *andante*, modulated to *allegro* and then built up inexorably to a thrilling *furioso*, before subsiding once again by stages to *lento*.' He fingered the strings of his violin as he spoke and gazed down into the street.

'Notice also the horse,' he said. 'It became somewhat

95

'Notice also the horse,' he said. 'It became somewhat agitated while the bout was at its most animated. The coachman had to hold its head as it attempted to back between the shafts. Even now its nostrils are flared and it is tossing its mane.

'Animals frequently respond with great excitement in the presence of human intercourse.'

I suppose that I had never properly considered this point before, but now I came to think on it, I recalled at least two occasions when the household cat had leaped upon the bed with a great purring and head-butting while I was in the process of grappling with one or other of Mrs P — 's daughters. Indeed I remembered Hannah, or was it Becky, bursting out in a fit of giggles as she attempted to push the persistent animal away as it tried to squeeze itself between our bodies.

'Come,' said Holmes, dragging my attention back to the present, 'We must prepare for our guest. Whatever her purpose in calling on us, she will be in sore need of something comfortable on which to recline. The sofa, I think. Help me spread this rug and pile up some cushions for her.'

Moments later the front door bell sounded and I heard the housekeeper shuffle down the hallway. Footsteps ascended the stairs and there came a quiet knock at the drawing room door.

'A lady to see you, Sir,' said Mrs Sayers, a gaunt woman who seldom if ever smiled but was fierce in her devotion to her employer. 'She prefers not to give her name but insists that you will be pleased to receive her.'

'Show her in, Mrs Sayers,' said Holmes.

As he said this, the door was pushed fully open and there entered an extremely handsome woman dressed in the height of fashion. Her bosom, a delightfully full bosom I could not fail to observe, rose and fell as though she was considerably out of breath. Her veil was flung back to reveal a pair of sparkling eyes with a faraway, dreamy look in them. Her lips were parted and her skin deliciously flushed.

As the door closed behind her, our visitor looked round in some state of agitation, then her glance fell on me and she started, backing away as though to leave the room.

'I had thought that you were alone,' she said to Holmes.

'My dear Lady M —,' he began.

'How . . . did you know my name?' she gasped.

'Suffice it to say that a trained eye and a trained memory are among the basic skills needed in my profession, while your face is not unknown in Society.'

Still exhibiting every sign of alarm, she looked questioningly in my direction.

'My assistant, Mr Andrew Scott,' said Holmes. 'I can assure you of his complete discretion. Everything you say will be in absolute confidence.'

As I rose to be introduced, I felt a familiar stirring as Mr Pego rose also, eager for his part for his own introduction to this enticing creature. I noticed that the all-seeing Holmes had spotted the tell-tale bulge in my trousers. One eyebrow was raised quizzically but he spared my embarrassment by keeping a straight face.

'Mr Holmes,' said our visitor, 'forgive me for my presumption in bursting in on you unannounced but the matter is urgent. I am being blackmailed.'

'By your husband, I suspect, Ma'am,' said the detective.

'How — how on earth did you deduce that?' she said with a little gasp of surprise.

'Elementary, my dear Lady M — ' he replied. 'You arrived in your own carriage. I have it on good authority that your husband is away on an official but secret mission to the Hapsburg Court concerning the recent unrest in the Balkans. Hence your dalliance at my doorstep has been with a man other than your spouse. I would add that your husband is well known for his enthusiasm for the science of photography.' He walked over to the bureau and produced a flat package from a pigeon hole. 'Indeed these are examples of his recent endeavours.'

Our visitor let out a little cry of distress and subsided in tears upon the sofa. 'Where . . . where did you get them?' she asked between sobs.

'My dear, you must pull yourself together,' said Holmes. 'Scott, there is brandy in that cabinet, and glasses. Lady M — is in need of a restorative. Help yourself as well.'

'And a glass for you?' I asked.

'My pipe will suffice,' he answered, reaching for the lady's laced boot on the mantel in which I had learned he kept the unusual smoking mixture he preferred and which was provided for him by a villainous-looking Lascar seaman who called clandestinely at regular intervals.

He tamped the mixture down in his pipe, struck a lucifer and inhaled deeply. 'Aaah, the Orient brings us many pleasures,' he murmured. 'But now, to the business in hand.'

Our visitor dabbed delicately at her eyes with a flimsy handkerchief, swallowed her brandy and mutely held out her glass for replenishment. As I bent to pour another libation, I caught the tantalising scent of a woman who, whatever her present distress, had but recently been wholeheartedly engaged in the pleasures of the flesh. Mr Pego gave another twitch. At once a warm, ungloved hand reached out and settled on the protruding source of my passions. She gave an unthinking little squeeze before realising what she was doing.

'I'm sorry,' she said pulling back from my aroused member. 'I hardly know what I am about. But thank you for your attentions.'

'Lady M – ' said Holmes, drawing on his pipe, 'We have here a most unusual coincidence. These photographs were handed to me in the strictest confidence by your husband. He asked me to discover the identity of the parties involved. With your permission, I would like to show them to my assistant. He is not inexperienced in such matters. You have my word, and his, that this matter will be handled in utter secrecy.'

'Indeed, yes,' I said, although truth to tell, I had not the slightest idea of what was depicted in this substantial portfolio of likenesses. 'I shall be the soul of discretion.'

'I can see that I will have to trust you both,' said Lady M – as a deep blush spread over her face. 'But I hope that you will not think too badly of me.'

'If I may speak frankly,' said Holmes, 'I have little other than contempt for many of the public conventions of the age. Providing only that such activities are not carried out in the street where they may frighten the horses, they are largely to

98

be encouraged. I am talking,' he said, turning to me, 'of fucking.'

Somewhat bemused by the turn of events, I could but stammer out my agreement. His opinions after all differed not one iota from those of my old headmaster, Dr White.

'But blackmail,' he continued, 'is the most loathsome of crimes. You are, Lady M— , a woman of considerable independent fortune, are you not? A fortune rather greater than that of your husband, particularly since he has lately been speculating rather unwisely in companies trading with the Baltic States and St Petersburg.'

'Indeed, yes,' she answered. 'His finances are now precarious in the extreme and he has become increasingly pressing in his suggestions that I should make over a substantial part of my capital to him so that he can avoid ruin.'

'But you have been thus far adamant in your refusal,' said Holmes.

'I have been for some years supporting a Home for Fallen Women as well as a retreat for disgraced and unfrocked clergymen, while much of the estate is entailed.

'My attorney tells me that legally I am bound to surrender all that I have to my husband if he so demands,' she continued. 'But this I will not do unless he forces the issue through the courts.'

'You do not like your husband, I take it?' said Holmes.

'Ours has not been a happy marriage,' she said. 'He is cold and domineering, obsessed with his position in Society and often unfeeling in his demands on me. For several years I have had to seek affection beyond the bonds of marriage.'

'And this search for affection has now led you to the point where he or some other who wishes you ill, has evidence that can destroy you in the eyes of the public,' said Holmes.

'Worse. He has already stated that he could have me put away in an asylum for the insane. Yet mine are surely the most natural of appetites.'

Again, an anxious hand reached out for me and clutched at my out-thrust manhood so convulsively that I flinched, fearing some damage to that most sensitive part of my anatomy.

'Ow!' I said.

'Oh, I am sorry,' she said. 'I have inadvertently hurt you. Here, let me kiss it better.'

My heart seemed to swell with pity and affection for this poor creature in distress. I vowed that I would do whatever was in my power to soothe her urgent needs. As I drew myself up to my full height and prepared a gallant speech to that effect, she unbuttoned me and my prick fairly leapt out into plain view. At once she lowered her head and gently enclosed its straining head with her lips. She licked eagerly at its tip before releasing me for a moment. 'You have a most understanding assistant, Mr Holmes,' she said.

'There are in fact considerable limits to his powers of understanding,' said Holmes, rather unfairly I thought, 'but his heart, and indeed his other organs, seem to be in the right place.'

She bent her head once more and without more ado took my whole swollen length into her mouth, sucking and nibbling with such expert concentration that I rapidly forgot the knotty problem that she had presented us with. I decided that I would leave the more cerebral aspects of the case to Holmes. He was already poring over the photographs, tapping the mouthpiece of his pipe against his teeth, his brow wrinkled with concentration.

'There are several members represented here,' he said. 'One I believe I can put a name to. Two, I believe may come from North of the Border. Another should be easily discovered since he has only one testicle, and this one,' he gestured towards it with his pipe, 'has a curious tattoo of a Masonic nature on the foreskin.' He scrutinised the print. 'I shall need my magnifying glass. I believe you may be sitting on it, Ma'am.'

'Wffflll, oooffl, gluppp,' she said, unable to speak with her mouth full.

Holmes looked at our visitor with a slight gesture of impatience.

'If I might prevail upon you to disengage yourself from my assistant, Ma'am, I must ask you some questions.'

With a guilty start, our delightful visitor withdrew her lips that had been so energetically sucking and teasing at the by now greatly swollen head and shaft of my member. I must have made some involuntary gesture of disappointment for I had been but moments away from discharging the full contents of my throbbing testicles down the length of my cock and into that warm, receptive mouth. Realising my distress, she took hold of Mr Pego in her hand and slipped one of her gloves on to him.

'I am sorry,' she said, 'but we have to attend to the subject of my visit. This will at least keep him warm until I am able to resume my ministrations. I know that it is unfair in the extreme to leave a man in such a state of expectation.'

How thoughtful she was, I thought to myself, although her kind action had left me in a rather delicate social dilemma. It would be ungallant to remove a lady's glove when it had been so understandingly pressed upon me, yet I could not easily thrust prick and glove together back inside my trousers. I realised that I should have to leave my unusually ornamented member protruding *en plein air* while I played my part in the consultation that was about to begin.

'Let us first consider whether the blackmailer is in fact your husband and not some other scoundrel who has gained access to the evidence of your extra-marital adventures,' said Holmes. 'May I ask you, Ma'am, to describe in detail the circumstances of the delivery of the threat.'

'Some three weeks ago,' said Lady M —, 'a large envelope was presented at the front door by a street urchin. He announced to my maid that he had been handed the package by a man he had never seen before, along with tuppence, and told to ensure that it was delivered to me personally, and that it contained documents of a strictly private nature and was to be opened by no-one but myself.'

'An impertinent demand,' said Holmes. 'But do you recall anything distinctive about your visitor?'

'He was an urchin like any other,' Lady M— replied. 'Badly dressed in hand-me-downs and clearly a stranger to soap and water.'

'And did you not ask about the stranger who had entrusted him with the errand?'

101

'Why, no,' she said hesitantly. 'You will understand that I am not unaccustomed to the clandestine delivery of *billets doux* and letters of assignation.'

'Of course,' said Holmes. 'Given the nature and, may I say, the complexity of your extra-domestic arrangements, such anonymous missives must arrive with some regularity.'

'That is so,' she said with a quick smile as she dropped her eyes in modesty. Unfortunately this caused her gaze to fasten upon my gloved member and she gave a little giggle. A consolatory hand reached out and, like a devout Catholic playing unconsciously with her rosary beads, she began to fiddle with me. Some instinct, most probably of neatness, led her to smooth the glove along my ramrod so that the head was forced into the opening of the middle finger of the glove. Such an entry was of course impossible and as the thin fabric stretched in its unachievable task of containment, I realised that if she continued with this course of action, however pleasant, some damage to the seams of the thin silk of her glove would inevitably be done.

I closed my hand over hers in warning. She ceased her stroking and pulling but continued to hold on to the tip between her thumb and first finger. Absent-mindedly she continued to toy with it, as though seeking some assurance.

At this juncture, Holmes smacked the dottle out of his pipe against the fender and held it out in my direction. 'A two pipe problem,' he said. 'If you would be so good as to replenish it. A generous filling, and packed well down.'

As I prised my prick somewhat reluctantly from the hands of Lady M — and her gentle kneadings, I took the proffered pipe and began to stuff it with the sweet-smelling oriental mixture.

'Now,' said Holmes, 'the note. Do you still have it?'

'I have brought it with me,' said Lady M — , 'together with the enclosures.'

'Enclosures?' said Holmes.

'A set of pictures that would appear to be duplicates of those that you have received. Although I have of course had but the briefest glimpse of your set.'

'May I inspect the note first of all,' said Holmes.

She reached into her reticule and drew out a well-folded piece of paper.

'An obviously disguised hand,' said Holmes, 'but clearly that of a man of some education, correct in the spelling and grammatical construction. We are not dealing with some working class fellow from the criminal classes.'

'A man?' I asked. 'How can you tell?'

'You will find in the library a monograph on the science of handwriting,' he said a little impatiently. 'Written by myself, it was, in all modesty, well received by the Society of Calligraphers when I presented it at their annual conference. The fruits of a lifetime's study. I have conclusively demonstrated that the gender, class and much of the character of any individual can be deduced from a careful examination of even the smallest sample of a script.

'I have attempted long and fruitlessly, I am sorry to say, to engage the interest of those clodhopping asses at Scotland Yard in my researches. It could in many cases be a valuable aid to detection. You may recall the Case of the One-Armed Plenipotentiary where I was able to render some small service to the forces of law and order. The Home Secretary of the time was rightfully very grateful and a discreet Honour was subsequently bestowed on me at a private investiture by Her Majesty. Not that I set any store by such baubles. The successful application of the Intellect in the solution of any problem is satisfaction enough, I find.'

I could not but notice that a note close to self-satisfaction had crept into his voice. Lady M — was also growing a little restless as he reminisced. She caught my eye, smiled, and fingered the top buttons of her dress in a most provocative fashion. As she drew a deep breath, her enticing bosom rose so that the shadowed valley between her creamy, plump titties was exposed. Mr Pego, who had been showing some signs of relaxing, re-erected in an instant.

Meanwhile Holmes took a deep suck at his pipe, drawing the smoke down into his lungs and holding it there. His eyes closed as though in a trance. 'Aaarrrgh,' he murmured as he exhaled. 'I feel my mental processes at work.'

Lady M — reached out and took my hand in hers. She

103

raised it to her lips and moistened a fingertip before inserting it deep down the front of her barely buttoned bodice and placing it on the unseen nipple that rose unhesitatingly to my touch. Gently I rubbed it and felt it hard and fat against my skin. She leaned forward so that her breast nestled in my cupped hand. I squeezed it carefully, trying not to disturb Holmes' cerebral concentration.

Holmes began to read, at first to himself but then out loud.

'"If you wish to retain your place in polite society, you will recognise, dear Lady M —, that it would be greatly to your advantage to obtain possession, not only of these prints but of the original photographic plates. These can be delivered to you with complete discretion at any time that you may choose. We both understand that the greatest care must be taken to ensure that they do not fall into the hands of any third party, in particular the editor of one of the public prints, nor, it goes without saying, of your husband.

'"There will of course be certain unavoidable expenses in order to assure both safe delivery of the originals and to ensure my continued silence in the matter."'

Holmes read on silently. Lady M — had frozen at his words, my hand still clamped firmly on her breast. I essayed a tentative squeeze to show my sympathy with her plight but she did not react. Mr Pego, sensitive as ever to the nuances of the situation, lowered his head. Holmes read on, once more out loud.

'The transfer of a very substantial amount of money will be necessary.'

Lady M — bowed her head and a tear trickled down her cheek. I pulled her glove off my prick and handed it to her so that she could mop her eyes. She sniffed.

'Thank you Mr — ?' she said.

'Scott,' I said. 'Andrew Scott.'

'Thank you, Andrew,' she said. 'You are most sympathetic.' She turned to Holmes. 'The sum demanded,' she said, 'will come close to beggaring me.'

She stood up suddenly and began to pace the room, unconscious that her splendid bosom was spilling out of her dress. So abrupt had been her movement that I fell forward on my knees, Mr Pego flopping on to the carpet as a milky bead of cum hung suspended from his tip. Holmes noticed.

'The rug is Turkish,' he said. 'From a village close to the Persian border. The same area from which I obtain my smoking mixture. I would be grateful if you can avoid staining it. It is very precious. The only other is in the Victoria and Albert Museum.'

I scooped my member up and wiped it with Lady M—'s discarded glove. 'My apologies,' I said, but Holmes' attention was once more directed to the matter of the blackmailing letter.

'But the money can be raised?' he went on.

'Just,' she said.

'Which suggests either that this is an improbable coincidence or that the demand comes from someone with an intimate knowledge of your financial affairs. We are dealing with a well-informed scoundrel. I notice however that there is no mention of the means by which these funds are to be transferred.'

'If you read on,' said Lady M—, 'you will see that he promises a further communication. All I am asked to do at this juncture is to assent in principle to his demands. A messenger is to call for my reply at some time in the next week.'

'Then we must be present also,' said Holmes.

'But he enjoins the strictest confidence,' she said.

'Never fear,' said Holmes, 'we shall be nearby but unnoticed when the agent of this diabolical plot arrives.'

'How will you ensure that?' she asked. 'The time is not stated. You might, I suppose, be lodged in my household.'

'That, alas, would be most unwise,' said Holmes. 'The arrival of two male guests while your husband is absent abroad would certainly be noticed in the neighbourhood. All my experience confirms that servants are inveterate gossips. Very little escapes their eyes and everything that is noticed becomes the subject of tittle-tattle amongst all their fellows in the vicinity. That is why I make the point of keeping the smallest establishment possible. Mrs Sayers is the soul of discretion while Mr Scott here will already have noticed that the boy and the maids speak only Portuguese: a language not generally understood in this country. I interviewed them all personally whilst in Oporto two years ago, where I was solving the Case of the Adulterated Wine.'

As with Colonel Moore (*see Oyster 2, 3,* and *4*), I realised that I was in the habit of falling in with men prone to digression.

'So what will we do?' I asked, dragging him back from triumphs past to problems present.

'That we will discuss later,' he said. 'But a scheme is forming in my mind. Rest assured, Lady M — that when the messenger returns, we will be present and observing all that transpires, although I suspect that you will not be aware of us.'

'So you are convinced that this vile plot is definitely all the work of my husband?' said Lady M —.

'In all probability,' said Holmes, 'although we must not discount the possibility that two separate attempts are being made to divest you of your fortune.'

'How horrible,' she said. 'I am ever too trusting of human nature.'

'And also somewhat careless with your affairs, Ma'am,' said Holmes. 'I would in future counsel some care in the bestowal of your favours.'

'I will try,' said our visitor, 'but you must understand that I am not one of your blue-stockinged, intellectual modern women. To put it bluntly, I have needs that have to be satisfied.'

'You like fucking,' said Holmes, bluntly.

'It is I suppose my chief enjoyment in life,' she said, drawing herself up to her full height and looking him straight in the eye.

'But until this frightful business is cleared up, I do most strongly suggest that you are, if not wholly continent, at least careful. Take for instance the gentleman who is waiting for you outside in your carriage.'

'An old friend,' she said. 'One who I can trust.'

'Will he not be becoming bored with the wait?' I asked.

'I suspect not,' Lady M — said with a roguish grin. 'He was

well drained from his exertions when I left him. He deserves some rest. But how did you know of his presence?'

'You were observed,' said Holmes. 'Or rather the vigorous motion of your carriage was observed.'

Lady M — blushed. 'I was so nervous concerning my visit to you that Matthew decided that I needed to have my mind taken off my plight for a few minutes.'

'Three quarters of an hour,' said Holmes.

'Good Gracious! Was it that long? How time does fly when one is fucking. Anyway, I did feel much better afterwards. But now I am beginning to feel rather tense.' Again she involuntarily reached out and clutched my member. I winced.

'Oh, sorry!' she said. 'I've squeezed you too hard.'

'Not at all,' I said, blinking a little as tears sprang to my eyes. She relaxed her grip and began to caress my prick with regular but gentle strokes. All the pain was quickly soothed away and it thrust boldly out once more.

'If you feel the need of some further relaxing exercise,' said Holmes, 'pray do not hesitate. I am certain that Scott will help you and I need to ponder some more on what is to be done.'

'That is very understanding of you,' she said. 'If Andrew is prepared to help a lady in distress — '

'By all means,' I answered, delighted at the realisation that I could actually help Holmes in his professional endeavours while at the same time assisting this poor suffering creature to gain some semblance of relief. 'Anything I can do to ease your anguish,' I said.

'I suggest that you ease your prick into my pussey,' she said with that commendable directness of expression that so often marks the upper *echelons* of our society. 'Now, off with your trousers!'

I did as I was told. She fairly threw herself backward upon the cushions, pulled up her dress and raised her knees. Without more ado, I lowered myself on to her.

Lady M — was clearly thoroughly experienced in such matters. There was none of that clumsy bumping and boring that so often attends the fumbling embraces of the novice. Mr Pego immediately slipped through the already damp thickets of her pussey hair and found the moist entrance to her cave of delights. At his touch, she wriggled her bum into a more comfortable position and opened up before me. Almost without effort, the entire length of my prick sank into her up to the hilt. I paused as she tightened her grip on me and a smile of pure pleasure lit up her face.

'That is just what I need,' she said, holding me for a moment or two.

Slowly I began to slide easily up and down her warmly clinging cunney. She in turn began to rise to meet my thrusting. Like any gentleman, I endeavoured to keep my weight on my elbows and, intent though I was on my delightful task, I could not help but notice that Holmes, not one whit put out by the scene that was being enacted in front of him, was scrutinising the photographic prints he held out before him. At one point he peered intently at some detail on a print using a magnifying glass. Then he screwed a monocle into place, raised his head and stared at Lady M – 's private parts now fully revealed as her dress rode up over her stomach with its deep-set navel.

'A memorable bush,' he murmured to himself. 'And a certain identification.'

Meanwhile the pace of our efforts had been increasing. It was as though we had fucked many times before. Our breathing was in unison, deeper now as a slight sheen of sweat oiled our bodies. My prick tingled with the firm pressure of her inner walls. We fitted together as though a benign Providence had designed each for the other.

Now she lifted up her legs still further and crossed them behind my waist, pressing me down into her, yet she did not grasp me so tightly as to inhibit my rhythm. We speeded up and then with a natural control, relaxed our efforts a little. Again our efforts increased and again slowed down. She had a wonderful sense of timing, understanding as though by instinct when to lower the tension so that our pleasure might be prolonged.

Holmes meanwhile had taken a pair of callipers from a desk drawer and was taking careful measurements from the photographs, noting down the results in a small book. His brow was a little furrowed as he concentrated on his task but there was a slight smile of satisfaction on his lips. Then he looked around him.

'Scott, could you — ' he began and then pulled himself together, realising that I was far too buried in my own work to assist him. 'I am sorry,' he said, 'Do carry on.'

We did indeed carry on. Lady M — had in any case clearly not heard his half-swallowed remarks. She was absolutely absorbed in our joint venture. Throughout our whole fuck she concentrated entirely on her pleasure and mine. Without any sense of artifice or unnatural effort, she both responded to my needs and attended to her own. She was of that admirable school of thought that holds that fucking is an activity for two. There was no mindless surrender to her own desires at the expense of my own. Nor was there any watchful deference to my will or possible demands such as is found in some of the more professional ladies that I have encountered.

So we fucked for a considerable time, locked together as one. Yet gradually the intensity of our activities increased. Each renewed level in tempo took us one step towards the final climax. From an easy canter, the pace was raised to a full yet sustainable gallop. I wondered at my own stamina. I was dimly aware that outside dusk must be falling as Holmes, with the thoughtful man's true patience, continued with his own intellectual efforts but allowed Mrs Sayers into the room to move softly about, lighting the gas and attending to the fire.

Then the rate of our striking increased still further as I drove in and out of my ever-responsive companion. Somewhere in the hallway I was aware of a clock chiming. At that moment I felt the first pulsation as my balls began to release what was to prove a veritable tidal wave of cum. As it began to flood unstoppably down my cock, I sensed that she also had reached that same point of abandonment to our bodily demands. It was as though she widened, opening out to receive my libations as they jetted time and time again into her. She did not cry out but moaned softly, then suddenly caught her breath. She matched my every surge as though she also was discharging her cum into me. But still there was no

109

sense of desperation but rather a feeling of inevitability as tide met tide and mingled in one rush and whirlpool of coming. So completely taken up was I by our climax that I swear the house could have burnt down without my noticing. Each jet felt now as though it must surely be the last, yet time and time again I felt one further eruption churning inside me. I was panting and shuddering as though I was emptying my entire being into her.

Then, imperceptibly, the pace began to slacken. Amazingly, we did not stop. There was no final exhausted thrust. No sudden collapse. Smoothly but inevitably we slowed, both breathing deeply, relaxing gently, still responding each to the other. Both of us began to be more aware of our surroundings. She turned her head to one side, a look of complete satisfaction and fulfilment spreading over her face.

'Stay inside me,' she said quietly. 'I can still feel you.' Then she hugged me to her, tucking her head into my shoulder. A last quiver of mixed emotion and cum flowed from me and we held each other silently.

'Forty-seven minutes,' said Holmes, fishing out a half hunter from his waistcoat pocket. 'A remarkable performance. I suggest a brandy, when you have disentangled yourselves.'

'I did not realise that we were being timed,' I said, a little put out by his attentions.

'Purely in the interests of Science,' said Holmes. 'The scientific measurement of all manifestations of human activity is one of my particular areas of intellectual endeavour. Alas, there has been as yet little published statistical evidence of the duration range of human sexual congress. A lack that I hope to remedy in a paper that I am preparing for private circulation within the next eighteen months. The evidence that I have collected so far is most interesting. One minute is the shortest time I have recorded. Yours was one of the more prolonged encounters I have been able to witness. However explorers in the East claim that four hours or more of *coitus uninterruptus* is regularly achieved among the adepts of some of the mystic sects of Tibet.'

'An indoor record, I imagine,' I said.

'A record but not necessarily indoors,' he replied. 'Well over two hours in a snow drift in the foothills of the Himalayas has been observed.'

'Both parties being well wrapped up?' said Lady M — , beginning to take an interest in the conversation.

'Stark naked, in fact,' said Holmes. 'Both of them.'

'Who was on top?' asked Lady M —.

'They changed positions several times,' said Holmes. 'The most fascinating fact is that none of the snow melted. It seems that through long training, they were able to retain all their body heat and concentrate exclusively on their exertions.'

'Amazing!' I said.

'On the contrary,' said Holmes. 'Through life-long spiritual immersion in the arts of Yoga, the *swamis*, as they are called, can attain complete control of all their bodily functions.'

'Like those pictures of old men with long beards, sitting on beds of nails and feeling no pain,' I said.

'But do they ever fuck on beds of nails?' asked Lady M —.

'Only the most advanced initiates,' said Holmes. 'There are dangers of course.'

'I shall stick to beds and sofas and carpets,' said Lady M —.

'And carriages,' I added, remembering the long session that Holmes at least had viewed from the window.

'I have tried it on a croquet lawn,' she went on. 'But we bent two of the hoops in our efforts.'

'But the hoops at croquet are set some considerable distance apart,' said Holmes thoughtfully. 'I must consult the rules for the correct spacing.'

'It was a rolling fuck,' said Lady M —. 'We did do some damage to the turf as I recall.'

'There was not a game actually in progress at the time, I assume?' I said.

'At the beginning,' said Lady M —. 'I have a distinct recollection of being struck by a croquet ball quite early on in our encounter, but then the other parties fell to fucking as well. Except for the bishop.'

'A bishop!' I exclaimed.

'I remember looking up and seeing a pair of clerical gaiters at my head, and above them a large pectoral cross dangling over a purple-clad paunch.'

'And was nothing said?' I asked.

'Nothing at the time,' she said. 'Although I recall afterwards that there was something of an atmosphere over tea. Meaningful looks exchanged over the scones. That sort of thing. Of course the silly man should have joined in instead of trying to play on and ending up losing his balls in the shrubbery.'

'What!' I said.

'Well, nearly,' said Lady M —. 'He became entangled in a snare that had been set by one of the keepers.'

'Shooting and sex,' said Holmes. 'The preoccupations of the Landed Gentry through the ages. However, we must return to the subject of your visit, Lady M —. A plan is beginning to form in my mind.'

I should at this point explain the rather unusual circumstances that had led to my acting as the temporary assistant to Mr Porlock Holmes who readers will recognise as being the greatest amateur detective of our age.

Mrs P —, the widow in whose house I lodged in Bayswater, had as I have previously mentioned in my memoirs (*see Oyster 2*), a considerable interest in certain aspects of the Classical and Oriental Arts. She was, for instance, one of a small group of *cognoscenti* who had long been urging Mr Richard Burton, the noted explorer, to translate into English such eastern texts as the *Perfumed Garden* and the *Karma Sutra*. She engaged in frequent and detailed correspondence with a learned circle of scholars of the erotic. In addition one of her daughters, Hannah, was an artist and potter of growing repute as well as being, along with her sister, a frequent partner of mine in the amatory arts. She was particularly interested in recreating the styles and techniques of some of the more unrestrained early Greek ceramic artists.

It happened one evening, just as I was looking forward to one of our regular postprandial entertainments of a sexual

112

nature, involving Hannah, her sister Becky and in all probability several of their friends, that Mrs P — announced towards the end of dinner that her friend Mr Porlock Holmes was interested in commissioning from Hannah a substantial vase, to be decorated with some scene from Greek mythology.

'What subject does he have in mind?' asked Hannah.

'He is as yet undecided,' her mother answered. 'Indeed he is prepared to be guided by you in the matter. He did though mention various subjects including Europa and the Bull and Prometheus Condemned to Eternal Punishment.'

'What about Leda and the Swan?' suggested Hannah.

'My grounding in the Greek myths is, I regret, uncertain,' I said.

'A constant theme,' said Mrs P —, 'is that of one of the Gods, in most cases Zeus, descending in various guises and surprising some hapless nymph or sprite and then leaping on her with great gusto. The unfortunate Leda was one such unwilling object of his attentions.'

'For the occasion, he took the form of a large swan,' said Hannah.

'What was the outcome?' I asked.

'An egg, or eggs,' said her mother. 'One hatched into the twins Castor and Pollux.'

'And according to some authorities of Antiquity, the fair Helen was also the fruit of their union,' Hannah added.

'That would seem a thoroughly suitable subject,' said Becky. 'I would be more than happy to pose as Leda. I see myself down on all fours, possibly looking at my reflection in the water and wearing something diaphanous in white.'

As I pictured the scene I began to see a part for myself. 'I would be more than happy to surprise you in such a position,' I offered.

'I don't doubt it,' said Becky. 'But you would have to be covered with feathers.'

'With his arms outstretched like wings,' said Hannah, clearly visualising the scene.'

'And a beak,' said Becky with a teasing smile.

'And webbed feet,' added her sister. I sensed a note of ridicule creeping into the conversation.

113

'Let us ring for cook,' said Becky. 'I know that she is intending to serve up a goose for tomorrow's dinner. I saw the poulterer delivering a large, well-feathered bird earlier today.'

By now I was beginning to have second thoughts about the whole endeavour but before I could protest, cook was summoned to confirm her plans. Moments later I found myself down in the kitchen, face to face with a substantial dead specimen of *Anser Domesticus*.

'Just the thing,' said Hannah, seized with enthusiasm. 'We shall pluck it immediately.'

'I, in the meantime, will go and pick out some suitable drapery,' said Becky.

'Give cook a hand,' said Hannah to me.

'Plucking is not one of my skills,' I said hastily.

'Then you must learn,' said Hannah firmly. 'First the plucking and then the fucking. You cannot take part in one without the other.'

'Don't worry, Mr Andrew,' said cook. 'Just watch what I do and follow me.'

Thus it was that some ten minutes later I found myself holding a stripped and naked bird while a stripped and naked Becky crouched invitingly in front of me.

'Are you certain that you will be able to perform to the satisfaction both of my sister and myself?'

'I have never failed yet,' I answered, my pride somewhat hurt.

'That is true,' said Becky. 'But in this case you will have to exercise a considerable degree of self-control. Several sessions will be necessary, so that my sister can sketch the tableau to her satisfaction. Are you sure that you will be able to hold your position without moving. Here!'

In an instant I had been forced down onto one knee while my arms were stretched out like wings. Becky and Hannah, quite ignoring my protestations, pushed and pulled me this way and that, standing back at intervals to scrutinise the effect.

'Right hand down a bit,' said Hannah. 'Can you get him to bend forward a little more.'

'Let's try him standing up and bending forward,' said Becky, dragging me to my feet.

'Legs a little apart,' said her sister. 'He's a bit stiff.'

'He frequently is,' said Becky with a grin. 'But not all over.'

The fact of the matter was that I was being so manipulated and shoved around that Mr Pego was at his most shrivelled and limp. This to my chagrin was revealed when both sisters began to divest me of all my clothing. Both looked sorrowfully at my state.

'Upstairs,' said Becky. 'At least it will be warmer, and I would prefer carpet rather than stone flags under me.'

Clutching a bowl of feathers, I was urged up the stairs. Once in the drawing room before a blazing fire, I felt more at ease. Hannah went off to bring her crayons and sketch pad, while Becky began to try various nymph-like positions in front of me. As she raised up her delicious bum, Mr Pego awoke from his slumber and jutted out in front of me. Unable to resist what was spread out before me, I dropped to a kneeling position behind her and with my hands on her hips, drew her to me. The tip of my prick slid easily between her thighs and began to probe at the entry to her lovely cunney.

'Can you keep it just like that,' said Hannah as she suddenly came into the room. I groaned with frustration and moved forward another inch or so.

'Don't let him in, Hannah,' said Becky. 'In this instance Nature must wait upon Art.'

'*I* seem to be suffering for *your* Art,' I said, a little bitterly, but, I thought, rather cleverly.

'Come out of my sister at once,' said Hannah, failing completely to respond to my witticism.

Becky it was who took pity on me. 'Later, Andrew,' she said, 'I can promise you an absolutely splendid fuck. And no doubt my sister can be prevailed upon to join in our activities. See, already I am quite damp with anticipation of what is to come. But now you must be greased and feathered. Arms out.'

Accepting my fate, I stood up. I was liberally smeared with what seemed to be lard, and first the down and then a selection of large wing feathers was pressed on to me. At this point both Becky and Hannah burst out laughing.

'Not at all like a Greek God,' said one.

'More like a scarecrow,' said the other.

At this point I became quite angry. 'You are making fun of me,' I said, making as though to leave the room.

'Come back at once,' said Hannah. 'Don't be so stuffy. See, we can all join in.' With that she slapped a pat of lard or butter on her sister's bared bottom and threw the rest of the feathers at her so that they stuck to her all over. Becky gave a squeal of protest and pulled at her sister's dress. In a trice they were wrestling over and over on the rug in a great confusion of discarded clothing and sticky feathers.

'Mr Porlock Holmes,' announced Emily the maid, suddenly appearing at the door. 'Shall I show him in?'

'The Library,' said Becky, choking with laughter and a mouthful of fluff. 'Mother will entertain him, at least until we are more presentable.'

So it was that a few minutes later I made my first acquaintance with the world's greatest detective. He was sitting at a desk in the library, smoking the oddly smelling pipe that I was later to come to know so well. Mrs P — was beside him and together they were poring over a large volume of what I later discovered to be Etruscan drawings.

'Mr Scott,' said Mrs P — as he looked up. 'He is presently staying with us. He is aware of the commission that you have in mind and has kindly offered to help in any way he can.'

'He is to be our Swan,' said Hannah. 'Although up to now he had not numbered bird impressions among his repertoire.'

'*Cygnus olor*, *gibbus* or *mansuetus*, the Mute Swan,' said our learned guest. 'A graceful creature, if one of uncertain temper. You are familiar with the genus *Cygnus* of the family *Anatidae*?'

'I have seen them swimming about,' I said. 'But must admit that I have not studied their habits in depth.'

'I am certain that the Misses P — will complete your education. As an artist, Hannah is well trained in observation while Becky has a nurse's interest in anatomy,' he said. 'I look forward to seeing the first sketches in due course but will not intrude on your work. I have, in any case, a small problem on which Mrs P — can in all probability give me the benefit of her considerable learning. The case I talk of,' he said, turning to his hostess, 'is that of the Incontinent Cabinet Minister. A matter of great delicacy for I fear that the Irish Question has raised its ever-importunate head. I sense a Fenian plot.'

'How much I regret the failure of Mr Gladstone's Home Rule Bill,' I said, determined to demonstrate to the great man that I had a sound grasp of the political issues of our time.

'He once accosted me in the street,' said Becky. 'I believe that he mistook me for one of his Fallen Women.'

'It is important for a man to have some interest in his life other than his work,' said Holmes. 'Even a Prime Minister. I myself, apart from my musical endeavours, am particularly interested in the problems posed by the employment of barmaids in many of our public houses. On the one hand it is argued that they are in a position of obvious moral danger, working as they do in close proximity to both men and strong liquors. On the other, the barmaid is in a situation, unusual particularly among working class women, of being able to dictate the behaviour of men. She can, for instance, refuse to serve any fellow who is being rowdy or objectionable. She can even order him out of the premises. So the question is raised as to whether the opportunities outweigh the dangers.

'Of course, in the interests of the Science of Detection, I have from time to time to enter, usually in disguise, many of the vilest drinking dens in the poorest parts of our city. It was on one such visit that I first became interested in the problem. I was, if I recall aright, at that time engaged on the Case of the Jaundiced Debutante, at the instigation of her mother, the Marchioness of Bolsover. But I am becoming indiscreet.'

He turned to Mrs P — . 'Have you a large-scale map of the County of Sligo in Ireland?' he asked. 'I must return to my intellectual labours and you to your artistic endeavours.'

Becky, Hannah and myself, thus dismissed, returned to the drawing room where Becky and I at once removed our clothing and I was greased and feathered before being pushed and patted into position, hovering, more like a vulture than a swan, as Hannah said, over Becky's invitingly bared bottom.

Hannah sketched industriously away. I was driven to shut my eyes in order to resist the temptation that stared me in the face. Crouching as I was with arms outstretched, down on one knee and with my eyes tight shut, I found it extraordinarily difficult to keep my balance. My plight was not helped when Becky could not resist the temptation to inch backwards so that I could feel the cleft of her buttocks pressing lightly against the tip of my engorged prick.

Hannah did not help matters. 'A little further forward,' she said. 'Can you open yourself up a bit, Becky.'

The strain was too much for me. Carefully I half opened one eye. Becky had reached back and with both hands had pulled her cheeks apart. Her tight little arsehole was flaunted, scarcely half an inch from my cock.

'He's peeking!' said Hannah to her sister. 'Supposing he was to enter just a little way into you. You could hold him fast in position and he could keep his balance. Don't drop your arms,' she said to me sharply. 'I'll arrange things.' She moved over to me and took my prick firmly in her hand.

'I've got it lined up,' she said to her sister. 'Just ease your way backwards on to him.'

Becky shuffled backwards and I inched my way into her.

'That's enough,' said Hannah. 'Now, hang on tight.'

'He's a bit big,' said Becky.

'Goose grease,' said Hannah. 'That will do the trick.' Carefully she smeared some of the by now warm fat on my cock. 'Try again,' she said.

This time I slid smoothly into her. Becky released her grip on her bum cheeks and as they closed about me, I was held fast.

'Just like that,' said Hannah. 'That's just about right. Andrew, you're sagging!' I must have looked surprised for seldom if ever had Mr Pego been more proudly erect.

'Your arms,' said Hannah, recognising my confusion. 'It's your arms. They're drooping.' She pulled both arms upwards so that I looked more like some great bird of prey swooping down on its victim. She stood back and scrutinised the scene that she had arranged.

118

'That will have to do,' she said and retreated to her sketch pad.

'I'm tired,' I said, for the strain on my shoulders was beginning to tell.

'We could prop him up,' said Hannah. 'I'll get one of the maids to bring up a couple of pieces of wood.'

'Like splints,' said Becky. 'We have been taught how to do that in the hospital. Andrew, you can relax for a minute or two until we get this fixed up.' With a sigh of relief I let my aching arms drop and at the same time surreptitiously pushed forward. Becky wriggled her bum and all of a sudden I had measured my full length into her. She let out a little yelp of pleasure and settled herself once more, gripping me round the base of my swollen member. I gritted my teeth and tried to keep control of myself.

It was in this position that Emily the maid found us when she answered the bell.

'This is Art,' said Hannah firmly to her. Instructions were issued to the startled servant. Two broomsticks were procured and bound firmly to my arms. The ends were jammed rather uncomfortably into my armpits while the heads, a mop in one case and a stiff yard broom in the other, projected out beyond my fingers' ends. Two chairs were propped under my splinted arms. Becky remained in position, clasping me warmly in her bum. I had seldom if ever felt so foolish. The situation was not improved when Emily stepped back from her handiwork and burst out laughing. At once she was all confusion and embarrassment.

'I'm sorry, Miss Hannah,' she said. 'But he does look so funny.'

Hannah joined in the laughter, clutching at Emily as they both gave way to complete hysterics. Becky also began to choke with uncontrollable giggles and the vibrations so teased my prick that I found myself being squeezed and teased to a point where I could no longer control myself. I began to thrust backwards and forwards into her. Becky, her head cradled in her arms, began to react as her desire for a good bum fucking fought with her determination to help her sister in her classical efforts.

With my arms still pinioned and propped, I was now driving energetically into Becky's eagerly responding bum. Suddenly one chair overbalanced and I half fell over sideways in a clatter of furniture. Becky reared up and I collapsed on to her, one wing sticking up in the air and the other trailing on the ground like a hen partridge feigning injury. So slippery were Becky and I with the now melting grease that only her tightly clamped sphincter prevented my complete downfall.

'How Athenian,' said a male voice. Unnoticed, Porlock Holmes had entered the room.

'A most interesting situation,' he said. Stepping forward, he set the overturned chair upright once more and set me on an even keel with each arm once more supported. Becky's succulent titties were still heaving and trembling with her half-stifled laughter. Fastidiously, he wiped the grease from his hands on the crumpled piece of drapery that had long since fallen off Becky's naked body. With his head set on one side he eyed his handiwork before arranging the thin material over her body. Seemingly satisfied, he seated himself at the table and took out his pipe.

'Mr Scott,' he said, 'I have a proposition for you. My assistant Dr Motson has had to leave the country for a few weeks. Some fuss with the governing body of the Royal College of Physicians. I regret that he has made enemies among the senior members of his Profession. Some trumped up charge involving medical ethics following his invaluable assistance to me in the Case of the Pregnant Mother Superior. It will all doubtless blow over as these things do, but meanwhile, I am without his help. I mentioned my problem to the good Lady of the House and she suggested that you might be interested in taking over Dr Motson's duties for a short while. She assures me that you have handled at least one delicate errand for her, concerning, I believe, Rosie, the Errant Schoolgirl and she further describes you as adaptable and resourceful.'

'He has indeed proved himself able and willing to rise to the occasion whatever has taken place in our house,' volunteered Hannah, rather nicely I thought.

'If a little clumsily,' added Becky, *sotto voce* from her

position on the carpet. She pushed backwards over-vigorously and I fell off my perch once more. She remained impaled on me and as I tried to scramble back into my classical pose, pushed again so that I fell over backwards, she sitting on my upthrust manhood. Holmes appeared to take no notice of the flailing and tumbling that was going on under his eyes. Swatting a couple of floating feathers away from his face, he sucked on his pipe and I smelt the exotic fumes with which I was later to grow so familiar.

It was in these unusual circumstances that I became the temporary assistant to the Greatest Detective of our Age. I had never before been offered employment while lying flat on my back with a naked woman speared on my prick, but my old headmaster had long since impressed on his pupils that opportunities must be seized with both hands, even if, as in this case, both hands were strapped to broomsticks. I assented to his interesting offer and arrangements were made for my new employment.

'I look forward to seeing the outcome of your artistic imagination,' Holmes said to Hannah courteously. Emily fetched his cape and rather odd hat and he made his Goodbyes. Prometheus was Unbound and we fucked merrily on the carpet, Hannah putting away her drawing materials and joining in, although not before she and Emily had thoroughly sponged down both her sister and I.

Two days later I was delivered, bag and baggage, to Porlock Holmes' rooms in a house close to the Metropolitan Railway Company's station on the Marylebone Road.

A further week and my involvement in the Case of the Blackmailed Wife was underway. I was impersonating a crossing sweeper and keeping watch on all who called at a house in Belgrave Square.

'What happened to the usual crossing sweeper?' asked the fellow in livery.

For a moment I was minded to tell him sharply that it was none of his business, but then remembered that I must behave according to my subservient situation. Holmes had taken up his duties early that morning and had instructed me firmly that I was to take over from him at midday.

'Every visitor to Lady M—'s Belgrave Square establishment is to be noted,' he had said. 'In particular any errand boy and member of the servant class must be regarded with suspicion. All we know is that a message is to be delivered from the blackmailer during the course of this week.'

Becky and Hannah, who had been made partially privy to my task, had fitted me out in an ill-fitting, shabby set of clothes, enlisting the services of Mary the maid.

Holmes, for his part, had been so thoroughly disguised that I had completely failed to recognise him when I presented myself at the street corner at the ordained time.

'Pssst!' A chesty but tremulous voice had whispered as I cast about me. He had entered thoroughly into the spirit of the adventure. Instead of the upright, elegant figure that I had come to know, a crabbed, bent creature approached me. Using all his theatrical skills, he had contrived a hare lip and the mottled complexion of one who spends too much of his time and money in sordid drinking dens.

I caught a pungent whiff of sweat and horse manure as he murmured his instructions in my ear. I recoiled as though by instinct from this stained, consumptively coughing figure.

'Scott!' he said urgently. 'It is I! Take this broom. I have to return to my rooms. I shall return later in the afternoon, around half past four. I have here a list of the regular callers, together with details of their appearance. If Lady M— has the opportunity to alert you, her lady's maid will appear at the window at the left hand side of the first floor. If you see her signal, you are to follow anyone not of the household who leaves.'

'Supposing he does not set off on foot?' I asked.

'There is a cab waiting round the corner. The driver is a reliable man whom I have used on many such occasions. He will do exactly as you say,' said Holmes. 'On no account are you to lose our quarry. If you are not present when I return, I shall assume that you are in hot pursuit. When you have some news, you are to return at once to my rooms, no matter what the hour.'

I had been engaged in my simulated employment for about an hour when this inquisitive servant accosted me.

'Old George is not well,' I said, remembering my script. 'His leg is troubling him more than usual. My uncle and I are taking it in turns to carry out his functions until he is recovered.'

'That would be the decrepid creature whom I saw this morning,' said the fellow. 'Don't go away. My mistress may have an errand for you.' With that, he turned on his heel and disappeared down the steps of one of the houses adjoining Lady M — 's.

This left me in something of a quandary since I could not desert my post without incurring the wrath of Holmes. However, I could hardly protest without my interlocutor becoming suspicious. I could but hope that his mistress would not have need of my services.

My hopes were to be dashed. Scarcely ten minutes had gone by when he returned.

'You are to come with me,' he said. 'My mistress needs your services.' He strode off haughtily without giving me the opportunity to demur. Reluctantly I tailed behind him. We went in through the servants' entrance and I was taken into a hallway and then upstairs, through a baize-covered door into the family's part of the house.

'In here!' he ordered brusquely, 'And wait. You will be given your instructions shortly. Nothing is to be made dirty.' Here he wrinkled his nose with disgust. 'Remain standing. The silver is all counted.'

I half opened my mouth in order to damn him for his impertinence when I recalled that I must, at all costs, remain in my character as a member of the lowest orders. I tugged at my forelock with a dirt-stained hand and cringed.

'Of course, Sir,' I said. 'I hope I know my place.'

He eyed me disdainfully, turned and left the room. I stood there, inwardly cursing my luck that had taken me from my observation station. As I stood at the window, the door opened and what was clearly the lady of the house swept in. She halted and ran an imperious eye over me.

'You're a thoroughly dirty fellow,' she said. 'And rather younger than the old man who performed this morning's duties.'

Obviously Holmes had also been dragged in from the street, although he had said nothing of this when I took over from him.

'My uncle, Ma'am,' I said.

'I hope you prove to be somewhat more vigorous in the discharge of your duties. He wheezed most horribly and indeed had to be revived by cook with a bowl of soup.'

Well-preserved would be the phrase that best described her. She was of middling age and height and full-bodied, tending a little to the stout.

'Now,' she said brusquely, 'I want you to enter me from behind!'

To my amazement she lifted her dress and leaned over an occasional table. A well-fleshed pair of buttocks was presented to my astonished gaze. Beneath the cleft I could see a dense, dark bush. She opened her legs a little and pulled apart her splendid cheeks.

'Come along,' she said. 'In there!'

I paused, still reluctant to obey her command.

'What are you waiting for,' she said.

Gingerly, I approached her, very aware of my grubby condition.

'It don't matter about the dirt,' she said. 'I want your hand on me and your cock in me. Get it out at once!'

Bemused, I did as I was told. Mr Pego hesitantly revealed himself. She looked at it.

'That won't do,' she said. 'Stick it between my legs. I see that I shall have to bring you to life.'

Cautiously I introduced my member to the indicated position. At once her thighs closed and she began to rub and coax it with a considerable degree of expertise. At her warm, skilled touch, my cock swelled and rose.

'That's better,' she said. She reached round behind her to grasp him in her hand.

'Much better,' she said. 'Big and hard, that's how I like it. Now, embrace me.'

'Beg Pardon, Ma'am,' I said. 'But I'm not very clean.'

'That's why I sent for you,' she said. 'I want to feel your hands on me.'

I grasped her tentatively, my hands on her hips.

'The waist, and then further up,' she ordered.

I did as I was told. Mr Pego at least declared his interest in these goings-on. Still with a degree of caution, I seized hold of her clearly voluptuous breasts, squeezing them and pressing them through her dress.

'Better,' she said. 'You're learning fast.' She began to breathe heavily and her own hands crushed mine against her. Her bared buttocks began to thrust and move against me. Mr Pego was by now rampant and I began to slip backwards and forwards between her firmly fleshed thighs. She began to twist this way and that.

'Push my clothes up,' she ordered, releasing her grip on my hands.

By now I was beginning to be quite carried away with my efforts. Sliding my hands up her thighs, I raised her dress well above her hips. My hands moved higher and encountered the large breasts which were quite unencumbered with any underthings. Again she gasped and then fairly threw herself forwards across the table so that her bum stuck proudly up in the air.

'Now!' she said and my engorged prick slipped directly into the opening of her cunney. She backed and forced herself along the full extent of my shaft. At once we fell to a completely abandoned bout of fucking. As I forced my way time and again into her, a little trickle of sweat made its way down her back and into the cleft. I rubbed my face eagerly in it. As she felt the stubble of my unshaven chin scratch her naked flesh she began to give out low groans of pleasure. By now the immaculate state of her clothing was becoming not just creased but torn. My begrimed fingers had left distinct prints on her damp-sheened body. Her hair was in a state of wild disorder. For my part I had been able to step neatly out of my trousers as they threatened to tangle round my ankles.

125

'More! More!' she cried out.

Ceaselessly I banged in and out of her now wide and wet cunt. My balls felt full to bursting but I attempted to control the eruption that was building to its climax. Drawing on all my experience, I first slowed down and then increased my pace. All of a sudden I felt the first unstoppable wave of my cum beginning to force its way down my prick. Before I had time to do anything, she had noticed what was about to happen.

'You're coming,' she said. 'Not inside me!' She bundled up the hem of her dress and used it like a handkerchief, wrapping it round the head of my prick just as the first milky spurt shot out. With one hand reaching down between her legs, she held me tightly as jet after jet was emptied into this hastily devised rag receptacle. I had been full to overflowing and soon my cum was smeared over her hand and seeping down her thighs. With an experienced hand she ran her fingers along my prick, urging every last drop of my spending out of me.

'Well done,' she said, as my discharge dwindled to nothing. Letting go of me, she twisted round and lowered her head to my still out-thrust member. With one mighty suck she emptied the last few drops and then, as my prick began to relax, she took it into her mouth in its entirety so that it lay along her tongue. She let it rest there, holding me firmly at the hips. Then, as Mr Pego shrank back to a more manageable state and size, she let me go.

'But I have not yet come,' she said. 'You must complete the job with your tongue.' She lay down on the carpet, quite oblivious to the mess that we were making, parted her legs once more and revealed the full splendour of her bush to me.

I kneeled before her and she reached out and pulled my head between her knees. Needing no further instruction, I at once began to feel my way with my mouth through the luxuriant undergrowth that hid her cave of delights. Already gaping and wet, her cunney lips welcomed me in. My tongue at once encountered the fullness of her clit which moments before I had been teasing into vigorous life with the thrusting of my prick. I began to lick it with quick, darting strokes. She rolled her hips, widening herself out under my attentions. The warmth of her pussey hair filled my nostrils and I breathed in the scent of her own coming.

By now she was crying out loud in a quite uncontrollable manner. A first shudder and then a second announced that she was reaching the final point of her ecstasy. Her bosom bounced up and down as she bucked and heaved like some thoroughbred trying to dismount its rider. I held on to her manfully however, my tongue clinging to her clit like a barebacked rider. Gasp after gasp forced its way from her and I was quite enveloped in the tides of her coming.

Soon her volcanic movements began to subside but not before I swear I felt the floorboards move and groan beneath us. Still panting with her exertions, she ceased all movement for a moment or two. Then she pushed my head away and drew her legs up with surprising flexibility for one of her age and build. With her own hands clamped firmly against her pubic parts, she rocked back and forth, a great smile of satisfaction spreading over her face.

'Very good,' she said. 'Very good indeed. Much better than your uncle.' So at least I had surpassed Holmes in one thing, I thought with satisfaction. I should call this the Case of the Satisfied Pussey. One that I had brought to a triumphant conclusion without any help from my mentor. Then I remembered that I had failed in my duties as observer at Lady M — 's. What would Holmes say? At once, I decided that since he had said nothing to me about the services he had been called on to render during his spell on watch, I was under no obligation to volunteer any description of the similarly unexpected summons that had drawn me away from my street-sweeping duties.

'Ring for the maid,' Her Ladyship ordered in her customary imperious tone.

'But . . . but . . . ' I stammered. 'Don't you need to, er . . . ?'

'Get on with it, young man,' she said. 'Abigail has been with me for years.'

I did as I was ordered. No doubt, I thought to myself, the maid must be used to such scenes, extraordinary though they

127

might seem to most people. And indeed the maid Abigail, when she answered, behaved as though it were the most natural thing in the world to find her mistress, half-naked, dampened and considerably dirtied, stretched out full length on the carpet while a ragged but untrousered member of the lower orders stood by the bell.

'If you would like to gather your things together,' she said to me. I collected myself up, adjusted my dress and followed her out of the room. Her Ladyship barely looked up.

'Take him out by the kitchen entrance,' she said. 'But he may have a wash first at the sink if he wants.'

Once outside, the maid said 'Her Ladyship would like you to take this as a reward for your efforts.'

With that, she slipped a half-sovereign into my hand. This was the first time that I had ever been offered money for satisfying a lady and for a moment I resisted. But then I remembered my assumed status and accepted my payment. 'The Labourer is Worthy of His Hire' was a proverb I recalled from my school scripture lessons.

'Her Ladyship is well satisfied,' said Abigail as I completed a perfunctory wash. 'She will in all probability send for you again. In addition, while there can be no question of a written reference, there is every likelihood that she will recommend you to Mrs Lucas across the street. She also has need of occasional assistance in these matters, seeing as how her husband is so often away on business.'

'I had no idea that this sort of thing went on,' I said.

'It's not for the likes of us to concern ourselves with the habits of the gentry,' said Abigail rather sniffily. 'Though I must say that I prefer my gentlemen callers to be clean at least.'

Thus dismissed, I returned to my duties at the street corner, hoping that there had been no need for my other clandestine services while I had been away. Cautiously, I looked across to Lady M — 's. All appeared to be as it had been. I fingered the half-sovereign in my pocket, hoping that there would be no further demands upon my time and energies.

About an hour later, Holmes returned.

'I take it that nothing of note has transpired,' he said.

'Er, no,' I said, a little worried that he might have returned while I had been called away and was testing my veracity.

'A completely uneventful spell?' he asked. Was it just my guilty conscience or did he suspect something.

'No unexpected callers at Lady M—'s,' I said, aware that I was being evasive. I spotted a raised eyebrow.

'I, er — ' Then I pulled myself together, remembering that he also had been plucked from his observation station to render the self-same service as myself. 'Honesty is surprisingly often the best policy,' had been one of the maxims most favoured by Dr White at Nottsgrove.

'I had to leave my post for a short while in order to answer a call of nature,' I said, edging towards a full confession.

'Your nature or another's?' asked Holmes with a thin smile. He had guessed. With a sense of relief, I admitted to my adventure. He listened.

'It's a damn nuisance,' he said when I had finished. 'I sometimes forget the demands of the flesh. I also received a similar call earlier.'

'You don't think that the woman is in league with our blackmailer and that it was done deliberately to draw us away from our vigil?' I suggested.

He pondered the point. 'Possible but not probable,' he said. 'Although of course, a neighbour would have every opportunity to observe the comings and goings at Lady M—'s. Discretion is clearly not among her more marked qualities. There is nothing for it. Tomorrow we will both have to be on duty at the same time, in case further calls are made upon your services.'

'Or indeed, yours,' I said.

'I suspect that I shall be spared the wretched woman's demands. I had the foresight to simulate considerable incompetence.'

For a moment I entertained the unworthy thought that his incompetence had not been deliberate but then remembered that he was an adept in the more demanding Oriental arts.

'At least I shall remain in a position to carry out our watching brief,' he went on.

'Two crossing sweepers?' I said. 'Will that not look a little odd.'

'You shall be the sweeper,' he said. 'I shall remain completely hidden.'

'How?' I asked.

'I am an expert in these matters,' he said. 'Never fear. I will be invisible but present.'

'In the meantime,' I said, 'how long are we to remain here?'

'All night, if needs be,' Holmes said. 'The criminal classes have a natural affinity with the hours of darkness.'

I began to have some doubts about the pleasures of the detective's life. Dusk was falling. A cold wind was beginning to blow and my ragged clothing was likely to prove quite inadequate in keeping out the nocturnal chill. I was also becoming extremely hungry.

'I wonder — ' I began.

'Ssssh,' Holmes said, holding up a warning finger.

'What?' I said.

'That tapping noise,' said Holmes.

I strained my ears. Sure enough, from some distance but nearing rapidly there came a sound of shuffling footsteps accompanied by a strange, insistent rapping.

'A blind man,' I said as I discerned a figure approaching in the gloom.

'Making surprisingly swift progress for one with his affliction,' said Holmes. 'Something's afoot.' Suddenly he turned in the other direction.

'A second blind man,' he said. 'An odd coincidence.'

We ducked down some area steps as he motioned me to silence. The two figures converged, each feeling along the kerbstone with his cane. Closer and closer they came. With a bump and a mutual cry of surprise, they collided. Each stood still as though waiting for the other to step out of the way. Then each began to mutter angrily as they measured up to each other. One waved his cane and made contact with the other.

'This is awful,' I whispered. Each obviously assumed that the other could see and expected him to stand aside. In a trice they were swearing and flailing at each other. I stepped forward.

Holmes pulled me back. 'Don't,' he hissed, 'I scent a diversionary tactic.' By now a grotesque fight had broken out. A carriage pulled up and the driver leaped down to pull the two apart. A passer-by joined in.

'There!' said Holmes.

'What?' I said.

'There! Getting out of the far side of the carriage.' Sure enough a shadowy figure had slipped out and quickly vanished towards the servants entrance to Lady M—'s establishment. 'That's our man,' said Holmes. 'Keep down!'

'How can you tell?' I asked.

'A well-dressed man in a top hat and with a silver-topped cane, descending to the *servants* entrance,' said Holmes. 'Even the most superior servant would not be so dressed. Note also the military bearing.'

There came the softest of raps at the door. At once it opened and our quarry was let in.

'Someone was waiting for him,' said Holmes. 'There is an accomplice inside the household.'

'What do we do?' I asked.

'We wait,' said Holmes.

We waited. The fighting blind men allowed themselves to be parted. They calmed down and tapped on down the road. The coach driver remounted, clicked his tongue at the horse and proceeded on his way, turning the corner and passing out of our sight. The passer-by, who had been the accidental recipient of a couple of stinging blows, patted himself down, wiped his face and walked on, limping a little. Silence fell. Holmes began to creep up the steps. Then as I followed, he crouched down, and I felt a pull at my elbow from behind. I turned, startled.

'Tuppence for a fuck,' said a small voice. 'Or thruppence for the both of you.' Angrily I pulled away.

'Not now!' I exclaimed, trying to keep my voice down.

'Tuppence for a very good fuck,' she insisted, and two thin but strong arms were flung round me. 'First of the evening,' she importuned. 'A good clean fuck.'

131

As I tried to wrestle her from me, my foot slipped and I fell down the steps and landed in a heap at the bottom, all entangled with her. As her body was squashed under mine, she wriggled and hung on to me.

At this point Mr Pego betrayed me and rose to attention. She felt my mutinous member pressing against her and quickly dropped her hands down, seizing hold of him through the unfortunately threadbare cloth of my disguise.

'My, he's a big, strong fellow,' she said. 'Surely you wouldn't deny a girl a chance of feeling that inside her.'

Despairingly I looked up but Holmes had vanished, leaving me to grapple with my seductress.

'Never mind about the other gentleman,' she said. 'You can catch him up in a minute or two.'

'He's not a gentleman,' I hissed. 'We're just a couple of poor crossing sweepers. You've made a mistake.'

'Crossing sweepers don't talk like that,' she said. 'You're gentry, no matter how you're dressed. On your way to a fancy dress ball, are you?'

'We're keeping watch — ' I started, nearly revealing all in my confusion.

'Never mind what you're doing,' she said. 'None of my business. In here!' She pushed open a door and dragged me into complete darkness. Something gave way under my feet and I fell over once more. There was a rumbling noise and what felt like a cascade of stones fell on me.

'We're in a coal hole!' I cried out, trying to regain my balance but falling over again as the mound of coal shifted under me. 'This is ridiculous!'

'Never mind,' she said, quite invisible in the Stygian blackness but still keeping firm hold of my prick. 'The dirt'll just add to your disguise. Now keep still while I get my gloves off. Don't want to get your prick all gritty. I'll have him out in an instant.'

Strong little hands unbuttoned me. As my eyes began to get used to the darkness, I could just about see my prick, ghostly white where the light from the half-closed door caught it.

'There,' she whispered. 'I'll guide you.'

132

All at once I felt the warmth of her bush rubbing against the tip of my already straining member. I stopped struggling. What else could I do? The quicker we got this over, the quicker I could get out and follow Holmes.

Now she was straddling me as I lay back. Expertly she lowered herself on to my prick, burying it entirely in her already wet cunney. Cautiously she began to ride up and down on me. I responded and felt the coal shift beneath me.

'Careful,' she said. 'We don't want to start an avalanche.'

I lay still once more. The idea of being buried alive while fucking did not appeal. She did not make any abrupt movements but just used her inside muscles, clenching and unclenching herself about my swollen cock. 'Cleopatra's grip,' I recalled Becky calling it. One of those feminine skills handed down from Antiquity in a centuries-old tradition. Never was it more needed now. One over-abrupt movement and catastrophe threatened.

Perilous though our situation was, I realised that I was beginning to thoroughly enjoy it. I was in the hands, or rather the cunney, of an expert.

As I surrendered to professional care, I forgot everything except the delicious rhythmic squeezing that was rapidly driving me towards my coming. I felt the first stirring as my jism began to churn inside my swollen balls. I must have made some slight sound.

'That's it,' she said, 'let it come. Everything you've got. Right into me.' I did as I was bid. Steadying myself on the ever-shifting coal slope with my outstretched arms, I began to pump spurt after spurt of my cum up and into her. After the events of the afternoon, I was surprised at how much I could summon up. Rising and falling a little now on me, she milked me as our juices were spread over my prick and began to trickle down into my hair.

'I call it my Wishing Well,' she said softly in my ear. 'When the last drop comes out, you must close your eyes and think of what you would most like to happen to you. I can see the whites of your eyes,' she went on. 'You're supposed to close 'em when you wish.'

I did as she commanded. All I could wish was that I could

133

get out of there as soon as possible and follow Holmes. My first Case and already I had a sense of failure.

'All done then?' she said.

I nodded and then coughed as some coal dust tickled my throat.

'Up we come then,' she said, carefully lifting herself off my discharged but still erect firing piece. 'A good two penn'orth, wasn't it?'

I nodded again, feeling in my pocket for some coins. As I began to lever myself up, I slipped.

'Blast this coal!' I said.

'Anthracite,' she said.

'What?' I said, still struggling to pick myself up.

'Good Welsh anthracite,' she said. 'Best there is for burning. Born and brought up in the Valleys, I was. Learned my trade at the pit head.'

'Young woman, this is not the time or place to discuss the merits of different types of coal,' I said, looking up at her. 'Help me up!'

She reached down, seized hold of my hands and pulled me to my feet.

'I must find my friend,' I said.

'I'll come with you,' she said. 'Maybe he'll want a quick fuck as well.'

'I think you'll find that he has other things on his mind,' I said, rummaging round in my pocket for the money to pay her off. My fingers closed round something. 'Here, take this!'

As she took the only coin I could find in my hurry, I realised from the milled edge that it was in fact the half-sovereign with which I had earlier been paid off after my own afternoon endeavours. However it was too late to take it back. Already she had hidden it about her person. For a moment I considered asking for my change but realised that as a Tuppenny Upright, she was hardly likely to have enough cash on her to be able to comply with such a request. I made a mental resolve to be more careful with money in the future.

'Now we must set out after your friend,' she said, yanking me out into the evening gloom. I saw a small smile flit across her face as she realised the extent of her luck and my mistake.

At least, I consoled myself, it would appear that I had a higher market value.

My immediate problem was to track Holmes down. Carefully I climbed up the area steps, my Welsh Undresser, as I had Christened her in my mind, rather wittily I considered, followed close behind. The road above was empty. I started across.

All at once there came a terrible moaning noise. 'My God!' I muttered out loud. 'Holmes!' He must have been attacked by the well-dressed fellow we had seen admitted to the servants entrance. I began to run towards the sound.

The door was still ajar and speedily but quietly I slipped inside, knowing not what scene of outrage I might find. The room was empty but through an open door and from down the passage, the unearthly moaning recommenced. I looked around wildly. Obviously Holmes must be in terrible trouble. If I was to be of any use to him, a weapon was needed. My eye lit upon a large rolling pin and I picked it up, feeling its reassuring weight in my hands.

'I don't think that will be needed, dearie,' said a small Welsh voice. I looked round. My Tuppenny Upright had followed me in.

'I must save my friend,' I said, rather impressed by my own heroism. 'Stay out of the way. This is man's work.'

'Woman's,' she said, contradicting me.

'What?' I said.

'It's all right,' she said. 'I know that sound — '

'Shhh!' I said, pulling away from her as she tugged at my sleeve.

'But — ' she said, refusing to let go so that I found myself dragging her in my wake as I raised the rolling pin and began to creep towards the bloodcurdling sound. I finally just about managed to shake her off but she insisted on following me, ignore her though I might.

The first two rooms we came to both had partly opened doors. There was no lighting but I realised that one was a larder and the other a store of some kind. The moaning sound came from ahead. I pressed cautiously on. All of a sudden my foot caught what appeared in the half-light to be a scrubbing brush. It skated across the stone flags and clanged against a bucket. As the sound echoed down the passage, the moaning came to an abrupt end. An ominous silence fell and then there came the patter of hasty footsteps. Casting caution to the winds, I rushed on. We came to a right-angled turn. I paused and edged forward. Another room opened off the corridor. Flattening myself against the wall, I inched my way onwards, trying to keep myself concealed until I could get a clear view through the doorway. From behind came a stifled, choking sound. I spun on my heel. My companion had her hand to her mouth.

'Shhh!' I said again. Again I paused, gathered up my reserves of courage and then fairly leaped in, ready to do battle.

'About time, too,' came a quiet voice.

'Holmes!' I cried out.

Holmes it was. He was standing by a small window, upright and wound about with what seemed to be a large sheet, his arms bound to his sides like an Egyptian mummy. He was pulling rather crossly at the ends of his imprisoning bandage which had been fed between the rollers of a large mangle.

'What — ' I exclaimed.

'The handle,' he said.

I strode across the room, seized the handle and quickly gave it a couple of brisk turns.

'The other way!' my employer cried out in a strangled voice. 'You're pulling me through the wringer!'

'Here, let me!' said my partner from the coal hole. 'I can see you've never been in service.'

She took the handle from me, reversed my efforts and began to release the Great Detective from his bondage.

'Now,' she said, as the ends were freed. 'You take one end and I'll take the other.' She laughed. 'Like a maypole. We've got to unwind him. Go round that way.' Obeying her, I set off clockwise. Ducking under my arms, she circled round in the opposite direction. Holmes, trying to help us, began to swivel round.

'It would be quicker, Sir,' she said, 'If you stayed still. We'll have you out of that in a trice.'

He did as he was told and with a few quick turns we had him disentangled. He stood there, swaying slightly on his feet.

'He's a bit dizzy,' she said. 'We'll turn him round the other way. That way he'll get his balance back.'

'You realise, of course, that these childish games are in fact connected with ancient fertility rites,' said Holmes, ever the teacher.

'Just what my old headmaster used to point out to us,' I responded, pleased to be able to demonstrate my knowledge of such things. 'I had not realised, Sir, that you had a particular interest in folklore.'

'A longtime but minor interest,' he said. 'Though one that has been useful to me before now in my detective work.'

I remembered the moaning and the sounds of hasty departure that had preceded our entrance, although all was now quiet.

'What happened?' I asked.

'As you should be able to deduce,' said Holmes, 'I have been assaulted in a most disgraceful fashion. They went that way,' he continued, pointing down the passage that stretched further ahead.

'How many were there?' I asked.

'Three,' he replied. 'One was the fellow we had been following. Or rather, *I* followed. You seem to have been somewhat delayed on the way. I notice also,' he said, 'that you appear also to have acquired a companion.'

'Er, this is er – ' realising as I began my introduction that of course I had no idea whatsoever of the name of my Welsh Encounter.

'Megan, Sir,' she said. 'Do you want a fuck? Only fourpence.'

'My dear young lady,' said Holmes, 'Grateful though I am for your assistance in releasing me, you must realise that this is neither the time nor the place for such a transaction. Evil is afoot and we must be in hot pursuit.'

'Did you get a good look at the other two?' I asked, somewhat concerned at the prospect of a hand-to-hand

137

engagement with no less than three opponents. For a moment Holmes appeared embarrassed.

'They were women.' Uncharacteristically he hesitated. 'Both substantially built and both, er, both stark naked.'

'Good God!' I exclaimed.

'Two large naked women. Probably of the servant class, judging by their coarse hands and coarse language.'

'What were they doing?' I asked.

'Behaving in a manner not dissimilar to that suggested by your friend here,' he said. 'They were accompanied in their activities by the well-dressed stranger.'

'Why did they tie you up?' asked Megan. Once more Holmes looked crestfallen.

'I had managed to approach the door, which was then half-closed, unnoticed,' he said. 'Believing from the noise that some foul crime was being perpetrated, I bent to observe what was going on through the crack between door and frame. Unfortunately, at that very moment, one of them looked up from their revels on the floor — '

'So *that* was the noise,' I said, enlightenment dawning.'

'If I might make so bold,' said Megan, 'that's what we in the trade call a screaming fuck.'

Holmes looked startled but I remembered the tremendous racket that had been set up by Mary the Maid at Mrs P — 's at the hands, or rather instrument, of Tom the Tool (*see Oyster 2*).

'I should have recognised it,' I said ruefully.

' — they looked up,' said Holmes, pressing on testily, 'and let out a great cry of "Peeping Tom!" Before I could either escape or explain myself, I had been roughly laid hold of, bound up in two large damp sheets and fed into the mangle.'

'How terrible!' I said.

All at once there came a spluttering sound. We both turned to see Megan bent over with laughter and pointing to the linen. As a consequence of our assignation in the coal cellar, there were now dozens of large black handprints all over the twisted remains of the sheets.

'They denounced me, using the foulest possible expletives,'

Holmes continued, clearly unamused by the turn of events. 'And then fled.'

'We must catch them,' I said.

'Why?' asked Megan.

'Because they have criminally attacked Mr Holmes,' I said. 'And the full rigour of the law must be visited upon them.'

'I concur with your sense of outrage,' said Holmes, 'But I have reservations as to your suggested course of action. Not only would they have some semblance of a defence in court but I should have to explain why I had been apparently spying on their perfectly legal sport. Such publicity would not help me in my endeavours to apprehend the blackmailing swine who is the cause of so much distress to Lady M.'

I could see the logic of his argument. 'But what then do we do?' I asked.

'May I remind you, Scott, that we are actually in the basement of Lady M — 's house. I suggest that we seek her out and find out if there have been any further developments in the affair while I have been unavoidably detained down here.'

'But what if we inadvertently happen upon your assailants?' I asked.

'I do not think we have to fear any further attack,' he said. 'Not only are we now their equal in numbers, but I strongly suspect that the two women will be chiefly concerned to reclaim their clothes and resume their domestic duties. As for the fellow, I would imagine that he has been either hidden away or pushed out into the street again.'

'Unless they hope to complete their fucking,' said Megan.

'That is a rather remote possibility,' said Holmes. 'We do not I think need unduly to concern ourselves with them any longer.'

'So we'd better go and look for Lady M — without further ado,' I said.

'May I remind you that we are both dressed as crossing sweepers,' said Holmes. 'I suggest that if we suddenly appeared before her looking like this, she might well become considerably upset. Also your friend here is not suitably dressed for a lady's drawing room.'

'I knew you wasn't a real crossing sweeper,' said Megan. 'A fancy dress ball is what I suggested if you recall.'

'Very observant of you, my dear,' said Holmes. 'You have the makings of a detective. It may be that I shall enlist your services. I would of course make it worth your while.' He fished out a small purse. 'Sixpence would seem an adequate sum for your services.'

'Make it ninepence and I will throw in a free fuck,' said Megan.

'That won't be necessary,' said Holmes. 'Although Mr Scott here might well be interested in your offer at some time later on.'

'He's already had his fuck,' she said.

'Which doubtless accounts for the delay in his arrival.' He turned to me. 'Scott, I am not unappreciative of your efforts to stand in for Dr Motson, but you might be more useful to me if you could remember to use your head rather than your balls from time to time.'

'Bit of a prick on wheels, is he?' said Megan brightly.

'Ah, yes, an army expression, is it not,' said Holmes. 'You have experience of the military?'

'The Barrackroom Bint of Blaenau Festiniog, I was known as at home,' she said. 'And then I served the Navy at Portsmouth before coming to London.'

'So you have considerable experience of the foibles and predelictions of humanity,' said Holmes. 'A veritable student of society.'

'I can tell the difference between a gentleman and a crossing sweeper,' she said quickly, 'However he may be turned out.'

'We must have a long talk together at some time in the future,' said Holmes. 'There are questions that I should like to put to you. Knowledge,' he said to me, 'must be sought in all quarters, even the most unlikely. But in the meantime, there is a problem to be solved.' He began to pace up and down. Then he patted his shabby pockets. 'Damn!' he said. 'I have mislaid my pipe in the *fracas*. I know I had it with me. It must be on the floor. You two look for it while I think.'

We searched and he pondered.

140

'We have to attract Lady M — 's attention without alarming her,' he said. 'We must also remember that the stranger we followed into the house may have come for reasons other than to engage the domestic staff in sexual intercourse. He may well be an emissary from the blackmailer. If so he could well still be on the premises, and one or more of the servants may be in league with him. We must be careful.'

'There is a maid's uniform hanging in one of the closets we passed,' said Megan. 'I could slip it on and go upstairs in search of her Ladyship. My appearance would not startle her and I could pass on a message to her.'

'A capital suggestion,' said Holmes. 'I will wait here, and Scott, you must resume your station in the street.'

'If you two gentlemen could help me get undressed and dressed again, it will speed things up,' said Megan.

'That would seem a task best suited to Mr Scott's talents,' said Holmes. 'Ah! My pipe!' He picked it up from a corner of the room where it had lain unnoticed. 'This will aid the thought processes.'

Megan sent me off to fetch the uniform from the closet we had passed earlier while she began to strip off her rather grubby woollen dress.

'A wash is called for,' said Holmes. 'You are rather dirty.'

'Comes of fucking in a coal hole,' she said, looking at herself. 'A quick all-over sluice will do. There is a sink over there. If the young gentleman will wash the grime off his own hands, he can help me.'

I noticed that she was shivering a little.

'No chance of some warm water, I suppose,' she said.

'No time,' said Holmes. 'Cold it will have to be.'

I washed myself, drying my hands and face on another sheet.

'Now,' she said. 'Give me a good splashing.' She was standing, almost naked in the middle of the floor.

'Your hat,' I reminded her.

'Silly me,' she said and raised her arms to take it off. Then she lifted her hair up and posed in front of me. In spite of the urgency of the moment, I could not help but notice how enticing she looked even though she was streaked with coal

141

dust. Mr Pego reacted and stood hungrily up. She of course spotted what was happening at once.

'Another fuck?' she said, licking her lips in a most provoking manner.

'Not now!' said Holmes sternly.

Picking up a large dishcloth, I began to wipe her down. At the touch of the cold, damp rag, she gave out a little squeal. As her bare titties shook, my virile member thrust out once more. Holmes noticed.

'I can see that I will have to attend to the young lady's ablutions,' he said. 'Get her domestic's uniform ready.'

As Megan, still shivering but well aware of the effect she was having on me, twisted first one way and then the other while Holmes plied the cloth, I meanwhile tried to regain my critical faculties.

'I think your young gentleman could do with a splash of cold water, too,' said Megan.

'That is up to him,' said Holmes, gruffly. 'Now, that will do. Where's the dress?'

I stepped forward and slipped it down over her head, although not without a twinge of disappointment as its voluminous folds hid her thin body from sight. Holmes stepped back to inspect the effect.

'That won't do at all,' he said. 'Far too large. Fetch a smaller uniform.'

'There's only one in there,' I said.

'Damn!' he said. 'We simply can't send her up into the house like this. She looks more like an entrant in some village sack race. Anyone will notice in an instant.'

'What shall we do?' I asked.

'I shall think,' said Holmes, puffing once more on his pipe.

'If you please, Sir?' said Megan. 'I have an idea.'

'Don't interrupt,' I said. 'Mr Holmes is thinking.'

'Don't be rude!' she said. She turned to Holmes. 'The young gentleman is the nearest in size. He can put the dress on.'

'Certainly not!' I said. 'I shall do no such thing.' I waited, confident that Holmes would come up with a more suitable scheme.

142

'That is not a bad idea,' said Holmes to my horror. 'He only has to escape the close attention of the rest of the household and make his way up to the drawing room. As long as Lady M – is alone, he should be able to creep quietly in and make himself known to her without causing her any great alarm.'

'But, but,' I stuttered, feeling that events were slipping beyond my control.

'Be quick,' said Holmes. 'Help him into the dress,' he said to Megan. 'But you'll have to get rid of his own clothing first.'

Megan wriggled out of the over-large garment and, naked once more, began to undress me. I surrendered to my fate. Once again Mr Pego rose up so that she had some difficulty in pulling my trousers down over his aroused projection. Quickly she took my balls in one hand and gave a sharp squeeze. I squealed with the pain and as Mr Pego drooped for a moment, she had me trouserless before her. I drew in a deep breath and as I tried to regain my composure, she dropped the dress down over my head, pulling the skirts right down and smoothing it into place.

'That's it,' she said with a mocking look. 'A much better fit. Now, turn round and I'll do up the back.'

I obeyed, still preoccupied with the ache in my balls. She busied herself with the fastenings and when all was to her satisfaction, stepped back to inspect her handiwork.

'He needs a cap,' she said. 'There must be one in the cupboard to go with the dress.'

A cap was found and placed on my head.

'What do you think, Sir?' she said to Holmes.

'He'll pass muster,' he said. 'Anyway we really have no other option. At least his shoes are hidden. Now,' he said to me, 'remember to take short steps and maintain a posture of deference. Take a turn about the room while I have a look at you.'

'Let me get into my own dress again,' Megan said, 'And we'll coach him.'

I tried to walk like a woman.

'Not very good,' said Holmes. 'You'll never make a

detective if you cannot master the arts of disguise. Why I remember I once had to play the part of a nursemaid for several days while solving the Case of the Kidnapped Heiress. I flatter myself that I became remarkably adept at the changing and bathing of infants, although it is not an experience I would choose to repeat. At least you only have to pass as a maid for a short while.'

I struggled manfully to perfect my impersonation.

'That will have to do,' said Holmes impatiently. 'Just try to keep out of sight until you find Lady M—.'

'Off you go,' said Megan, patting me on the bottom. 'And try not to clump as you walk.'

And so I was sent out on my errand.

As I crept towards the servants stairs, I took stock of the situation. Somewhere in the house were the two maids. Since they had fled without their uniforms, which were still in the laundry along with Holmes and Megan, they would be immediately pre-occupied with finding some alternative clothing. Also possibly in the house was the well-dressed stranger, although if he were simply in the habit of calling at the house in order to fuck the maids he had doubtless slipped out again into the evening. If on the other hand he was indeed the blackmailer's emissary, he would have sought out Lady M— in order to deliver his message. On balance, this was the more likely situation since Holmes had clearly worked out that some member of the household was in league with the blackmailer and was supplying details of who was entertained in the absence abroad of Lord M—. It was therefore safer to assume that the well-dressed man was part of the plot. I had to keep out of his sight. I had no knowledge of how many other staff might be kept apart from the two who had been surprised by Holmes. One could assume at least a cook, possibly a housekeeper, a lady's maid and a manservant. I had to take care.

I further recalled that the arrangement had been that a servant would make a signal from an upstairs window on behalf of Lady M— when the message arrived. Clearly Lady M— had one trusted confidante among her staff. Unless she had mistakenly relied on one of the two denuded maids in

144

the basement, this was a certain argument for at least one further domestic somewhere in the house.

At the top of the stairs I looked round cautiously. All was clear. I moved into the hallway. There was no sound. At the front of the house were doors to the left and the right. One would be the drawing room in which I might hope to find Lady M — . I looked into the room on the right. It was a dining room and empty of people although a cold meal of substantial proportions was laid out on the side. I thought again.

The signs suggested that this was cook's night off. This would account for the cold cuts that had been left. At least that was one less unwelcome surprise in waiting. However the quantity of food made it plain that guests were expected. I would have to hurry. I looked into the other room. The drawing room. Then I breathed a sigh of relief. Over by the window was Lady M — . She was alone, looking thoughtfully out into the street.

I entered and coughed. Lady M — turned round.

'What is it — ' she began. Then she looked more closely at me and started back.

'Who are you?' she said imperiously. 'Where is Esther?'

'Don't be alarmed, Lady M —' I said. 'It is I, Andrew Scott, Mr Holmes' assistant.'

'Good God!' she said. 'You gave me a terrible start. Why on earth are you dressed like that?'

I began to explain as well as I could. However I was barely halfway through the story when to my horror a door at the far end of the room opened and there stood the well-dressed stranger. 'Ah, Dear Lady,' he said, addressing himself to Lady M — . 'I think I have found the papers that your husband asked me to collect, so my business is completed.'

He looked in my direction. Luckily he seemed not to notice anything untoward about my appearance. Then he looked back towards Lady M — , plainly waiting for her to react to his statement.

'Ah, er, Hetty,' she said to me, at the same time screwing up her face and generally making it clear to me that I would have to act out my part for the moment. 'Hetty, would you serve drinks?' Then she walked over to me and said in a low voice, 'I've no idea what is going on. The butler's pantry is at the foot of the stairs. You will have to carry out Esther's duties.'

Downstairs, no-one was to be seen and there was no time to go looking for Holmes and Megan and find out what they were doing. I returned with glasses and a decanter of what looked like sherry. Lady M — was in deep conversation with the stranger.

'Put them down over there, Hetty,' she said.

I did as I was bid and withdrew. I must own to the fact that I was becoming considerably hot and bothered. As I stood in the hall wondering what to do next, to my alarm there was a ring at the front door.

'Answer it will you, Hetty,' Lady M — called out. 'John has the evening off and Esther is busy upstairs.' At least she had managed to pass on much-needed information about the disposition of the other members of the household. Nonetheless I had been placed in the awkward position of having to cope with whoever was on the steps outside. With lowered eyes and ready to bob demurely, I opened the front door.

Two women stood there, dressed in the height of fashion.

'The Honourable Gwendolen Fairfax and Miss Cecily Cardew,' said a familiar voice. 'Lady M — is expecting us.'

I leaped backwards in surprise. Gwendolen and Cecily! Two of my dearest and most intimate friends (*see Oyster 3*).

'What is it, girl?' said Cecily sharply. 'You look as though you've seen a ghost.'

'It's Andrew,' I hissed, knowing that I could not escape recognition and hoping to get the surprise over with there and then without any exclamations that would draw attention to us. 'It's me — ' Unfortunately I was so overcome by the surprise of our encounter that I choked and began to cough.

'What!' said Gwendolen. Then she looked at me carefully. Her eyes widened with amazement.

'It can't be! Stop coughing and stand up straight so we can get a good look at you.'

My eyes streaming, I spluttered, 'It is, but for Heaven's Sake, keep your voices down.'

'Well, it could be him,' murmured Cecily sweetly to her companion. 'But it's hard to tell in this light and him dressed up like that.'

In desperation, knowing that I had only seconds to make the situation clear to them, I recalled the one thing that was most likely to convince them that I was in fact Andrew. Abruptly I pulled up my dress. Underneath, of course, I had nothing on. Like a faithful hound responding to its master, my cock leaped into sight. Cecily and Gwendolen both let out simultaneous cries of recognition.

'It is him,' said Cecily. 'I'd recognise that Thing anywhere.'

'True, Cecily,' said Gwendolen. She looked carefully at me. 'I did not know that you numbered dressing up in women's clothes among your interests.' She walked up to me, took my engorged prick in her hand and looked back at Cecily. 'Who could overlook something like that,' she said. She began to rub her hand up and down the charged length of my member. 'And to think that we believed we were invited for a quiet meal with our friend Priscilla. Mind you,' she went on to Cecily, 'she has always been fond of contriving unusual entertainment for her friends. This promises to be an excellent evening as long as Andrew is not the only man present. Maybe they are all to be attired in this way.'

'No! It's not like that at all,' I whispered urgently. Quickly I gave the two of them a brief description of the events that had transpired. All the while Gwendolen was playing most teasingly with my prick so that I had great difficulty in keeping my mind on my tale.

'Hetty! Show my guests in,' came Lady M — 's voice.

Pulling myself together, I disentangled myself from Gwendolen's grip, tugged my dress down, and adjusted my maid's cap. 'Not a word in front of the stranger,' I managed to hiss. 'I suspect that he is part of another plot altogether.'

I ushered them into the drawing room and closed the door behind them. Outside I took a deep breath and tried once more to think. The situation was that Lady M — knew that I was Andrew Scott, assistant to Porlock Holmes, the Great Detective. Cecily and Gwendolen also knew that I was

Andrew Scott but did not know that Lady M – was privy to this information. And *vice versa*. The well-dressed stranger, as far as he had noticed me, thought that I was Hetty the maid. Neither Lady M –, Gwendolen nor Cecily had more than a sketchy idea of the events that had brought me to this state of frantic impersonation. I needed help in order to decide what to do next. It would have to be Holmes.

I picked my way carefully down the servants' stairs once more, hoping that I would stumble upon my friends rather than the two scullery maids. The laundry room would be the place to start. I minced towards it.

'Sixpence for a fuck,' said a quiet voice behind me.

I nearly jumped out of my skin. Megan! Then I let out a yelp of surprise as an intruding finger was shoved forcefully between the cheeks of my bum, probing through the thin material of my dress. As I turned, she turned with me, nipping me sharply in the nape of my neck with her teeth.

'Not now!' I said, reaching behind me to fend her off. Suddenly a door opened.

'Who are you?' said a new voice. Someone who was clearly a *bone fide* ladies' maid was looking at the two of us.

'You must be Lady M – 's personal maid,' came a further voice. Holmes had emerged from the laundry. 'Don't worry, my dear,' he said. 'I can explain everything. We are all friends of your mistress.'

The newcomer looked as though she was about to bolt in confusion and fright.

'We must keep our voices down,' said Holmes. 'Are you indeed Esther?'

'Yes – ' she said reluctantly, still poised like a nervous gazelle, ready for flight.

'I know from Lady M – that you can be trusted. You have been commissioned to pass on a message from the window to a crossing sweeper in the event of some unwelcome visitor to the house. I am that crossing sweeper and this,' he pointed at me, 'is my assistant.'

'Dr Motson, I presume,' said the maid Esther, relief spreading over her face.

'Scott, actually,' I said. 'Dr Motson is on holiday.'

148

Holmes took her, still trembling, by the arm and led her into the laundry. Megan and I followed. Rapidly he explained the situation as far as he knew it. When he had finished, I in turn brought him up-to-date with the events upstairs. It remained only to ascertain the whereabouts of the two naked domestics who had been so heartily engaged in sexual congress with the stranger before our arrival upon the scene.

'They are locked in a store cupboard,' volunteered Megan. 'They were hiding inside and I turned the key on them. The stranger must have told them to keep out of the way. They still do not have any clothes.'

Esther, by now more or less calmed, offered her services in furthering our endeavours. 'Her Ladyship's guests are expecting supper,' she said. 'But I do not know if the strange gentleman is also to eat with them. I have to wait on them.'

'And Mr Scott, also,' said Holmes.

'Noooo!' I howled. 'I can't do that!'

'Yes you can and will,' said Holmes firmly. 'As long as you do not arouse the suspicion of the stranger, you will be quite safe. Everyone else knows of your imposture, if not the whole story that accounts for it, so none of them will give you away in front of him. But I need you to be there to observe what happens and to get a message to Lady M –'

'What is that?' I asked.

'She must be reassured that I am on call below stairs. I also need to know whether she understands that we need confirmation that the stranger is indeed part of the conspiracy with her husband.'

At that moment a bell jangled.

'That will be Her Ladyship,' said Esther. 'If Mr Scott, or Hetty, will accompany me, we must serve supper.'

Before I could protest any further, I was shoved up the stairs behind her by Holmes and Megan.

My first venture into domestic service was growing more fraught by the minute. It was not an easy meal. The stranger had indeed stayed for dinner. By dint of great concentration, I managed to perform my duties with a degree of verisimilitude, coached and watched over as I was by Esther the maid. However I had reckoned without the unfortunate

149

sense of humour of Cecily. I was standing dutifully at Lady M – 's shoulder while she helped herself to a plateful of soup when I felt a hand slide under the hem of my dress, run rapidly up my thighs and begin to insinuate itself between them. Instinctively I clenched my buttocks but too late. A delicate hand cupped my balls and began to squeeze them rhythmically.

I lurched forward, slopping the soup into Lady M – 's lap. She shot backwards in her chair, just managing to avoid the deluge but bumping into me as she did so. The soup ladle dropped to the floor and I hastily banged the tureen on to the table before ducking down on hands and knees to retrieve it. My testicles were released but the same hand flipped my skirt over my bum. The strange man was seated on the other side of the table so that at least I was concealed from his gaze. As I groped around for the ladle, I was assaulted in a most outrageous fashion from left and right as Lady M – joined in the sport. I felt a stinging pinch to the cheek.

'Do be careful, Hetty,' said Lady M – . 'You have nearly spoilt my dress. Help her up, Esther.'

Flustered and humiliated, I scrambled up.

'Fetch a cloth and mop up this mess,' Lady M – continued, before turning back to the strange man and resuming her polite dinner table chit chat. I retrieved the tureen, found another ladle and, struggling to regain some composure, went round to serve the stranger.

To my horror, as I bent over him, he also patted me on the bum. Of course I had to submit to his coarse advances without flinching. Such is ever the lot of the servant, I remembered as he managed to press himself against me with impudent familiarity.

By now I realised that I was likely to be grabbed and fondled every time I approached the table. Only Gwendolen had so far kept her hands off me, but I knew her too well to regard her as trustworthy. Esther, bless her, did her best to keep me out of harm's way. Somehow the meal was served and eaten. As it wore on, I became considerably adept at avoiding any surreptitious strokings and intrusions into my private parts.

Then, just as we were serving the dessert, the stranger asked to be excused for a moment. Esther directed him down the hallway to the cloakroom and at last I could speak my mind.

'That was most unfair,' I said, coming up to the table. 'You very nearly gave the game away.'

'I am sorry,' said Cecily contritely. Then she whipped up my skirt from the front and her sister pushed me rudely forward. My prick slapped down on the table, landing on the edge of a plate. Before I had the time to whisk it away under cover again, Gwendolen trapped it with her hand.

'What an interesting object to see served up to one,' she said to Lady M —. 'What a pity that we cannot have one each.'

'We shall have to sample it in turns,' said her hostess.

I tried to pull myself free.

'Lady M —' I said desperately, 'I have an urgent communication from Mr Holmes.'

'Of course,' she said, 'I had quite forgotten. There is another prick downstairs. As soon as we have bidden Mr Pride goodnight, we can bring him up from below.'

'Lady M —' I said, 'Mr Holmes suspects that your visitor is in league with the blackmailer. Has he attempted to pass on any message from the scoundrel?'

'Yes,' said Lady M —, 'but there is no time to explain further. He will be coming back in a minute. Let him go,' she continued to Gwendolen and Cecily. 'We can resume our entertainment in a little while.' I was released. Mr Pego, who in spite of my confusion had shown every sign of wanting to come out and take part in the engagement, was hidden once more from sight. Esther took over the task of bringing coffee and I made my escape once more below stairs.

A muffled thudding was coming from the cupboard where the two maids were imprisoned. Then I heard the sound of a struggle. I dashed into the laundry fearing the worst. Holmes was helpless on his back in a large wickerwork basket, trying to get up again. However Megan had him pinned down, her legs on each side of his waist and was fairly bouncing up and down on him.

'Get this woman off me!' he cried out as he saw me. 'I have an injured back.'

I stooped forward to pull her off but she instantly reached under my dress and once more Mr Pego was hauled out into full view.

'What a sorry looking fellow,' she said. 'I must lick it into shape.'

I realised that she was thoroughly enthroned on Holmes and thus securely seated, she proceeded to bend forward and take me in her mouth. With the expertise of her profession, she all but swallowed my member while her tongue cradled its underside. Clasping me tightly round the backs of my thighs, she began to suck and lap me into such a state of excitement that I became quite incapable of any further resistance.

Soon, as she lifted herself up and down on the still protesting Holmes, I began to respond, thrusting in and out of her eager mouth. Yet, ever mindful of my errand, I attempted at the same time to inform Holmes of what Lady M — had said concerning her visitor.

'I knew he was a wrong 'un,' he said, beginning in spite of himself to enter into the spirit of the occasion. His eyes closed and he frowned with concentration even as he started to pant with his efforts.

'One of us must follow him when he leaves,' he gasped.

'I think,' I panted, 'that it had better be you. I have to attend to the two young ladies upstairs.'

'Who are they?' he asked breathlessly.

'It's a long story but I know them both,' I said. Then I felt the first stirrings from my swollen balls as the beginnings of my cum began to spurt along my cock. Megan sucked hungrily at me and I began to discharge myself into her warm, wet mouth. Thirstily she swallowed my copious bounty while still levering herself up and down on Holmes like one possessed.

'If I ever get out of here and am still able to walk,' he said, 'I shall attempt the task. But first, I'd better get on with my immediate duties, or your Welsh friend will never let me go.'

I realised that in spite of his verbal reluctance he also had been provoked to his coming. Fairly snorting with his efforts, he was matching Megan stroke for stroke. For a man of such cerebral habits he was proving surprisingly athletic, although I recalled that he was used to long moorland excursions according to Mrs P – 's account.

By now I was becoming quite drained with the activities of the day. A last jet of cum trickled rather than gushed down Megan's throat and she began to lick me clean. My prick slipped from her mouth and a final milky dribble fell on Holmes. Luckily he failed to notice its descent as he also was completing his spending. Satisfied at last, Megan ceased her writhing and let him slip free as well.

'That should be sevenpence each,' she said. 'But since we had not come to any agreement beforehand, I shall have to rely on your generosity.'

'Now, Madam, will you please release me,' said Holmes, 'or our quarry will escape.'

Megan lifted herself up. 'All sweaty , I am,' she said. 'I need another wash.'

'Well, you stay down here and clean yourself up,' I said. 'I have to get back to the dining room at once.'

Once more pulling my dress down, I looked about me.

'Your cap is all awry,' she said. 'Here, let me straighten it.'

'Give me a hand with Mr Holmes, first,' I said. 'He seems to be stuck in the basket.' Together we took him by the arms and hauled him to his feet. As we let him go, he clutched his back and winced.

'An old campaign injury,' he said. 'South Africa.' For a moment he stood, bent double and then took a deep breath and drew himself up. 'My pipe. It's gone again.' Megan fussed round him like a mother hen, tucking his shirt into his trousers, before retrieving his pipe and other belongings.

'I shall go outside and wait in the street,' he said. 'When you have finished your duties upstairs, you must make your way round to my rooms. If I have not returned, Mrs Sayers will look after you. Now, I must be gone.' So saying he let himself out into the darkness.

'What are you going to do?' I asked Megan. 'I don't think you should linger. Remember that there are two maids, in all

153

probability still naked, locked in the cupboard. It would never do if they managed to get out and found you here. One at least is implicated in the plot.'

'Don't worry yourself about me,' she said. 'I promise to avoid detection.' There was no point in interrogating her further on her intentions. I would have to trust to her common sense. Then a thought struck me.

'Where are my clothes?' I said. 'I shall have to change back out of this dress before I leave.'

'Oh, you don't want to bother with those raggedy old things,' she said. 'You look very fetching as you are.'

'But where are they?' I insisted.

'In the corner over there. You get upstairs and I'll fish them out and leave them where you can find them later.' Once again I was propelled back into the fray.

At the top of the stairs I stumbled. The fatigue of the day was beginning to affect me. As I entered the dining room, Lady M— looked up.

'Back again so soon, Hetty?' she said.

'I would prefer to be called by my correct name,' I said.

'Not dressed like that,' she said, tweaking provocatively at the hem of my dress. 'Cecily and Gwendolen have been telling me all about your artistic interests (*see Oyster 3*). But where is Mr Holmes? I think it is time he was brought up from below stairs so we can have a council of war and then possibly some entertainment.'

'He has resumed his watch in the street,' I said. 'Your gentleman caller has to be followed when he leaves.'

'That should be in a minute or two,' she said. 'Esther is seeing him out.'

'He brought some message from the blackmailer, I presume,' I said.

'A demand that I hand over a letter signing away much of my fortune. I told him that I would have to see my attorney. The letters of assignment have to be prepared within two days. He will call again to collect them.'

'I am certain that Mr Holmes will be able to apprehend the principal in this diabolic scheme.'

'Then there is nothing more that we can do for the

moment,' she said. 'Cecily has a plan to take our minds off this sorry affair.'

The splendidly full-bosomed Cecily stood up. I realised that the back of her dress was already unbuttoned.

'Since Esther is otherwise engaged for the moment, you must play the part of ladies' maid. There are a couple of fastenings that I cannot easily reach.' She presented her back to me. Already her creamy shoulders and back were partly exposed. Fumbling slightly, I undid the remaining restraints on her freedom. Under instruction, I pushed her dress and chemise off her shoulders. Her splendidly lush titties sprang into view.

'Your hands,' she said. Obediently I reached round her from behind. She took my hands and placed them firmly on her breasts. They were warm and plump in my palms.

'A little attention to my nipples, I think,' she said. My fingers closed over her already protruding nipples. I felt them harden under my touch.

'Squeeze them,' Cecily said. I began to rub and fondle her. All fatigue was forgotten as I felt her respond to me.

'A little harder,' she said. 'Oh! That feels so lovely.' Nestling her bum against Mr Pego, she started to twist and sway, forcing her titties into the palms of my hands. As I began to stroke her, she was breathing more and more heavily.

'Keep going!' she gasped. 'A bit harder. Don't be afraid of hurting me. I am quite impervious to pain when my breasts are being massaged. Oh! Lady M — ' she said to our hostess, 'Is it not simply the most delightful experience to feel a man's hands on one's bosom?'

I looked over in Lady M — 's direction. She had flung herself down in an upholstered chair and I noticed that one hand had crept under her skirt and she was beginning to frig herself into a state of excitement.

'Gwendolen, please,' she said. 'Hetty has got her hands full. I wonder if you could be of assistance.'

Gwendolen, ever the courteous guest, rose and knelt down in front of her. Carefully she drew Lady M — 's skirt up. She responded by leaning back and parting her thighs. I saw the

155

forest of her quim spread out before me. As though unveiling some rare treasure to an expectant audience, Gwendolen slipped one finger under her and felt for a moment. Lady M — gave a shudder of pleasure as the finger disappeared into her. Then it was slowly drawn upwards. A second finger joined it in its unseen cave, then her lips were carefully parted and Lady M — 's cunney was opened out to the public gaze. Instinctively I clutched Cecily harder and began to rub my hands up and down her glorious breasts. My prick jutted out, pressing into her. Cecily lifted up both her skirts and mine and as the embroidered material rubbed against the very tip of my distended member, I was brought to a state of almost uncomfortable readiness. I felt her cheeks part and she reached down, taking hold of the end of my prick and guiding it easily into her. Once I was properly seated, she stopped all movement, and paused expectantly.

As though recognising her cue, Gwendolen began to rub her fingers up and down in Lady M — 's cunney. She slipped still further down in her chair and spread herself wide. She let out a sudden cry of pleasure and I realised that Gwendolen's assiduous fingers had encountered Lady M — 's clit. As the slow but regular movements of her rubbing and caressing continued, I found myself automatically rubbing Cecily's nipples in a similar circular fashion. She was now bumping her cheeks against me, forcing me still deeper into her. Then she started to slip backwards and forwards on me, bending down so that I could thrust my entire member into her wet and welcoming tunnel.

Still watching the lovely display facing me, I kept time with Gwendolen's efforts. Lady M — began to turn her head from side to side, her mouth open and her eyes closed. She was moaning and quite oblivious to the rest of the world. I was banging and thrusting against Cecily like a man possessed. My knees were beginning to tremble with my exertions but so enervated was I from my day's repeated sexual exploits that although Mr Pego was in an almost painful state of excitement, there was no sign of that relieving gush that would mark the culmination of my efforts.

'More! More!' Cecily cried out, continuing to buck and

writhe on my impaling instrument. Gamely, I drove on, my balls smacking against her widespread thighs. In and out I thrust. Then, over-vigorous in my motion, my prick slipped out of her. Hungrily, she seized hold of it and almost rammed it up inside her again. Then as Lady M — began to cry out loud, Cecily also increased her pace to a frenzy. I sensed a final hot flush of ecstasy inside her and she and Lady M — came together, their near-delirious pleasure cries mingling.

Although my prick was wet and slippery with Cecily's copious juices, there was a hollow dryness within and a dull ache in my balls. Desperately I drove like a piston into her. She was in the full flow of her coming and her own juices were trickling down her thighs. She gave one last gasp and staggered. In my determination I had forced my whole weight on her. Weak from my efforts, I buckled at the knees and in an instant we had fallen forward onto the carpet. I lay on top of her, sapped of all energy as if I had also come. Yet my undischarged member remained obstinately and adamantly erect. Cecily slipped off me once more and we both fell over, she on her back with her legs raised, her hands rubbing and pressing against her bush, savouring the last moments of her spending.

I for my part was also flat on my back, my dress rucked up somewhere around my armpits and my prick bolt upright like a flagstaff. Dimly I realised that Esther the maid had entered the room. Obviously she was used to such scenes in the house for when Lady M — said 'The fanny fan!' to her, she immediately picked up some sort of Spanish lace fan from where it lay, obviously in readiness, on a shelf and began to waft it vigorously in front of her mistress's bared quim.

Gwendolen, her own needs as yet unattended to, was nonetheless looking quite happy, sitting back on her heels beside Lady M — and sucking the fingers that had just been so busily and skilfully engaged in their stimulating work.

'Our guest has gone?' asked Lady M — .

'Yes, Ma'am,' Esther answered, still fanning away.

'Good,' said Lady M — , continuing to expose herself to Esther's cooling mission. 'We must hope that Mr Holmes is successful in tracking him to his lair.' She glanced over to me.

'Gracious,' she said. 'You look as though you could do with some help.'

'May I rest here for a little while, Lady M – ' I said feebly. 'I fear I am quite worn out with events.'

'Of course,' she said understandingly. 'But there is Gwendolen to think of. I would like to think that you can satisfy her in due course.'

'I will try,' I said. 'Please do not take offence. I should like nothing better than to help her. I will do what I can as soon as possible.'

'Don't worry,' said Gwendolen. 'I have an idea. Don't move.'

As I gazed up at the ceiling, I became aware of a rustle of clothing. Suddenly everything went black. Gwendolen had lowered her quim onto my face!

For a moment I thought I would faint from lack of air as darkness enveloped me. Then she lifted herself up a fraction and I took a deep breath, drawing in the scent of her eager pussey while her dense hair filled my mouth and nostrils.

'Don't smother him,' came a voice, seemingly from far away. 'Esther, can you put a cushion behind his head. He needs to be lifted up a bit.' Lady M – was issuing orders like an experienced mistress of ceremonies. 'Gwendolen, if you lean forward you should be able to take him in your mouth.'

I felt warm lips nuzzling at the end of my prick. As her bum was raised, I could see once more. My head was carefully propped up. 'Be gentle with him,' ordered Lady M –. 'He must have had a hard day. Andrew, if you could just use your tongue on Gwendolen, I am certain she will be more than grateful.'

Gallantly I began to lick and tease at Gwendolen's cunney. Such was our position that I could not enter into her properly but I managed to rub against her delicately parted lips.

'That's lovely,' she said sympathetically. 'It's all I want for the moment. Just a lick and a promise.' Then she bent down and dabbed lightly at the very tip of my prick. Now at last I felt a quick contraction in my sorely tried balls. From deep inside me a small rivulet of cum pulsed up my prick. Just as it reached the top, Gwendolen withdrew. A rather feeble fountain shot up into the air.

'Poor thing,' said Cecily. 'A spent force. I suspect that that is all he has to offer for the time being. We must let him recover.'

I carried on tonguing Gwendolen as best I could. Delicious though the sensation was, I was near exhaustion, as well as thoroughly mortified that I had not been able to satisfy her. As waves of fatigue coursed through me, I was dimly aware that she had lifted herself from me.

'Fucked dry,' said a voice. 'Gwendolen, come over here and let us complete what he has started.' All went blank and I lapsed into near unconsciousness.

Coming as though from a great distance, I heard the murmur of voices. I was half aware of a door opening and closing. Time passed. More voices and the sound of low, earnest conversation seeped into my fatigue-dulled brain. I turned over on my side as though I were in bed.

'How unfortunate,' I heard someone say. 'He has been taxed beyond human endurance.'

'Unfortunate, indeed!' came a scornful voice. 'Look what he's doing! The dirty beast is playing with himself!'

Coming to with a start I realised that my hands had sought out the warmth and comfort of my prick and I was clasping it between them. Other hands turned me over on to my back once more.

'Don't be so harsh, Cecily,' said a more concerned voice. 'Look at his Thing. I've never seen it like that before. I much prefer it in its more usual state. I only hope it gets better soon.'

'If I might offer my advice Ma'am,' said a soft Welsh voice, 'We should let him lie for a few minutes more. If nothing happens then, I have a trick or two up my sleeve. It is a problem that I have often encountered in my trade.' Megan had been brought into the room.

Bewildered, I tried to sit up. 'What's happening?' I said.

'Nothing,' said Lady M —. 'That's the problem.'

My stomach rumbled.

'Too much fucking on an empty stomach,' said

159

Gwendolen. 'We must give him something to restore him to life.'

A bowl of by now cold soup was thrust under my chin. Then I was lifted into a sitting position while Gwendolen plied me with several spoonfulls. I swallowed obediently but as my strength returned, so did a feeling of mortification. I was being nursed like an invalid or worse still, a baby. I pushed the spoon away.

'I am quite capable of feeding myself,' I said crossly.

'Well, I suppose that's some improvement,' said Cecily. 'But I am being altogether too severe on you,' she continued, a note of contrition creeping into her voice. 'Maybe there's something more that can be done.'

At that, she lowered her still naked breasts so that they brushed against my dormant member. She began to swing them back and forth. Lady M — and Gwendolen crowded in on me, first one and then the other lowering themselves onto the carpet so that they could carry out a close inspection of Cecily's efforts.

'Nothing happening so far,' said Lady M — .

'I know it will work,' said Cecily. 'My great aunt was a nurse in the Crimea under Florence Nightingale. She said that she often did this to restore some unfortunate injured soldier to life. Indeed most of the nurses did. Of course they had to wait until the Lady with the Lamp had returned to her quarters.' As she talked, she continued her healing ministrations.

'Look! Something's happening now,' said Gwendolen. 'I saw a distinct sign of life.' Sure enough, Cecily's gentle persistence was bearing fruit. Mr Pego stirred and straightened. Struggling against the Law of Gravity, he began to raise himself up, inch by inch.

'*Penis redivivus*,' said Lady M — displaying an unexpected acquaintance with the language of the Classics.

'Like Excalibur emerging from the Lake,' said Gwendolen, not to be outdone in this display of learning.

'Not yet,' said Megan, practically. 'There's still a bend in it.'

'Some extra help is needed,' said Lady M — . Pressing her face close to my valiantly straining member, she began to lick carefully both at its tip and at Cecily's swollen nipples. Gwendolen joined in. Under their combined care, Mr Pego's revival continued.

'Now we must get him completely upright,' said Megan. 'He still needs some more time before he is completely ready to enter into any further activity.' I was hauled to my feet and released. As my dress dropped into position, I stood there, my legs apart, trying to steady myself.

'Fetch a chair,' said Lady M— and as Esther hurried forward with an upright, I sank gratefully down, my knees almost giving way once more.

'At least we can bring him up to date with what has been occurring,' said Lady M—.

I listened, glad that for the moment there were no further calls upon my energies. It transpired that the stranger had left the house and that Esther had managed to dash upstairs and give the pre-arranged signal from the window. She had caught sight of Holmes waiting up the street under a gas lamp. The stranger had walked off down the road and had then hailed a passing cab. Esther was sure that Holmes had set off after him. I remembered that Holmes had had his own cab waiting round the corner for just such an eventuality. I also recalled that I was under orders to return to his Marylebone Road rooms and report what had gone on in the house. I explained what had to be done to Lady M— and the others.

'First I must find my clothes,' I said. 'Megan, you were going to have them ready for me.'

'They're very dirty,' she said. 'And there is still the problem of the two incarcerated maids.'

'Esther, you must go down and release them at once. Bring them up here. I must have a severe word with them. One at least is betraying my confidences. We must find out which is the guilty party and she must leave immediately.'

'If it please you, Ma'am,' said Esther, 'I don't think that it is Olive. She's fresh from the country and none too bright, but I don't think there's an ounce of malice in her. She's just very fond of fucking.'

'Very well,' said Lady M—. 'I shall have to question them one by one.'

'But if you will forgive me,' I said. 'I must return to Mr Holmes' rooms as soon as possible.'

'You'll have to go like that,' said Lady M — . 'We can send your sweeper's rags round in the morning.'

'Is that wise, Ma'am,' said Megan. 'Dressed like that, he will have to make the entire journey on foot. If he gets a cab he will surely betray himself by his voice, if nothing else.'

'You're right,' said Lady M — . She paused, deep in thought. 'I know, someone must go with him. You can take my carriage. Send for James.'

'Lady M — ,' said Cecily, 'may I suggest that Gwendolen and myself go with him? He is not yet fully restored to health.'

'On second thoughts, we will all accompany him,' said Lady M — . 'The problem of the maids can be dealt with tomorrow. Esther, let them out but make sure neither of them leaves the house.'

So all of us, Megan included in the party at Lady M — 's insistence, crowded into her carriage and set off through the night to beard Holmes in his den.

Of the journey, I can remember little. I was still considerably fatigued and such was the warmth engendered by our densely packed confinement that I dozed throughout, lulled by the motion of our passage. I was aware of low conversation and the occasional squeal of pleasure but all was subdued and relaxed.

Some while later the carriage drew to a halt and I came to.

'We have arrived at Mr Holmes' place,' said Lady M — and we all piled out and swarmed up the front steps.

'Good Gracious!' came Mrs Sayers' voice. '*Five* ladies come to call and at such a late hour. However I am afraid that Mr Holmes is not at home, nor is his assistant, Mr Scott. They went out much earlier and neither has been seen since.' She peered at us more closely. 'Lady M — !' she said. 'If it is in connection with the case that he is working on, I can only suggest that you come in and wait for him. I am sure that one or other of them will return soon.'

I realised that dressed as I was she had not recognised me, but before I could make my identity known to her, Lady M — swept in and we were all ushered upstairs to Holmes' study. Mrs Sayers poked the fire into life and then bustled out with the promise of a pot of coffee to come. We settled down to wait.

'What shall we do to pass the time?' said Cecily. Several glances were turned in my direction. 'Andrew, we need entertainment. There must be some parlour game that you can suggest.'

'I would like first of all to change back into some of my own clothes, if I might be excused for a short while.'

'Certainly not,' said Lady M — . 'We've grown used to you in that rather fetching outfit. It suits you.'

I opened my mouth to protest at being so bullied and ordered about but then remembered that Lady M — had engaged Holmes to act on her behalf and, while I had no idea of the financial arrangements involved, it seemed to me in all probability that I was under some quasi-contractual obligation to do as she said. More to the point, I knew that she was under some considerable strain from the whole affair and that it would be kind to humour her. Holmes in any case would not be best pleased if I managed to upset his client over what I suspected he would feel was a trivial matter.

I accepted that for the time being I would have to remain in women's clothing, and that my more pressing worry was that I should not be able to take any part demanded of me in any game suggested by those present. I would have to offer an alternative proposition.

'A game of whist?' I suggested. 'There are cards in the bureau.'

'Too boring,' said Lady M — .

'Bezique?' I tried.

'You'll have to do better than that,' she said.

'I'd like to fuck,' said Gwendolen. I must have looked alarmed because Megan, bless her, came to my rescue.

'I know a game that I learned from a gentleman friend in Portsmouth. We used to play it in his lodgings with his companions.' The other looked rather unimpressed. 'It really is great fun,' she went on brightly.

'It is not some intellectual pursuit, I hope,' said Gwendolen. 'It is not *intellectual* stimulation that I need.

'Fucking would be nice,' said Cecily.

'It is quite simple,' said Megan supportively, 'And it is probably the nearest thing to fucking that can be arranged until Mr Scott has gathered his strength.'

'Tell us about it,' said Lady M — .

'And while you do,' said Gwendolen, 'I have just had an idea. Look!' She had been busily rooting around in her bag as she spoke. Now she triumphantly drew out a familiar object.

'A dildo!' came a chorus of delighted recognition.

'But no ordinary dildo,' she said. She walked over to me, holding the object in her hand. Once more my dress was pulled up and Mr Pego put on display.

'See!' she said. 'Do you not see the similarity?'

'Not much,' said Lady M — . 'One is up and the other is down. If we are to make comparisons, they will both have to be in the same state.'

'Both up would be the more pleasing prospect,' said Cecily. 'In any case, we can hardly bend the delightful object that dear Gwendolen has procured for us. One of us must help Andrew in an attempt at re-erection.'

'I might manage it, if I may,' said Megan. 'My gentleman friend in the Navy often had such a problem when he had just returned from a long sea voyage.'

'By all means, go ahead,' said Lady M — . 'We will watch.'

'I need some butter,' said Megan. 'Perhaps we might ring for the housekeeper?'

'Mrs Sayers is of a rather puritan disposition,' I said. 'It would be better if any object that could cause offence were hidden from her.'

In truth, I had no idea whatsoever if there was any truth in what I said. Indeed I surmised that in her capacity as Holmes' housekeeper, she had long grown used to an array of odd happenings and strange habits. However I was quite determined not to be confronted by her in my present revealing state. In any case, she was of advancing years and since she had not so far recognised me, got up as I was, I did not want to cause her a fright.

'I accept your point,' said Lady M —. 'Let us present a united and decorous front.' So both dildo and member were put away and I moved over into a corner where the light did not catch me. Megan came and stood beside me while the others arranged themselves elegantly on a *chaise longue* and Holmes' leather bound armchair. Mrs Sayers was sent for and butter ordered.

'A tray of sandwiches, Your Ladyship?' asked Mrs Sayers, having no inkling of course as to the purpose for which the butter was needed.

'That would be nice,' said Cecily. 'But make sure there is plenty of butter on them.'

'Ham sandwiches?' asked Mrs Sayers. 'We have a large smoked ham, just delivered from the country at the behest of one of Mr Holmes' acquaintances.'

'That sounds splendid,' said Lady M —. 'With mustard.'

'But not *in* the sandwiches,' said Megan hastily, from her semi-obscurity. She had obviously foreseen the possibility of a painful problem as far as I was concerned, if, as I suspected, I had accurately divined the use to which the butter might be put.

The arrangements were made and we awaited her return. The others turned to talk of intimate encounters while I took the opportunity to sit down once more. Megan sat beside me, keeping a watchful eye and indeed hand on my recovery. Such was her closeness that I relaxed and began to hope that I should be able to regain my full faculties in the not too distant future. She gave my thigh a little squeeze.

'Don't look so worried,' she whispered. 'We'll soon have you up and about again.' Cecily and Gwendolen were entertaining Lady M— with stories of their schooldays in Somerset (*see Oyster 3*) when Mrs Sayers returned with a large salver of sandwiches, mustard in a pot and coffee. Putting it all down on an occasional table that I had earlier noticed because of its marquetry inlay depicting an Eastern scene of astonishing complexity and frankness, she retired. She volunteered the information that she was more than used to having to wait up all hours for Holmes, so we could safely leave any callers to her. The fire was stoked up once more and we were left to our own devices.

Hands reached out for the sandwiches, then Gwendolen paused. 'Megan has first call on them,' she said, 'or at least on the butter in them.'

With a well-mannered curtsy, Megan opened up one sandwich and inspected it. 'That'll do nicely,' she said. 'Just the thing to produce an inflexible friend. Lift your skirt up, Hetty!'

'Andrew, please!' I said.

'You're Hetty until I've dealt with you. Then maybe you'll be an Andrew again.' I stood up and hiked up my skirt. Megan extracted the ham from the sandwich, took a good bite out of it and then scraped a generous helping of butter into the palm of her hand. After she had rubbed it into a suitably soft state, she bent down and began anointing my prick. As she rubbed it into my rather wretched member with her gentle hands, I began to perk up a little. The others looked on with deep interest.

'Can't we speed things up a bit,' said Lady M— rather unhelpfully. 'A good dollop of mustard should produce some reaction.'

At such an idea, I flinched and wilted once more.

'Please, Ma'am,' said Megan. 'Now see what you've done.' Not knowing how Lady M— would take such a reprimand from one of the lower orders, I pursed my lips. Then I realised with a sense of relief that she had been teasing me all along. She burst out laughing.

'I'm sorry, Andrew,' she said. 'How we are mocking you. It is only in fun. Let me reassure you that whatever happens or does not happen tonight, I have every confidence that we can have a most delightful fuck in the near future.'

'And me,' said Gwendolen.

'Me, too,' said Cecily.

At this chorus of assent I relaxed, knowing I was truly among friends. In response to both my easier mood and Megan's renewed buttering, Mr Pego began to recover. There was a round of applause. Emboldened, I strode over to the centre of the room, flourishing my awakened manhood. Megan carefully stroked its underside and then withdrew her hand.

166

'I don't think you need propping up any further,' she said, standing back to admire her handiwork. There were nods of approval all round. Then Gwendolen delved into her bag and drew out the dildo again.

'Now,' she said, coming over and holding it parallel to my prick, 'What do you notice?'

'It's Andrew! To the life!' exclaimed Lady M — with delight. 'How on earth did you get hold of such a Thing?'

'It's a long story,' said Gwendolen, 'but it was given to me by a mutual friend when we were on a bicycling holiday in Northamptonshire (*see Oyster 4*). She is an artist and potter of considerable skill and persuaded him to model for it.'

'I should dearly like to have such a memento of him for my own entertainment,' said Lady M —. 'Are there more copies to be had?'

'I am certain that can be arranged,' said Gwendolen. 'But in the meantime, I realise that I have a further example of her craft.'

Another dildo was produced. At once I recognised it but the others looked most puzzled. Lady M — reached out to inspect it more closely. 'But, it's got *writing* on it,' she cried out. 'I can't quite make out what it says. This is a very strange Thing indeed.'

'It is a signature,' I said, holding it up to the light. 'Count Johann Gewirtz.' I showed the other side and read on. 'The Gobbling Galician.' (*see Oyster 4*).

'I know him! I know him!' Lady M — exclaimed. She took the dildo in her hand. A frown of concentration appeared on her forehead and she closed her eyes as though trying to recall some memory. 'It's just how I remember it.' She hefted it in her hand. 'Just like the original.'

'I'm sure I've never met a gentleman with his name inscribed on his prick, although I've seen some strange tattoos in Portsmouth,' said Megan.

'I don't mean the writing!' Lady M — said. 'But everything else is to the life.' She fondled it and pressed it to her. 'Would you mind, Gwendolen, if I were to use it? See,' she ran her finger down one side, 'where the lettering is raised up. That could stimulate fond recollections indeed.'

167

'I would be delighted if it would help you bring back the past,' said Gwendolen.

'I have every hope that it will also be a foretaste of things to come,' said Lady M —, 'for I have every expectation that he will be in these parts again shortly. He travels frequently.'

'There is one small problem,' said Cecily. 'If you are to enjoy Count Gewirtz and Gwendolen can make use of Andrew's facsimile, what am I to do? I am not sure that the original is yet in full working order.' Here she glanced at me.

Megan, who had been completely ignored during this division of the spoils, spoke up.

'There is my game,' she said. 'A game of chance with the winner taking first pick. Or prick?'

'A pottery lottery,' I said, rather pleased with my witticism.

'What an awful joke,' said Cecily. 'You will certainly have to pay a forfeit for that.'

'What *is* the game?' said Gwendolen. 'I can hardly wait to win. I am always lucky at cards.'

'Yes, we must get on with it,' said Lady M —. 'We have no idea when Mr Holmes may walk in and it would be nice to have a round or two completed before that happens.'

'It is simplicity itself,' said Megan. 'After I have shuffled the pack, we all take a card. The one with the lowest card has to take off some item of clothing. Then we repeat the procedure.'

'This could go on for hours,' said Lady M —.

'Not if we are quick about it,' said Cecily. 'Deal the cards!'

'Two!' said Cecily, peering under her card without turning it over. 'I lose.' With that she unbuttoned her dress and let it fall to the ground. Under her chemise, her splendid titties were delightfully outlined. Mr Pego responded happily.

'Cheat,' said Gwendolen. 'Turn it over. That's the rule. We must all see.'

'Oh Gwendolen, do you not trust me?' said Cecily. 'Surely old schoolfriends should have faith in one another. Do you not remember the School Motto?'

'No,' said Gwendolen. 'Anyway, it was in Latin and I

abhorred the language.' She turned Cecily's card over. 'Ten!'
she said. 'I knew you were cheating. You must put your dress
back on again this instant.'

'I don't think I can,' said Cecily. 'There are so many
complicated buttons and things. You know I have never been
very good at dressing myself.'

'Well, *I* have a five,' said Lady M —. 'I am certain that is
a winning score.' She removed a glove.

I looked at her with admiration. I should explain that she
had been a winner in previous rounds but had chosen to
undress in an unorthodox order. Apart from her remaining
glove she was completely naked. As the firelight played on
her naked body, I began to have every confidence of being
able to enter the game in the near future.

Again Megan dealt the cards. Again Cecily peeked at her
card without letting the rest of us see. 'The Joker!' she said,
a mischievous smile flitting across her face. 'That means I
can take off ten items of clothing.'

'I don't remember that rule,' I said.

'Ask Megan,' said Cecily. 'You cannot have been paying
proper attention when the rules were set out. I distinctly recall
Megan saying so.'

Megan, sensing no doubt a certain mood of impatience
among the assembled company, agreed to Cecily's statement
with great promptness. 'I think that you were too tired to
listen carefully at the beginning.'

'Very well,' I said. 'Ten items of clothing it shall be.'

Cecily, barely waiting for my concurrence, had slipped out
of her chemise as well as her remaining underclothes.

'Seven choices left,' she said. 'But I have nothing left to
remove. I believe that I have the right to allot my spare turns
to anyone I may choose.' She looked round the room to see
if there was any further disagreement.

'Dear Cecily,' said Gwendolen, 'I do hope that I can be
the recipient of your generosity. I have been so unlucky in
this game. I've hardly lost a stitch and I am beginning to find
the heat from the fire quite enervating. I am sure I shall fall
into a swoon unless I am able to get rid of some of these
clothes.'

'But what about Megan,' I said. 'She also is unfortunately fully dressed. I think the two of you should share Cecily's gift.'

'Don't worry about me,' said Megan. 'Remember that if we all end up unclothed at the same time, the whole point of the game is lost.'

'You're right,' said Lady M —. 'Cecily and I are already out of the game, with nothing left to lose.'

With that, she picked up the two dildoes that had been left to warm in front of the grate.

'Cecily, if you would like to take Andrew, I have an urgent need to refresh my memory of dear Johnny.'

She flung herself down on the *chaise longue* and I watched with some envy as the Gewirtz dildo was thrust between her legs. Without any further ado, she began to slide it repeatedly in and out of her obviously eager quim. A satisfied look spread across her face.

'It's all coming back to me,' she said. 'Johnny Gewirtz to the life! It was at the Duchess of Hallamshire's Ball last winter. My husband was talking to some thoroughly boring people. I managed to evade his notice for a few minutes and Johnny Gewirtz and I escaped into a side room. I was simply dying for a fuck and he responded with all the gallantry for which foreign gentlemen are renowned. Although the fact that he was in the full dress uniform of some regiment or other delayed things for a while. The Gallician Cuirassiers! That was it. A very fanciful creation. A lot of gold and a positive chestful of medals, as well as a sword and spurs on his boots. There was no time to get that lot off so I pulled his trousers down and his military accoutrement fairly leaped out before me.'

As she reminisced, she was plying the object of her recollections rhythmically to and fro. Meanwhile Cecily, who had accepted her lot without complaint, was licking my likeness while making herself ready with her other hand. Then she knelt down on the hearth rug, facing the fire so that her splendid bum was staring us in the face. I realised from her movements that she was rubbing the dildo against her succulent breasts. Her back being turned to us as it was, I

170

could only guess what happened next. She gave an excited cry of pleasure and twitched her bottom. I realised that my likeness had been inserted into her delicious cunney.

So delightful was the scene that I at once knew that I should be able to take part in the activities without further delay.

'Would anyone like to sample the original?' I asked, taking hold of my prick and offering it to the room.

'Mine!' said Gwendolen, struggling frantically to get out of her clothes.

'Me!' said Cecily, looking round.

'Don't be selfish,' Gwendolen replied. 'You've got your plaything already.'

'Well, you're not ready,' said Cecily. 'Andrew, come over here!'

Rather ungallantly, I must admit, I abandoned poor Gwendolen to her disrobing and lined myself up behind Cecily. As soon as I grasped her by the hips, she lifted herself up and I entered into her from behind. She sighed and settled. Then she pulled forward again and removed herself from my impaling instrument.

'Both,' she said. 'I want to try both the copy and the original. They will have to take turns.' As Mr Pego stayed lodged between her thighs, she inserted my counterfeit into her and thrust it backwards and forwards several times. Then she pulled it out.

'Now the other,' she said. I slipped into her once more and drove on. Again she pulled clear and again I was replaced by my replica.

'All change again,' she cried out.

I realised that it was all a matter of timing. Three or four strokes were completed and then there was an exchange of instruments. Unusual though the situation was, it was nonetheless an exciting new sport. 'Always seek to broaden your experience,' I recalled young Fanny saying to me back in what now seemed my far distant school days. She had been parting the cheeks of her bum as she spoke, opening out her back passage into which she was urging me to enter. 'Tools rush in where angels fear to tread.' That had been another of her sayings. I had embraced her philosophy with gratitude.

Meanwhile Cecily had been speeding up her alternating members. As she became more rapid in her comings and goings, some confusions as to timing were beginning to creep in. More than once I found myself driving into her just as my other half was being withdrawn. She herself was now so widened that there was no question of her lips closing as one member slipped out. What with the heat from the fire and the heat of her exertions, she had become quite slippery with perspiration and her cunney juices were soaking into her bush and running down her thighs. I took my place once more.

'Stay in, Andrew!' she said, letting my replica fall from her hand. 'I want to be finished off by the real Thing.'

I took full responsibility and thrust on. Out of the corner of my eye, I spotted the approach of Gwendolen. Still partly dressed, she swooped on the discarded member and carried it off in triumph. Suddenly Cecily began to come.

While I tried to hold myself steady, she shuddered and started to moan, forcing herself onto me while her hands opened and closed, clawing at the rug, her whole body trembling with ecstasy. Like a stout anchor in a gale, I kept us safe and sound as the full storm of her coming burst upon us. Spasm after spasm coursed through her as she choked and gasped. Then she paused and gave out one last cry of delight before subsiding, still clamped about me, to the floor.

As I struggled to remain in her, I took the chance to survey the scene. Lady M— seemed quite transported by her memories of Johnny Gewirtz and was stretched out full length on her couch, one leg hooked up over the back and the other trailing on the ground, her hands grasping the object of her desire and forcing it slowly but regularly in and out of her tunnel of love.

Gwendolen was sitting on the floor, backed up against a comfortably upholstered chair. She had not bothered to complete her unrobing and her dress was pushed up to her waist. My discarded replica was being put to good use.

Megan, who was also fully dressed, was playing no part in the activities except that one hand had disappeared under her skirt. She was playing with herself as she stood by the window looking out into the street. All of a sudden she turned back into the room.

'Someone is coming,' she said.

'Almost everyone is coming,' I said.

'No! I mean outside!' she said urgently. 'There's a cab at the door and someone is getting out of it. It's Mr Holmes!'

Interesting though this news was, there was no-one other than myself sufficiently *compos mentis* to pay the least attention to it.

Withdrawing from Cecily's embrace, I joined Megan at the window, my prick still standing out like a tea-clipper's bowsprit.

'You could hang washing on that,' said Megan, taking hold of it and inspecting it with professionally dispassionate skill. 'But keep it away from the window panes, you're making them mist up with the heat.'

In spite of the rather domestic nature of her metaphor, I took it as a compliment. 'If you can make use of it,' I said, 'please do so.'

'As a working girl, I usually charge for such things,' she said. 'But I believe I may owe you some change from our first encounter. Anyway, there isn't the time now. Your Master is here.'

Sure enough, at that moment the door was opened and Holmes strode in.

'I see that you have been entertaining our guests,' he said, looking about him. Instinctively I dropped my hands, trying to conceal my straining member. Megan stood beside me, keeping her composure admirably in the circumstances. Neither Cecily, Gwendolen nor Lady M— reacted in any way whatsoever, so intent were they all on their activities.

'I, — I can explain — ' I said nervously.

'There is no need for explanations, Scott,' he said. 'It does not take a detective's training to understand what is going on. Pray, continue, Ladies,' he said to the others. 'But it would be nice if there was somewhere to sit.'

I pulled the only spare easy chair in the room over to him, but instead he remained standing. Then he began his familiar pacing to and fro.

'The plot is developing fast,' he said. 'I have uncovered the blackmailing swine who is behind it all.'

'Possibly we should attempt to engage Lady M—'s attention,' I said.

'She does not look like a woman who is capable of coherent thought at the moment,' he said, casting an eye on the display revealed to all and sundry on the *chaise longue*. 'My experience in these matters tells me that we will have to wait a little while longer.'

Lady M— was indeed oblivious to everything but her own imminent coming. She was spreadeagled, her head thrown back and clutching at Count Gewirtz' memento as though it was the last hold on life of a drowning sailor. Her magnificent breasts were rising and falling as she busied herself with her fast approaching climax.

As for the others, Cecily appeared to have fallen into a light sleep curled up in front of the fire, her hands between her thighs. Gwendolen, not yet so far gone along the path of pleasure, was backed up against her chair, her knees raised, making repeated insertions of my likeness. There was a frown of concentration on her face as she looked down on her deft probing and teasing. It was clear that she was concentrating all her efforts on her clit, rather than seeking the deepest penetration.

'Ring for Mrs Sayers, will you,' said Holmes to Megan. 'We are all about to need some restorative draft. Some Canary would be the most appropriate.' Then he looked at the mantelshelf. A small lacquered box that I had not seen before stood there. 'Fresh supplies from the Orient,' he said, picking it up. 'Lloyds confirmed that the ship was safely arrived in the Pool.'

The reference meant nothing to me but Holmes was obviously pleased. He prised open the tight-fitting lid of the box and sniffed delicately at the contents before reaching for his pipe. There followed the now familiar ritual of stuffing and tamping the smoking mixture into its capacious bowl. Finally he lit his pipe and sucked appreciatively at the stem.

'Not a habit of yours?' he asked me.

'I am a cigar man rather than a pipe smoker,' I answered.

'I have never been able to understand the enjoyment that there is to be got from such things.'

'There are pleasures in life that you have yet to sample, Scott,' he said. 'But you will come to them in your own good time.'

Megan meanwhile had been twitching her nostrils as the aromatic smoke rose. 'From the Levant,' she said.

'Ah, my dear, so you have a connoisseur's nose for such things,' said Holmes.

'I came across it when I was working in Portsmouth,' she said. 'When the Fleet was in. Particularly when any ship had returned from station in the Mediterranean.'

They exchanged little grins of complicity while I was left with the uneasy feeling that I was missing the point of their exchanges.

'But what of the plot?' I asked.

Holmes took his pipe out of his mouth and looked me up and down. I was suddenly conscious of the fact that I was stark naked and that Mr Pego was waving about as I talked. Holmes continued to look thoughtfully at me, one eyebrow raised as was his wont.

'Where is that charming dress you were wearing when I saw you last?' he said.

'Over there,' said Megan before I could gather my wits. 'On the floor in the corner. He threw it there when we started to play cards.'

'My dear,' he said to Megan, 'Could you do something about that?' He pointed to my plainly displayed pikestaff. 'I find it something of a distraction when I am trying to think.'

'Certainly, Sir,' she said.

Taking me carefully between finger and thumb she drew me aside. She began to squeeze my balls delicately but insistently. Then she knelt down in front of me. 'Soon have him discharged,' she said, looking up at Holmes. Then she took me in her mouth and, still massaging my balls, began to suck my straining cock. After my encounter with Cecily I was already close to my coming. Megan's skilled attentions soon provoked a first tingling response from my recharged

175

testicles and then in no time at all I was beginning to feel a first surge of cum jetting down my prick. Megan held me in place and swallowed everything I could produce with consummate ease. After such an arduous day's duty, I was soon at the end although my pleasure remained unimpaired.

'That was quick,' said Holmes a moment or two later.

'He's had a busy time,' said Megan, practically wiping her lips delicately as the last drops leaked from my cock.

'And yours is a practised hand,' said Holmes.

'I am practised in all parts,' said Megan brightly. 'See, he's retreating out of sight already.'

'I suppose I owe you something for that?' I said to Megan, slightly put out by the way that I was being handled.

'No, no, allow me!' said Holmes, reaching into his pocket. 'I commissioned the job.'

'Sixpence, Sir,' said Megan.

'Your prices seem to be going up,' said Holmes.

'Special rates for the Gentry,' said Megan. 'I want to better myself in life.'

'Very sensible,' said Holmes. 'Always charge what the market will bear. One of the first lessons to be learned in commercial circles. However, now that Mr Scott is no longer intruding on my thought processes quite so visibly, I should perhaps begin to explain what I have been about since I left Lady M—'s.'

'And I shall account for myself also,' I said, anxious to demonstrate that I had not been delinquent in my duties as his assistant.

'I have a pretty shrewd idea of what has been happening as far as you and your friends are concerned,' said Holmes.

As he said this there was a positive howl of pleasure from the corner of the room. Gwendolen had achieved her aim of the moment. With a flamboyant gesture she fairly threw down my replica and began to laugh in sheer relief.

'I am sorry,' she said. 'But I did so need that. I do apologise for having interrupted your conversation. Pray continue. I will be quiet now.' She lay stretched out on the carpet like a cat in front of a fire, quite unconcerned that her bush was thus casually displayed.

'As I was saying,' said Holmes, 'much has taken place. I followed Lady M — 's visitor. He had his cab drop him off on the edge of Kensington Gardens. A man was waiting for him under a tree. A horse chestnut. *Aesculus Hippocastanum*, as it is known to the botanist.'

'Yes,' I said, somewhat impatiently.

'A man was waiting for him,' Holmes continued. 'They at once fell into urgent conversation. So intent were they that I was able to creep up on them unobserved.'

'So you were able to overhear what was said,' I interjected.

'Not a word,' said Holmes. 'Far too much wind. A south easterly.'

'How unfortunate,' I said.

'Not at all,' said Holmes. 'I was able to ascertain that money changed hands and that orders were being given. When, shortly afterwards, they parted, I followed the second man as he set off across the park. I had already made a tentative identification but my suspicions were soon confirmed. He crossed Bayswater Road and went into a house near Lancaster Gate. As he was admitted, he was clearly illuminated.'

'Who was it?' I asked eagerly.

'None other than Lord M — himself,' said Holmes. 'My earlier surmise was proved correct.' At this point there was a gasp. Lady M — had caught the sound of the name. She sat bolt upright, her breasts swaying most fetchingly as she clasped her knees together and looked up on us.

'My husband!' she said.

'Indeed yes,' said Holmes. 'You have been the victim of a dastardly scheme.'

'But what am I to do?' she said. 'He must have returned incognito from the Continent in order to spy on me. What a vile thing to do.'

'Do not upset yourself,' said Holmes. 'Now that we have found out all about his nasty little scheme, we can confront him with our knowledge and threaten to expose him to the Authorities.'

'But if this should become *public* knowledge, I shall never again be able to hold my head up in Society. I shall not be received anywhere and will have to retire to the country. I simply can't abide our place down in Wiltshire. It is huge and draughty and there is hardly anyone there one can fuck.'

'I do not think it will have to come to that,' said Holmes. 'I had in mind not some legal proceedings but a quiet word in the ear of one or two men of affairs close to the Prime Minister. That would be enough to ensure that he is never again employed on any missions of a diplomatic nature and that the Honour he so eagerly covets is never bestowed. There would be no public disgrace but word would get around and he would have to resign from his clubs. His days of influence would be at an end. Blackmail is frowned on in such circles. It casts doubt on one's suitability for much government work.'

'Nor can I bear the thought of having to confront him myself,' said Lady M — . 'In fact I never want to see the brute again. If he insists on taking up residence again in our house, I will have to leave at once and seek admission to some nunnery where he cannot find me.'

'I hardly think such drastic measures will be called for,' said Holmes. 'I will undertake to handle the whole distasteful business myself. I hope he does not become violent or I may be forced to knock the blackguard down.'

'His is a choleric disposition,' said Lady M — , 'and he is handy with his fists. He once brutally assaulted our Vicar in Wiltshire.'

'An unprovoked attack?' asked Holmes.

'Almost entirely so,' said Lady M — . 'I had had occasion to seek some spiritual comfort and advice and the Vicar had come to the house for that purpose. We were discussing my problems which involved, among others, a nice point of Trinitarian doctrine, when my husband burst into the bedroom quite unannounced and beside himself with rage. He accused the Vicar of intentions of a substantially secular nature and attacked him. The poor man was only able to save himself from further punishment by leaping from the window.

'Luckily there is a well-grown Virginia Creeper on that side of the house — '

'*Parthenocissus quinquefolia* or *tricuspidata*?' interrupted Holmes with his customary insistence on scientific accuracy.

'And he was able to scramble down to safety,' went on Lady M —, ignoring the interjection with aristocratic nonchalance. 'My husband flung his cassock, trousers and camera after him but he was in too much of a hurry to stop and pick them up. The curate was sent round for them the next day.

'After that, of course, I was no longer able to attend his services. Luckily the Living is in the gift of a neighbour with whom I have a close understanding, otherwise I am certain that the poor creature would have been turned out of pulpit and vicarage.'

'He sounds the sort of cleric a parish can ill afford to lose,' said Holmes. 'An incumbent with an understanding of the Sins of the Flesh from first hand experience is an asset to his flock.'

'He didn't have a very big Thing,' went on Lady M —, 'but he used it with a surprising degree of invention and precision, unlike my husband who is hung like a prize bull but who wields his weapon more like some medieval seige piece than an instrument of pleasure.

'The vicar also had the sweetest set of balls you have ever seen. When he became agitated, which was often in my presence, they used to swing from side to side like an incense censer being processed down the aisle in a Roman church.'

'A charming picture,' said Holmes, 'but we must complete our plans. Have you any idea who may own the Lancaster Gate house where he appears to be staying?'

'In all probability his cousin Humphrey, a morbid sort of fellow; tall, cadaverous and unsmiling with a stern moral view of Humanity. I only once saw him show any signs of animation and that was when I was telling him of my work with Fallen Women. He expressed deep interest in the Home I was establishing for them and enquired after the means of Correction that were to be used on the inmates.

'I recall that he gave me something of a lecture on the virtues of physical chastisement in cases of moral backsliding. He seemed to regard his own hand as an extension of the

Divine Will. He belongs to a like-minded group who call themselves Spankers for the Lord. They devote much of their spare time to what they call Visitations. As many as a dozen of them will descend on a place, usually one of the poorer parts of some Northern manufacturing town, and seek out women of the streets and back alleys. They urge them into the Paths of Repentance, exhorting them to bend before the storms of Righteousness and belabouring their buttocks to drive out Sinfulness. I am told that the sounds of their Redemptive Onslaughts fairly ring through the meaner streets of the North. They have a particular liking for Oldham. At the end of their expeditions, they repair to Buxton or Matlock, sore-handed and worn out with their efforts, and take the waters.'

'I had a Gentleman in Wales who was similarly inclined,' said Megan. 'An Elder of one of the stricter Chapels in Aberavon I think it was. He used to seek me out every Thursday. I had to lean over a table while he smacked my bum and cried out to the Heavens that here was a miserable sinner who had to be driven firmly along the road to Rectitude. I charged him sixpence. I used to point out that he could have a fuck for tuppence but he didn't seem to be interested in that sort of thing.

'He used to sing a sort of hymn while he was chastising me. "Spanking out the Sin" it was called. He used to beat out the time on my bottom. Of course, we Welsh are a musical nation.'

At this point I recalled the apoplectic man in the upturned dogcart whom we had encountered while bicycling in Northamptonshire (*see Oyster 4*). However Holmes, who had been listening to these digressions with avid interest, decided now to recall us to our present planning before I could recount my own tale of Fundamental Practices.

'Is Cousin Humphrey likely to be a party to your husband's blackmail plot?' he asked Lady M — . 'Is he for instance likely to be in need of additional funds in order to finance his spanking expeditions?'

'I doubt it very much,' said Lady M — . 'He has a substantial private income. He is in any case by profession an attorney and I have never found such people to be short of funds.'

'In that case,' said Holmes, 'I will call at the house in the morning. I think you had better accompany me, Scott. The presence of two able-bodied visitors will dissuade our quarry from attempting any violence when we confront him with our suspicions.'

'What if he is not at home?' I asked.

'We will wait for him,' said Holmes. 'We can explain that we have an urgent communication of a confidential nature from the Foreign Office. We must take the photographs with us and ensure that we do not come away without the original plates.'

'But what shall *I* do?' said Lady M — . 'I do not want to return home until I am assured that my husband is not likely to call.'

'You must stay here,' said Holmes. 'Mrs Sayers will see that you have every comfort.'

'And we can safely go home,' said Cecily, 'unless, dear Priscilla, you would feel more at ease if we stayed here with you.'

'Thank you, I should like that,' said Lady M — .

'In that case,' said Holmes, 'Megan might like to stay as well. She is already so involved in the case that I am sure she would like to know of the outcome. I would also like to discuss the possibility of the payment of a retainer fee. An occasional additional pair of eyes and ears is always of use to someone in my line of business.'

'Thank you, Sir,' said Megan. 'Would you like a fuck on account?'

'Not now,' said Holmes hastily. 'I need to consider tomorrow's encounter. Possibly Mr Scott would like to act on my behalf.'

'I doubt if he has got it in him,' said Gwendolen sweetly.

'Please do not make such assumptions,' I said stiffly.

'Now we've upset him,' said Cecily. 'Andrew,' she continued, 'I for one do not want to cast aspersions on your prowess. Possibly a good hot bath would restore you to your customary vigour.'

'That is easily arranged,' said Holmes, 'but I shall have to leave it to you to attend to his recuperation. I am certain he will be in good hands.'

Lady M — looked up. 'What an excellent idea,' she said. 'I would like to see him revived and besides, the endeavour would help me take my mind off this whole sorry business.'

Soon afterwards I found myself happily immersed in a hot bath. Megan was holding Mr Pego up out of the water as she soaped and sponged my sorely tried balls, while Gwendolen and Cecily knelt beside the bath, scrutinising her efforts.

'I do not think there is any more need to hold him up,' said Cecily. 'He seems to be recovering.' Megan released me and sure enough, Mr Pego managed to stay upright. She stepped back in order to inspect me.

'We'd better give him a complete scrubbing,' said Cecily. 'Gwendolen and I will start with his feet.'

In no time at all, three pairs of hands were employed about my person.

'Close your eyes,' said Cecily, 'We've got to get you clean from head to toe.'

I did as I was told and surrendered myself to their solicitous attentions. Gentle hands soaped and lathered my body. Fatigue and pleasure coursed through me and lulled me into a half-conscious daze. My eyes closed and I drifted while the pains and strains of the day were drained from my over-taxed body.

Suddenly I jumped convulsively as though an electric shock has been passed through me. A sharp fingernail had been run up the tender underside of my prick.

'Keep your eyes shut or you will get soap in them,' said a stern voice.

Lady M — had decided to take charge. There came a sound of giggling and my legs were lifted up and parted so that my ankles rested on the rim on either side of the bath. An unseen hand began gently to massage my balls. Then first one and then the other big toe was encircled by a warm mouth. I flinched.

'He's ticklish!' came a gleeful voice. 'What fun!'

Two tongues licked and rasped at the soles of my feet. I struggled convulsively to get free but as I thrashed about, my head went under the water just as I tried to draw in a deep breath. As my lungs filled, I spluttered, spouted and flailed wildly about. Water cascaded everywhere and there were peals of laughter. I sat bolt upright, blinking vigorously to get the water out of my eyes.

'Now look what you've done,' said Lady M –. 'His Thing has sunk down out of sight. Just lie back again Andrew and think of England. We have no intention of drowning you.'

Pinioned as I was, I had no real option but to obey. As I lowered myself backwards, Mr Pego floated back up from the depths to lie on the surface and then slowly begin his resurrection.

'That's better,' said Megan.

'I can think of a part for me in all this,' said Lady M –. Unbuttoning herself, she leaned over me. Two dark nipples swayed like forbidden fruit just above my face. Tantalisingly they were lowered to within an inch of my mouth. I strained up towards them, poking out my tongue to touch them but they trembled teasingly just out of reach.

'Like a stranded fish, he is,' said Megan. 'Don't be so cruel, Ma'am.'

Lady M – cupped her breasts in her hands, pushing them out towards me and letting them brush my face. Then like a suckling infant, I managed to latch on to a nipple and began to suck hungrily at it. Lady M – pulled away slightly and, for a distressing moment, I thought I was to be deprived of my comfort. Craning my head upwards I tried to retain my hold. Then she relented and lowered herself once more. Greedily I pulled at her swollen nipple, aware at the same time that Mr Pego was standing proudly above the water like a palm tree on a desert island, except in his case the nuts were at the bottom rather than hanging from the top.

With Lady M – 's splendid bosom now pressed against my face and my vision thus delightfully obscured, I was unable to see whose was the mouth that now descended on my upright member, taking in half of his length in one gulp. At

183

the same time I became aware that other soft breasts were stroking my feet, one to either side of the bath. More water was displaced as I stretched out, rubbing against them while at the same time forcing Mr Pego up and further into the friendly mouth.

'The floor is absolutely soaking,' came a voice. 'Shouldn't we get him out of there before the whole place is turned into a swamp.'

'It's far too late to worry about a thing like that,' came an answer. 'As long as we all help to clear up afterwards, I expect we will be able to make our peace with Mr Holmes and the housekeeper. Besides, I've just had an idea!'

As I nuzzled at Lady M — 's plump and responsive titties, moving from one to the other and feeling first one nipple and then the other harden in my mouth, I was aware of whispering. All at once there was an almighty splash and a veritable tidal wave shot along the bath. Still clinging on to Lady M — 's bountiful breast, I nearly disappeared under water once again as a soapy torrent filled my eyes and nostrils. I spluttered and lost my grip but as the waters washed over me and I went down for the second time, I was dimly aware that I was no longer alone in the bath.

A naked woman was kneeling between my legs while Megan held out my cock to her like the priest of some strange religion holding out a votive offering. Before I could ascertain whether it was Cecily or Gwendolen who had joined me in my ablutions, I was once more submerged. Peering up through the water, I saw the distorted outlines of Lady M — 's wonderful breasts looming above me. As the tide swirled over me and then began to recede, I bobbed to the surface again, only to collide with her generous flesh. This had the unfortunate effect of pushing me under once more just as I reached up with my mouth to the life-saving nipple that swam before me.

With a gurgle I sank to the bottom but, as all my past life began to pass before me, someone grabbed me by the hair and I was jerked upwards.

'Quick, pull out the plug,' came Megan's voice. Spluttering and spitting out water, I took in a much-needed lungful of air. In my struggles I had thoroughly drenched Lady M—. Trickles of water ran down her succulent breasts and dripped from her nipples into my open mouth. I swallowed once and then again, licking the droplets as they hung, ready to fall.

Then, as the receding water flowed past me, my newly-arrived companion slid towards me along the fast-emptying bath and with the truest of aims, impaled herself on my prick. Easing herself backwards and forwards, she began to fuck me. Lady M—'s hands were cradling the back of my head, pulling me on to her and keeping me away from any abrupt and painful contact with the taps. Realising that I was not about to die and that I was in safe hands, I began to respond, pushing forward to help my member in its repeated entries into that warm, receptive cunney.

'He's better,' came a voice. 'For an awful moment I thought he'd overtaxed his strength.'

'At least his most vital part is back in the land of the living,' said another. 'Just look at it!'

'Thank Heavens,' said the first voice. 'I'm certain Mr Holmes would never have forgiven us if he'd lost his new assistant so suddenly.'

'He would indeed have been a great loss to the world,' said another. 'Although, of course, there would always have been the Scott dildo to remember him by.'

'I for one would have insisted that it was placed in perpetuity on his gravestone. At least it wouldn't have wilted like a bunch of flowers and future generations would have been able to appreciate what had distinguished him in life.'

'People would have come from miles around to stroke it for luck and in fond remembrance. It would have become all worn and shiny like the toe on that saint's statue in Rome that the pilgrims always kiss.'

'Or the Blarney stone.'

'Except that as it became all weathered and worn down, no one would think it was anything out of the ordinary any more and they'd stop coming.'

'And the moss would grow over it.'

'Sad.'

'*Sic transit gloria pudendi.*'

I tried to interrupt this increasingly heartless conversation but Lady M — 's bountiful bosom once more stopped up my mouth. Meanwhile I was slipping and squeaking my way up and down the nearly empty bath in my efforts to keep pace with the eager quim that had swallowed up my revived member and was now bumping and boring against me.

'Ow!' said a Welsh voice as someone fell over with a thump. 'The whole floor is sopping wet and slippery. Help me up someone, please!'

'Your dress is wringing wet,' came what I dimly realised was Gwendolen's voice. 'Here let me help you off with it. It will have to be hung up somewhere to dry.'

By now I was growing increasingly uncaring of what exactly was going on around me as the excitement of my fuck in the bath grew with every stroke. I drove on, thrust following thrust until, locked together, we began to skid wildly along the bath.

'He's got the soap wedged under his bum,' said Megan, spotting that something was awry. 'He's going to do himself an injury if we don't get it out.'

I was grasped under the cheeks of my bum and hoisted up while another hand insinuated itself under me, groping around until it closed on the unwanted bar of soap.

'Bother,' came Megan's voice, 'it's got away again. I can't see where it's gone. We'll have to try and anchor him in position until Miss Cardew has finished.'

I was steadied and held in position as Cecily moved more and more vigorously up and down my prick. She was beginning to breathe heavily. With Gwendolen and Megan holding on to my feet and Lady M — supporting my head, I was able to hold steady as her movements rose to a frenzy.

'The insatiable in pursuit of the immovable,' observed Gwendolen as she gritted her teeth, clinging on to me for dear life.

'I'm coming! I'm coming!' Cecily cried out.

My knuckles were white with the effort of holding on to the sides of the bath. I tensed myself as her cunney almost swallowed me up. She let out a great shriek of pleasure and I felt her shudder all over as her juices flowed down. I was so deep in her that it felt as though I should never be able to retrace her passage. I could feel the sorely tried end of my prick probing her innermost being while she seized me by the hips and tried to force me even further into her. Desperately I thrust back, aware that the mixture of cum and soap had made the bath so treacherous that any slip could result in serious injury. She shrieked again and gave one last heave before almost collapsing. A couple of great sighs wracked her body and she lay back, her breasts rising and falling with the effort that she had put into her fucking.

We lay still for a moment and then, as the others relaxed their grip on me, inch by inch my swollen, glistening member slipped out of her. Lady M — 's generous bosom ceased to press against me. I licked feebly at a passing nipple and then, utterly exhausted, lay still, my undischarged firing piece pointing at the ceiling.

'He can't go to sleep there,' said Gwendolen firmly, after a blissful moment or two of rest. 'Andrew! Pull yourself together and get up!'

Wearily, I struggled upright. Willing arms supported me as I stepped out on to the wet floor. With the whole bath now to herself, Cecily stretched out full length. I looked down at her. Drops of water hung like fresh dew on the hairs of her pussey, trembling slightly as she breathed. Her wonderful big titties stood proud above her ribcage. Her eyes were open but with a faraway look in them, while a big silly grin spread over her face.

Pride stirred in me at the thought that even in my exhausted state, I had been able to satisfy her once more. I lifted my chin and squared my shoulders.

'It's all right,' I said, shrugging off my supporters. 'I can stand up.' Megan, Gwendolen and Lady M — let go of me and I collapsed.

That night, or rather during the remainder of the night, I slept the sleep of the dead. Who put me to bed I do not know, nor who brought the bowl of sustaining broth. Truly I had been driven to the limits of human endurance. Like some explorer in the Dark Continent struggling through the jungles, or the master of a ship, thrusting its way through the ice floes of the Greenland Sea in search of the North West Passage, I had endured and survived. As I closed my eyes, visions of pussies swam before me. I reached down to touch my trusty tool. It was also dead to the world. All I could hope was that we would both wake in the morning. I snuggled down and lapsed into unconsciousness.

'Mrs Sayers reports that you acquitted yourself nobly last night,' said Holmes.

We were swaying along in a cab, *en route* to the Lancaster Gate house and our rendezvous with the unsuspecting Lord M —. I had been roused at what had seemed an unearthly hour. I was still deeply fatigued but determined not to let Holmes realise my weakened state.

'Although she was left with rather a lot of clearing up to do,' he went on. 'Wet clothing everywhere. She's getting rather rheumaticky in the knees and all that bending down and picking things up is not good for her. Luckily Megan helped. When I left they were doing the washing up together.'

'Washing up?' I said. 'I do not recall a meal.'

'Soup bowls and dildoes,' said Holmes. 'At least two of the latter, recently used. Obviously they belonged to our guests. If they have need of them again while we are out, they can be found on the draining board.'

I accepted the reprimand. It was true that his rooms had been left in some disarray, although I had not personally been responsible for much that had gone on and for the life of me I did not know what I could have done to persuade our guests to behave with more decorum. I decided to change the subject.

'The blackmailer's photographs,' I said. 'There appear to be two sets: one that was presented to Lady M — as evidence of her activities, and a second, sent to you by her husband with a request that you discover the identities of the intruding members. You suggested when Lady M — first arrived that the pictures had been taken by her husband. Surely he would have recognised the gentlemen involved. Or at least some of them?'

'The answer to your question, Scott, is that, whilst he took the photographs, he was not actually present at the time.'

'I don't understand,' I said.

'The explanation is quite simple,' said Holmes. 'Last night, I took the liberty of inspecting the marital bedroom at Lady M – 's. I found a thin but strong wire attached to one of the legs of the bed. It led through a small hole carefully bored in the wainscoting, into the next room, up the wall and back into a loft space immediately above the bedroom. A spyhole had been cut in the ceiling. It was almost invisible from below since there is some intricate plaster moulding that hides it. I peered through the hole. It is lined up precisely on the bed. In the loft were traces of powder burns and indentations in the dust.

'A camera must have been positioned there, lined up on the bed. Because of the restricted field of vision, only a few square inches of any visitor could be seen.'

'And the camera would be triggered off by any pronounced movement of the bed,' I said. 'Such as that occasioned by a bout of fucking.'

'Precisely,' said Holmes. 'Exposure below would be followed by exposure above. No doubt there were many times when the bodies were not lined up with the lens and nothing of interest was recorded, but so great and so frequent is that poor creature's need for consolation in her unhappy marriage, that some at least were likely to be recorded *in flagrante delicto* as the lawyers would say.'

'And you have in fact made some identifications of the instruments of pleasure involved?' I asked.

'I have narrowed down the field considerably,' said Holmes, 'to the point where I could make a positive identification with only a little more research if I so chose.' He drew out the portfolio and showed it to me.

'For instance, this fellow here,' he continued, picking one specimen out. 'What do you make of that?'

I scrutinised the proffered print. 'There seem to be indentations on it,' I said.

189

'Precisely,' Holmes said. 'Those are literally indentations. It has been recently bitten. Notice an irregularity in the markings. You will have discerned when Lady M – smiles, that she has a small gap between two of her front teeth. I am prepared to wager that she is the biter. In addition Dr Motson, if he were here, would doubtless be able to confirm that the extent of the injuries is such that the victim would have had to seek medical treatment after the event. There are only two doctors in London who specialise in such matters. I will not name names but one is By Appointment to the Prince of Wales while the other is a Harley Street man with a practice consisting largely of military patients. Either, if it was explained that this was a matter of National importance, would doubtless be prepared to tell me in the strictest confidence if they had treated such a wound recently. However, as I said, I do not intend to pursue the matter any further.'

'What of the others?' I asked.

'The one with the Masonic insignia tattooed on the foreskin: that is the mark of a very secret lodge restricted to senior members of the Church of England. Among their number, the Bishop of Y – has a reputation in clerical circles for his zealousness in offering spiritual comfort to unhappy women, especially among the aristocracy.'

'And the remainder?'

'These two would appear to be identical twins. They could almost be the same member except that in one case, it has been recently exposed to the elements while the other is a very pale specimen. So we are looking for brothers, one of whom regularly engages in open air fucking. A countryman, in all probability a Scotsman, ever prepared to lift up his kilt as he goes about his country pursuits. His brother I suspect would prove to be a town dweller. Both were captured on the same occasion judging by the similar wrinkles in the small area of bed linen visible. So I suspect that we are looking at a Scotsman who is in Town, visiting his twin brother. An estate North of the Border and a business in London points to an interest in the whisky trade. The McShaftoe of that Ilk and his brother, known in his locality as the Bane of Speyside, are the most likely candidates.'

'Amazing!' I said. 'And have you made any more identifications?'

'One,' he said. 'Where have you seen something like this before?'

He held out a further print. I peered closely at it. There was indeed a familiarity about the object of our attentions. Suddenly I remembered.

'The other dildo!' I said. 'This is the original of the Gewirtz instrument. The one that was signed.'

'I took the liberty of inspecting it after it had been laid out to dry by the sink in the kitchen,' said Holmes. 'A remarkable piece of work.'

'What do you intend to do with the photographs, assuming that we are successful in our interview with Lord M — ?' I asked.

'Lady M — 's set, I will return to her. She may wish to destroy them or to keep them as souvenirs. That is up to her. The original plates will be destroyed and the second set of prints will be lodged in my forensic library. They may come in handy at some time in the future. A good reference library is invaluable to the detective.'

I recalled Rosie the Errant Schoolgirl (*see Oyster 3*).

'A friend of mine is in a position to lay her hands on a magnificent collection of photographic records of female bottoms,' I said. 'Many of them are those of the pupils at a well-thought-of school in the West Country. The owner is in the process of developing a system of identification and classification of types based on the human bum. It is his life's work and he has sacrificed much to continue his work.'

'I should like to hear his theory,' said Holmes. 'You must put me in touch with him. The scientific mind must be encouraged.'

Shortly afterwards, the cab slowed to a halt.

'Ah, we have arrived,' said Holmes. 'Now to beard the beast in his den.'

I do not intend to describe the painful interview that followed. Suffice it to say that we left a broken man in

Lancaster Gate. The threat of exposure was enough. The plates were handed over and we returned to Marylebone Road. Lady M – was so delighted at the successful outcome of our visit that she left me with a standing invitation to visit her and enjoy her hospitality as soon as I was sufficiently recovered to pay her the attentions she sought.

'We shall be At Home on Wednesday,' said Cecily as she and Gwendolen left. 'A Musical Afternoon. You might consider bringing a friend with you. It will be an energetic occasion.'

'A quick fuck?' offered Megan, before she too went on her way.

I had to decline her offer, being still somewhat drained by the events of the last few days. She was most understanding and announced that in any case, she would be a regular visitor to Holmes' establishment since it had been agreed that she would be assisting him as the occasion demanded.

It remains only to be said that a small paragraph in *The Times*, a day or so later, noted that Lord M – had sailed from Liverpool on a prolonged visit to one of our more obscure Colonies. He was not expected to return in the foreseeable future.

By then I was safely ensconced in Mrs P – 's Bayswater house where I had been given a rapturous welcome by her daughters. So ended my first exhausting venture into the world of Crime and Punishment.

THE OYSTER
VOLUME VI

This is for Jennie and Ronald
– two jolly good sports.

INTRODUCTION

The world of our great-grandparents was one in which an astonishingly high number of men and women lived in ignorance of many important aspects of human sexuality. Their natural feelings were deliberately numbed and inhibited by an over-strict and often unpleasantly hypocritical morality strenuously propounded by the ruling Establishment.

But by the end of Queen Victoria's long reign in 1901, universal basic adult literacy had almost been achieved and amongst the most popular entertainments for young Edwardians was the illicit 'horn' magazine of which *The Oyster* – which flourished from the late 1880s until 1909 – is a typical example.

Not only did these bawdy publications provide valuable instruction in sexual techniques but they preached a gospel that sexuality was to be actively enjoyed. Thus they offered a platform of resistance to the suffocating and guilt-ridden climate of the times. This was, after all, an era when Society insisted that decent women had no sexual passions (though if they felt twinges of desire it was their bounden duty to suppress them) and even leading physicians warned that masturbation would lead to blindness and insanity!

However, the basic urges of human nature can never ultimately be denied. The recent republication of turn-of-the-century underground erotica such as *The Oyster, The Black Pearl* and *Cremorne Scandals* reveals to the modern reader that, under the all-enveloping public respectability of the age, there existed a parallel world peopled by consenting adults who revelled in high-spirited sexual frolics.

Earlier extracts from the pseudonymous Sir Andrew Scott's novel *A Fond Recollection of Youthful Days* were published in *The Oyster: Books 1–5* [New English Library]. Whilst we will probably never find out his true identity, one would imagine that 'Sir Andrew Scott' was indeed born into one of the extremely wealthy upper-middle-class families of the time and was thus fortunate enough to lead the leisured, luxurious life of a young man about town in the fashionable West End of London during the early years of the twentieth century.

And while certain details might have been altered to amuse the reader, there is no reason to doubt the veracity of the author's wide variety of erotic escapades about which he writes with a vivid liveliness. For whilst lip service was still being paid to the stern ideals of the Victorian Age, the Edwardian aristocracy enjoyed a secret world of sensuality, of illicit liaison and secret rendezvous, of Bohemian bawdiness in intimate circles where blissful hours were spent behind closed doors and the Eleventh Commandment – Thou Must Never Be Found Out – was deemed of far more importance than the sum of the other Ten.

As Professor Louis Lombert remarks in his seminal study of Edwardian erotic writing *His Mighty Engine* [Vancouver University Press, 1969]: 'Young members of this hedonistic *jeunesse dorée* such as "Sir Andrew Scott" were ready and eager to challenge the dominant stiff-necked, sanctimonious morality of the age and they pursued high-spirited, free-wheeling lives in which frequent sensual relationships played a major role.

'This was of course in direct contrast to the stern dictates of the propagated established doctrine (a doctrine never upheld by King Edward VII and rarely by those in the highest echelons of London Society) of sexual abstinence even within marriage. For those who questioned the prevailing taboos the only available forums for discussion of their experiments with copulation were the popular "horn magazines".

Even if we do not know the real identity of 'Sir Andrew Scott' – although circumstantial evidence has recently been offered that this might have been an alias used by the rakish young *bon viveur* Lord Philip Pelham – he appears to have been an amiable chap of a kindly, liberal disposition. True, he may have over-indulged himself in what his contemporaries called 'The Pleasures of the Flesh', but it should be noted that he eschews pederasty and the dark sado-masochism associated with the age as well as other acts of truly gross perversion which litter the pages of similar publications of the era.

And though he certainly wrote his unashamedly erotic memoirs to titillate the appetite of the reader, he was also a blatant propagandist for contemporary radical new ideas. There was indeed a more serious if secondary purpose in the writing of his salacious life story.

In the first few pages of this extract from *A Fond Recollection of Youthful Days*, 'Sir Andrew' quotes with approval the words of Dr Simon White, the headmaster of his old school, the Nottgrove Academy for the Sons of Gentlefolk, who told him: 'My boy, it is nothing short of a tragedy that the lives of so many young people are being blighted by an insane prudery which prevents the merest discussion of a morality based upon a saner understanding of our own natural desires. Surely it can be no great sin to enjoy those delicious sensations for which a beneficent Creator has so amply fitted both sexes?'

As Professor Lombert has stated, it is undoubted fact that 'Sir Andrew' and his friends used the columns of the 'horn magazines' to debate such forbidden subjects as bondage, lesbianism, masturbation and oral sex. It is now widely accepted that this enquiring attitude was an important factor in leading to the far more relaxed, self-understanding state which exists today, concomitant with the multiplicity of positions on sexuality which currently exist as our own century draws to its close.

Desmond Foxton-Smith
Port Elizabeth
August, 1996

3

It's the same the whole world over,
It's the poor wot gets the blame,
It's the rich wot gets the gravy,
Ain't it all a bleedin' shame?

Angus Ridout [1844–1932]

CHAPTER ONE

On The Town

'Never look back for the best is yet to come' is, by and large, a sensible philosophy to which I have adhered since my schooldays. Mind, I doubt if I would be able to continue to live by that maxim if I ever contracted such an unfortunate condition as my poor Uncle Bertram who, since his prick began playing him up last year, needs Aunt Rosina to stick a dildo up his arse in order to stiffen the most important muscle in his body.

However, whatever the future may hold, I shall always be able to look back fondly upon the lascivious memories of my boisterous youth, especially those of such vintage months as the autumn of 1906. It is my ardent wish that readers will find much to amuse and excite them in my candid reminiscences of those occasionally riotous times.

As it happened, that particular season of mists and mellow fruitfulness began in difficult circumstances. My dear father – Sir Radleigh Wellington Scott, Bt, O.B.E. – wanted me to take more than a passing interest in the business affairs of our sizeable country estate in Hampshire and it needed all my powers of persuasion to make him agree that I should first live in London for a spell with my chum, Teddy Carmichael.

'I know what the pair of you have in mind, my lad,' he snorted as he rose from behind his desk and glared at me. 'So let me make it crystal clear that I have no intention of allowing you to join that crowd of idle young fellows who take morning rides down Rotten Row and spend lazy afternoons at their clubs before going out to parties, theatres and what-have-you.'

I was sorely tempted to remark that I was far more interested in the what-have-you than anything else, but wisely I kept my counsel and let my father vent his feelings upon the matter. In any case, I was not totally displeased when Papa informed me that he would agree to my leaving the family home in deepest Surrey for what he termed 'The Fleshpots of the Metropolis' on the understanding that I would take up part-time employment as an editorial consultant at the old-established publishing house of Hartfield and Moser in Bloomsbury.

He growled: 'The company is owned by Lord Neumann, an old friend of your mother's family. Not that Freddie actually does anything except attend the annual directors' meeting, of course, but naturally his word is law. So you'll report to Mr Geoffrey MacArthur, the managing editor, within a week of your arrival in London or I'll withdraw your allowance.' Nevertheless, I was happy enough to promise my compliance with this condition although as I suspected, Mr MacArthur was hardly brimming with enthusiasm at this idea. However, we rapidly reached a most satisfactory understanding about my duties, the most important feature of which was that I was not expected to put in a daily appearance at Hartfield and Moser's offices in Bedford Square. But I did agree to keep an appointment with MacArthur's secretary every Thursday morning at eleven o'clock to pick up a bundle of unsolicited manuscripts sent in to the firm by hopeful budding authors.

'Like our fellow publishers, we call it the "slush" pile,' explained Mr MacArthur. 'Perhaps this is because it usually consists of revoltingly sentimental novels written by genteel maiden ladies living in places like Chichester, Frinton-on-Sea or Tewkesbury.

'Still, as it is just within the bounds of possibility that a new Ouida or George Eliot *may* be lurking in the dross of the "slush" pile, all these stories have to be read. So I'm giving you this responsible job, Andrew. You might as well take the scripts home to read and the following week you can return those you have ploughed through to my secretary who will then send them back to their authors with a rejection slip.'

'Suppose I do come across anything which actually does have some literary merit?' I asked. He grunted: 'That would be extremely unlikely, but by all means let Miss Caughey know if you do find anything genuinely readable.'

This arrangement suited both of us down to the ground and although by late September I had not found a single decent manuscript to show to him, Mr MacArthur nevertheless invited me to a slap-up dinner at the Savoy Hotel to celebrate the fiftieth anniversary of the founding of Hartfield and Moser Ltd.

Perhaps it was an over-indulgence when the excellent vintage port was passed round the table, but I didn't wake up until slightly after quarter past eight the following morning. On most days this would have been of little consequence, but today I was due to meet Lord Philip Pelham at half past ten and take a spin out of town in his new motor car with two young ladies from the chorus line of *Hold Your Hand Out, Naughty Boy*, the latest musical show at the Empire, Leicester Square.

So on the count of three I leaped out of bed to welcome the rays of bright sunshine which were shining through the bedroom curtains. I drew them back before divesting myself of my nightshirt to stand stark naked in front of the window which I opened – only to hear a shocked giggle floating up from our small back garden.

Alas, I had forgotten that at this time young Sally, our daily domestic, might be hanging up the washing. As luck would have it, I looked down at the buxom girl just as she glanced up in my direction with a saucy smile on her face and my best shirt draped over her arm. But the grandstand view of my nude torso did not appear to bother Sally overmuch, even though my cock was standing up stiffly against my tummy (for in these youthful days I invariably woke up with a tremendous hard-on).

Nevertheless, I hastily moved away from the window, although not before my cheeks flushed crimson with embarrassment when Sally called out: 'It's all right, Mister Andrew. Believe me, I've seen more than that on a Saturday night after a good party.'

Oh well, I said to myself as I padded across to my *en suite* bathroom and switched on the hot water tap, at least this accidental exposure of my prick to feminine eyes would thankfully not lead to such an unpleasant experience as had recently been suffered by my house-mate, Teddy Carmichael.

True, my closest chum had only himself to blame for his misfortune since no one else had suggested that, after a convivial evening at the Jim Jam Club *[A raffish gentleman's club in Great Windmill Street which flourished during the Edwardian era – Editor]*, he should be so foolish as to unbutton his trousers and relieve himself against a lamp-post. Anyhow, the long and short of it was that Teddy was charged with being drunk and indecent. After an uncomfortable night in the cells at Vine Street, he was hauled up at the police court and fined five pounds.

I chuckled as I recalled Teddy's gloomy observation that being a fiver out of pocket was bad enough but that the magistrate who had inflicted this monstrous sentence to the accompaniment of some very offensive remarks was none other than his godfather. This worthy would doubtless be writing to Teddy's parents before poor Teddy could dream up an excuse for his peccadillo.

With a savage scowl on his face, my pal had added: 'To add insult to injury, less than a week later there was an announcement in the *Evening News* that the old bugger was about to retire from the bench. I happen to know that my beloved godfather has a nice pot of money in the bank as well as a country seat and a thousand acres down in Devon. I'm telling you, Andrew, I wouldn't be surprised if the old swine stuck to some of the fines. Let's face it, five quid here, five quid there – you can see for yourself how it would mount up over a period of time.'

In honour of my forthcoming tryst with Lord Philip Pelham and the two chorus girls, I lathered my face with Roger & Gallet Heliotrope Shaving Cream and carefully scraped away the facial hair from my top lip with my new Wilkinson's Safety Razor. Even though moustaches are again coming back into fashion, both Teddy Carmichael and myself prefer to keep a clean shaven face. On the other hand, Phil Pelham insists that girls enjoy the feel of his 'tache against the lips of their cunnies when he takes part in his favourite sport of muff-diving.

The bath was now ready and I was about to step into the warm water when I heard a knock on my bedroom door. 'Just a moment,' I shouted out as I slipped on my dressing gown and rushed out of the bathroom to discover who wanted to speak to me. To my astonishment, my unexpected guest turned out to be none other than the pert little maid who had been out in the garden a few minutes ago.

'Hello, Sally, what can I do for you?' I gulped, feeling my cheeks colour up again. She giggled: 'Well, sir, please don't think me too forward but I was so shocked to see you standing at the window in the altogether that I've come over all hot and bothered and wondered if you would let me have a bath in your tub. The hot-water tank's full but it'll need at least two hours to heat up again so I'll need to use your bathwater after you've finished with it.'

I looked at her blankly and Sally patiently repeated her request which in the circumstances I felt unable to refuse. Two charming dimples appeared on either side of the pretty girl's rich red lips when she smiled her thanks and followed me into the bathroom.

'You can sit on my bed and read the magazine on the side table,' I said to her, but the little vixen twinkled: 'Oh, if you like, Mister Andrew, but I think I have a far better idea. My friend Ellen works at Mrs Shackleton's Salon in Wardour Street and she says her clients really enjoy a Continental-style assisted bath. Let me give you one – Ellen's told me what I have to do and I think we would both enjoy the experience.'

'An assisted bath, eh?' I queried in all innocence. 'But isn't this a service for elderly sufferers from rheumatic complaints who find it too difficult to stand up and sit down by themselves?'

'Oh no, sir, it's nothing like that,' she answered with a broad smile. 'What happens is that I soap you down and sponge off the suds before drying you off with a nice warm towel. Then you lie down and I give you a very special massage.'

'H'm, I must say that all sounds very nice, but why are you unbuttoning your blouse?' I asked her. Sally replied. 'Well, I have to undress, Mister Andrew, or my clothes will get soaking wet.'

She shrugged off her blouse and not surprisingly my cock began to thicken at the sight of the firm swell of her creamy breasts and I could also see the dark outline of her nipples thrusting against the fine white cotton of her chemise.

But this was just a foretaste of what was to come. I drew a sharp intake of breath when Sally unhooked her skirt which fell to the ground. She fleetingly exposed her luscious backside when she turned and lifted the chemise to her hips in order to yank down her knickers which she rolled down to her feet.

The frisky miss swiftly wriggled the flimsy garment off as she turned round again. Not surprisingly I found it quite impossible to avert my eyes from either her heaving breasts or the dark patch of hair I could make out between her exquisitely formed thighs before she lowered her chemise.

'Come on, sir, get into the bath and I can start work,' she said briskly. So I slipped off my dressing gown and stepped into the bath. I was about to kneel down in the tub when to my astonishment Sally took hold of her chemise again, lifting it high over her head before she threw it gracefully behind her. I watched it flutter to the floor as she joined me in the tub, standing in front of me with a sensual smile on her face. Naturally my shaft shot up to its full height, twitching wildly against my tummy as I drank in the thrilling naked charms of Sally's supple young body.

Her bare breasts jiggled delightfully as she rubbed a bar of soap over the honeycombed natural sponge. Her red-berried nipples jutted out proudly towards me as she smoothed the soapy sponge over my torso, dropping the cleansing item into the water after brushing it across the pit of my stomach.

Then she squeezed my stiffie, sliding her fist up and down the rock-hard shaft as she murmured: 'My, aren't you a big boy, Mister Andrew. Your prick must be near enough two inches longer than my boyfriend's and it's much thicker too.'

'Thank you very much,' I said modestly. 'But as I always say to any envious chaps in the dressing room after a game of footer, dimensions don't matter, it's how you use your equipment that counts.'

'That's true enough,' agreed Sally, cupping my balls in her hand and jiggling them up and down in her grasp. 'Still, I must admit that a nice big cock like yours does make me feel very naughty.'

Without further ado she went down on her knees and planted a slurping wet kiss on my knob. Then she washed me all over and, after soaping herself down with the sponge, we rinsed off the water and towelled ourselves dry. We used two of the set of luxuriously soft blanket towels I had purchased from the Army and Navy Stores, an admitted extravagance at 19/2½d [96p! – Editor] but I do enjoy wrapping myself up in a large towel after a bath or shower.

When we had finished, I was about to shake a little

13

Johnson's Powder over my body when Sally said hastily: 'No, no, don't do that, Andrew, come into the bedroom with me.'

I had no objection to this request although, quite frankly, I had no choice but to obey her command. For, gripping my erect tool tightly in her hand, Sally pulled me out of the bathroom before instructing me to lie down on my bed. Nothing loath, I lay on my back with my head on the pillow. I discovered instantly why Sally had not wanted me to dust my body with talcum for the feisty vixen now knelt down beside me and began to lick my toes. This was the first time any girl had done this to me and the sensation was truly incredible! Sally worked her way slowly up my legs, twirling her teasing tongue along my thighs until she reached my groin. She glanced upwards and gave me a wide, voluptuous smile as she brought my uncapped ruby helmet to her waiting lips.

I let out a hoarse groan as this ravishing naked creature proceeded to give me a most delightful sucking-off, beginning by tracing hot wet kisses all over my cock and balls, pushing me to the very edge of a spend. Then she swirled her magic tongue around my knob, savouring its firm texture as she sucked me in between her luscious lips, gobbling my shaft from top to base and back again, sending almost unbearable waves of pleasure coursing throughout my entire body. Every time Sally sensed I was on the verge of a cum, she would take my cock out of her mouth for a moment or two to prolong our mutual pleasure which was reaching ever higher peaks of ecstatic delight.

Sally's cheeks bulged as she virtually devoured my cock, sucking my shaft with gusto whilst I ran my hands through her shiny brown hair. All too soon I felt the seed boiling up in my balls (though I would have defied even noted connoisseurs of *l'art de faire l'amour* such as Lord Dunn of Stamford Bridge or Sir Robert Bladen to have lasted any longer) and I filled her eager mouth with spurt after spurt of salty spunk which she gulped down with relish, licking her lips as she milked my prick of every last drop of my copious emission.

14

'Now will you be kind enough to return the compliment, Mister Andrew?' breathed Sally as she swung herself over me and squatted on my face with her hairy quim pressing down upon my face.

'By all means, you dear girl, one good turn deserves another,' I murmured, kissing her pussey before taking her protruding clitty between my lips and sucking on it for all I was worth.

'Oooh, that feels so good,' Sally groaned as I lapped up the jaunty lass's love juice which was dribbling out of her juicy quim. She clamped her thighs around my head and squealed with delight when I began to finger-fuck her sopping slit with my thumb, her lusty moans growing louder and louder until her pussey walls spasmed around my thumb and a spray of spend came shooting out of her cunt as if from the nozzle of a hose.

Then Sally reached back with her hand and raised her eyebrows when she discovered that my sturdy shaft had fully recovered and was again standing as stiff as a poker. 'My word, you *are* a randy lad, aren't you?' she said with an appreciative little chuckle.

'Well, waste not, want not,' she went on and hauled herself backwards until she was sitting on my thighs and my throbbing tool was pushing against her slick, wet crack. I took her jutting breasts in my hands, lifting the firm globes and marvelling at their lightness whilst I rubbed the pointed tawny nipples between my fingers. Sally lifted herself slightly, taking hold of my straining shaft and pushing herself down upon it, her slippery cunt effortlessly stretching to accommodate its rampant fleshy visitor.

'H—a-r-g-h! H-a-r-g-h! H-a-r-g-h!' gasped my feisty partner as she rocked upon my cock which was buried to the hilt inside her. I soon caught the insatiable girl's rhythm, lifting her up and pulling her down as she threw back her head and hunched her dripping cunney up and down the length of my twitching love truncheon.

Oh, how we both enjoyed this magnificent ride, for my big cock filled Sally's narrow sheath to the full and she squeezed the muscles of her cunt so expertly around my tool that I was swiftly transported to the seventh heaven of delight. We spent simultaneously shortly after she began moving her hips even faster, her delicious cunney gripping and releasing my cock so exquisitely that a gush of frothy white spunk soon shot up into the furthest recesses of her sticky honeypot, flooding her snatch and trickling down in tiny rivulets onto her thighs.

We fell back exhausted onto the bed in a tangled flurry of limbs. Perhaps it was just as well that Sally had several urgent domestic duties to perform before Mrs Pelgram, our cook-housekeeper, arrived to prepare our meals because, given half a chance, I would rather have waited for my cock to recover from its delicious exercise and fucked Sally once more than been on time for my appointment with Lord Philip Pelham.

However, the opportunity to choose between these alternatives did not arise for after a minute or two Sally swung her shapely legs over the side of the bed and padded into the bathroom to pick up her clothes. I followed her and was greatly tempted to slide my thickening todger between her beautifully rounded bum cheeks when she bent down to pick up her knickers. But I managed to resist this ungentlemanly urge and instead towelled the perspiration from my face as it occurred to me that my flatmate was spending a week in Paris with his Uncle Gerald and that I had the maisonette to myself. So I asked Sally whether she would like to return to the house this evening for a light supper and some further frolics.

'Mister Teddy won't be back from his trip to Paris till tomorrow afternoon and I'll tell Mrs Pelgram that she can leave after she has prepared a nice cold collation for us,' I said. But she shook her head and replied: 'Not tonight I can't, sir, because my boyfriend promised to take me to the first house at the Tivoli and actually I'm really looking forward to it

16

because Harry Tate's top of the bill and he always makes me laugh.

'But I can be here half an hour earlier tomorrow morning, if that would be convenient,' she said with a wink which caused the cloud of disappointment to disappear from my face. I returned the wink and remarked that this was a splendid idea.

When Sally had finished dressing herself she hurried out to prepare my breakfast and fifteen minutes later when I strolled into the dining room I was greeted by the appetizing aroma of frying bacon. 'Two eggs enough for you, Mister Andrew?' called out Sally. I replied in the affirmative as I poured out a cup of tea from the silver pot which she had placed on a tiny spirit lamp on the sideboard and helped myself to a slice of toast from the rack on the table.

I scanned through the headlines in the *Daily Chronicle*, then picked up the clutch of letters by my plate and put aside unopened the bills from local tradesmen which would be settled at the end of the month. But I slit open the envelope with an Irish postmark for I rightly surmised that this contained a letter from Lady 'Madcap Molly' Southard, the outrageous daughter of the Duke and Duchess of Hampshire who had told me that she was spending a few weeks with her relations in Killarney. Molly was a close acquaintance of both Teddy and myself, although I hasten to state that neither of us had made love to the extremely pretty girl. In fact, I doubt if any man had ever graced Molly's bed for her sapphic propensities were well-known to all the young blades in London.

Be that as it may, Molly was a great correspondent – as one of her three brothers wittily wrote back to her in Tennysonian parody:

Such newsy letters you send each week
To Mother, Clive and Trevor
At fifteen sheets most ladies end,
But you go on for ever!

Nevertheless, it was always a pleasure to receive one of Molly's multi-page missives and after I had tucked in to my plate of bacon and eggs I poured myself another cup of tea and sat back to peruse Molly's uninhibited letter, which began innocently enough by praising the beauties of the countryside around Killarney. She continued as follows:

I suppose the principal charm of the place lies in its magical variety. There is no monotonous perfection but an ever-changing fascination which every mist that sleeps on its waters, every ray that glances on its mountain tops, every season that clothes its woods in different garb, exhibits under a fresh aspect of loveliness, imbued afresh with a thousand prismatic colours.

My principal companion has been my second cousin Geraldine, a shapely nineteen-year-old blonde girl with whom I had only corresponded and had never actually met before this trip. I fell in love with her from the first, for what a lovely girl she was, with soft honey-blonde hair that shone like gold, large melting eyes of the lightest blue and cheeks tinted with the softest brush of the rose. Within only hours of seeing Gerry (as she preferred to be called) I knew I had to fuck this gorgeous girl or go out of my mind frigging myself every night as I lay in bed thinking of her.

Luckily, I soon discovered that my pretty young cousin and I shared the same sexual propensities. My chance came after a picnic tea one afternoon on my Uncle Clarence's estate. The weather was exceptionally warm and Gerry and I decided to cool ourselves off by bathing in a pool which was hidden from general view by a surrounding clump of beech trees.

'It's far more fun swimming in the nude, don't you think?' I observed as I unbuttoned my dress whilst I watched Gerry pull her chemise over her head to reveal

18

her lithe, supple figure. Her breasts were small but perfectly rounded with large dark red areolae in the middle of which were placed delicious berry-like nipples which I longed to tweak between my fingers.

'Oh yes, I just love the feel of the rays of warm sunshine on my body,' Gerry replied and a wave of desire swept through my entire body when she rolled down her silk knickers to reveal a golden thatch of fluffy pussey hair between her slender thighs.

I quickly finished undressing. Hand in hand we waded into the pool and playfully splashed each other with the cool, clear water. We had not brought any towels so when we came out of the water we spread the tablecloth which we had used for our picnic on a patch of grass and laid ourselves down on it to dry off in the sun. I confess that it took all my willpower to stop myself from throwing my arms around the dear girl there and then.

The opportunity to find out whether she had any similar desires came when I recalled that I had brought a small pot of Professor Pethick's Skin Care cream with me. I reached over for my handbag and brought it out as I said: 'Gerry, we should rub some of this stuff on us to protect ourselves from the sun. If you'll slide over onto your tummy I'll rub some on your back and then perhaps you would do the same for me.'

The sweet girl thanked me as she obediently turned herself over to lie on her front and I smoothed the cream onto the upper parts of her back with my fingertips. Then I looked down at her dimpled peaches of her bum cheeks and said huskily: 'Now I'd better put some on your botty. It's all white and will burn if you're not careful.'

My pussey was already damp when I massaged Gerry's beautiful bottom and my heart began to pound when, without my asking, she moved her legs slightly apart to enable my fingertips to dip between her thighs and lightly graze the edge of her pussey bush. However,

19

I made no attempt to proceed further and gnawing my lower lip in frustration I merely gulped: 'Good girl, now turn over and I'll finish you off.'

She swung herself round to lie on her back and I smeared the cream on her breasts, lightly cupping the gorgeous globes as I said with a smile: 'Well, we mustn't let these pretties become red and sore.'

Frankly, I was soon carried away as I began kneading her superb bosoms and finding it impossible to contain myself any longer, I shamelessly let my fingers stray over her hardening nipples. To my immense relief, Gerry did not push my hand away but sensually wriggled her body and whispered: 'You may kiss them if you like, Molly.'

I needed no further invitation and a tiny whimper escaped from Gerry's lips as my lips fastened on one of her rubbery nipples whilst I rolled the other between the fingers of my right hand. I sucked greedily on the stiffening nipple whilst my hand dropped down until my fingers were entangled in the delicate fluffy hair which lightly covered the swell of her mound. My finger gently probed lower until it lightly grazed the lips of her pussey and now Gerry gasped and pulled me on top of her, seizing my hand in her own as she guided two of my fingers into her sticky wetness.

With mounting excitement I finger-fucked the delicious girl and Gerry had no qualms about making my hand the instrument of her pleasure, rubbing her clitty against it until it protruded beyond her outer cunney lips. I squeezed the fleshy love button between my fingers and she drove me on with increasing urgency as I frigged her faster and faster.

Then I dropped my head downwards, fastening my lips onto Gerry's dripping love funnel as my tongue flicked inside her cunt. I sucked in her tangy love juice whilst she jerked up and down in a frenzy of salacious excitement. I varied the cuntal stimulation by opening

*her velvety folds and stroking her twitching clitty which
sent fresh tremors of ecstasy coursing through her body
from the epicentre of pleasure between her legs.*

*'Have you come, darling?' I enquired, lifting my
mouth from her sopping slit when Gerry screamed out
her pleasure. Her blissful sigh was answer enough and
so I now rolled over on my back, my thighs spread wide
and my legs raised as I massaged my own auburn-haired
pussey, my left hand moving rapidly over my already
swollen clitty and two fingers of my right hand working
in and out of my cunt from which trickles of love juice
were already dribbling down my thighs.*

*'Wait for me!' cried Gerry, throwing herself on top of
me. Taking my face in her hands, she pressed her lips
against mine. We exchanged a fiery open-mouthed kiss,
our tongues waggling in each other's mouths until Gerry
withdrew to slide her mouth downwards, breaking her
journey first to one nipple and then the other before
slipping down my trembling belly to my thick brown
bush.*

*'Ahhh, that's so lovely,' I murmured as my delectable
cousin carefully moistened my inner thighs and then
teased the tip of her tongue along the length of my
tingling love slit before gently inserting two of her long
fingers between my pouting pussey lips. She brought me
off quite beautifully with her thumb and fingers pressed
together, stroking, circling and then plunging in and out
of my clinging quim. I writhed from side to side in the
most delicious agony as Gerry slurped the cuntal juice
which was now freely flowing out of my hairy snatch as I
shuddered my way to a wonderful orgasm.*

*'You clever darling, you've made me spend,' I panted
as I fought to regain my breath. 'Can you feel my juices
running over your face?'*

*'Oh, I think you can cum again,' she muttered. I fairly
screamed with delight as the impudent girl slipped her*

21

hand underneath me and frigged my arsehole with the tip of her little finger as she continued to lick and lap inside my dripping honeypot, flicking her tongue around my erect clitty.

In no time at all, I did indeed climax again in a mad frenzy of passion as she pressed her mouth up to my soaking slit, working her tongue deeper and deeper as a second copious flow of cum gushed over her nose and lips.

Our surging desires were still not fully satisfied for we were still at that joyful early stage in a physical relationship when we still had to find out the particular likes and dislikes of the new partner. Fortunately, our tastes were very similar and I immediately nodded my agreement when Gerry suggested a naughty and novel love-play which she said she adored. After the usual foreplay of kissing and cuddling whilst we pinched each other's titties, she rolled on top of me and, parting my pussey lips with her fingers, Gerry directed her erect clitty into my open cunt. Without separating for a moment, our bodies writhed from side to side, swimming in a veritable sea of lubricity as we spent within seconds of each other, feeling the force of our orgasms rushing through our bodies.

We threw ourselves back on the tablecloth which was now much stained with the evidence of our naughtiness. Suddenly Gerry sat up and cocked her head as she said quietly: 'Molly, I could swear I heard footsteps coming from near that big tree in front of us.'

I struggled into a sitting position. I replied that she must have been mistaken for all I could hear was the faint sound of birdsong from some distance away.

'No, I'll bet you a thousand pounds that there's someone watching us from behind that old oak,' she insisted. Scrambling to her feet she darted towards the gnarled trunk and shouted out triumphantly: 'I can see

22

you, young man! Come out here and show yourself!'

With some reluctance, a boy slowly moved out from behind the tree. Being slightly short-sighted, I peered across to see for myself who had been spying on us whilst Gerry ran towards the culprit and, grabbing him by the arm, marched him towards me.

Gerry called out that she knew the identity of this youthful Peeping Tom who was dressed only in a white running vest and a pair of brief athletic shorts. 'Molly, this young fellow is Master Christopher Lewis-Tucker. He's the youngest son of Major Fortescue Lewis-Tucker who happens to be the Mayor of Killarney.'

She turned to the good-looking youth who was tall and well-made for his age and went on: 'What do you think your father would say if he found out what you had been up to, young man?'

Poor Christopher was rooted to the spot, unable to speak or move as a crimson blush of shame spread over his cheeks as he stood with his head hung down on his chest. I could not but feel somewhat sorry for him for it seemed to me that he was embarrassed rather than excited by the sight of two naked girls.

'Well then, what do you have to say for yourself, h'm?' Gerry demanded. With obvious effort he replied in a shy, apprehensive voice that he had had no idea of our presence when he had decided to take a few minutes' rest whilst running through the woods in preparation for the cross-country race which would be taking place locally on the coming Saturday afternoon.

'Please don't report me to my father or I'll be in terrible hot water because I'm supposed to be swotting for a geography exam next week,' he begged. Gerry winked at me whilst she pretended to consider his plea.

'Very well, I suppose we must give you the benefit of the doubt, Christopher,' she said finally. 'Anyhow, I dare say that Molly and I must rely on you not to sneak on us.'

The boy found his voice and he said: 'Oh, you have my word of honour that my lips will be sealed, Miss Geraldine.'

Gerry grinned at me and then chuckled openly at his discomfiture as she said as bold as brass: 'Good lad, that's all I need to know. But you must answer one more question – am I correct in thinking that this is the first time you have ever clapped eyes on the nude female body?'

Christopher lifted his head to steal a quick gaze at the fluffy triangle of flaxen hair between Gerry's thighs as he replied in a hoarse croak: 'You're right, I've never seen any girl in the nude before.'

To my surprise she said delightedly: 'So it must follow that you are still virgo intacto. Don't be embarrassed, I'll wager there aren't many boys of your age who have crossed the Rubicon. But I know from my own experience how tiresome it is to be a virgin even at your tender age, especially when you are physically ready to enjoy your first fuck. You are physically ready for sexual initiation, I presume?'

Christopher's eyes lit up and he said excitedly: 'I should say I am, Miss Geraldine! Why, I've been more than ready for a long time!'

'Have you now?' she continued with a lusty look in her eyes. 'Well, my young feller-me-lad, it would be best if you stripped off and let me see for myself whether this is so. There's no need to be shy, my dear – Molly and I have already exhibited our naked charms to you so now it's your turn to show us what you have to offer.'

She need not have bothered to encourage him because Christopher instantly whipped off his vest and pulled down his shorts to exhibit a thick cock which appeared to me to be surprisingly big for a lad of his age. Gerry reached out and clasped his prick which swelled up to a state of throbbing erection against his

24

flat belly as she fisted her hand up and down the blue-veined shaft.

'Hasn't Christopher been lucky to be blessed with such a thick prick, Molly?' she said to me. But I shrugged my shoulders and said: 'I suppose so but, to be quite candid, I haven't the slightest interest in cocks of any shape or size.'

Gerry looked at me in great astonishment. 'Well, it's entirely up to you, of course, but I do think you're missing out on a great deal of fun if the sight of a juicy big todger doesn't make you feel even a tiny bit randy. You really should try one out, darling, there's a lot to be said for being fucked by a real prick as opposed to even the wickedest tongue or fingers.'

She turned to Christopher and said: 'This is one of the nicest cocks I've ever handled, Master Lewis-Tucker. I can't believe that all the local lasses would let such a splendid shaft go to waste. Are you absolutely sure it has never been inserted inside a cunney before?'

Christopher shook his head and answered in a voice cracking with emotion: 'No, it never has, though not from want of trying. But the only time I ever came close was when I had a snog after my birthday party with our kitchen-maid who let me play with her pussey whilst she tossed me off.'

'And it has had to be satisfied with the ministrations of Mother Thumb and her four daughters?' enquired my sweet cousin with a lascivious grin as she continued to slide her hand slowly up and down his pulsating pole. 'Well, see how you like this, young man.'

Gerry sank to her knees and delicately licked all round the ridge of his uncapped helmet before jamming her luscious lips over the mushroom dome and lashing her tongue around his rigid rod. She sucked at least half of Christopher's exceptionally thick cock into her mouth whilst her hands played with his dangling balls.

Then she began to gobble him in earnest, drawing her hot wet tongue from the base of his throbbing tool right up to the tiny 'eye' on his gleaming bell-end. He clutched at her hair and shuddered all over: Gerry only had time to swish her tongue over his knob one more time before the coup de grace *and Christopher expelled a stream of frothy jism into her mouth which she gulped down whilst she gently squeezed his balls to milk his virgin cock of every drop of sticky seed.*

Unfortunately for the eager boy, Gerry had no time to continue this lewd playfulness because we had promised to attend an evening reception at Southard Lodge which my Uncle Lionel and Aunt Rosina had planned for our neighbours and to which Christopher's parents had been invited. And here I must confess that I was slightly miffed when Gerry arranged to meet Christopher at this secluded spot in three days' time when she would complete his first practical lesson in fucking.

Anyhow, enough of such rudery – let me now tell you of the wonderful excursion we made yesterday to Glengariff which must be the most beautiful area in the whole of Ireland. It is set in a deep Alpine valley seldom exceeding a quarter of a mile in breadth and of about three miles in length enclosed by precipitous hills.

At this point I folded the letter and stuffed it back inside the envelope, for to be honest I was far less interested in the beauties of South-west Ireland than in Lady Molly Southard's escapades with her lusty young cousin! In any case, I had no time to read any more or I would be late for my meeting with Lord Philip Pelham whose pet hate is unpunctuality. *'L'exactitude est la politesse des rois'* he would say severely to any errant guests and I had no desire to receive a wigging from my chum.

But, more importantly, Lady Molly's uninhibited epistle had made me feel extremely raunchy and I could hardly wait to be acquainted with the two chorus girls my chum had invited to join us for a drive in his new motor car. I squinted out of the window and, seeing there was hardly a cloud in the sky, I decided to wear my best summer coat, a smart unlined Alpaca which Mr Motkalevitch had made for me back in April. I made a mental note to send him a cheque at the end of the month because I don't believe in keeping a tailor waiting for more than six months to be paid.

[This should not be taken as a sarcastic comment. A tailor, dressmaker or bootmaker might have to wait up to two years for young gentlemen like Andrew Scott to settle their accounts because small tradesmen did not dare to press for payment for fear of offending their uppercrust clientele – Editor]

I called out a goodbye to Sally and dashed out into Kendal Street where I hailed a passing taxi to take me to Lord Philip's luxurious apartment in Berkeley Square. Thankfully the traffic was relatively light and the driver was not held up for too long at Marble Arch so it was only ten thirty-five when I knocked on Phil's front door. He opened the door himself and clapped me on the shoulder.

''Morning, Andrew, isn't it a glorious day?' he said cheerfully as I followed him through the hall into his spacious living room. 'Come and have a glass of bubbly. I've just ordered Mutkin to bring a bottle out of the ice-box as the girls arrived only a moment ago and are taking their coats off in one of the bedrooms.'

'How disappointing! I had hoped they would be taking off more than that!' I observed. Phil chortled: 'Have patience, old boy, the day is young. Now take a pew, the girls will be in very shortly. They're both simply terrific fun and I've been wondering which one you will find the most attractive.

'I rather fancy Becky myself but I've no objection to pairing off with Claire instead because I know that you're a real sucker for blondes,' he added generously.

27

'Aren't we all?' I retorted and rose to my feet as the two girls swept into the room, followed by Mutkin bearing a tray with four glasses of chilled champagne.

Phil swiftly made the introductions and it was clear why he had been bowled over by Becky Fairweather's charms. She was a petite, well-rounded young lady with twinkly blue eyes and a saucy face with a small, slightly *retroussé* nose and full red lips. Not that Claire Blakemore was any less lovely! She was taller than her friend and her large brown eyes were set in soft, classical features whilst there were deep, natural waves in the long tresses of her shiny hair which reached down to her shoulders.

Mutkin stepped forward. I passed Claire a glass of champagne from his tray and said: 'Phil tells me that you and Becky are in the new revue at the Empire, Leicester Square. You must be jolly good dancers to have been chosen to play at the top music hall theatre in London. I'll wager there were twenty girls battling for every place in the line.'

Claire smiled and exchanged a fleeting smile with Becky as she replied: 'Yes, it's not easy finding work, although Becky and I are both on the books of a leading theatrical agent. As you say, there are lots of girls who can sing and dance well enough and you just have to hope that the director likes the look of your face.'

'And your legs,' chuckled Phil as he clinked glasses with the girls. 'I wouldn't mind being the choreographer at a place like the Empire or the Hippodrome with lots of pretty girls wanting to do their best to attract my attention. Between ourselves, do any of these fellows ask for any special favours, so to speak?'

'Occasionally, but most of them are nancy boys so we don't often get asked for a bit of slap and tickle on the side,' answered Becky with a giggle. 'But there are one or two exceptions like Mike Burge at Drury Lane. He likes girls, all right, doesn't he, Claire?'

28

'You can say that again!' said Claire with great feeling. 'But he was a real gentleman because he didn't ask me out to dinner until after he chose me as one of the tavern girls in *Hallo, Sailor*. Mind you, it was a terrible show and closed after only three weeks!'

'I never knew he took you out to dinner, you naughty thing,' said Becky. Phil remarked that the girls could probably write a jolly interesting play about their experiences in the theatre. He winked at me as he continued: 'And it wouldn't be hard to find backers for the production either, though I suppose the best bits couldn't be staged as we would have to tone it down too much because of the Lord Chamberlain's office!'

[The Lord Chamberlain's Examiner of Plays censored the British theatre until 1967 – Editor]

Becky finished her drink and grinned: 'Not if you could put it on at one of those private theatres a few of those toffs have built in their big country houses. Why, Claire and I could tell you some tales about one or two of the shows the Earl of Hampshire puts on down at his place at Laverstoke Hall near Basingstoke. Why, we had three costumes and if we wore them all at once you could still see our titties!'

'I've never seen anything untoward when I've been in the audience in the theatre at Laverstoke Hall,' I commented ruefully. 'Of course, that may be because I've only been there as a guest of his daughter, Lady Molly Southard. Funnily enough, I received a letter from her only this morning. Did either of you meet Molly, by any chance?'

'No, but I've heard all about her,' laughed Claire. 'Isn't she the lusty tribade the weekly journals call "Madcap Molly"?'

'How did you know she's a tribade? That information was never printed in *The Tatler* or *The Illustrated London News*!' I said in some surprise. Claire shrugged her shoulders as she answered: 'Oh, come on, Andrew, don't tell me that you never read any of the "horn" magazines! There was a long article about Molly Southard and her naughty nights at the Arcadian Society for Ladies in *The Cremorne*.'

[The Arcadian Society in the Bayswater Road was a well-known haunt for lesbians like Lady Molly Southard. Female homosexuality was not per se illegal and the Club flourished during the first decade of the century. However, it was dramatically shut down in 1911 when a police raid resulted in the owners being accused of keeping a disorderly house. No charges were ever brought as any case would have involved several well-known ladies from the very highest families in the land, but the Society closed its doors shortly afterwards and never re-opened – Editor]

Phil rubbed his hands together and said: 'I'd love to hear more about these private performances, but let's wait till we get to Putney Heath. Mutkin, will you be good enough to refill the glasses whilst I check with Mrs Angel that she's packed all the goodies for our picnic.'

'M'mm, I adore good bubbly,' said Claire, holding out her goblet which the butler filled to the brim. 'Andrew, have you tried this new drink called Buck's Fizz? It's all the rage in the West End these days. The recipe is simple enough, three-quarters of a glass of champagne to a quarter of fresh orange juice.'

'Yes, and I find it very refreshing although it would be rather wasteful to prepare it with 1902 Moet et Chandon,' I remarked whilst Mutkin emptied the bottle into the remaining three glasses. 'Still, if you're keen on Buck's Fizz, we can stop at a greengrocer on our way to Putney and I'll buy some oranges so you can make up a jar for us.'

'Oh, I don't know whether that would be such a good idea because that particular cocktail makes me feel frisky,' giggled Becky and Phil caught these last words as he came back from the kitchen.

'Whose cock makes you feel frisky, m'dear?' demanded our

30

host with a smile on his face. 'Has the infamous Jerry Fenner been poking you again?'

Phil turned to me and continued: 'I tell you what, old boy, I don't think that there can be any pretty soubrettes left on the London stage who have been able to resist Jerry's charms. My God, don't you wish we had his *savoir faire*? Why, only a couple of months ago I saw with my own eyes how this year's crop of debutantes were actually queueing up to be shagged by Jerry after the Berkeley Square Summer Ball.'

Becky downed her glass and wagged a reproving finger at Phil. 'I said "cocktail" not "cock", your naughty lordship,' she replied lightly. 'Anyhow, I haven't seen Jerry Fenner for ages. The last I heard of him was that he took Lady Daplen's twin eighteen-year-old daughters to Bournemouth at the beginning of the month for a holiday and he won't be returning till next week at the earliest.

'But never mind about Jerry, I'm looking forward to a picnic and a ride in your motor car,' added the perky blonde.

We trooped downstairs and piled into Phil's brand new canvas-covered Rover tourer whilst Mutkin attached a large hamper to the back of the vehicle. The girls sat in the back whilst I sat next to Phil who adjusted his goggles – *[this early Rover had a windscreen but open side doors – Editor]* – and my chum gave a happy chuckle as the engine roared into life at the first time of asking. 'Here we go,' he cried and we shot out into the traffic, narrowly missing a passing horse and cart whose driver bellowed a curse at Phil as my pal swung the car into Hill Street.

'What did that cheeky blighter shout out?' asked Phil as we chugged our way towards Park Lane.

'I wouldn't worry about it,' I said comfortingly. 'In any case, even if you wanted to, I should think it's anatomically impossible. But take it easy, old bean, we want to get to Putney in one piece.'

'Andrew, don't be such a spoilsport, I love going fast!' cried out Claire. Of course, this was all Phil needed to hear and he drove at speed through Hyde Park. Now, if I had been called as a witness at the magistrate's court I would have had to perjure myself if I testified that we had been travelling at less than forty miles an hour on the Carriage Road when a policeman stepped from behind a tree as we approached the Prince of Wales's Gate and waved us down.

'Buggeration!' muttered Phil as he brought the car to a stop and waited for the constable to approach us. 'I've already been summoned for speeding this month. Oh well, let's see if I can persuade this fellow to let me off with a wigging.'

I didn't give much for his chances when the policeman arrived and said sternly: 'Good morning, sir. Do you realize what speed your car reached just now? The limit in the park is fifteen miles an hour but since you passed my colleague at Park Close, you were driving at forty-four mile an hour.'

He pulled his notebook out of his pocket and Phil smacked his cheek in horror. 'Dear me, is that so? Then I must offer you my sincere apologies but the truth is that I only purchased this car a few days ago and I'm not really used to driving such a powerful machine.'

'All the more reason for taking extra care, sir,' said the constable. But as he brought out his pencil to write down Phil's particulars, my chum alighted from the car and said: 'Hold on a tick, officer, I'm a founder member of the Courtesy Motorists Club. Let me show you my membership card.'

Claire leaned forward and whispered to me: 'What on earth is the Courtesy Motorists Club? Becky and I have never heard of it.'

'Neither have I, and I read *The Motor* every month,' I muttered as I watched Phil pass a small piece of blue cardboard to the policeman who unfolded it and immediately slipped a folded leaf of paper into his pocket whilst he studied the cardboard intently for a few moments.

To my astonishment the policeman refolded the board and gave it back to Phil as he said in a gruff voice: 'Well, in the circumstances, I'll let you off with a caution this time as the

32

road was clear, but you must be more careful in future, sir.'

'Oh, I will be, officer, you can depend on it,' said Phil as he climbed back into the car and let off the handbrake.

I looked at him and scratched my head whilst he drove slowly up to the line of cars waiting at Prince's Gate to cross into Exhibition Road and said: 'Well now, I would have put a tenner on your getting a ticket back there. How did you make that bobby change his mind? Does membership of the Courtesy Motorists Club confer any special privileges as far as the police are concerned? If so, tell me how I can join it.'

He said drily: 'Don't be daft, Andrew, I'm the founder, secretary and only member of that fraternity. The reason why the copper let me go is not unconnected to the view I've often expressed to you that a judicious financial gift to persons in petty authority works wonders. I'm a little surprised that you didn't guess that I had a banknote tucked inside that piece of board.'

'Gosh, wasn't that a rather dangerous gambit?' I said excitedly. 'Suppose he had taken offence at the offer of a bribe to let you off scot-free?'

'Not much chance of that,' retorted Phil. 'Aren't you aware that our coppers are the best money can buy! Anyway, I didn't get off scot-free, it cost me a pound note. Sure, I would probably have been fined only double that amount if I had been brought up before a beak – but think of all the time and trouble I've saved by paying off the chap now.'

'H'm, I'm not too certain whether that argument would hold up if you were ever charged with perverting the cause of justice,' I declared doubtfully – and then burst out laughing as I realized just how pompous I had sounded!

The girls joined in the laughter as we made our way through the crowded streets towards Putney Bridge. Once over the river, though, the traffic thinned out and Phil pressed his foot down on the throttle when we reached Putney Hill. Expertly, he changed to a lower gear as we sped up the incline and by half past twelve we parked the car and Phil and myself carried the heavy wicker hamper to a quiet secluded spot near Scio Pond.

We opened the hamper and it was clear that Mrs Angel had packed enough food and drink for double our number. There was cold roast chicken, a veal and ham pie, brisket of beef and rolled tongue as well as two large bowls of salad, rolls and butter and pastries.

'What a bumper spread! I hope you boys are hungry,' exclaimed Claire. I grinned: 'And I hope you girls are thirsty, because even though I forgot to ask Phil to stop so I could buy some oranges to make Buck's Fizz, we have four small bottles of champagne, two bottles of seltzer, a bottle of claret and a bottle of hock to knock back!'

'Well, we'll just have to do our best,' Phil declared as he helped Becky spread out the linen tablecloth. 'Tuck in, everybody.'

After this magnificent feast the four of us all agreed that a pleasant post-prandial snooze was now in order. We found comfortable places to rest some twenty yards away from each other and to Phil's obvious delight, he was able to pair off with Becky who snuggled her curvy body next to his lean, supple frame. This did not bother me in the slightest for I was happy enough to have Claire resting her pretty head on my shoulder as I snaked my arm round her waist and brought her closer to me as we lay back on a hillock of dry grass.

Claire let out a little chuckle. When I asked what was amusing her, she replied: 'I was just thinking about Phil's friend, Jerry Fenner. Are you also one of his chums?'

I replied: 'Not exactly, although we have met at the occasional house party. I know he's a good-looking brute, but I've often wondered how he got such a reputation as a gay Lothario and whether indeed it is justified.'

Claire gave a broad smile. 'Oh, it's justified, all right. But then, what would you expect from a young man who moves in one of the fastest sets in the entire country? I don't know how he is regarded in Society but he's a real stage door Johnny.

Most girls I know have been sent one of his special bunches of red roses with an invitation to dine at Romano's.'

The champagne had loosened my tongue and I blurted out: 'How about you, Claire? Did you ever succumb to his advances?'

'Just the once,' she replied quietly. 'You probably know that Jerry is reckoned by many to be one of the most talented amateur portrait painters in London. Well, he approached me one afternoon as I was going in to the theatre for the last matinée of *Hallo, Sailor*, my first West End show which you recall had poor reviews and ran for only three weeks. I was feeling very low and he really cheered me up by asking me if I would sit for him one day after the final performance.

'His offer boosted my morale and, to cut short the story, he arranged for his chauffeur to pick me up from my lodgings. He took me to Jerry's posh house in St John's Wood.

' "Mr Fenner's expecting you, Miss," said the driver as he opened the door for me. Jerry must have been watching out for my arrival for he opened the door himself whilst I was walking up the garden path. "Hello, Claire, how lovely to see you again," he beamed, planting a chaste little kiss on my cheek as he helped me take off my hat and coat. He ushered me into the drawing room and gestured me to a comfortable armchair.

' "Do join me in a glass of chilled white wine," he smiled. Jerry soon put me at ease as we exchanged the latest bits of theatrical gossip. Like many girls, I was quickly taken with this witty and handsome young man. He had dressed himself for the part in a pair of purple velveteen trousers, a loose white shirt with a colourfully embroidered waistcoat and a floppy silk tie secured with a glowing moonstone.

'Anyhow, we chatted away and I am not ashamed to admit that I blushed with pride at the realization that Jerry was obviously rather keen on me. Happily, this was very much a mutual feeling – so much so that I really thought little of it when Jerry announced that he wanted me to model for a nude study.

35

' "I hope you're not offended by this suggestion but I cannot tell you how excited I am by the thought of capturing your unadorned beauty on canvas," he went on, looking searchingly at me from across the room.

'Well, if I say so myself, I've never suffered from false modesty, so I rose from my seat and said to him: "You've never seen me *au naturel*. Suppose you find my figure isn't to your liking?"

' "I can't believe that will happen," Jerry replied huskily as I reached up and unpinned my hair which cascaded down in tresses down the sides of my face. Then I turned round and kicked off my shoes as I let my jacket fall from my shoulders. I followed this by unbuttoning my blouse and swivelled back to face him whilst I slipped off the garment and threw it across the arm of my chair. With a soft smile playing about my lips, I unhooked my dress and let it slide to the floor with a gentle swish. I stepped out of the crumpled heap of cloth and when I pulled my chemise over my head, Jerry gasped audibly at the sight of my creamy bare breasts.

'Next I sat down and peeled off my stockings and as I stood up, bending my knees whilst I wiggled down my knickers to my feet, I said lightly: "There you are, Mr Fenner. Do you like what you see or shall I wrap the goods up again?"

'He took in a deep breath and I grinned as I saw his eyes rove up and down my naked body. In a cracked voice he answered: "My dear Claire, even though I have never made any secret of my affection for you, I truly never imagined that my senses would be assailed by such gorgeous feminine beauty. You are so very, very lovely . . ."

'Jerry's voice trailed off as he took my hand and led me to a carved cheval mirror on the far wall where I delightedly contemplated my nude body in the glass.

'Now nudity – even my own – always awakens my sensual passions and a delicious, liquid sensation was already suffusing my pussey as I looked at myself in the mirror with unashamed delight. With my eyes shining, I allowed my tongue to emerge from between my parted lips and I turned my head from side to side whilst I admired my elegant profile. Locks of silky chestnut hair fell forward, the ends caressing my breasts, and this sent further electric sparks shooting through my body, causing my rosy nipples to harden and rise. Glancing down at my heaving bosoms, I cupped the globular spheres in my hands, squeezing the soft, yielding flesh and tickling the hardening rubbery nipples.

'A wordless growl escaped from Jerry's throat as, watching myself even more intently, I massaged the rounded cheeks of my bottom and then brought my hands round to my gently curving belly until I finally reached the fluffy thatch of curls between my thighs. The merest touch of my fingertips on my outer cunney lips was enough to make me quiver with unslaked sensual lust and a lightning flash of liquid fire shot through my entire body when a stray finger brushed the edge of my swollen clitty.'

It was evident to me that recounting this erotic episode was affecting Claire's composure as she paused to moisten her lips with her tongue before she continued: 'With my eyes blazing with passion, I turned to Jerry and, with my hips undulating in a lascivious rhythm, I pressed myself against him, crushing my breasts against his chest as I felt his steely stiffstander throbbing against my crotch. My arms snaked around his shoulders, caressing the hard musculature at the back of his neck as his mouth opened to receive my darting tongue.

'Now it was Jerry's body that trembled all over as he took my jiggling bum cheeks in his strong hands, kneading the jouncy globes as he pressed my cunt even more firmly against his erection and making me gasp with excitement. Suddenly I was filled with an overwhelming desire to take this palpitating shaft into my mouth and Jerry's eyes lit up in joyful anticipation when I dropped to my knees and ripped open his fly buttons, plunging my right hand inside the open slit to release his twitching todger. I rubbed the palm of my left hand against my love lips when I found his huge boner and immediately bent my head forward to kiss the glowing red helmet, licking up a blob of "pre-cum" which had formed around the tiny "eye" whilst I clasped his meaty chopper between my fingers and filled my nostrils with his distinctive musky maleness.

'He groaned in exquisite agony when I ran the tip of my tongue from the base to the tip of his cock. I followed this by feeding as much of his thick tool as possible into my mouth, sucking strongly and rhythmically as my lips moved backwards and forwards along the hot, smooth shaft.

'My pussey was getting wetter and wetter and an overwhelming sensual craving for Jerry to make love to me shuddered through my veins as I gobbled greedily on my fleshy sweetmeat. So I pulled his gorgeous cock out of my mouth and implored this elegant man to fuck me without further delay.

'I reached for a cushion from the sofa to slide under my head as I laid down on the carpet and he scrambled on top of me, pushing my thighs wide apart so that he could insert his knob between the love-puffed lips of my clingy snatch. I worked my legs upwards, wrapping them around his back whilst he pumped wildly in and out of my soaking slit and soon I had his cock in to the hilt, his heavy balls banging against my bum cheeks as his helmet reached the very back of my love funnel.

' "Fuck me, Jerry, fuck me with your big fat cock!" I urged him, and the dear man responded with renewed vigour, thrusting his tool at speed in and out of my juicy cunt. Like the crack of a starting gun, our thighs slapped together with every pistoning stroke as he corked my cunney to the limit with his pistoning shaft.

'The sensations were simply too wonderful to describe and we gloried in a magnificent simultaneous spend when, after a series of tempestuous spasms, Jerry creamed my cunney with a fountain of spunk and I reached my own superb climax, climbing the highest peaks of pleasure as we thrashed around in those unique magical moments of erotic delirium.

'Jerry rolled off me and instantly I realized why his tool is in such demand amongst young Society ladies, for his thick prick was still as stiff as a poker!

' "Would you care to continue?" he asked as I reached down to clasp the warm wet shaft, wrapping my finger around the base. I was greatly tempted to accept this invitation, but my pussey had been so well stretched by Jerry's colossal chopper that it needed a rest. So I murmured: "To be honest with you, darling, my cunt isn't yet ready for another joust. However, if you would like to lie back, I would love to finish you off by sucking your delicious cock."

'He promptly lay back. I scrambled up on my knees and, still holding his blue-veined love truncheon, I leaned forward to close my lips over his gleaming uncapped dome. With my free hand I massaged his balls as I slid my lips up and down his swollen shaft, sucking with relish until he began to thrust upwards, in and out of my mouth in time with my own lewd rhythm.

'Soon Jerry's balls began to tremble inside their wrinkled hairy pink sack and I guessed correctly that he was about to spend again. A few moments later a long stream of sticky sperm spurted into my mouth and his massive member bucked uncontrollably as I held his knob lightly between my teeth. My own supreme pleasure flowed over me as I sucked and swallowed the fierce spouts of jism which poured out of his prick.

'I licked up the last drops of tangy cum with my flickering tongue and his silky-textured tool finally softened as I rolled my lips around it. Jerry heaved a long sigh of relief as he lay sated. I straightened up and said with genuine admiration: "My word, Mr Fenner, your cock certainly has been blessed with an unusual power. Do you perform any special exercises or take any kind of secret medicine to keep your equipment in such good order?"

'Jerry laughed heartily as he replied: "Of course not, you

silly goose. Believe me, if such an elixir or exercises existed and a medical man wrote a treatise about them, the queues around the bookshops would stretch for miles! No, the simple fact of the matter is that I am lucky enough to have a strong constitution. Also, I do not indulge in the foul habit of smoking and I drink only sparingly to keep myself in good trim." '

Claire smiled to herself as she took a bite of one of Mrs Angel's delectable apple tarts and I said with a hint of asperity in my voice: 'So tell me, did you ever get round to sitting for Jerry Fenner?'

She shook her head and answered: 'Unfortunately not, because by the time he set up his easel and began to make a preliminary charcoal sketch, I could see his shaft was beginning to thicken once more and at my instigation we enjoyed a further doggie-style fuck. I bent over the arm of the sofa with my legs slightly apart and Jerry guided his cock between my bum cheeks and into my impatient cunt. He slid his arms around me and cupped my breasts in his hands as he slewed in and out of my squishy quim. This time we enjoyed a long, leisurely fuck and again I was able to enjoy to the full the mingling of my love juices with Jerry's creamy jism when he shot a copious emission of spunk inside my tingling snatch.

'There was no further time to carry on because he had arranged with a friend to play billiards at the Jim Jam Club before supper and since then our paths have not crossed again. Still, I hope we will see each other again soon and that Jerry will keep his promise to paint me.'

I heard a heartfelt sigh from behind me and turned to see that Phil and Becky had sidled up to us whilst Claire was recounting the details of her rude encounter with Jerry Fenner. Clearly, Claire's confessions had aroused their own lascivious desires for the lusty couple were now lying on a raised grassy hillock glued together in an impassioned embrace. I instinctively moved nearer to Claire and slipped my arm around her waist whilst we watched Phil slide his hands over

Becky's body, moulding the linen blouse against the rounded curves of her bosom. Indeed, she made no move to repulse him when Phil fumbled with the hook of her skirt. Becky herself unbuttoned her blouse and slid down the straps of her chemise over her arms whilst he tugged down her crisp white knickers and slid his right hand in between her legs.

'Oooh, now you know that you shouldn't do that, Phil. What would happen if somebody came walking by?' asked Becky with a mischievous twinkle in her blue eyes. She neatly trapped his hand by squeezing her thighs together whilst he tickled the entrance of her honeypot with his imprisoned fingers.

'Who cares? If anyone wants to watch, Andrew and Claire can pass the hat round for a collection,' he blurted out breathlessly. 'Now let go my hand, Becky, let me stick my prick in your cunney instead and we'll have a jolly little fuck.'

'Oh, all right then, though it'll have to be a quickie,' she giggled as she released his trapped hand. Phil nodded as he smartly tore off his trousers and drawers. Becky fondled his erect shaft whilst he gently massaged the pouting pink pussey lips peeking out of her curly thatch of flaxen pussey hair.

'Gad, Becky, you really are a delicious little filly,' Phil murmured as their lips met. The ripe young blonde smiled at the compliment, holding his cock in her fist whilst his searching fingertips continued to trace the outline of Becky's crack through the fine bush of golden hair which lightly covered her cunney.

Phil's prick leaped and pranced in her hand as he inserted his finger inside her moist cunney. Becky wrenched her mouth away and pulled his head to her breasts where he turned his lips from side to side to kiss each of her raised-up rubbery nipples.

'Now fuck me, you big-cocked boy,' she whispered. Phil was more than happy to oblige, his entire frame quivering with anticipation as he rolled on top of her and positioned himself along the luscious length of her warm, naked body.

My own cock also swelled up to a throbbing erection. From the gasps of ragged breath emanating from Claire, I could tell that she too was aroused at watching our mutual chums enjoy each other's bodies.

'My word, there's no stopping those two now,' I said quietly as Becky clasped hold of Phil's raging cock to guide it carefully between her yielding love lips and into her juicy wet cunt. Phil gently embedded his shaft inside her luscious love channel, moving only very slowly as he revelled in the heavenly sensations afforded by her clingy cunney muscles. Then he began to fuck the blonde beauty in earnest, pistoning his prick in and out of her flaxen muff until their pubic hairs were entwined before withdrawing all but the very tip of his knob and then plunging its whole length in again to the very root.

This controlled, rhythmic fucking had the desired effect upon Becky whose rounded bum cheeks left the ground as she arched her back, cleverly working her cunney back and forth against the ramming of Phil's rampant chopper. Soon he groaned hoarsely that he could no longer hold back the tide of sticky spunk in his tightening ballsack which was now shooting up his rod stem.

'Haaah! Haaah! I'm going to cum!' Phil wailed. Becky shrieked: 'Let it go! Let it go!' as she grabbed his arse cheeks in her hands and pulled him forward so that every last inch of his beefy prick was sheathed inside her cunt. Their pubic bones ground together as she jerked her hips up and down to meet his pounding thrusts.

'A-a-r-g-h!' gurgled Phil as he exploded into her squishy quim, showering the walls of her cunney with jism during his copious ejaculation. Becky sighed with delight when he kept his throbbing tool pulsing inside her tingling notch, sending a series of tiny electric shocks speeding to every part of her trembling torso as he shot spasm after spasm of creamy seed into her sated slit.

Phil rolled off the girl and lay by her side, his chest heaving as he recovered from his voluptuous coupling. He gasped: 'Phew! That was a truly wonderful fuck, m'dear, but I'm sorry I spent before you climaxed.'

But Becky smiled and said: 'You don't have to apologize, Phil, it's partly my fault because I shouldn't have squeezed your tool so hard with my cunney muscles.'

He smiled, gave her a grateful look and swung himself over her again, nibbling on the nubile dancer's pointy red nipples before lowering his head and planting a wet kiss in her golden thatch of fine pussey hair. Then he moved himself round to kneel between her legs and declared: 'No, no, I insist on putting matters right. Believe me, Becky, it will be my very real pleasure to do so!'

He parted her thighs. The cute little blonde let out a blissful sigh when he lovingly kissed her pouting crack and ran his tongue down the full length of her rolled love lips.

'Oooh, you lovely licker!' she murmured as Phil moved his tongue sensually along her slit, savouring the tangy essence of their joint love juices. Up and down he licked and lapped. Becky breathed deeply as she wound her thighs around Phil's neck and lost herself in the excitement of having her new lover eat her pussey. To her great delight, Lord Philip Pelham was proving himself to be an experienced and expert cunnilinguist, as many young ladies, from humble chambermaids to those in the highest strata of Society, could already have testified.

Claire and I leaned forward to watch Phil in action. He began by parting the pussey lips with the utmost care before running the tip of his tongue very lightly along the edges of Becky's crack, sending shivers of sheer ecstasy racing out of her cunt. Then his tongue suddenly darted in and out of her dripping snatch, and she wriggled wildly, tossing her head from side to side when he started to quicken the pace.

'Oh, that's marvellous, it's just like being fucked by your cock,' gasped the ecstatic girl when Phil found the swollen little button of her clitty. He nipped at it playfully with his teeth, rolling his tongue all around the fleshy nut whilst he slid his forefinger into her open wetness.

She clutched his head, scrunching her thighs tightly around it, her cunt spasming as he lapped up the oozing cuntal juices which now flowed freely from her pussey.

Becky was now eager to repay the compliment and as Phil's cock had already hardened up again to its full majestic stiffness, she settled him nicely on his back. Then she climbed on top of him, bending forward to kiss his lips as Phil cupped her luscious breasts in his hands, feeling her stiffened strawberry nipples rub against his fingers whilst she lowered herself upon his cock with tantalizing slowness. Phil growled with unslaked passion as her oily cunney lips brushed against the tip of his uncapped helmet.

Then he let out a deep breath of satisfaction when Becky moved her hips so that her cunney lips slid over his knob: he thrilled to her clinging wetness as she lowered herself fully upon his palpitating length.

'Here we go again,' she said cheerfully as she raised herself up and then plumped herself down hard, impaling her shuddering torso on his rock-hard lust truncheon which slid right up inside her warm, wet love funnel.

Now Phil slipped his hands under her shoulders and bounced the nubile girl up and down. She used her thighs to ride him, and her breasts jiggled invitingly as she bobbed up and down on his cock as he met each of her downward thrusts with an upward jerk of his hips. However, it was Becky who was directing the pace of their frantic love-making and soon Phil was panting furiously whilst she heaved herself up and down on his twitching tool, taking every inch of his cock deep into her juicy honeypot. The continual contractions of her wickedly clever little cunney soon brought him to the brink of a second rip-roaring spend.

His face contorted with effort as he shot a tremendous jet of jism into Becky's cunt as she rocked from side to side, faster and faster until the force of a fierce orgasm swept over her. With a shriek of joy she achieved her climax, almost swooning away as her cunney disgorged a rivulet of cuntal fluids over Phil's matted pubic curls.

She sank down into his arms and he declared with no little satisfaction: 'H'm, you certainly spent that time even if you had to do most of the work!'

Becky looked up with a happy smile on her face and kissed his chin. 'Oh, don't worry about that, my lord, it was well worth the effort! I love to shag in that way although some of my friends grumble about being asked to go on top, saying that it's a lazy man's way of making love. But I don't mind it at all because I've found that fucking this way always makes the boy's cock rub against my clitty!'

I had been so engrossed by this erotic exhibition that I genuinely had not realized that Claire had become so excited by the lusty scene that she had undone my fly buttons and was wanking my erect shaft up and down in her hand.

She swung herself over to sit on my thighs and, as I glanced at her flushed face, the thought flashed across my mind that Phil's ploy with the constable on traffic duty would be unlikely to bail us out if we were reported to the police by an outraged passer-by. But, as the old saying goes, when the cock goes stiff, common sense flies out of the window. So I said nothing but simply closed my eyes and moaned with delight as Claire washed her tongue all around my bared crimson helmet.

'Woooh!' I gurgled as Claire nibbled at the edges of my knob with her even white teeth before gently easing my cock into her mouth. She gobbled with gusto as I instinctively put my hands up to cup her breasts which swung so invitingly inside the thin covering of her taffeta blouse.

Claire slurped on her fleshy lollipop and wave after wave of exquisite pleasure crashed through my body as I thrust my shaft forward, pressing the crown against the roof of her warm, wet mouth. No cock could resist such a wickedly clever stimulation and just as Phil had notified Becky when he was about to cum, so I called out hoarsely that I would be unable to hold back my spend for much longer.

(In reply to readers who may ask why I bothered to do so, my answer is that I deem it to be a necessary courtesy. For there are some girls, admittedly few in number, who enjoy sucking pricks but do not wish to swallow their boyfriends' spunk. I find this difficult to understand as it can do them no harm. Indeed, masculine seed contains a highly nutritious mix of minerals and vitamins. But, of course, a partner's wishes must always be respected. Only a cad would try to bully his lover into doing something she wasn't happy about but there is absolutely nothing wrong in asking your *amorata* whether she would be willing to pleasure you in a particular way.)

Happily, I had no need to make any such enquiry of Claire. She clearly adored the taste of sperm for she nodded as she squeezed my balls inside their wrinkled pink sack. With a loud groan I expelled down her throat a torrent of creamy jism which she swallowed with evident enjoyment. She continued to suck my cock with great skill until it had been milked dry and then she lifted her head and smacked her lips in satisfaction.

'Now how about a proper fuck, Andrew? I'm dying for a good poke,' she brazenly declared as she kept my cock stiff by slicking her hand up and down the quivering shaft.

'So am I, but let's wait till we get back to Phil's flat,' I smiled as I gently moved the voracious girl off my legs. 'It will be far more comfortable because we'll be able to take off all our clothes and won't have to be on the look-out for any Peeping Toms!'

'Quite right, old boy,' interjected Phil with a grin. 'With a bit of luck my chopper will have recovered and if you and the girls are willing we could have a smashing whoresome foursome.'

Naturally, I was all in favour of this idea which also found favour with Becky and Claire so we gathered up the detritus of our picnic and walked briskly back to the car. After the incident with the police in Hyde Park, Phil kept strictly to the speed limit on our journey home but despite some heavy traffic, less than three-quarters of an hour later my chum was ushering us in to his apartment.

'What can I offer anyone?' he asked us as we settled ourselves down in the living room. 'Ladies, how about a liqueur to refresh you after our journey? There's cognac, cherry brandy, chartreuse, crème de menthe, kummel, drambuie. Andrew, I dare say you'll join me in a whisky and soda?'

'By all means,' I replied genially but Claire thought hard for a moment and said: 'Phil, I might have a crème de menthe later, if I may, but what I would really like now is a nice cup of tea.'

'Me too,' piped up Becky which caused Phil to frown and pull his hand slowly down his cheek as he said: 'Ah, now I'm afraid that tea might be a bit of a problem. You see, Mrs Angel and Mutkin have the afternoon off today so we would have to make it ourselves.'

Becky gave a broad chuckle and wagged her finger at him. 'Blimey, it looks as if my Dad was right after all. He says that toffs like you don't know their arses from their elbows which is why they always need so many servants hanging about around them.'

'He's probably right at that,' grinned Phil as he opened a bottle of Martell's V.S.O.P cognac. 'Nevertheless, you can tell your father that I can tie my shoelaces without any assistance, find my way to and from the bathroom and, believe it or not, my dears, I'll be pleased to prove to the pair of you that I can make a very good cup of tea. So is your liking for Indian or for Chinese?'

'We both prefer Indian, thank you,' Becky replied and Phil winked at me as he asked: 'Darjeeling, or a blend of Ceylon and Congou?'

'Darjeeling will be fine,' said Claire, who had not yet cottoned on that her host was gently teasing them, although she furrowed her brow when Phil continued: 'Lemon or milk?'

'Milk, please,' she replied sweetly, and still keeping a

47

straight face, Phil enquired: 'Jersey, Hereford or Shortthorn?'

The puzzled girl shrugged her shoulders and was about to reply when Becky caught sight of the smile playing on my lips. She threw a cushion at Phil as she called out: 'You rotten beast! Just for that I've a good mind to pull your cock!'

However, Claire and Becky were both good sports and neither of them were really annoyed with Phil, especially when a few minutes later he wheeled in a tea trolley loaded with plates of plum cake and shorbread biscuits and cups, saucers, tea-pot and hot water jug in the new French fire-proof china.

'Here we are, honoured guests,' Phil commented as he sat down on the sofa next to Becky. 'Now all we have to do is wait for a minute or two to let the tea brew.'

'Well done, sir! If you don't mind, I'll join the girls and have that cognac with you afterwards. There's no doubt about it, Phil, you'll make a good housekeeper should there ever be a Revolution in England which sweeps away the aristocracy,' I remarked. But my old chum shook his head and said: 'No chance of that, Andrew. Remember what poor old Oscar Wilde said: "In England, education produces no effect whatsoever. If it did, it would prove a serious danger to the upper classes and probably lead to acts of violence in Grosvenor Square." '

'Oscar Wilde, did you say? Wasn't he the poofy writer who picked up nancy boys in Piccadilly?' enquired Becky. This caused Phil to frown and say: 'That's the man, but you really shouldn't disparage the fellow simply because he was a pansy.

'Let me ask you something, Becky. Do you eat meat?'

'Of course I do,' she answered promptly. Phil said: 'Very good, so at the table you wouldn't turn away a beefsteak or an escalope of veal?'

'No, I like them both,' said Becky. He nodded: 'Exactly so! Well, if I may take this analogy a little further, Oscar Wilde didn't really enjoy eating beef or veal. He only liked pork and always paid handsomely for his dinners. Therefore I don't believe Wilde should have been sent to jail because in my opinion this is not a question of morality but a simple matter of taste.'

'I agree with you,' said Claire warmly. 'It's nothing to do with anyone else what anyone wants to do in private.

'So long as their partners are happy about what's happening and children are protected,' she added hastily and then tut-tutted when she saw Phil pouring tea into the cups.

'Aren't you supposed to pour in the milk first?' she asked, a view with which Claire and I concurred.

However, my chum would have none of it. 'That's just an old wives' tale,' he scoffed. 'It doesn't make a scrap of difference either way, although it's true that everyone has their own way of making a "cuppa". It's quite extraordinary how the preparation and drinking of tea is very much ritualized all over the world. When I went out to India last year, I could see that the tea stall is a veritable institution in every town and village and each *chai wallah* has his own way of making tea, though it usually comes ready mixed with milk and sugar.'

'Ugh! I don't like the sound of that,' remarked Becky but Phil gave a throaty chuckle as he went on: 'Come to think of it, the best cup of tea I ever had was in India. By Gad, I won't forget that afternoon in a hurry. My brother Cuthbert and I were staying in Agra with General Sir Barnett and Lady Hazel Meade, who are very good friends of my parents. Naturally the first trip on our itinerary was a walk around the Taj Mahal.

'Well, I was so fascinated by the building that the next day I returned for a second visit whilst Cuthbert went off with General Meade to a polo match in Delhi. After a couple of hours sauntering through the magnificent gardens I was feeling thirsty so I bought a cup of tea from an elderly man who had set up his stall on a wooden pallet underneath an awning.

'Now I had been told by Sir Barnett that many of these were great characters and were often the founts of local gossip so I was not entirely surprised when he said to me in that inimitable Indian sing-song fashion: "Sahib, please do not take offence at my asking you this question, but are you not the young lordship from England who is staying with his young brother at the home of General Meade?"

' "Yes, that's right," I replied in an amused tone, feeling slightly flattered that my arrival in Agra was deemed worthy of talk amongst the local inhabitants.

'What did surprise me, though, was that a gleam appeared in the old chap's eyes and he shouted some words in Hindi to a wiry youth who was lounging against the wall before turning back to me in great excitement and saying: "Lordship, I have been a *chai wallah* here for many years and am well known to all the highest-ranking officers and their families who are stationed at Fort Vedgama. Often I carry messages for them and I have one for you from the General Meade's daughter, Miss Fiona, who for a reason of which I am not aware was not able to speak to you in person before you left for the Taj Mahal this morning. But she sent a servant down here with a note for you in case you walked through this street and so now it is my pleasure to give this letter to you."

'He called out again to the young man who ambled up and with a bow produced a sealed white envelope from his tunic which he gave to me. I tore it open and swigged down a gulp of sweet warm tea whilst I read:

Dear Phil,

I had to leave home at an early hour this morning because Mama commanded me to accompany her whilst she carried out an inspection of the regiment's new medical clinic. But thankfully she has gone with Papa and everyone else to the polo match which means that I will be all alone this afternoon. So please do hurry back from the Taj Mahal and join me for tea.

Fiona Meade

' "I'll say I will," I muttered to myself as I passed my glass back to the old *chai wallah* and gave him a generous tip. He blessed me in English and Hindi and insisted that I allow the young man (who happened to be his nephew) to take me to the Meades' residence in his donkey cart. Well, it might not have been the most elegant form of transport but it was much better than walking and would get me to the fair Fiona that much quicker!'

'Oh, ho, a bit of a corker, was she, then?' Becky laughed and Phil could not prevent a smirk from spreading over his face as he answered: 'I won't lie, m'dear, Fiona was a real smasher. She was a bonny lass of nineteen with gold-dusted light brown hair and, being of a light-hearted disposition, her pretty face was more often than not lit up by a merry smile. Both my brother and I were also entranced by the feminine curves of her figure which were, to say the least, extremely well proportioned and I must confess that during the previous evening I had found it difficult to keep my eyes away from the two proud spheres of her gorgeous breasts.

'Fiona had been eager to hear all the latest news about what people were doing in London and it was as plain as a pikestaff that she was bored with life in India. This was not surprising because there was very little social life for a lively girl like Fiona – although I am sure that there must have been a great many young officers who would have given their eye-teeth for an introduction.'

'Presumably her Pa kept her on a very tight rein,' I remarked. But Phil replied: 'No, not really, Andrew. General Meade was an amiable old buffer, not like a lot of those chaps who come back here with their brains addled by the heat and dust to spend their declining days writing tracts about the secrets of the Pyramids or propounding some fanciful idea about a secret conspiracy of one-legged Spaniards who are planning to take over the British Empire. Her Ma was a bit of a tartar, though, and the poor girl had almost no opportunity to meet any boys of her own age.

'Anyhow, Fiona was delighted to see me and we chatted avidly during tea. Then we decided to take a stroll in the garden. As we left the room, I asked to be excused for a few moments as I needed to wash my hands.

' "I'll wait for you on the patio," said Fiona as I made my way upstairs to the bathroom where I relieved my bladder of all the tea I had been drinking that afternoon. Then, as I was about to button up my trousers, my eyes fell upon a magazine which had been left on the window-ledge. "Good heavens!" I gasped as I thumbed through the pages of *The Star of India*. It was nothing less than an Indian version of *The Oyster*. My shaft stiffened up as I gazed at the randy photographs which showed a good-looking native couple in a variety of revealing sexual poses. Almost unconsciously, I clutched my rock-hard chopper in my hand and slowly rubbed it up and down, closing my eyes as I fantasized about how marvellous it would be to run my hands over Fiona's beautiful breasts, fondling her delectable ripe titties as I slid my hot, throbbing cock into her juicy cunt.

'I was on the verge of spunking when my reverie was disturbed by a gentle knock on the door. "Who's that?" I called out, my hand leaping away like lightning from my prick. Then my heart began to pound when I heard the soft reply: "It's only me, Phil. Are you all right?"

' "Yes, yes, I'm fine, thank you," I panted and rushed across to open the door where Fiona stood with a worried expression on her face. "You're not suffering from what we call 'Delhi belly', I hope?" she asked anxiously. Then, before I could even answer, she looked fleetingly down at my tummy and burst immediately into a fit of giggles.

"What's so funny?" I asked as I followed Fiona's amused gaze downwards. Then I let out a little cry of sheer horror when I saw that I had forgotten to button up my trousers: my erect throbbing truncheon was poking out in a lewd salute towards her!

'I sat down heavily on the side of the bath, my face burning

52

bright red as I stammered out an apology whilst I stuffed my fast-shrinking shaft back inside my trousers. I could see myself being expelled in disgrace from the Meade household. But, to my overwhelming relief, Fiona assured me that she had not been offended by this unintended exposure of my cock. Far from being annoyed at my discourtesy, the sweet girl smiled whilst she sat down next to me and slid her hand inside my flies to bring out my flaccid prick. She murmured: "Oh dear, I didn't mean to upset your shy little cockie. Shall I bring him out again and see if he would care to be petted?"

'Her words shocked me, but somehow I managed to recover enough composure to reply in a husky whisper: "Please do, Fiona, I'm sure he would like nothing better."

'So she reached into my trousers and slipped her fingers around my limp truncheon. As if by magic, it immediately began to swell up again, rapidly returning to its former length and strength as the gorgeous girl slowly tossed me off, squeezing and rubbing my cock whilst we exchanged a passionate open-mouthed kiss.

'Now, I hadn't enjoyed a romp since Cuthbert and I left England so not surprisingly Fiona's soft, warm hand quickly brought me to the brink of a cum. However, when she realized I was about to spend, she let go my excited shaft and muttered: "Quick, let's go to my bedroom where we can enjoy ourselves properly without being disturbed."

'I could hardly believe that this ravishing lass was so brazenly offering herself to me! Nevertheless, I wasn't going to look a gift horse (or in this case, a gift fuck) in the mouth. So, hand in hand, we dashed across the landing to the safety of her bedroom. We were both trembling with excitement but fortunately Fiona had enough of her senses about her to lock the door before we crashed down upon her bed and began tearing off our clothes. Quite honestly, I almost spent then and there at the sight of her jiggling bare breasts and I tugged down her knickers myself before clasping her thrilling young body to me.

'Our mouths met as we embraced and my hands ran over her pert, rubbery nipples as we thrashed around, bucking and writhing in each other's arms. I kissed her again and again, almost afraid of hurting her with the intensity of my need. My fingers now strayed downwards to trace a path through the curly hairs which formed a light veil across her pouting pussey lips. Then she wrenched her lips away from mine, saying softly: "Take me, Phil, please take me. I want to be fucked by your lovely big cock!"

'As you might expect, I could hardly wait to obey this sweet command. Quivering with anticipation, I mounted the delectable girl. A low moan escaped from her throat as she grasped my thick prick and guided it firmly inside her juicy cunt.

' "Ooooh! Ooooh! Ooooh! Oh Phil, how splendidly your cock fits inside me!" gasped Fiona as I embedded my trusty tool inside her luscious sheath. Then I began to fuck her nice and slowly, revelling in the sensations afforded by the muscles of her tight, clinging cunney as I plunged my shaft forward until our pubic hairs were entwined. Then I pulled out all but the tip of my knob before swiftly pistoning it in again. This rich, deep fucking had the desired effect upon Fiona whose rounded bottom cheeks rolled from side to side as she arched her back to work her cunt back and forth while I reamed out her dripping quim.

' "Can I cum inside you?" I panted. She replied with a quick nod as she grabbed my buttocks and pressed me tightly against her so that every last inch of my cock was enveloped inside her tingling sheath. She moved her hips up and down and, with her hands still clutching my bum cheeks, I matched her movements so that my throbbing tool slid in and out of her sopping crack at an even faster pace.

'With a hoarse cry I exploded into her, creaming her cunney with a flood of sticky jism. My fierce ejaculation instantly brought about Fiona's own orgasm. Her body stiffened whilst I rubbed her clitty with my hand and the sweet girl shuddered

54

in ecstacy as the powerful force of her spend swept through her. When I felt Fiona's body relax, I rolled off her and we lay panting with exhaustion in each other's arms.'

Phil paused for a moment and gave a lascivious grin as he savoured the remembrance of his voluptuous coupling. Then he continued: 'Once we had recovered our senses, Fiona played with my balls and asked me if I would—'

But at this point Becky interrupted him. 'Oh, never mind all that! Enough of words, let's have some action!' declared the clearly aroused blonde as she stood up and kicked off her shoes.

Then the wanton young vixen swiftly shucked off her blouse and tugged down her skirt – to reveal that she had not bothered to replace her underwear after her romp with Phil on Putney Heath. My cock shot up as I stared at Becky who now stood stark naked in a lascivious pose, running one hand over her jiggling breasts and letting the other fall down so that she could run her fingers through the flaxen bush of hair at the base of her snow-white belly.

Phil chuckled openly as she stretched out her hand and rubbed her palm against the swollen bulge in his trousers. 'Oooh, Phil,' she said sweetly. 'Have you put a banana in your pocket or do I really excite you?'

Without waiting for an answer Becky unbuttoned his flies to draw out his thick prick which stood stiffly to attention between her long fingers. She looked at Phil's shaft critically for a moment. Then, grasping it firmly and giving it a friendly squeeze, she turned to Claire and declared: 'H'm, I must say that this is certainly a handsome weapon. But it isn't as big a cock as I had imagined it would be after reading about Phil's naughty escapades with Rosie d'Argosse and Sheena Walshaw in *The Cremorne*.'

*[*The Cremorne *was a contemporary 'horn book' similar in content to* The Oyster *which was published for members of the Cremornite Society, ostensibly a dining club for men-about-*

55

*town but in reality a notorious group of wealthy libertines who
held wild parties and published a rude monthly magazine.
Rosie d'Argosse's own memoirs have been recently republished
in paperback by New English Library – Editor]*

'What on earth do you mean by that?' frowned Phil. But this
only made Becky and Claire break out into a fit of giggles. I
smiled too because I knew what had caused their merriment. I
said soothingly: 'Don't fret, Phil, you evidently haven't read
the report on your sexual prowess by Rosie d'Argosse. You can
be proud of yourself, old boy, she gave you top marks for
quality *and* quantity. In fact, she wrote that your boner was one
of the biggest she had ever entertained in her cunt.'

Now this news might have upset some gentlemen but my
best chum had been favoured with a light-hearted sense of
humour as well as a goodly amount of *savoir faire*. He simply
joined in the laughter and announced: 'Well, what can I say,
girls? I'm sorry if my prick disappoints you but size alone is
of very little importance and I am happy enough with the
dimensions of the equipment which has been given to me.'

'Well said, Phil,' cried Claire as she bent down and planted
a smacking wet kiss on Phil's uncapped purple helmet. 'As the
Yankees say, it isn't the size of the ship that counts, it's the
motion of the ocean.'

I must confess to feeling slightly irritated at watching the
girl I was itching to fuck wrap her lips around Phil's rigid rod,
especially when Becky joined in the fun and licked his
wrinkled scrotum whilst Claire lustily sucked on his blue-
veined shaft.

The only consolation was looking at the ecstatic expression
on my chum's face as their moist mouths sent spasms of sheer
bliss racing up and down his spine. The feel of their tongues
slithering around his cock and balls soon brought him past the
point of no return. Phil gasped out a warning that he was about
to cum, but Claire made no move to extract his jerking prick
from the sweet captivity of her mouth. Indeed, she grasped the

firm, muscular cheeks of his bum, moving him backwards and forwards until, with a final juddering throb, he spurted an abundant emission of sticky spunk into her willing mouth. She gulped down his spunk-flood, smacking her lips with gusto as the spicy jism slid down her throat. Phil trembled with delight when Claire pulled back her head, leaving Becky to lick up the last drains of cum whilst Claire and Phil sealed their new bond of friendship with a loving kiss.

Becky had no complaint to make about her friend sucking off her lover, but when she bent down to pick up her clothes, she wrinkled her brow and exclaimed: 'Oh my, Phil, I'm afraid that some of your spend has dribbled onto this lovely Persian rug.'

'That's all right,' he replied cheerfully. 'I'll just pop into the kitchen and get a bottle of Professor Goulthorp's All-Purpose Cleaning Cream. A few dabs with this excellent American product will do the trick.'

Phil hurried out and when he returned he sponged the spunky spots with the pungent liquid. 'Now leave it to dry and within the hour you'll see that the stain will have vanished. Honestly, some enterprising trader would make a small fortune if he gained the rights to import it into this country.'

The four of us then retired to the bedroom where Claire, Phil and I stripped off our clothes. Now, though I say so myself, by nature I am not a jealous kind of chap. But watching Claire gobble Phil's todger had done nothing to stimulate my desire to fuck the lissome girl. Rather the opposite, in fact, for when Phil went out to the toilet, despite the close attentions of both Becky and Claire, my cock obstinately refused to budge from its sorry state of dangling limply between my thighs. The girls tried rubbing and squeezing it and Becky even swirled her tongue up and down the sensitive underside. But to no avail.

'I'll have to bow out of the fun for a little while,' I said sadly as Phil returned, his beefy prick already semi-erect when he bounced onto the bed.

'No, you don't have to do that, Andrew,' said Claire comfortingly. 'You don't necessarily need a stiffie to bring me off, do you?'

How could I have been so foolish! I brightened up and moved across the bed to kneel in front of her as Claire spread her legs invitingly and afforded me a delicious view of her pouting love lips peeping through her thatch of pussey curls. Next, she took hold of my hand and placed it directly onto her hairy mound, purring with pleasure as I ran the tip of my forefinger up and down her long crack.

'Haaagh!' she gasped when without warning I buried my head between her thighs and kissed the opening of her moist honeypot. Almost of their own volition, her legs splayed even wider when my tongue raked across her hardening clitty. I feasted my eyes on the glowing red chink before drawing her cunney lips into my mouth, delighting in the musky feminine odour whilst Claire's hips rose and fell with added urgency.

The excited girl groaned with joy as I lapped up the free-flowing love juice which was now pouring out of her cunt. How the honey ran when I nibbled at her clitty. She cried out: 'Fuck me, Andrew! Fuck me, you lovely cunney licker!'

Alas, despite this erotic foreplay, I was still unable to oblige her. I raised my head and sighed: 'I'm dreadfully sorry, Claire, but I'm afraid I just can't get a hard-on. Phil, perhaps you will do the honours for me.'

'Only too glad to help out, my dear chap,' he answered as I scrambled away. With a wolfish growl Phil took my place, mounting the lissome girl who grabbed hold of his cock and guided his knob into her aching quim. Once his cock was snugly inside Claire's snatch, she brought her legs up against the small of Phil's back, humping the lower half of her body to meet the plunges of his pistoning prick. He sank his fingers into the soft flesh of her bum cheeks and then inserted the tip of his finger into her arsehole, making her squeal in fresh ecstasies of erotic fervour as he slammed his throbbing todger in and out of her slick, squelchy cunt.

Claire clawed at his back and jerked her hips upward to pull his cock even further inside her as she screamed: 'A-h-r-e! I'm going to spend, Phil! Cum with me, darling! Empty your balls, you randy rogue!'

Phil bore down on Claire yet again, jamming his bursting tool inside her oily orifice. Then he climaxed in great wheezing shudders as he creamed her cunt with a coating of frothy jism. Claire squeezed her thighs tightly together to trap Phil's cock inside her until she achieved her own orgasm, and a blissful smile lit up her lovely face as the ecstatic sensations swept through her.

Now Becky turned to me and asked if I would care to fuck her from behind, doggie style – but, to my abject discomfiture, my cock rebuffed her advances even when she fisted my flaccid shaft up and down in her soft hand. So when Phil recovered from his previous exertions, for a second time I was forced to watch my chum take my place as Becky slipped out of bed to stand with her feet on the floor, leaning forward with her arms held straight out and the palms of her hands flat against the wall. Phil followed Becky and stood behind her as the luscious girl thrust out her chubby bum cheeks. Taking a deep breath, he guided his thick prick between the rounded globes and into her juicy quim.

'Yes! Yes! Crack away!' cried out Becky as Phil slewed his sturdy shaft to and fro, squelching a passage in and out of her delicious honeypot. She worked her hips in rhythm with his eager thrusts and spent just as Phil made one last lunge forward, his balls cracking against her thighs as he sent a stream of sticky spunk hurtling into her sopping snatch.

Even the two randy girls had to take a breather after these frenetic fucks and the four of us cuddled up under the eiderdown for a refreshing nap. Of course, by the time I woke up about thirty minutes later my cock was as stiff as could be and fairly aching to slide into a welcoming wet cunney. Alas, this was not possible because Becky and Claire had to be back at the theatre for the first house *[Edwardian music hall artistes were expected to give two performances nightly – Editor]* and I felt quite wretched as we dressed ourselves. Claire kindly said to me that she was sure it was only fatigue which had caused my naughty cock to behave so badly and that all it needed was a good rest to regain its potency.

CHAPTER TWO

Lascivious Liaisons

Despite Claire's optimistic forecast that I would soon regain my potency, I refused Phil's offer to take me out for a slap-up dinner at his club, saying I had indeed been overdoing it a bit lately and that an early night would do me good.

When I returned home I was puzzled for a brief moment to find myself alone. Then I remembered that my house-mate Teddy Carmichael would not be back from his trip to Paris until the following afternoon. Gloomily, I searched in the larder for something tasty for my supper and was comforted to find one of Mrs Pelgram's veal and ham pies. I cut off a generous portion and washed it down with a bottle of Heineken Pilsener lager.

After I finished this meagre meal, I retired to the living-room and picked up one of the manuscripts I had brought home from the office. As Mr MacArthur had forecast, nothing I had yet read had warranted further consideration by an experienced editor at Hartfield and Moser, and I expected nothing to change as I stared balefully at the title page of *Modern Daughters* by one Miss Abigail Wiggins.

But as I riffled through the pages, I imagined I saw the phrase 'She begged him to fuck her' appear before my eyes. I was so surprised that the script dropped out of my hands onto the floor. Luckily the pages had been stapled together in bunches which I was able to pick up with ease. I turned to the first page where Miss Wiggins had thoughtfully written a summary of the plot [*a good tip for contemporary aspiring authors when sending a submission to a publisher! – Editor*] and discovered that the story involved a group of wild women from the suffragette movement who would do anything to secure for their sisters the right to vote.

Therefore it was with an unexpected eagerness that I waded into the novel. I discovered that the heroine of the stirring tale was a feisty girl named Danielle who had planned to seduce Sir James Horobin, a junior Government Minister, in order to win his support for the cause, but had fallen hopelessly in love with him and thus placed herself on the horns of an awkward dilemma.

I read with interest how the affair began when she succeeded in attracting the attention of Sir James who had been quickly smitten by her charms. A few days later she accepted his invitation to accompany him to Covent Garden to hear Signor Caruso and Madame Melba in a gala performance of *Carmen*. Danielle was aware of Sir James's reputation as a ladies' man but, after they had dined at Jackson's Restaurant opposite the Opera House, she agreed to go back with the elegant M.P. to his rooms in nearby Bloomsbury Way. Told in Danielle's own words, the story continued as follows:

Sir James placed a bottle of champagne in an ice-bucket and sat down next to me on the sofa. Then he drew me close to him and we exchanged a brief kiss whilst he caressed my body with long, sensual strokes. Gently he took my face in his hands and now we kissed more passionately, our tongues sliding in each other's mouths whilst his hands prowled beneath my clothes, enticing me to surrender to the feel of his fingertips on my tingling skin.

In a low voice he whispered, 'Danielle, I have no right to speak in this way after only such a brief acquaintance, but you have bewitched me, you dear girl. I must tell you desperately I want to make love to you tonight.'

Intrigued and excited by the sensations which were coursing through me, I said nothing, blocking out everything in my mind except for the excitement I felt when Sir James began to undress me. I helped him by scurrying out of my dress and very soon he was passing his lips over my bare breasts, licking and lapping my erect tawny nipples in great style.

Meanwhile I allowed my hand to glide over the huge bulge in his crotch and this aroused Sir James almost beyond endurance. He groaned as I touched the tip of his pulsing prick through the fine material of his black evening trousers. The feel of his cock made me desperate to get rid of whatever separated his body from mine and Sir James smiled whilst I delicately unbuttoned his flies. He slipped off his braces from his shoulders as he breathed: 'Yes, my darling, please release my imprisoned cock or I may well spunk inside my expensive silk drawers.'

'Well, we wouldn't want that to happen, would we?' I murmured, slipping my hand inside his trousers to pull out his hot swollen shaft which stood bolt upright in salute. Sir James closed his eyes and slowly exhaled a long deep sigh of relief.

He could be justifiably proud of his prick which was one of the largest I had ever seen with a wide ruby knob crowning a thick, barrel-like shaft. I wrapped my fingers around the palpitating pole and gave the ivory column a tiny tug whilst Sir James raised my head upwards. Our mouths melted together again and I trembled all over with unashamed longing for this handsome man to make love to me.

Our lips remained fastened together as we fell back on the sofa and now, secure in the knowledge that he was pleasing me, Sir James journeyed further. Sharing his sense of urgency, I lifted my bottom so he could tug down my knickers. Then he swiftly disrobed and I was able to explore the hard muscular masculinity of his lean body.

Now his hand worked its way inexorably up my thigh towards my groin and two of his fingers slid between my yielding love lips. I lay back and parted my legs to await the arrival of the smooth helmet of Sir James's cock pushing through my eager lust portal and I purred with delight as he continued to press forward into my welcoming wetness.

'Ooooh, that's nice,' I whispered and for a moment our eyes locked together before he covered my mouth with his own. Clutching my bum cheeks in his hands, he inserted the full pulsing length of his lovely thick prick inside my dripping sheath which magically expanded itself to receive its plump visitor. I could hardly speak for my love tunnel was totally filled by him. His cock squished in and out of my honeypot and his balls slapped against my bum as, with a powerful jolt of his loins, he embedded his mighty weapon to the very root.

Reader, I do realize that some measure of modesty should be preserved at all times – even during these ecstatic moments of erotic ecstasy. Yet I am not ashamed to admit that I immediately cried out for Sir James Horobin to thrust his rampant truncheon back inside my juicy cunt when he playfully teased me by pulling out all but the tip of his knob from my tingling notch.

'H-a-a-r! H-a-a-r! H-a-a-r!' he gasped as we fucked away in joyful unison, our bottoms heaving in rhythm as he slewed his sinewy shaft in and out of my luscious crack. 'What an exquisite cunt you have, Danielle! How tightly it clasps my cock! Carry on, my precious, work your bum up and down in time with my thrusts – but not

so wildly or I will cum too quickly!'

We lost ourselves in blissful fulfilment as Sir James's throbbing tool pistoned back and forth. I gloried in each of his powerful strokes as my own juices dribbled down my thighs and sprinkled his ballsack. Cupped in his broad palms, the dimpled cheeks of my backside rotated in lascivious rhythm as his magnificent prick rammed home at ever-increasing speed.

Alas, although both of us wanted this superb fuck to continue for ever, Nature was not to be denied and when I felt the initial waves of an approaching spend rising in my cunney, I panted, 'I'm cumming, I'm cumming! I'm almost there! Y-e-s-s-s! Y-e-s-s-s! Y-e-s-s-s!'

'So am I!' croaked Sir James and buried his face in my neck as he began the climb to the highest peaks of pleasure. We were swiftly lost in the delicious throes of a mutual spend and my quim was soon awash with Sir James's sticky spunk as well as with a flood of my own cuntal juices.

Needless to say, I spent the rest of the night with him and the dear man fucked me three more times before I woke to see the first rays of dawn shining through the curtains of his bedroom. I cradled his head in my arms and smoothed my hand through his hair whilst I reflected on how much I had enjoyed my night with Sir James Horobin, a gentleman who not only possessed a powerful prick but, even more importantly, also took the necessary time and trouble to cater for the needs of his partner as well as his own.

Here the chapter ended. I let out a deep sigh as I carefully placed the script on the floor before unbuttoning my trousers to release my own throbbing todger which had been aching for relief from the moment I began to read Miss Wiggins's manuscript. I squeezed my shaft but, remembering Claire's farewell comment about needing to give my wedding tackle a rest, I resisted the temptation to treat myself to a five-knuckle shuffle.

Not that I believed that tossing off would do me any harm *per se*. As I have stated in earlier chapters of this unexpurgated autobiography *[see 'The Oyster, Volumes One to Three: Omnibus, New English Library – Editor]*, I am convinced that a great deal of nonsense is talked about 'the solitary vice'. When poor old Teddy Carmichael was caught having one off the wrist while reading *The Cremorne* by his school chaplain, the benighted cleric ordered him to dip his cock in a glass of cold water every morning as a punishment.

[Ludicrous though this may sound at the end of the twentieth century, there is no reason to doubt the veracity of this story. Until the early 1920s, many physicians were convinced that 'self-abuse' led to weak eyesight, poor hearing and even mental instability in later life – Editor]

However, it proved impossible for me not to succumb to the blandishments of Sally the lusty chambermaid who – as readers will recall – had promised to come in half an hour earlier the next day for an early morning fuck. I was fast asleep when I was woken out of my slumber by a gentle shaking of my shoulders. As my eyes fluttered open I heard Sally's voice whisper in my ear: 'Hallo there, Mister Andrew. It's half past six and time for some rumpy pumpy.'

'Six o'clock! My God, that's almost the middle of the night!' I yawned as I hauled myself up to a sitting position and watched the buxom girl slip out of her clothes.

'Not for me, it isn't, sir,' commented Sally as she stepped out of her skirt and sat herself down on the bed to roll down her stockings. 'But I'm afraid that's the price of an early morning fuck.'

'Yes, and I'm delighted to pay it,' I said hastily. 'I'm just not used to being roused at this time of day, that's all.'

She gave a sardonic little laugh. 'Hah! I wish I could say the same, Mister Andrew,' she said fervently. 'I always have to get up at six o'clock, come rain or shine, and when I leave here at about ten, I work with my Mum on her market stall in Paddington Street till tea-time. Not that I'm complaining, you understand, all my friends who are in full-time service work much longer hours for the same money than you and Mister Teddy pay me.'

Quite frankly, although I was pleased to be considered a kindly employer, I could take little credit for any liberality because Teddy had made all our domestic arrangements and I simply paid my share of the household expenses. Nevertheless, after hearing Sally's remark, I resolved never to grumble about any small problems that affected my own easy-going lifestyle.

Meanwhile the lusty lass finished undressing. The sight of her nubile nude body sent my cock shooting up as she pulled back the sheets to slide herself into bed next to me. I had slept without a nightshirt as it had been a warm night and automatically I covered my crotch with my hands. This caused an impish smile to form on Sally's lips as she said: 'Now then, Mister Andrew, why are you being so bashful? It's not as if I've never seen your naughty bits – crikey, have you forgotten already that I not only tossed you off yesterday but that I also gave your prick a nice juicy gobble before you fucked me!'

'Sally, you're absolutely right and I am well rebuked,' I said firmly as I took the impudent girl in my arms. 'What can I do to apologize?'

'Well, you've had my cunney and I've tasted your cock so why don't you give my bum a good seeing-to?' she answered brightly as she scrambled to her knees and jiggled her luscious bum cheeks.

'There's nothing I'd like better,' I declared as I heaved myself up to place myself behind her but Sally said: 'Hold on a moment, Mister Andrew. Your cock is so thick that you'll need to lubricate it first. Pomade [an oily brilliantine – Editor] would be very suitable.'

I jumped off the bed and rushed across the room to pick up

67

a jar of Golden Macassar Oil from my dressing table. I lobbed it back to Sally who unscrewed the top. As soon as I returned she slicked such a liberal amount of the greasy liquid on my shaft that my balls threatened to release their spermy contents before my tool had even begun to burrow its way between Sally's jouncy buttocks.

To prevent such a disaster, I gritted my teeth and forced my brain to concentrate upon answering a question so tedious that the flow of jism would reverse itself back to my scrotum. The problem I set myself was how many English towns I could think of whose names began with the letter B. As usual, this stratagem did not fail me and I recommend it to any gentleman who wishes to hold back his cum until his bed-mate is ready to receive his spunky libation.

Be that as it may, once I had overcome this hurdle, I parted the young chambermaid's bum cheeks and slid my knob straight into her miniature starfish-shaped rear dimple. Thanks to Sally's anointment of my prick with pomade I was able to slip my shaft directly into the narrow sheath until it was completely embedded inside her bottom and my balls swung against the backs of her upper thighs.

Holding onto her shoulders, I began to bum-fuck the voluptuous girl with long, deep strokes, raising the tempo from *lento* to *andante* and building up the speed to an inevitable *furioso*. Together we rode the wind as I slid my greasy cock backwards and forwards. It was clear from Sally's high-pitched yelps and the artful wriggling of her beautiful backside that she was enjoying herself as much as I was.

'Go on, sir, shove it in as far up as you can! Then wrap your arm around my waist and play with my quim,' she cried out. This I was, naturally, happy to do. A veritable flood of love juice flowed out of Sally's cunt when I twiddled her clitty and the contractions of her back passage soon brought a torrential discharge of seed spurting out of my cock into her bottom.

'Oh yes, yes, what a lovely cum! Whoooh! Keep frigging my cunney, Mister Andrew, I'm cumming too!' shrieked Sally who almost fainted away as, with a last maddened shudder, she spent copiously over my hand. I furiously pumped out the final creamy drainings of my spunk and with a 'pop' pulled out my shrinking shaft from the sticky embrace of her arse. I rolled over onto my back, my chest heaving up and down as I recovered my breath after these salacious exertions.

Yet, despite this tremendous cum, my cock was still semi-erect as it swung lazily between my thighs. When Sally squeezed my shaft and fisted it up and down in her clenched hand, my treacherous truncheon stood up again as stiff as a poker! Sally relinquished her grip on my tool briefly to go and fetch a bowl of warm water, some soap and a flannel. She washed my now rampant rod with slow, caressing movements, teasing it with sensual strokes until I felt almost on the brink of another spend.

So why hadn't my prick swollen up to its full majestic height for the lovely Claire only a few hours ago, I asked myself silently. But there was no time to ponder on this question because Sally had now clasped my cock between both her hands. I could feel my scrotum tightening as she said: 'Well, Mister Andrew, I must say that you do have a thick todger. It looks good enough to eat, so if you have no objection . . .'

Sally's voice trailed off and in a trice her tousled head was between my legs. I let out a gasp of delight when she kissed my cock and washed the uncapped helmet with long slow swirls of her pink wet tongue. The hot-blooded young minx looked up at me with a smile on her pretty face and then, bringing her mouth down over my bell-end, she ran the tip of her tongue along the length of my throbbing tool, sending electric shock waves through every fibre of my body.

These erotic sensations were heightened as Sally continued to suck my cock with great relish, cleverly moving her mouth along my shaft to cover every inch of my palpitating prick. At the same time I hauled myself up and slid my hand between her bum cheeks to diddle her clitty as she lightly grazed the wrinkled skin of my scrotum with her fingernails, smoothing her hand gently underneath my ballsack. Soon I began to tremble all over when I felt the approach of a searing wave which was building up at an ever-quickening pace inside me.

My cock started to shiver uncontrollably as Sally's sweet wet tongue slid up and down the sensitive underside of my swollen shaft. I cried out hoarsely: 'I'm cumming, Sally! I'm going to shoot all my sticky spunk down your throat, you ravishing little vixen!'

This lewd warning seemed to make Sally suck even more frantically on my quivering cock and within seconds a fountain of creamy jism spurted out of my prick into her receptive mouth. Sally smacked her lips as she gulped down every last drop of my tangy seed.

I fell back on the bed utterly exhausted from this second ejaculation of my vital fluids but well pleased that, when called upon to perform its party piece, my cock had not repeated its embarrassing reluctance of the day before. For when all was said and done, it didn't matter a jot whether one had the thickest or the longest chopper in the entire country so long as one could count on simply having a prick which worked to order. With this comforting thought in my mind I slipped into a pleasant after-fuck doze but was soon woken by my insatiable bed-mate shaking my shoulder.

'For heaven's sake, Sally,' I spluttered irritably. 'You surely don't expect me to shag you again so soon.'

When she saw the look of annoyance on my face, she put her forefinger on my lips and said apologetically: 'Oh, Mister Andrew, of course not, my cunney needs a rest just as much as your cock. Please don't be cross with me, but I want to ask you to do me a very personal favour.'

I raised my eyebrows and enquired: 'A personal favour, eh? And just what might that be?'

Even though we were alone in the house, Sally cupped her hand around my ear and whispered: 'Don't be shocked, sir, but I want you to shave the hair around my pussey.'

70

I was staggered by this extraordinary suggestion and, being rather fond of twirling my fingers inside a hirsute bush of cuntal curls, I tried to dissuade her from this drastic course of action. However, Sally was not to be dissuaded and she insisted: 'Doesn't a hairless notch appeal to you, sir? My boy friend prefers my slit to be shaved when he brings me off with his tongue. He calls it a shaven haven and I must say that I find it very exciting to look at my bare pussey in the mirror.'

She kissed me on the cheek and added: 'Come on, sir, be a sport. Whilst you were having your nap, I took the liberty of putting out a fresh bowl of hot water, a pair of scissors and a safety razor.'

Well now, I thought to myself, it would be easy enough to remove Sally's fluffy thatch and if this was what she really wanted me to do, it would be churlish not to oblige the girl. So I shrugged my shoulders and said: 'Lead on then, Sally, I'll be happy to shave off your pussey hair.'

'Oh thank you, Mister Andrew,' she beamed happily as she jumped out of bed. Although I still felt slightly apprehensive about the proposed operation, I followed Sally into the bathroom.

'This is the first time I've ever done this, but I'll do my best not to nick your skin,' I said as she stood stark naked on the bathmat with her legs slightly apart while I carefully clipped her curly thatch with a small pair of scissors. When I had finished, I spread my best shaving soap – Guerlain's Crème d'Amandes – on a new badger-hair shaving brush and, after thoroughly sponging her crotch with warm water, I spread a blanket of creamy lather all over the remaining patch of pussey hair.

My cock began to thicken whilst I carefully shaved around Sally's puffy pink cunney lips with a safety razor. I was sporting a full-blown stiffie by the time I cleaned off the remaining hairs with a flannel and handed her a mirror to inspect my handiwork.

'Well done, sir, you've done an excellent job,' said Sally

gratefully and unfortunately my good resolution not to over-tire my cock flew out of my mind when she grasped hold of my boner and led me back to the bedroom. She laid herself down on the eiderdown and stuffed a pillow under her bum to elevate her crotch as I leaped on the bed between her outstretched legs and buried my face between her thighs to chew and nibble on her cunney lips.

'Don't you find it easier to lick my pussey now?' she chuckled. It was certainly true enough that there were no stray hairs to get into my mouth whilst I sucked her sopping snatch. So I pulled my head up and panted: 'Yes, I must agree that a shaved quim tastes even better.'

Then I resumed my tonguing. Sally threshed her buxom young body from side to side as I flicked the fleshy bud of her clitty until, with a high-pitched scream of delight, she achieved her climax and filled my mouth with a flood of salty cuntal juice.

'Oooh, what a gorgeous spend! I love being brought off like that, but not many men can use their tongues as cleverly as you can, Mister Andrew,' she gasped huskily as she slid her hands underneath my shoulders and pulled me up over her. 'Now fuck me with your thick prick and fill my quim with jism.'

Naturally, I was eager to comply with this demand. When I substituted the bulbous knob of my cock for my mouth, Sally thrust her hips upwards as my throbbing tool squished its way into her clingy wet crack. She threw her legs over my back and heaved her body in time with me as we commenced a lively fuck. Despite her juicy lubrication, Sally's cunt was still exquisitely tight, holding me in such a sweet vice that I could feel my foreskin being drawn backwards and forwards with each shove as my cock slid into the folds of her shaven slit.

'Go on, sir, go on!' she beseeched me when I paused for a moment to catch my breath. 'Fuck me harder, Mister Andrew! Slam in you cock! H-a-a-r! That's it, sir, I'm there, I'm there!'

I lunged forward one last time. My balls slapped against her bum cheeks as, with a growl, I spurted a stream of spunk into her cunt. I wriggled my twitching tool around inside her quim as the creamy jism gushed out of my knob, making Sally scream out joyfully as she achieved a second delicious spend.

This lively fuck exhausted even this insatiable girl. Once she had recovered her composure, at my request she ran me a hot bath which I shared with her before we went downstairs. I read the newspaper while Sally prepared breakfast.

Afterwards I decided to catch up with some outstanding correspondence (I owed my parents the monthly letter I had promised to send them). But no sooner had I sat down at the desk in the library than Sally came in with the top buttons of her blouse undone and sat herself on my lap.

'Mr Andrew, I'm sorry to disturb you but I still feel so randy,' she said playfully while she took hold of my hand and slipped it inside her blouse. 'Can you spare the time for just one more poke before Mister Teddy comes back from Paris?'

I wasn't angry with the lusty girl but my cock refused to rise as I cupped one of her pert breasts in my hand. I released the quivering globe and shook my head. 'I'm sorry, Sally, that won't be possible. I have some important letters to write and then I'll be going out.'

She was clearly disappointed and said anxiously as she slid off my lap: 'You're not giving me the brush-off, are you?'

'No, of course not, you can wake me up like you did this morning any time you want,' I said, thinking how foolish I had been to ignore the advice of my father which he had given me along with a ten-pound note on my last birthday. 'Never form liaisons with the servant girls, Andrew,' he had said solemnly. 'If for no other reason than that if you poke one, it will invariably end in tears.'

However, I was more concerned to hear what my physician, Doctor Jonathan Elstree, had to say about my prick's refusal to obey orders and I marched out into the hall to telephone his surgery. Except in cases of emergency, it was usually impossible to make an appointment on the same day but luckily there had been a cancellation and he was able to fit me in at noon. The sun was still shining so I decided to walk to the good doctor's rooms in Harley Street. However, before I left the house, I also telephoned Mr MacArthur at Hartfield and Moser as I couldn't wait till Wednesday to see his face when he scanned the pages of Miss Abigail Wiggins's risqué manuscript!

Mr MacArthur was at a meeting but his secretary said that he would be in his office after luncheon. So I popped the manuscript into a holdall along with the single yet unopened letter for me which had arrived in the morning post. After saying good-bye to Sally, I set off to see Doctor Elstree, a physician who could certainly tell a few fascinating stories if he ever broke his Hippocratic oath and revealed the secrets of certain high-placed members of London Society.

Far from being tired from the strenuous indoor exercises with Sally, I felt fighting fit and there was a jaunty spring in my step as I mulled over the events of the morning in my mind whilst I strolled through Portman Square. However, when I arrived at Doctor Elstree's rooms almost spot on twelve o'clock, I was slightly disappointed to be informed by his receptionist that he had been called out on an emergency soon after I had spoken to him.

She looked at her watch and added: 'My apologies for the delay, Mr Scott, but he only had to go round the corner to Devonshire Street and he telephoned just now to say he would be back in about twenty-five minutes. So if you would care to take a seat in the waiting-room, he'll be able to see you as soon as he returns because the lady he was supposed to examine at eleven-thirty didn't want to stay and made a new appointment.'

'Fair enough, I've something to read while I wait,' I said and marched through to the waiting-room. After fishing out my letter from my case, I sat myself in an armchair to read it. I opened the envelope and was pleasantly surprised to find that it had been sent by the aptly-named Hilary Pokingham, one of my first conquests with whom I had kept on friendly terms after our romance had ended some three years ago. Nevertheless, we still corresponded on an irregular basis and, as the pair of us had agreed, whenever we wrote to each other we penned in great detail all the juicy details of our current love life! So, with a grin on my face, I settled down and perused Hilary's epistle which, after asking after my health, continued in the following fashion:

As for me, Andrew, I've been bored silly these last two weeks stuck with the family in our country house in the wilds of deepest Herefordshire. However, relief came last week with the arrival for a weekend's shooting of Major William Bucknall of the Honourable Artillery Company and my ennui was shattered in a most delightful way by this gallant soldier.

Before I recount my naught adventure with Willie Bucknall, let me tell you that he is forty-four – more than twice my age – and is thus the oldest gentleman ever to have poked me. But believe me, dear Andrew, I can now say from experience that there is much truth in the saying about how the best tunes are played on old fiddles!

So now I will tell you exactly how Willie and I came to find ourselves entwined together in the nude on top of a pile of straw in our stables! He had arrived earlier than the other guests on the Thursday evening because, like myself, he is a keen water-colourist and wished to spend a day with a brush, palette and easel before going out to bag a brace of quail. So after breakfast on Friday morning I offered to take him to the banks of the River Teme where he would have a marvellous view of the beautiful rolling hills around us.

Willie thanked me and as we strolled through our grounds he regaled me with a string of fascinating anecdotes about what has been happening in London

75

lately, for it must be admitted that Willie is not only well-connected but is also a shameless gossip. In fact, we were both roaring with laughter about a tale he had heard about the recent exploits of your friend Lord Philip Pelham at the Jim Jam Club when Willie unluckily placed his foot in some very fresh evidence of a herd of cows having passed by not long before us.

He ripped out a colourful oath and his artist's case went flying as he executed a wild ballet before he fell awkwardly to the ground. I rushed over to assist him to his feet but Willie had twisted his right ankle quite badly and even when leaning on my shoulder, the poor man could only walk with great difficulty.

As fate would have it, the wind now began to freshen appreciably and a grey cloud scudded over the sun. I said to him: 'Look, let's get you over to the stables where you can rest whilst I run to the house and bring a couple of servants to help you back.'

'I think that might be best, Hilary,' he replied as he bent down to pick up his case. 'I'm sorry to put you to all this trouble.'

'Oh, that's all right, Willie, accidents will happen,' I said. As I assisted him to hobble towards the stable door the first drops of a sharp summer shower pattered down upon us.

'Ah, that's much better,' he sighed with relief when I helped him sit down on a pile of fresh straw. 'My ankle only hurts when I put any pressure on it. So there's no need for you to get soaked, Hilary: wait till the rain dies away before you make your way back to the house.'

'Very well,' I agreed. Then I suddenly realized that at least this unfortunate situation gave me the perfect opportunity to practise my skill at Chinese massage, a technique which had recently been shown to me by none other than Lady Molly Southard at one of Johnny Wood's wild parties in Chelsea before I was summoned back home. Of course, being Molly she was only interested in massaging my pussey. But in the end she did agree to demonstrate this technique – which she had learned on her visit to Hong Kong last year – on a less private part of my anatomy.

'Well, I don't suppose it could do any harm,' said Willie doubtfully. But he complied with my instruction to divest himself of his shoes, socks and of course his trousers which were badly soiled with cow dung whilst I took off my jacket and rolled up the sleeves of my dress.

'Now just lie back and relax,' I said and, laying my hands carefully around his lower leg, I began to massage the affected ankle. At first Willie grimaced with pain but after a minute or so he remarked: 'My dear Hilary, there's no doubt about it, you have been blessed with healing hands. My ankle feels much less painful already.'

I smiled at him and replied: 'I'm so pleased, Willie. It's a simple enough technique used in the Orient by friends to ease away aches and pains.

'The girl who taught it to me says that it is also a wonderful way to enhance friendships,' I added softly as I moved my hands up to stroke his muscular thighs. I could see the outline of what appeared to be a sizeable cock begin to twitch against the white cotton of his drawers.

Willie looked at me with a twinkle in his steely grey eyes as he murmured: ' "Voilà où menent les chemins du plaisir."

'The paths of pleasure lead here,' I translated, showing him that my stay at an expensive Swiss finishing school for Young Ladies had not been entirely wasted. There was a brief silence. Then he took me in his arms and our mouths clamped together in a passionate open-mouthed kiss. Willie's tongue thrust sinuously against mine as we rolled together in the straw. In no time at all he had opened up my blouse and pulled down the straps *of my chemise to expose the firm swell of my bare bosom to his lustful gaze.*

We helped each other ease off our clothes. I shuddered with desire when Willie's head moved down towards my breasts and his wicked tongue curled over their hardening tips. As you might remember, my nipples have always been terribly sensitive and my pussey began to moisten as he sucked on one erect bud while tweaking the other between his fingers. I was further aroused when I reached down to clasp his stiff shaft which was throbbing insistently against my leg for Willie's cock was indeed something special: it was so thick that I could scarcely wrap my fingers around the blue-veined barrel of his shaft.

I licked my lips as I capped and uncapped this fiery red-headed truncheon and, foregoing any further preliminaries, I lowered my head and began to suck lustily on this delicious sweetmeat. Willie moaned with pleasure as I washed his knob with saliva and licked and lapped all round the ridge of his helmet whilst his palm rubbed against my damp bush of pussey hair. Gradually we moved into the soixante-neuf *position and when my crotch was level with his face he pressed his lips against my pouting slit and wiggled his tongue inside my tingling cunney. He licked out my love funnel with stylish aplomb, lapping up the freely flowing juices which were now gushing out of my excited cunt.*

However, just as my pussey was about to explode into orgasm, Willie lifted his face from between my thighs and pulled my lips away from his pulsating prick. I let out a kittenish miaow of protest but Willie swallowed hard and said in a husky voice: 'I'm sorry, Hilary, but I can only cum once these days and I desperately want to make love to you.'

'That would be very nice,' I replied as I caressed his

quivering cock. 'So tell me how you want to do so.'

He caressed my breasts as he continued: 'I want to fuck you at the gallop, you ravishing creature. I'm going to cram my cock into your squelchy slit and pump my prick in and out of your juicy snatch.'

'Yes! Yes! Yes!' I hissed into his ear. 'My cunney will cling to your cock and we'll cum together in a glorious spend!'

With a low growl, Willie rolled me over on my back. I lay trembling with desire, my legs apart, as he grasped his colossal cock and rubbed the huge head up and down against my puffy pussy lips.

Now, Andrew, you know that I have sampled perhaps more than my fair share of pricks, but I must tell you that I was genuinely worried that my little quim would not be able to accommodate Major William Bucknall's formidable weapon. Happily, though, my fear quickly proved to be unfounded and when he pressed home, my sopping sheath expanded to receive his massive member. I was overwhelmed by the exquisite sensations as slowly but surely he gained entry into my eager cunt.

Strands of his pubic hair entangled with mine as our groins touched and Willie whispered: 'I'm fully in you, every inch of me — and now I'm going to fuck you, my sweet girl.'

'Go on, then, fuck my arse off if you can,' I replied saucily, wrapping my legs around his tight bum cheeks whilst Willie slewed his superb shaft to and fro. We began what was to be a glorious fuck at a leisurely speed, lingering over each delicious stroke.

Then he quickened the tempo. I lifted my hips to meet his thrusts and love juices started to pour out of my cunt as his rock-hard rod squished its way in and out of my dripping snatch.

'Haaah! Go on, big boy!' I gasped as the gallant

soldier speeded up the pace to a wild, frenetic pumping. I squealed with delight as my pussey pulsed furiously around Willie's colossal column as we fucked away in a savage, tempestuous rhythm.

'Oh God! What a wonderful fucker you are, Willie!' I whispered breathlessly. 'But I'm ready to spend, darling, so you can cream my little cunney whenever you like!'

'I'm almost there myself,' he panted. 'Watch out, Hilary, here it comes!'

As his huge cock began to vibrate I felt the approach of the first tiny spasms of my own spend and then – whoosh! – I screamed with joy as my climax arrived just as Willie spurted a copious emission of frothy cum into my cunt. Billowing waves of ecstasy flowed out throughout my body from my saturated slit. Then to my surprise I felt a second sticky gush of spunk burst out of his knob while Willie shot another jet of jism inside me. What a man! What a cock! I would have loved to stay in the stables with him until his shaft had recovered its strength for another fuck, but the rain had stopped and one of the grooms might soon have come by to take out a horse for my father who often takes a mid-morning ride around the estate.

However, after everyone had retired later that night, Willie crept into my bedroom and we spent the wee small hours in fucking and sucking to our mutual pleasure. You will be pleased to know that by the morning Willie's ankle was much improved and only a colourful bruise advertised his accident which he agreed with me was well worth the discomfort.

'It only goes to show the truth in the old maxim that there's no gain without pain,' he commented, stealing back to his room before the servants came upstairs with trays of early morning tea.

I must close now, Andrew. Write back soon and tell me all about your own latest amatory adventures. But make

sure you keep some spunk in your balls for me when we
see each other next moth at Richard Tucker's birthday
bash.

All my love

Hilary

I laid down her explicit letter and gave a little chuckle as I mopped beads of perspiration from my brow. Gad! Hilary was quite a girl, always ready to call a spade a spade – or in her case, as Teddy Carmichael once acidly remarked, to call it a bloody shovel.

With excellent timing, the receptionist came into the waiting room just as I folded Hilary's letter back into my pocket. She announced that Doctor Elstree had just returned and was ready to see me.

She escorted me through to his surgery where my physician was busy washing his hands. 'Hallo there, Andrew, I'm sorry to keep you waiting. Lady Gaiman wasn't due to give birth till tomorrow but her son had other ideas. Still, she won't grumble especially as she was lucky enough to have a short labour and a nice easy birth.

'So what can I do for you, young man?' he asked as he waved me to a chair and sat down behind his desk. 'You look healthy enough to me.'

'Well, as it happens I *do* feel very well,' I said and then paused to pass my hand slowly across my mouth. 'There's nothing physically wrong with me, as such. Um, it's rather embarrassing, really, you see—'

'All right, say no more. What's wrong with your prick?' Doctor Elstree interrupted me. 'It is something about your prick which has brought you here, am I right?' When I nodded wordlessly he added: 'Now, I can't believe you've been foolish enough to consort with low women, so what exactly *is* the matter with your todger, Andrew? Crabs, a red rash round your shaft or some other similar complaint?'

'No, no, nothing like that,' I said hastily and proceeded to tell him how, on the previous afternoon, my rebellious member had failed to rise to the occasion at Lord Philip Pelham's apartment.

'I see,' said the good doctor. I might have imagined it but I thought I detected a twinkle in his eye when he went on: 'Well, I doubt very much if there's anything really wrong with your tool. Still, I'd better have a look at it to make sure all is in working order. Go behind that screen, drop your trousers and I'll be with you in a jiffy.'

I did as he asked and sure enough, after a brief examination and a few questions about my recent sexual encounters, he said: 'Just as I thought, there's nothing to worry about. Mind you, if there *were* any problems, I realize what a tragedy it would be for a sophisticated young chap like yourself. After all, your cock would really be in danger of dropping off through over-use if there were any justice in the world.'

He leaned back in his chair and grinned at me as he continued: 'If I subscribed to some of my colleagues' more peculiar ideas, my diagnosis would be that you were suffering from satyriasis, the name given to what they would call an abnormally intense desire for sexual intercourse. But then, I happen to believe that this affliction affects us all to some degree, so there's absolutely no need to panic!

'Actually, that's the most important rule to keep in mind if ever this condition occurs again. In your case, Andrew, I am certain that the inability of your prick to perform was caused solely through physical tiredness. Remember, men reach the peak of their sexual prowess at eighteen and I'm afraid that even at the tender age of twenty-three, you possibly can't fuck for hours and hours without a break like you could five years ago. But I'll wager a pound to a penny that you now possess greater control, have more knowledge of *l'art de faire l'amour* and your *amorata* enjoy themselves far more since you gained the experience essential to extract the maximum pleasure from activities between the sheets.'

Doctor Elstree clearly welcomed an opportunity to ride his hobby-horse and I later discovered that he had written a paper on this delicate subject for an illustrious American journal *[this refers to the* New England Journal of Medicine *which published his article in November, 1907 – Editor]*. He rose from his chair as he declared: 'A number of gentlemen with similar worries to your own have come to see me and in almost every case the difficulty was solely in the mind.

'Nervousness is often a key factor. As I told a patient only a few days ago, it is only natural to feel slightly apprehensive before intercourse if it happens to be the first time you have ever fucked the lady. You may even have drunk a little too much to steady your nerves. Or in this particular case because he was worried that his lover's husband might return home early and catch the pair of them *in flagrante delicto*!

'Anyhow, my advice to you is simple enough – you should give up fucking for a couple of days, take yourself off to the country for a week or so and have a damned good rest. Take my word for it, that will refresh you more than any pills or potions which I could prescribe. And I guarantee you'll come back to town so completely revitalized that you'll fuck the arse off any girl who tickles your fancy.'

'Thank you, doctor,' I said. When I stood up to leave, he patted me on the back and said: 'My pleasure, dear boy, I only wish I could cure all my other patients so easily. Goodbye then, Andrew, and please pass on my kindest regards to your parents when you next write to them.'

'I certainly will, sir,' I promised him as we shook hands. I left the surgery quite elated by Doctor Elstree's professional confirmation of Claire's opinion that all I needed was a short spell far from the madding crowd to restore my cock's ability to perform on demand.

It was now nearly one o'clock so I walked briskly down towards Oxford Circus where I bought an afternoon newspaper and sat down to a light luncheon of tomato soup, fried fish and chipped potatoes and a vanilla ice, washed down by a pint of bottled beer, in a nearby small restaurant. The service had been friendly and efficient so, even though I thought that the three shillings *[fifteen pence – Editor]* that it cost was somewhat on the steep side, I was fumbling in my pocket for a sixpence *[two and a half pence! – Editor]* to leave the waiter a generous gratuity when I felt someone tap me on my shoulder. I looked up to see the face of Sid Cohen, the Jim Jam Club's bookmaker looking down at me.

'Hallo there, Mister Scott, studying form for the big race at Kempton Park tomorrow?' he enquired, jabbing his finger at the newspaper which I had left open on the sports page. 'Your chum Mr Carmichael has put a fiver on the favourite, Fletcher's Folly, at seven to two. Do you want something on it too? She's a fine little filly but between ourselves I don't think she'll stay for a mile and a half. Still, it's up to you, of course.'

'Well, let's see,' I said as I cast an eye over the page and then turned sharply away before jabbing my thumb down onto the list of runners. 'No, I won't back Teddy Carmichael's horse, as I've picked What A Cracker to earn a few bob for me. What sort of price will you give me, Sid?'

'Twenty-five to one, as it's you, sir,' he answered. I pulled out a sovereign and gave it to him saying: 'Yes, and the nag would be thirty to one to anyone else! Still, I'm feeling lucky today so I'll have a pound on the nose, please.'

'As you like, Mister Scott,' he shrugged as he slipped the coin into his pocket. 'Sure you wouldn't prefer to have ten bob each way? Because you've chosen a rank outsider, even though Martin Neild's a good jockey and will give the others a run for their money, especially if the going stays soft.'

'No, thank you, Sid,' I said lightly as I looked at my watch. 'Just leave the winnings with the porter at the Jim Jam Club on Saturday night, I could do with the twenty-five smackers.'

'So could I,' said the bookmaker with a friendly grin. 'That's fine with me, I'll be only to happy to pay you out at the Jim Jam if What A Cracker does the trick for you. I might even throw in a bottle of champagne because I've probably taken more than I should on Fletcher's Folly and we'll both be celebrating if What A Cracker wins the blooming race.'

'I'll hold you to that promise,' I said as I picked up my holdall, walked out of the restaurant and jumped on a passing omnibus to Bedford Square. As we rattled our way down Oxford Street I chuckled to myself as I wondered how Geoffrey MacArthur might react to Abigail Wiggins's steamy manuscript. There was still a happy smile on my face as I opened the front door of Hartfield and Moser's offices.

I made my way to my employer's office but neither he nor Miss Thompson, his personal secretary, were to be seen. I was about to sit down and wait for their return when a typist came in and told me that Mr MacArthur had taken Miss Thompson to the third floor boardroom for a private conference, leaving strict instructions that they were not to be disturbed.

'Well, on my head be it, but I must interrupt them for just a couple of moments because it would be best not to leave this particular manuscript lying around. Don't worry, I know where to go,' I said to her as I picked up my bag.

So I trudged up the stairs, the thick carpeting muffling the sound of my footsteps, although when I reached the third floor the silence was broken by a familiar gasping noise that emanated from behind the frosted glass door of the boardroom. There was no mistaking these sounds and a wide grin spread across my face as I realized just why Mr MacArthur had not wanted to be disturbed! I would have wagered a thousand pounds with Sid Cohen that, rather than planning the publication schedule for the busy Autumn months, my boss was engaged in a rattling good fuck with Miss Thompson, his attractive assistant who had always caught my eye on my weekly visits to the office.

It was inconceivable that the raunchy couple had forgotten to bolt the door so I shamelessly dropped down to my knees and peered through the key-hole. A scene which instantly confirmed my suspicions about this 'private conference' met my gaze!

The large mahogany table had been cleared of all papers and lying across it, stark naked, was Mr MacArthur. His somewhat corpulent belly sagged without the restriction of the abdominal belt I saw lying across the back of a chair, but he could still be proud of the state of his thick prick which was standing up smartly enough and looked to be in fine fettle. Keeping his pulsing cock as stiff as a poker was Miss Thompson who was standing at his side and whose out-stretched hand was rubbing his rigid rod. She occasionally varied the frigging by bending down and planting a wet kiss on his bared helmet. The pretty slim brunette was only half dressed, because Mr MacArthur had undone the top buttons of her dress: her pert breasts had freed themselves and jiggled saucily up and down, mouth-wateringly ripe for the touch of lips or fingers.

'Rub harder, Annabel, there's a good girl,' grunted Mr MacArthur. 'Ah yes, that's lovely. Now put your other hand round my balls and give them a gentle squeeze.'

Annabel Thompson obliged the managing editor of Hartfield and Moser by caressing his ballsack in her hand while she continued to toss him off until, with a hoarse growl, Mr MacArthur shuddered and a fountain of frothy jism shot our from the 'eye' of his knob, drenching her hands and liberally anointing the boardroom table.

'Oh dear, I hope the charwoman will be able to get rid of those spunky stains,' she remarked, sliding her hand up and down his shaft to milk the last drops of spermy cum from Mr MacArthur's twitching tool.

I would have liked to call out to them that a dab or two of Professor Goulthorpe's All-Purpose Cleaner would remove all traces of their audacious tryst, but this would hardly have been wise in the circumstances. So I said nothing and kept my eye glued to the key-hole.

'Fuck the charwoman,' said Mr MacArthur thickly as he pulled Annabel towards him and manoeuvred his hands round her back to unbutton the remaining buttons of her dress.

'That's a job for you rather than me,' she giggled as she stepped out of her dress and pulled her slip over her head. 'My word, Geoffrey, your prick has only gone down a little bit. How does a man of your age manage to keep himself so virile?'

Naturally, Mr MacArthur was flattered by this compliment. He winked at her and said: 'It may merely be the luck of the draw, I suppose, but for what it's worth, I've found that eating only a light breakfast and taking regular exercise keeps me fighting fit. Now, my dear Annabel, if you would just give my cock a little suck whilst you take off your knickers, I think you'll find I'll be more than ready to fuck the arse off you.'

The willing girl obeyed and swirled her tongue over his knob whilst she divested herself of her drawers. Then she let out a tiny squeal as Mr MacArthur pulled her up onto the table next to him and, grabbing her luscious bottom, pressed his mouth against hers. Annabel responded by wrapping her arms around him. However, Mr MacArthur drew back to feast his eyes on her jutting young breasts and on the curly fleece of chestnut hair which covered her cuntal mount.

He slowly moved himself on top of her and pressed her knees apart to admire the glistening moist folds of her cunt. Holding his throbbing tool in his hand, he placed his straining bell-end between her puffy pussey lips and guided his cock into her juicy crack.

'Ahhh!' groaned Mr MacArthur, swivelling round on the table so that his back was now directly in front of me as he slid into Annabel's slippery sheath. He began to fuck the delectable girl with short bucking movements, making his buttocks wobble in a sensual animated rhythm. She matched him thrust for thrust and they were soon rocking so fiercely that they seemed in danger of falling to the floor!

Her legs shook and trembled but it became clear that Mr MacArthur would be first to cross the finishing line when he growled: 'I'm going to shoot into you now, Annabel! That's it, my girl, frig my cock with your magic little cunney muscles!'

'Yes! Yes! Oh, Geoffrey, I'm cumming with you!' she

howled as she continued to squirm under the surging strokes of his pulsing prick.

'I'm spunking, Annabel! Feel it! Take it all!' he panted breathlessly. The raunchy pair moaned in a voluptuous orchestration of lustful sighs as they climaxed together. Mr MacArthur pumped jet after jet of love juice into his secretary's eager quim as she gripped his bum cheeks and pulled his spurting shaft deeper inside her.

Now I would do myself a kindness by drawing a veil over the next minute or so. But I promised to set down an uncensored account of my private life so I will record the fact that, as I moved back a step to straighten up from my eavesdropping position at the door, I tripped over my holdall and a wordless cry escaped from my lips as I went down with a thud onto the carpet.

I scrambled to my feet but, of course, Annabel and Mr MacArthur were now aware that there was somebody outside. I heard Annabel shout out in panic: 'Who's there? Who's there?'

'It's only me, Andrew Scott,' I called back and, after giving a perfunctory knock on the door, I attempted to open it, not expecting for one second to find it open.

However, to my astonishment, it became plain that Mr MacArthur *had* forgotten to take the most elementary precaution against being discovered and had left the door unlocked. I sailed into the room to catch my boss ejaculating the final drops of his spunky emission into Annabel's cunt.

To his credit, my boss instantly hauled himself up and attempted to shield Annabel's naked body with his own. 'Andrew, would you please wait for me downstairs in my office,' he said coolly with an admirable level of composure in his voice. 'I will be with you as soon as possible but you must allow me time to get dressed.'

'Of course, sir,' I murmured and backed out of the room, taking care to close the door firmly behind me.

Five minutes later he came into his office together with

Annabel whose face was flushed. She was the first to speak, blurting out her apologies, but I held up my hand and interrupted her by declaring: 'Please say no more, Miss Thompson, you had no reason to expect me to breach your privacy. Why, I shouldn't even be in the office today! So if any apology is due it should be from me for my unwelcome intrusion.'

Naturally this fine speech impressed Mr MacArthur who told Annabel to make the three of us a nice pot of tea. After she had scurried out of the office, he turned to me and shook me warmly by the hand. 'Thank you, my boy. I said to Miss Thompson as we came downstairs that I knew you could be relied on to be discreet.

'How could I have been so foolish? It was almost criminally stupid not to have locked the door. My goodness, it's as well that it was you who caught us in the act and not someone like our chairman who would affect great shock and displeasure at my immoral behaviour and then demand my immediate resignation.'

I gave a wry smile. 'Would he really? Well, that's not my style and not only because I too have been surprised in a similar embarrassing situation *[see* The Oyster 3 *–Editor]*. No, it is because, in my experience, moral indignation is often simple jealousy with the addition of a halo instead of a hat!'

'I couldn't agree more though, to be fair to Lord Neumann, I don't know whether that stricture would apply as far as he is concerned,' said Mr MacArthur as he plumped himself down in his chair. 'Still, I've learned my lesson, Andrew. If I ever manage to persuade Annabel up to the boardroom again, I'll make damned sure to lock the blasted door! It's not as if either of us are married but as Molière's sardonic little couplet puts it: *"Le scandale du monde est ce qui fait l'offence: et ce n'est pas pécher que pécher en silence."* ' *[It is public scandal which gives offence and it is no sin to sin in secret – Editor]*

Mr MacArthur let out a thoughtful sigh and continued: 'Anyhow, what brings you here today, Andrew? Are you going to tell me you have found a nugget amongst the dross of the "slush" pile?'

'Well, I don't know if this novel could be called a nugget,' I said doubtfully as I unbuckled the catch on my holdall and passed Miss Wiggins's manuscript across the desk to him. 'But it's certainly very different from anything else I've been given to read.'

However, somewhat to my chagrin, Mr MacArthur only glanced at the top page before handing the sheaf of paper back to me. With a slight smile on his face, he said: '*Mea culpa*, I should have warned you about Abigail Wiggins, she's been sending us one of these racy stories about every six months since the old Queen died. This one must have slipped through the net because these days we return them to her promptly with only a printed rejection slip. I'll give this latest effort to Annabel and she'll put it in this afternoon's post.

'I do hope you didn't get too excited about your find, Andrew, though I dare say you didn't find it too much of a chore to read through Miss Wiggins's latest steamy story. As it happens, her scripts *are* rather well-written – but of course I would find myself at the Old Bailey if I tried to publish them! Really, the only way she will ever get into print is if she goes to Paris and shows her stuff to a French publisher. I can think of two or three firms there who would be very interested in her naughty novels.'

Annabel now came into the room bearing a tray with a silver teapot and jugs of milk and hot water. But, feeling rather crestfallen about the dismissal of Miss Wiggins's script, I politely declined the offer of tea and made my way out into the bright sunshine. I decided to go home and see if Teddy Carmichael had returned from Paris but as I was walking towards the taxi-rank in Tottenham Court Road, I heard someone behind me shout out: 'Hey, Andrew! Andrew Scott!'

I turned round to see a swarthy well-built chap of my own age walking briskly towards me from the corner of Bedford Square. At first I had no idea who he could be but as he came nearer I recognized him as Antonio Rubira, a delightful Spanish gentleman with whom I had chummed up when we had met some two years before at a house party given by Lord Philip Pelham's parents, the Earl and Countess of Cheshire.

So I held out my arms and we hugged each other in the Continental style as I greeted him. '*Buenas dias, mi amigo viejo, que tal?*'

'*Soy muy bien, gracias* and all the better for seeing you, my dear fellow,' he exclaimed (and I should add here that Antonio spoke perfect English for his half-Scottish mother brought him up to be bi-lingual). 'Do you know, I was just on my way back to the Savoy where I was going to telephone you to see if you were free to dine with me tonight at Bickler's.'

'Well, if nothing else I have saved you the cost of a telephone call,' I replied. 'And I am free this evening. But I'll be frank with you, Antonio, I can't really afford to go to such an expensive restaurant.'

Antonio smiled broadly and grinned: 'Your father keeping you on a tight rein as usual? Well, that won't matter because our dinner will be on the house. You see, my father has an account with Bickler's because he comes to London quite frequently since the Spanish government invited him to lead a committee to promote Anglo-Spanish trade. He was told that it would be more convenient for the bureaucrats if he would arrange for his bills to be sent directly to the Foreign Ministry in Madrid.

'Mrs Bickler caters all his receptions in the restaurant or at the Embassy and she's so grateful for the business that she insists on treating me every time I come over here,' he explained. Then he clicked his fingers and said: 'Andrew, I must rush away as I'm having tea with a distant relative of my mother's. But I'm so pleased we can meet up again later. Eight o'clock all right for you?'

'That would be lovely,' I answered as I hailed a passing cab which I insisted Antonio should take as I was in no particular hurry. I waved goodbye to him as I decided that, although I would have a free feed tonight, it was unnecessary to splash out one and six *[seven pence! – Editor]* on a taxi when I could sit on an omnibus which would take me to within some hundred and fifty yards of my front door for twopence.

I came home to find that Teddy Carmichael had returned from France just after mid-day. Whilst we munched through the cucumber sandwiches left by Mrs Pelgram, he recounted the details of an extraordinary sensual affair in which he had been involved during his brief stay in Paris. He leaned forward over the tea-table and said: 'Andrew, you might not believe me, but the day before yesterday after a slap-up luncheon, I fucked the pretty young wife of the naval attaché at the American Embassy.'

'Well, lucky old you,' I rejoined with a chuckle. 'But what was so extraordinary about this occurrence? Many ladies attached to naval officers find themselves with an itch which occasionally they find it necessary to scratch in a discreet manner. To be blunt, it must be especially tempting for them to enjoy the cocks of passing acquaintances such as yourself who can be relied upon to keep their secrets and are most unlikely ever to be seen again by their husbands.'

'Yes, yes, I realize this,' he said impatiently. 'However, in this case it was not the lady in question but her husband who asked me to poke her!'

I stared at him in amazement and exclaimed: 'Oh come now, Teddy! Are you trying to pull my leg?'

'Not at all,' he said sturdily. 'Without a word of exaggeration, I tell you that's precisely what happened. Look, it all began the night before when I met Captain Gordon Dashwood at a private view of the latest works of Alfred Kleiman, the German abstract painter whose paintings are the current rage in highbrow Parisian circles. He was sitting by himself on a sofa with a glass of wine in his hand and I could see from the glum expression on his face exactly what he thought about Kleiman's colourful daubs. Anyway, I sat down next to him and when I cautiously mentioned how difficult I found it to see the merits of *avante garde* art, his face lit up and, putting down his glass, he grasped my hand and shook it vigorously.

' "Let me shake you by the hand, sir," he said in a pleasant Yankee drawl. "In my opinion, if you showed this crowd a canvas of six splodges of red paint and informed them that the picture was the famous *Donkey's Backside* by Alfred Kleiman, some idiot would pronounce it a masterpiece."

'You're probably right,' I said cheerfully.

' "Oh Gordon, you're not boring this gentleman with your reactionary views about modern art?" said a sweet voice behind me and I turned my head to see a pretty young woman standing behind me.

'She really was exceptionally attractive, Andrew, with a well-proportioned figure, a graceful white-skinned complexion, large brown eyes and rich red lips which, when she smiled, revealed sparkling white, even teeth. I was delighted when she sat down next to my companion who sighed: "Very well, my dear, I know you think I am an old fuddy-duddy but I believe that my friend here will stand on my side of the barricades if you want to discuss the merits of Herr Kleiman." '

Teddy paused and let out a hoarse guffaw as he went on: 'Naturally I leaped to her defence because to gain an introduction to this ravishing creature I would have taken her side in any dispute even if she had argued that two and two made five! I said: "Well, let's not be too hasty. Painters like Kleiman are expressing their ideas in an intensely personal, private fashion which it totally different to the traditional, accepted techniques and I don't think they should be dismissed out of hand."

'To my delight, the stunning girl clapped her hands and said: "Bravo! Well said, Mister—"

' "Carmichael, Teddy Carmichael," I smiled, standing up to shake her hand. Two delectable dimples appeared on her cheeks when she smiled at me and said: "How do you do,

93

Mister Carmichael. My name is Valerie Dashwood and this is my husband, Gordon."

' "A pleasure to meet you, sir," I said with a bow. To cut short the story, we chatted very pleasantly until the Dashwoods had to leave the gallery, but before they left me, Captain Dashwood insisted that on the following day I should join them for luncheon at *Chez Nicole*, one of the swankiest restaurants in Paris.

'Quite frankly, I would have accepted an invitation to eat at a workman's café in Belleville. Not that I complained at the delicious food at *Chez Nicole*. We started with caviare followed by sole poached in white wine and then a *coq au vin* which fairly melted in the mouth, all washed down with a splendid white Sauterne.

'Then Valerie left the table to go to the ladies' room. As soon as she was out of earshot, Captain Dashwood frowned as he looked at his watch and said: "Dear Lord, is that the time? Teddy, forgive me but I've just remembered that I have to see the Ambassador at three o'clock and there are one or two papers I should run my eye over beforehand. So please do not think me rude, but I really must get back to the Embassy. I've already settled the check but I would appreciate it if you would be kind enough to escort Valerie home."

' "Of course, it will be my pleasure to take Valerie home," I said. Then I nearly fell of my chair when Captain Dashwood leaned over the table and added quietly: "Thank you, Teddy, and in that case, I should mention that there is one further service you could perform for my dear wife. This morning Valerie told me how delighted she would be if I could persuade you to fuck her."

'I could hardly believe my ears and I spluttered: "What did you say?" He calmly repeated: "I said that Valerie wants you to fuck her."

' "That's a pretty poor joke," I commented. But he shook his head and continued: "It's no joke, Teddy. Don't look so shocked – we've been happily married for eight years but since our first date I've always known that I could never satisfy Valerie's tremendous appetite for fucking."

'Captain Dashwood stood up to leave us as I slowly digested this information. Seeing the dazed look of astonishment on my face, he shrugged his shoulders and added: "Teddy, it's a price well worth paying to be married to such a luscious woman. Anyhow, I'm truly proud that so many men desire her."

'I could not refrain from blurting out: "Yes, I suppose I can understand that, although there can only be a small minority of men who are happy to share their wives' favours."

' "Maybe so," he agreed. "But it doesn't bother me that Valerie takes lovers now and then. Honestly, I really don't mind because her affairs keep her happy and fulfil her needs."

'With those words, he waved goodbye and left me with my mind in a whirl. Then it struck me that perhaps I might be the victim of a practical joke (albeit in the worst possible taste) played by Captain Dashwood on both his lovely wife and myself. My hands began to tremble as I thought how dreadful it would be if her husband had been spinning me a barely plausible yarn. The consequences would be hugely embarrassing not only for me but also for Valerie. What a bounder she would think me when out of the blue I suddenly proclaimed my desire to make mad, passionate love to her!

'On the other hand, I had no wish to pass up the opportunity of poking the gorgeous woman who was now making her way back to our table. I decided that I would say nothing about the amazing conversation with her husband until I could somehow determine the truth of his remarks.

'I rose to my feet as a waiter pulled back Valerie's chair for her, but my heart sank when she said to me lightly: "You poor man, has Gordon also deserted you?"

'Of course at this time I was still unaware that this short charade had been carefully planned by the Dashwoods beforehand so I found it difficult to answer this seemingly innocent query. I felt a blush spreading across my cheeks as I mumbled some words about how her husband had been called away on Embassy business.

' "Oh dear, how very naughty of him," remarked Valerie. I hastily added: "But he has asked me to escort you back to your apartment which I hope you will allow me to do."

'She gave me a dazzling smile and answered: "That's most kind of you, Teddy, I would be most grateful for your company if you can spare the time."

'Well, here was an opportunity to test the water. Summoning up my courage, I cleared my throat and said: "Valerie, I can always find time to spend with such a charming companion."

'She flashed a strange glance at me and I held my breath as I anxiously waited for her reply – would she give me any sign of encouragement or just ignore the remark? Or, worse still, might she take umbrage at my words and flounce out of the restaurant in a huff?

'So I almost cried out with relief when the stunningly beautiful girl murmured: "And so can I, my dear and I do hope you won't have to rush away when we get home."

'Then as if to leave me in no doubt of the meaning of her words, Valerie reached out and gently squeezed my hand whilst, under the cover of the long white tablecloth which almost reached the ground, she sensually rubbed her foot against the side of my leg. Throwing caution to the winds, I leaned across the table and whispered: "Rush away, did you say? No, I certainly won't do that because I have this overwhelming desire to make mad, passionate love to you."

'She said nothing but ran her tongue between her lips in a lascivious smile. She made no complaint when a waiter came to enquire if we would like some coffee and without even consulting her I shook my head and told him to bring our coats.

'Minutes later we were sitting together in a *fiacre [a horse-*

drawn cab – Editor] wrapped in a wild embrace, our lips melded together in an uninhibited open-mouthed kiss. Valerie seemed to melt against me as my arms went around her, my hands sliding up to cover her breasts and feel under the fine cloth her nipples hardening against my palms.

'I let my hand fall to her lap, pressing it against her pussey, but with obvious reluctance she drew away and breathed in my ear: "Not now, Teddy, we're almost home."

'However, once we were safely inside the Dashwoods' spacious apartment on the Rue de la Paix, we took up from where we left off in the hallway until Valerie suggested that we moved into the bedroom. There, she pushed me back onto the bed and said: "Teddy, I must go into the dressing room and take off this nice new frock before it creases up. Stay here, I shan't be very long."

' "Don't worry, I'll be ready and waiting for you," I replied and as she closed the door behind her, I pulled off my shoes and socks. After all, it didn't need a Sherlock Holmes to know what Valerie had in mind, so I proceeded to undress down to my drawers and hung my jacket, shirt and trousers over a chair. Then, just as I sat down on the bed, Valerie returned, wearing only a diaphanous silk robe.

' "Ah, I'm glad to see that you haven't wasted any more precious time," she said huskily as she slipped the robe off her shoulders and let it fall to the floor whilst I gazed in awe at her flawless naked body.

'Andrew, my dear chap, I swear to you that mere words are inadequate to describe her beauty and it needed not a weird artist like Kleiman but a da Vinci, Rubens or Van Dyck to capture this perfect picture of feminine pulchritude. My heart began to beat faster when she lifted her arms to unpin her reddish-brown hair and free her long shiny tresses which now tumbled down to her shoulders whilst her superb uptilted breasts and cherry-sized nipples jiggled up and down with the movement. As you might expect, my shaft shot up like a rocket as my eyes swivelled down to her smooth white-skinned belly and the curly bush of auburn hair which nestled between her ivory thighs.

'I was transfixed by this sensuous vision and sat stock-still, wondering how any girl could have breasts so exquisitely rounded with nipples that thrust out so tight, so hard. Valerie looked at me with an amused smile on her face as she walked slowly towards me with outstretched hands.

'The dappled light streaming in through the net curtains shone on the ravishing girl as I pulled her down onto the bed. Our mouths fused together as I gathered her into my arms. My hands flew to her breasts which I squeezed and rubbed whilst I lifted my hips to enable her to yank down my drawers and gasp hold of my throbbing cock.

'But, probably because this was the first time I had fucked another man's wife, there remained a tiny glimmer of concern in my mind despite Captain Dashwood's encouragement of this adulterous affair. For just a moment I drew back and whispered: "Valerie, you are sure you want to continue? I mean, if Gordon unexpectedly came back—"

'She interrupted me by kissing me on the lips and confirmed the truth of her husband's assertion about his wife's high sexual drive by saying: "Hush now, Teddy, didn't Gordon inform you at the restaurant that he and I have a special understanding?"

'This was all I needed to hear and I wrapped my arms around her again as we locked together in a passionate exploration of each other's bodies. She responded to my every move. Later, Valerie told me how she had meant to take her time but her pussey was juicing so quickly that without further ado she straddled herself over me and impaled herself on my cock.

'She rode me like she would a bucking bronco, pounding the gorgeous soft cheeks of her arse against my thighs as I gyrated my hips upwards and felt her cunney muscles grip my shaft as my knob pounded the depths of her clingy, moist quim. For at least two full minutes we fucked without a pause until I could hold back no longer and, with a low, wordless growl, I flooded her cunt with a deluge of frothy jism. This fierce gush quickly brought on Valerie's own climax and she shuddered to a thunderous orgasm as if an electric shock had crackled through her cunney. With my quivering cock trapped inside her cunt, she clenched her thighs together for one last ecstatic spend.

'I fell back exhausted but was given little time to recover! With a gay laugh, Valerie swung herself round so that she now faced the window. Then she leaned forward, pushing out the glowing cheeks of her shapely bottom so that they were only inches away from my face as she closed her lips over the bulbous helmet of my shaft which was still liberally coated with our mingled love juices.

'Valerie's delicious sucking made my shaft stiffen again and I gasped with pleasure at the ecstatic sensations caused by her warm, moist tongue as she gulped more of my cock further inside her mouth. With the tip of her tongue she began to strum the underside of my shaft, working her way wetly along its full twitching length. I closed my eyes and gurgled with delight as, after just two or three swipes of her wicked tongue, my fully erect chopper was once more as hard as iron.

'Then she pulled her mouth away and murmured: "M'm, what a tasty cock! But rather than suck you off, I would far rather you poked me doggie-style, if you would be so kind."

' "With the greatest of pleasure," I answered although, truth to tell, I would have liked a longer period of recuperation because I had just spent copiously after a wild fuck which itself had come after a sumptuous luncheon. Nevertheless, it would have been grossly impolite to refuse her request so I hauled myself up to my knees. Valerie leaned forward and impudently stuck her creamy bum cheeks in the air as she called out: "Go on, dear, my nice wet love funnel is ready and waiting for you."

'I took a deep breath and guided my pulsing prick beneath

her rolling buttocks, sighing with delight as my knob squelched its way into her dripping quim. Valerie squealed happily as we fell into a fresh bout of wild fucking. She pushed her bottom back to force her cunney along the full length of my throbbing boner and beads of perspiration trickled down my face as I slewed my tired but still eager shaft in and out of Valerie's exquisite cunt.

'My balls felt full to bursting and, quite candidly, I made little attempt to delay the ultimate pleasure, quickly exploding into a climactic release. However, Valerie had already milked my cock so expertly that only a feeble rivulet of jism spurted out of my knob as waves of sheer fatigue coursed through me. My shaft softened straight after this paltry emission and I lapsed into a comatose state of complete and utter exhaustion. Much to Valerie's displeasure because, believe it or not, Andrew, the insatiable floozie now wanted me to fuck her jouncy bottom.'

'Well, couldn't you have obliged her after a refreshing little nap?' I enquired, trying in vain to keep a straight face as a tiny smile played about my lips.

'There just wasn't time, old boy, because I had to attend an important auction of eighteenth century silver at Reis et Cie at five o'clock,' he answered gloomily. 'Valerie was clearly very disappointed but she shrugged her shoulders and said: "Oh well, then we'll just have to call it a day. Thank you for the fuck, Teddy, I really enjoyed myself – and so will Gordon when he comes home because he loves listening to me telling him all the exciting details about how my latest lover poked me." '

'Captain Dashwood likes to hear his wife talk about her affairs with other men?' I said incredulously. Teddy spread out his hands and shrugged: 'Oh yes, Valerie swore to me that he actually encouraged her to get shagged by whoever she fancied so long as she told him all about it afterwards. Interestingly enough, without divulging the names of the couple involved, I mentioned the incident to a French friend that evening, but to

100

my surprise he wasn't particularly shocked. He said to me that such behaviour is not that uncommon amongst men who are not confident of satisfying their wives and have an overwhelming need to be humiliated.'

'*De gustibus non est disputandum*,' I commented and he nodded: 'Absolutely so, old boy – though I find it difficult to imagine myself wanting to share my wife's favours even with you! Nevertheless, as you rightly say, there is certainly no accounting for tastes!'

Teddy went into the study to write a letter of thanks to his cousin in whose home he had been staying in Paris. Whilst I mulled over his extraordinary story, I heard the sound of a letter sliding thought the flap of our front door so I hauled myself out of my chair and walked to the front door.

[There were at least four deliveries of mail every weekday in Central London before World War One! – Editor]

The solitary envelope was addressed to me. I raised my eyebrows when I opened it and pulled out the letter which was from Katie Judson, an engaging girl with whom I had enjoyed a platonic friendship during a country house weekend some two months before at her parents' beautiful home in the charming Cotswolds hamlet of Upper Chagford situated in Oxfordshire about seven miles from the border with Gloucestershire.

I hasten to add that the platonic nature of our friendship was not from any lack of ardour on my part. But Katie had been in no state to begin any fresh relationships. The reason for this was that she had only recently broken off her engagement to Anthony G—, a gentleman who soon afterwards was packed off to New Zealand by his family after narrowly escaping criminal prosecution for the foul crime of blackmail. However, since copies of *The Oyster* now reach Antipodean shores, I will not reveal his full name in the hope that he has changed his ways for the better. Be that as it may, I was delighted to receive this letter from Katie Judson which read:

Judson Manor, Upper Chagford, Oxfordshire

Dear Andrew,

I am counting on you to help a damsel (well, several damsels) in distress! Forgive the short notice, but are you able to accept an invitation to come up to Judson Manor on Friday for a long weekend? The reason why I would be hugely grateful is not just that it would be lovely to see you again but because I have my cousin Susie and two of my closest friends, Alexa and Erika Hansen from Denmark, staying here. Alexa and Erika are twins and their mother is distantly related to Queen Alexandra.

Anyhow, we are all alone here because my father received a telegram yesterday about his Aunt Maude who had reached the great age of ninety-seven but whose health is now giving great cause for concern. Do not think me over-cynical, but as my Great Aunt Maude is thought to have a fortune of more than a quarter of a million pounds, my parents have rushed up to Warwick to be at the old lady's bedside for what are probably her last hours. Of course, this act of kindness has nothing to do with any worry they might have that other unscrupulous relatives might also make a similar journey in order to persuade her to change her will or even – as my father has more than once hinted with regard to his brother Osborn, the black sheep of the family – attempt to forge a codicil or gain a power of attorney over her affairs.

Be that as it may, we four girls have the house to ourselves for at least a week and Susie suggested to me that we should invite some young gentlemen to make up a jolly party whilst my parents are away. Do you recall Ian Pethick, the young Leicestershire landowner, from your last visit here? He is sweet on Susie and as soon as he received an invitation from her, he wired back his acceptance. Our neighbour Colonel Dennison's son, Jack, will also make himself available so we need two more boys to make up the numbers – perhaps your friend Teddy Carmichael would be interested? I would be so pleased if you could both accept this admittedly last-minute invitation.

Perhaps you would send me a telegram saying yea or nay as soon as you receive this letter.

With all my love

Katie

Naturally, I was thrilled to receive this letter – my only arrangements for the weekend consisted of a half-promise to some chaps to take part in a charity bridge evening at the Jim Jam Club in aid of Princess Louise's East End Milk Funds and a duty visit to my Uncle Hubert and Aunt Gertrude in Ecclestone Square. Well, a cheque to the Funds and a letter of apology to my aunt and uncle would suffice and I hurried into the study to ask Teddy if he were free to accompany me to Upper Chagford on the coming weekend.

'Excellent,' I said when Teddy informed me that he was indeed free and would be very happy to make the journey up to the Cotswolds. 'I'll send a telegram to Katie right now.'

I performed my chores and took a shower before changing into an evening suit for my dinner at Bickler's with Antonio Rubira. I arrived at the restaurant at eight o'clock precisely but it was almost a quarter past eight before Antonio appeared. I was startled to see that he was sporting a large sticking plaster over his left eyebrow and looked far from his usual ebullient self. Therefore I interrupted his fulsome apologies for his late arrival and asked if he had been involved in a traffic accident.

He gave me a rueful look and replied: 'Well, that's exactly

what I said to the constable who found me lying on the pavement in a side alley off Dover Street this afternoon. But in fact I had been assaulted and robbed.'

'Good heavens, how terrible!' I gasped. 'But why didn't you tell that to the policeman? Were you in shock? It's not too late to make a statement at the nearest station, you know. I'll go with you if you like.'

'No, no, no, that's that last thing I want to do, my dear friend,' he said quickly. 'After all, the news of what happened might leak out to the newspapers and it would embarrass my father. Besides, I don't want the whole world to know how damned stupid I have been.'

He called over the waiter and went on: 'Let's choose what we want to eat and then after our meal I'll tell you what really happened to me.'

Naturally I dropped the subject although, of course, I was dying to hear what had befallen poor Antonio! Anyhow, we enjoyed a splendid dinner and I followed him upstairs to one of the small private sitting-rooms where we took our coffee and brandy. I settled down in a comfortable armchair but Antonio preferred to stand at the window looking down at the bustle of Piccadilly whilst he sipped his Courvoisier. Then he turned away from the window and said: 'Andrew, I'm so ashamed! I've been a perfect bloody fool!'

He plumped himself down on a small sofa opposite me and sighed: 'Do you remember that when I left you this afternoon I had to rush to meet a second cousin of my mother's at the Ritz? Well, I arrived in good time but a note was waiting there for me to say that he was unable to meet me as he was suffering from a bad cold.

'I won't pretend that I was dreadfully upset and I went back out into Piccadilly and strolled through Green Park. I was about to sit down in a deckchair for a snooze when an attractive girl in a grey coat handed me an advertisement leaflet. Normally, I would have thrown the cheaply printed paper away, but I had nothing to read so I eased myself into my deckchair and saw that the leaflet offered a twenty-five per cent discount off the price of an entrance ticket to anyone who brought it with them to the private *poses plastiques* entertainment being staged daily on the hour every hour only five minutes' walk away at 3, Albermarle Street.

[The Victorian/Edwardian equivalent of contemporary striptease. Girls would pose in classical scenes which gave the necessary excuse for them to appear scantily clad or semi-nude – Editor]

'Well, now, I thought to myself, if any of the performers in this *poses plastiques* were as pretty as the girl who had given me the leaflet, they would be worth a visit. When I looked at my watch I saw that it was ten minutes to four which was more than enough time for me to catch the next show. Still, I hesitated, but then as if – how do you say in English – to egg me on, the sun began to move behind a cloud so I decided to heave myself out of my deckchair and saunter across to Albermarle Street.

'I rang the bell and a stout fair-haired man opened the door and ushered me into a small room off the hallway. He demanded a sovereign but accepted fifteen shillings when I showed him the leaflet which he took from me.

' "Very good, sir," he said greasily. "Stay here, please, and someone will be with you in just a moment."

'Sure enough, a minute or two later the door was thrown open and who should be standing there but the very same girl who had given me the leaflet in Green Park! However, she had now divested herself of her coat and was wearing only a tightly fitting white tennis shirt and a short sports skirt which barely reached down to her shapely calves.

'She flashed me a bright smile and said: "Hallo there, didn't I see you in the park just now? What's your name? My name is Sheena and I am you own personal *pose plastique* performer."

' "Yes, you gave me a leaflet," I stammered. "My name is

Arthur (I find it easier to give this English equivalent rather than have to start explaining how to pronounce or spell Antonio). But I have never heard of a personal *pose plastique* performance before – what does it mean?"

' "Why, it can mean just about anything you want," she cooed as she stepped forward and provocatively thrust her large rounded breasts almost into my face. Instinctively I nuzzled my face into her cleavage but Sheena skipped back a pace and giggled: "Not so fast, Arthur, not so fast. What performance you get depends on what you pay – so far all you've bought is a ticket for the basic ten-minute show in which I pose in scanty costumes as Diana the huntress, Boadicea the Warrior Queen and so on. However, if you want to see my breasts, you'll have to pay another pound for a special performance."

'I was about to say that I wouldn't part with a sovereign just to see her titties when the luscious girl nudged me in the ribs and whispered: "But if you can afford it, I recommend that you splash out another four pounds for the extra-special show. You won't regret it, Arthur, I promise you."

'And as if to prove her point, Sheena moved close to me again and lightly rubbed her hand against the outline of my thickening cock as she went on: "For instance, wouldn't you love me to suck your big stiff cock?"

'Well, of course I gave her another four pounds for the extra-special show. As she slipped the money into a pocket in her skirt, the little hussey smiled sweetly and moved her mouth to my ear, gently biting on the lobe before she said: "Oh good, I'm really pleased because I really do fancy you and I'm going to enjoy the next hour as much as you."

'Then she beckoned me to follow her upstairs into a well-appointed bedroom where she began to undress until she was stark naked. My rock-hard cock was now making a huge bulge in my lap as I sat on the bed and watched Sheena slide her hands over her beautiful big breasts and tweak her nut-brown nipples between her fingers. I licked my lips as I stared at the neatly trimmed bush of brown curls between her thighs. Seeing the direction of my gaze, Sheena said: "Do you like my pussey, Arthur? Why don't you ream it out with your tongue?"

' "With pleasure," I croaked. And without further ado, I knelt down in front of her and immediately buried my face in the furry cuntal thatch whilst I grabbed Sheena's chubby bum cheeks and pulled her closer to me.

' "My word, you're a fast worker and no mistake," she gasped as she clamped her hands on the back of my head and forced my face further inside her moist quim. I worked my tongue in between her pussey lips and soon found her clitty. Sheena let out a delighted squeal when I began chewing on the delicious fleshy morsel.

' "Wooooh!" she yelped as I licked out her dripping love funnel until, with a violent shudder, Sheena achieved her spend and drenched my face with a copious flood of cunt juice. When she had finished she patted me on the head and said in a husky voice: "Thank you, Arthur, that was absolutely divine. Now let me do something for you."

'I rose to my feet as Sheena fell down to her knees and ripped open my flies, sending my trousers sliding down to my ankles as she slipped her hand inside my drawers to bring my swollen shaft out into view. In a trice her tousled chestnut hair was between my thighs as she kissed my knob and twirled her tongue along the ridge of the bulbous helmet. Her teeth scraped the dome as she drew me in between those luscious red lips, sucking hard as her smooth soft fingers clenched themselves around my throbbing tool.

'Andrew, *mi amigo*, the lusty girl then gave me one of the best gobbles I have ever experienced. Her mouth was like a cave of fire that warmed yet did not burn whilst her wicked wet tongue circled my cock, savouring the tasty love juice which was already trickling out of my knob. It must have been clear to Sheena that I was almost ready to spend and she began to suck my prick even harder as she reached down and gently

107

squeezed my balls. This had the desired effect and seconds later a low wordless growl escaped from my mouth as I shot a tremendous stream of foamy jism into her mouth, its powerful force sending the sticky cream to the back of her throat. Sheena smacked her lips as she swallowed my seed, fisting her hand up and down my pulsating pole until my shaft began to soften in her grasp. When she had licked up the last dribbles of cum, I helped her scramble to her feet and we laid down on the bed together whilst I played with her jouncy breasts and she toyed with my limp cock.'

Antonio gave a satisfied grunt as he gulped down his brandy. I scratched my head and said: 'Well, I don't see what's so terrible about that, even though four pounds, fifteen shillings is a great deal of money to pay to be sucked off – or did you recover in time to fuck this frisky wench?'

'Ah, if only this encounter had ended there, I would not have begrudged Sheena a penny,' sighed Antonio whilst he refilled his crystal goblet. 'Alas, the story now takes on a far less pleasant turn.

'As I said, we were resting on the bed when in flounced a nubile auburn-haired girl of no more than eighteen wearing only a diaphanous beige robe through which I could make out the contours of her breasts. "Hallo, you two," she said perkily. "Can I get either of you a drink?"

' "Oh, I would adore a glass of champagne, wouldn't you, Arthur?" said Sheena. I nodded my head lazily as she continued to stroke my cock. The girl came back less than a minute later with a tray on which stood a bottle of champagne and three glasses. She set down the tray on the bedside table and unknotted the cloth belt of her robe which opened up to reveal her firm, succulent young breasts. She smoothed her hand along my thigh as she asked politely if she could join the party.

' "Please do," I replied. Whilst I watched the girl pop open the bottle, (which, incidentally, turned out not to be champagne but a cheap though drinkable sparking Moselle), Sheena

108

said: "Arthur dear, you must give Patsy ten shillings for the bubbly."

'I reached for my wallet and thought I detected a gleam in their eyes when I extracted a Treasury note from a tight wad of its fellows. Anyway, I forget exactly how it came about, but after we had drunk a glass or two of wine, the girls suggested that, like most men, I would be unable to tell the difference between their pussies with my eyes closed.

' "What nonsense! Of course I could," I said indignantly. My cock began to stir again as Patsy rolled down her knickers and I gaped at the pouting pussey lips I could see poking out of her thick fleece of curls at the base of her belly. Then Sheena took charge of the proceedings and, after telling me to lie back and close my eyes, she blindfolded me with the belt from Patsy's robe. She said that they would take turns to sit on my chest and press their pussies against my lips.

' "First wash your mouth out with another drink to clear your palate," she instructed as she placed a brimming glass in my hand. As I obediently swigged it down, I thought the taste was slightly different from that of the previous glass I had drunk.'

I held up my hands in horror and exclaimed: 'Oh no, don't tell me that one of the girls had slipped a sleeping draught into your drink.'

Antonio gave a rueful grimace and replied: 'I'm afraid that's exactly what happened. Suddenly there was a rushing noise in my ears, I felt myself falling back on the pillow and the next thing I knew was I was sitting up fully clothed against a wall in a side alley nearby the house being shaken into consciousness by a kindly passer-by who anxiously asked me if I needed any help. I put a hand up to my head and discovered that I was bleeding from a cut over my eye (they must have banged my face when carrying me downstairs or out through the back door). I staunched the flow of blood with a handkerchief whilst I thanked the elderly gentleman who had woken me up, assuring him that I was all right.

'After a while I managed to haul myself to my feet and staggered across Piccadilly in a dishevelled state back to the Ritz where, after a soak in a warm bath, I began to feel much better.'

'I suppose the girls had stolen your wallet,' I commented but my Spanish chum shook his head: 'No, surprisingly enough. Even though it was an expensive crocodile leather one, it was still inside the inside pocket of my jacket – though it was now empty, of course!'

'Oh dear, how much money did you lose?' I enquired. He answered sheepishly: 'About seventy-five pounds, and they also stole my gold watch.'

'The scoundrels! You really should lay an information against the girls at the police station,' I said warmly.

But Antonio demurred: 'I don't think that would be a good idea, Andrew. Listen, my friend, the fact is that it's my word against theirs and even if the police believed me, the case would come to trial. Besides causing embarrassment to my father, I would also hate to see my name plastered over the pages of the popular newspapers.'

I slowly nodded my head and mulled over his predicament. Finally I sighed: 'Yes, I'm sorry to say that it would probably do you no good to go to the police. So it would be best to enter the incident into the ledger of experience and then forget about the whole sorry business.'

'That's precisely what I plan to do,' he agreed and clapped me on the shoulder. 'So finish your drink and let's finish the evening at the Jim Jam Club. There's a special French *café-conc'* evening tonight which should be quite fun.'

[A Café-concert, or 'café-conc' as it was popularly known, was the French equivalent of the British music hall with a stage, footlights and an orchestra. But a café-conc' would take place in large cafés which could seat up to a couple of hundred people rather than in a theatre – Editor.]

I hesitated as Doctor Elstree's advice to rest my wedding tackle crossed my mind, but Antonio would not take no for an answer. So I allowed myself to be bundled into a cab which less than ten minutes later had deposited us outside the doors of the Jim Jam Club in Great Windmill Street.

'Do you know, I'm rather worried that they'll not let us in as I've forgotten to pay this year's subscription,' I remarked. But Antonio waved aside this objection and produced his own membership card for the duty supervisor to inspect. Coincidentally, this evening this official happened to be Colonel Aspis, the Club secretary, who sat at his rosewood desk in the hallway flanked by two burly doormen who were always on hand to escort would be gate-crashers off the premises. This happened quite frequently these days as rumours about the raffish goings-on at the Jim Jam had recently begun to circulate amongst the *hoi polloi* and the Club had been forced to operate a strict policy of admitting only members and their guests at all times.

'Good evening, Andrew, are you keeping well?' he greeted me whilst Antonio signed me in as his guest. 'Forgive me mentioning it, but you must send me a cheque soon or I'll have to suspend your membership. We've a long waiting-list of gentlemen who are eager to take your place if you want to resign.'

'I'll post you a cheque first thing tomorrow,' I promised him. The Colonel gave a wan little smile and said: 'I've heard that phrase so many times, Andrew. As Harry Tate – *[a tremendously popular music hall comedian of the era – Editor]* – joked at a gentlemen-only cabaret here only last week, that's one of the three greatest lies ever told.'

In spite of his stricture, I chuckled: 'And what are the other two, sir?'

'Both very simple, my boy,' he answered promptly. 'Specifically, at the dentist's when he says: "This won't hurt at all," and in general terms whenever a young man swears: "I promise I won't cum in your mouth"!'

111

Nevertheless, Antonio and I were ushered into the Club. In the large restaurant area the *café-conc'* was in full swing. To a roar of applause from the audience, a line of scantily-dressed chorus girls had just finished their routine as the head waiter came up and managed to find us a free table for two at the back of the room. He took Antonio's order for two large cognacs whilst the chairman stood up and, rapping his gavel on his table for silence, announced that for our entertainment, the Jim Jam Club was proud to present a performance by two leading members of the *Nouveau Ballet Parisienne*, Monsieur Leon Chauvineau and Mademoiselle Juliette Lebrun.

We joined in the polite round of applause as the lights were lowered and the orchestra struck up a romantic air although, to be frank, I must confess that Antonio and I were a mite disappointed at this news. However, little did we know just how enthralled we would soon be by the sensual performance of these magnificent young dancers.

We watched with growing interest as a spotlight shone on the lissome young ballerina as, dressed in a skimpy silver top and matching tutu skirt, she gracefully moved around the stationary figure of the gleaming, bronzed body of her partner who was bare-chested and wore only a pair of white tights. At first he stood facing the side of the room. But when he turned face on towards the audience, a lady sitting at a nearby table muttered: 'Good gracious! Either that young man has stuffed something down between his legs or else he must be hung like a donkey.'

She was soon to discover that Leon Chauvineau was guiltless of any deception. But my attention was principally drawn to his partner who was now sensually divesting herself of all her clothes to a ripple of appreciative applause before finally standing totally naked in the spotlight. Juliette's haughty high-cheekboned face and slim figure were ravishingly beautiful: naturally, my cock started to swell as I goggled unashamedly at her small but splendidly firm breasts with their perky berry-like nipples which stood out so firmly as she tweaked them up to erection between her long fingers.

My eyes now dropped to her snow-white tummy and dimpled navel below which lay a curly bush of chestnut pussey hair. I heard a collective drawing in of breath as Juliette ran her hand suggestively along Leon's hairless chest before rolling down his tights to expose his enormous thick prick. I could see it spring up and quiver stiffly against his belly before he skipped behind her and slid his arms around her sides and fondled her bare breasts in his hands.

Then Leon moved round and dropped to his knees between her parted legs. He pressed his face into her thatch of glossy pussey hair: she threw back her head and moaned with joy as his tongue found the crack of her cunney. However, he quickly raised himself up and sucked on Juliette's firm titties whilst he dipped his forefinger in and out of her moistening quim.

She used both her hands to hold his huge cock which was truly of an awesome girth. Her own elongated nipples appeared to jut out even more stiffly as her eager companion caressed each of her jiggling breasts in turn.

To the rhythm of the soulful music, they moved towards the side of the stage. Juliette placed herself with her back against the wall and a wide smile lit up Leon's boyish features when she opened her legs and pulled his thick prick towards the waiting wet haven of her cunney, easing the purple knob between her pouting pussey lips and drawing it in inch by inch until their pubic muffs were matted together.

It occurred to me that his colossal cock might cause the slimly built girl some discomfort. But Juliette showed no signs of unease when Leon began fucking her with powerful strokes of his enormous todger. Indeed, she urged him on by throwing her arms around his neck, clasping her legs together around his waist to force even more of his huge prick inside her snatch.

Antonio and I were not the only spectators to be excited by this grand exhibition and behind me I heard a familiar fruity voice declare: 'Go on, you lucky lad! Crash your cock into her juicy cunt and rattle your balls against her bum!'

113

I turned my head and smiled when I saw that this encouraging comment had come from none other than Lord Philip Pelham, standing against a pillar with a tall fluted glass of champagne in his hand. However, I was more interested in what was happening on the stage where Leon had now increased the pace of the poke, sliding his tool to and fro faster and faster whilst Juliette threshed wildly from side to side, panting with passion as she clung to him, humping the lower half of her body upwards to meet the violent pounding of her lover's rampant red rod.

Leon bore down on her one final time, his youthful torso now shining with perspiration. Then his body tensed and he slammed his shaft into her, jetting his emission inside her juicy cunt as Juliette squeezed her thighs tightly around him. She did not release her grip until she had milked every drop of sticky seed from his spurting length.

A mighty roar of applause broke out as the couple disengaged themselves and slipped on red silk robes before taking a well-deserved bow to a standing ovation. Lord Philip Pelham went round the tables with a small china bowl to make a silver collection which he then presented to the artistes as they left the stage.

After the lights came up, Philip strolled over to our table. As he was chatting to Antonio, I plucked at his sleeve and pointed to a small group of men clustered around a thick-set older gentleman – whose face seemed curiously familiar – as they hurried past our table on their way to the exit. My eyebrows shot up and I turned to Philip and said: 'Am I suffering from an hallucination or did I just see—'

'Yes, you did,' he confirmed with a chuckle. 'It was no mirage, that portly chap with a neat grey beard is our sovereign lord, His Majesty Edward VII. I'm surprised you haven't seen the king in here before. He often comes to the Jim Jam with some friends to see a *risqué* cabaret. Now unless I'm very much mistaken, His Majesty has gone upstairs to a private room for an assignment with Mademoiselle Juliette or one of his favourite girls from Mrs Sylvano's establishment across the street.'

[Hilary Sylvano's bordello in Great Windmill Street catered to an exclusive clientele which included many foreign dignitaries on their visits to London, including the Kaiser and the Shah of Persia, as well as many members of the British Establishment. Mrs Sylvano planned to close down in 1915 but at the urging of Lloyd George – himself a frequent patron – the house remained open for the benefit of high-ranking Army officers until the end of World War One when she retired to a villa in Tuscany – Editor.]

'Actually, I think that old Tum-Tum' *[Society's private name for the portly monarch – Editor]* 'has the right idea,' added Philip, rubbing his hands together. 'Now, I've booked a private room for myself upstairs tonight and you gentlemen are very welcome to join me. Antonio, I've also arranged for two chorus girls whom Andrew met yesterday to meet me there for a late-night supper and it'll be no problem finding a third girl to join the party.'

Antonio looked at me questioningly but I shook my head and said: 'That's very kind of you, Philip, but I must have an early night.' Then I turned to Antonio and said: 'However, don't let me stop you, *mi amigo*. Becky and Claire are two very jolly girls and you'll have a fine time. Thank you again for a lovely dinner and don't forget to contact me when you next come to London.'

On that note I parted from my friends and took a taxi back home to Kendal Street. To my surprise Teddy Carmichael had not yet gone to bed but was sitting in the lounge in his dressing gown and pyjamas, leafing through the pages of a magazine.

'Are you all right, Teddy? I thought you would be fast asleep by now after such an exhausting day,' I remarked. He looked up and answered: 'Yes, so did I. Truth to tell, Andrew, I'm feeling rather wretched but I simply can't get to sleep.'

'Oh dear, I hope you're not coming down with a chill,' I said whilst I unravelled my bow tie. 'Go to bed, old boy, perhaps you'll be able to doze off now. It's a shame we can't telephone Mrs Dashwood to visit you because half an hour with her would put you in the Land of Nod!'

He gave a wan smile and wished me good night as I walked through to my bedroom. I finished undressing and, after washing my hands and face, I slumped into bed and fell fast asleep.

Sally woke me up as usual the next day. But instead of diving under the cover for a quick fuck, she stood at the side of the bed with a worried expression on her face and informed me that Teddy had looked very poorly when she brought him in his early morning cup of tea.

I pulled back the eiderdown and swung myself our of bed as I sighed: 'Oh dear, he wasn't feeling too well last night. I'll go and see if there's anything I can do for him.'

Well, one look at his flushed face was enough to see that he was feverish. I said: 'Right, you stay there and try to rest. After I've dressed myself, I'll telephone Jonathan Elstree and ask him if he will come round and see you.'

'Thanks, Andrew, I'm so sorry to be such a nuisance,' he wheezed whilst I drew his curtains and said heartily: 'Don't be silly, old boy, it's no trouble. Anyhow, it's in my interest to have you fighting fit for the weekend with Katie Judson and her pals.'

Luckily, Doctor Elstree lived less than a mile away in Gloucester Place and agreed to see Teddy before his first appointment in Harley Street. As I expected, after examining him, the good doctor announced that Teddy was running a temperature of just over 100 degrees. He went on: 'I don't think he's contracted influenza but he still has a nasty summer chill. But if he stays in bed, has plenty of hot drinks and doses himself up with these new aspirin tablets, he should be able to shake it off pretty quickly.'

116

I looked in the bathroom medicine chest and found it to be empty. Doctor Elstree said: 'Ah, that's a pity, because this sort of fever should be treated as quickly as possible. Unfortunately, I don't have any aspirin in my bag.'

'Blast! None of the pharmacies around here open till ten o'clock,' I muttered but he said: 'No, Andrew, haven't you noticed that Nugent's have opened up a branch round the corner in Edgeware Road? Their shops open at eight-thirty so you can go there now and buy the aspirin for Teddy.

'And while you're there you should also purchase half a dozen tubes of Vaseline,' he added with a low chuckle.

'Why should we do that?' I enquired. He promptly replied: 'Because it's a product which you and Teddy always need to keep in stock if I'm any judge of character. Come on, Andrew, put on your jacket and I'll show you where this new pharmacy has opened up.'

'Thank you very much, doctor,' I said gratefully. But when I arrived at the shop I found a *Closed* sign on the door although the lights had been switched on and when I peered through the window I could see a pair of long silk-stockinged legs and a shapely bottom sticking out from underneath one of the cabinets.

I knocked on the door and a buxom lady in her mid-thirties scrambled up from the floor. She walked up to the door which she opened, saying apologetically: 'I'm so sorry, sir, but I'm afraid we're shut. For some reason, our chemist hasn't arrived yet. I'm only an assistant and not allowed to sell medicines so I've closed up to do some stocktaking until Mr Horne arrives.'

Then she looked at me closely and said: 'Excuse me, sir, aren't you Mr Scott from over the road in Kendal Street?'

'Yes, I am,' I said and she gave me a charming smile. 'You don't recognize me, do you? Well, we only met once, about three months ago in the queue outside the Palace Theatre. My name is Edwina Robertson and I was with my best friend, your housekeeper, Mrs Pelgram.'

Now at first I thought it impossible at such an early hour of the day, but I could have sworn I detected the smell of gin on her breath and when Mrs Robertson went on: 'Beth Macdougall was top of the bill that week and when you told us that the bearded young gentleman standing beside you – a Mr Hammond, if my memory serves me right – was her press agent I asked if he could get her autograph for us. Do thank Mr Hammond when you next see him, sir, because, as he promised, signed photos of Miss Macdougall were waiting for us at the stage door after the performance.'

'Your memory does indeed serve you well,' I replied. I was now somewhat concerned because for no real reason my cock began to thicken and push itself out into a tenting bulge in the front of my trousers even though little more than performing my errand of mercy for Teddy was on my mind. Yet again, I failed to understand why my love truncheon was behaving as if it were an autonomous entity with a will of its own. Mrs Robertson told me to come inside if there was anything I needed, saying that so long as I did not need to have a prescription made up, there was really no reason why she could not serve me.

So I entered the shop and she locked the door behind us as I mumbled that all I required was a bottle of aspirin tablets for my friend who was feeling unwell. Mrs Roberston said: 'Ah! We've just taken delivery of a box of Professor Anthony Mulliken's Aspirins. These are a little more expensive, but they're supposed to be the best in the trade. Just a moment and I'll see if I can find them.'

She knelt down and searched through some half-opened boxes. When she triumphantly brought out the bottle she had been looking for, her face was level with the bulge in my crotch. I noticed her eyes widen and felt my cheeks begin to burn as I blushed with embarrassment. I cleared my throat and thanked her as Mrs Robertson rose and pressed the bottle into my hand.

'It's very thoughtful of you to take such trouble for a friend,' she said. Now I was certain that I could smell alcohol when she breathed deeply and added: 'I wish there was somebody who cared enough about me to go out on my behalf if I fell ill. But my sister has moved down to Maidstone and Mr Robertson has been away since April – he won't be back till next February at the earliest.'

I wondered what circumstances had forced her husband to leave the matrimonial home for such a length of time. But I thought it impolite to ask, so I simply nodded my head sympathetically and enquired whether I might also purchase half a dozen fourpenny tubes of Vaseline.

'Yes, of course you can,' replied the buxom lady, giving me a grandstand view of the swell of her ample breasts as she bent down again to open another box. 'Six tubes, did you say? Who's the lucky girl, then?'

And then before I could make any rejoinder to this impertinent question, Mrs Robertson's face crumpled up and her eyes filled with tears as she sobbed: 'Oh, Mr Scott, I'm so sorry, please forgive me, that was the gin speaking. Please don't report me to Mr Horne or I'll get the sack. The fact is that since Herbert, my husband, has been away I've been so lonely and I won't deny that this isn't the first time I've popped a pocket flask into my handbag before leaving the house.'

So she *had* been drinking, after all! I felt I had to speak out and I said: 'Mrs Robertson, forgive me saying so but in a responsible job like yours, that's really most unwise. Suppose you made a mistake and gave a customer the wrong medicine whilst you were under the influence of alcohol? The consequences could be tragic.'

To my discomfiture, she continued crying so bitterly that I moved round behind the counter and put my arms around her shoulders to comfort her, saying: 'There, there, Mrs Robertson, I didn't mean to upset you, though I hope you will consider what I said. But what is troubling you so much? Would you like to tell me why you need to drown your sorrows with drink before you go to work?'

She looked up at me and wiped her eyes. 'I can see that

119

Hettie Pelgram was right when she told me that you were a very kind-hearted gentleman,' she said in a low voice. 'So don't you know what happened to my husband? I thought it was common knowledge in West London as the court case was in all the newspapers. Well, not to beat about the bush, poor Herbert's doing twelve months in Wormwood Scrubs. Oh, he's not a real criminal, sir, but the silly fool fell in with a fast crowd and he tried to pay off his gambling debts by letting himself get involved in some City swindle.

'So, I've been on my own since April and I do miss him, Mr Scott,' she sighed, putting her head against my chest as she continued: 'And I'll be frank with you, I'm a hot-blooded woman and I haven't had a good night's sleep since the day Herbert was arrested and taken to Paddington Green police station.'

Now what was I to do? It was quite obvious that the poor lady was extremely distressed, and I felt it incumbent on me to provide such comfort as I could.

It was difficult to realize what Mrs Robertson wanted. Happily, she made it crystal clear when she whispered: 'The truth is that when I saw you standing outside the shop with a big hard-on between your legs, it brought back memories of how, when Mr Horne asked me to work late, Herbert used to come here at closing time and we would have a lovely little quickie in the stockroom before we went home. Oh, I can hardly tell you how frustrated it made me feel!'

'Well, if there is any way I can help ease this feeling,' I murmured softly. Her eyes lit up as she instantly replied: 'Oh yes, you certainly can, young man. Go into the back of the shop whilst I switch off all these lights.'

The thought of fucking this pretty lady had made my cock swell up to bursting point and I unbuttoned my flies in anticipation whilst I walked through into the stockroom. Seconds later I was standing against the wall with Mrs Robertson's warm body pressed against me. As our lips met, she stuck her tongue deep into my mouth and ground her pussey against my stiff shaft.

We exchanged a passionate kiss. Then she muttered fiercely: 'Ahhh! How exciting to feel a thick prick rubbing against me again! Oooh, Mr Scott, the very idea of having your cock slide into my cunt had made me all wet. Feel my quim and see for yourself.'

I ran my hand up her dress and found out that, after turning off the electric lights, Mrs Robertson had also taken off her knickers because there was no impediment to my fingers slithering into her damp pussey bush. Her body trembled when I began to toy with her clitty and she moaned: 'Oh! Oh! Oh! Quickly now, take off your clothes and fuck me, you dear boy!'

Who could resist such a sweet command? Whilst I tore off my trousers, she too undressed swiftly and in no time at all we were locked in a naked embrace. The underside of my stiff shaft throbbed against her belly as our mouths meshed together and I fondled her large, pendulous breasts.

She reached out, grabbed my palpitating prick and guided me gently inside her. My knob sank between her cunney lips and into the welcoming love channel beyond, the walls of which closed deliciously over my cock, pulling me in deeper and deeper until my chopper was completely engulfed in her squelchy cunt. I drew back and she squealed with joy as I thrust myself into her again. I leaned back against the wall when the happy lady threw her arms around my neck and, with surprising dexterity, wrapped her legs around my waist, locking them behind me so that my prick was fully ensconced inside her sopping cunt.

However, I found the position a trifle uncomfortable and I slid slowly down the wall as she released me from the scissor-like hold in which she had held my frame between her legs. By chance there happened to be a pile of huckaback towels on the floor and I pulled one out to slip under my bottom as Mrs Robertson straddled me and lowered herself onto me, holding my straining shaft lightly in her hand as it slowly disappeared into her dripping shaft.

The raunchy lady settled herself and then, sitting bolt upright, arched her back so that her big jouncy titties jutted out proudly. She purred with pleasure as I reached up and squeezed them in my hands. Then, putting both hands behind her neck, she shook her head, tossing free her dark mane of hair before taking her weight on her hands. She kissed me wetly on the lips, moving her body upwards so that she was almost clear of my glistening cock.

However, she soon lowered herself again onto my throbbing tool. Now it was my turn to gasp with delight when her puffy pussey lips brushed the mushroom dome of my helmet as she slipped her luscious love funnel down the stiffstanding length of my shaft.

'Oh yes!' I panted as the slick, warm walls of her cunney closed tightly around my swollen lust truncheon. I quickly shunted my shaft up and down in swift, short jabs which brought us both to the very brink of ecstasy as I increased the pace to a near-frenzied speed. At every thrust downwards, Mrs Robertson's plump backside smacked against the top of my thighs and her juicy quim seemed to tighten its fleshy grip all the more, as if a suction pump had been applied to the bell-end of my rampant todger.

Suddenly the massaging muscles of her juicy cunney tightened about me in a long, rippling seizure which ran from the base of my cock to the very tip of my knob. This clutching spasm sent me to lust's Elysium: a torrent of spunk burst out of my cockend and creamed the inner crannies of her cunt. Gush after gush of milky jism jetted out of my knob, spurting deep up inside her. She cried out in joy as she achieved a glorious climax.

We shouted our ecstasy together in a delirium of delight. As I continued to pump upwards, Mrs Robertson ground her pussey against my groin while she surrendered to the pleasures of her spend. She crushed her breasts against my chest as my fingers dug into the fleshy cheeks of her generous backside, pulling her forwards against me.

When the exquisite sensations finally subsided I pulled her off my cock and reached down into her sopping sheath, dipping my little finger in our mingled love juices. Then I rubbed the pungent wetness over her succulent breasts, anointing her titties with our cum whilst we recovered our composure after the spirited if unexpected coupling.

Then I recalled the original purpose of my visit. So I hauled myself to my feet and searched for my drawers as I said jokingly: 'Well now, after such wonderful service, you can be sure that my future patronage is assured. But I must be going now, Mrs Robertson, because my poor friend is waiting anxiously for his aspirin tablets.'

She nodded her head, then grasped hold of my cock and gave it a fervent kiss. 'Yes, of course, I quite understand, sir. But if you would like to return here tonight just before we close at seven o'clock, I'll give you a sucking-off you won't forget in a hurry.'

This was a tempting invitation indeed. But I hedged about giving Mrs Robertson an outright acceptance as I felt it would put me under an obligation to form an on-going relationship into which I had no desire to enter. So I grinned: 'I'll do my best to come back for that sounds too good to miss. But I believe I have to see some relations who live in Belgravia this evening so if I'm not here by seven, don't wait for me.'

Let me hasten to add that my reluctance was not on the grounds of involvement with a woman of a lower social class – if nothing else, my previous liaisons will bear this out – but because I have always steered clear of any attachments with married ladies. I have seen several chaps find themselves in the most devilishly awkward situations through their injudicious poking of other men's wives. Furthermore, in this case Mrs Robertson's other half might at the time have been incarcerated in Wormwood Scrubs, but with remission for good conduct, he could well have been released even earlier than the following February.

Nevertheless, I had no wish to hurt her feelings, so I added: 'If I don't turn up tonight, you won't see me for a while as Mr Carmichael and I are going to the country on Friday for a few days. But I'll contact you when we come back to town next week.

'Now before I go, I must pay you,' I concluded. She looked at me in horror but burst out laughing when I quickly added: 'For the aspirins and the Vaseline, you naughty thing. What else did you think I had in mind?'

I walked briskly back to the house and after Sally took my coat, I handed her the bottle of aspirin. I asked her how Teddy was feeling. 'He dozed off a few minutes ago,' she replied and I said: 'Good, let's hope he can sleep off his cold. Now it's a shame to have to disturb him, but he must take two of the pills every six hours. So in about an hour we'll wake him up. Then I want you to make Mister Teddy a hot cup of tea and I'll bring him a glass of water and make sure he takes two of these tablets.'

The salacious little minx looked at me slyly and answered: 'Very good, Mister Andrew, and shall I bring you a cup of tea as well? You look a bit tired, if you don't mind me saying so. Did you run all the way to and from the chemist's shop?'

'Er, yes I did,' I fibbed, but this only caused the impudent girl to break into a fit of giggles. 'Did you really?' she said with obvious disbelief. 'Well, you must have taken the scenic route because it's taken you ever such a long time. Why don't you go and lie down on your bed for a rest? After I've finished my chores we can finish what we didn't really start this morning because of Mister Teddy's illness. Then I'd be grateful if you could give me some advice that I could pass onto one of my girlfriends who has a worrying problem regarding her boyfriend.'

I looked at the cheeky girl and gave a heartfelt sigh as Doctor Elstree's admonition to abstain from rumpy-pumpy for a few days flitted across my mind. I had already disregarded his advice by shagging Mrs Robertson and once I let Sally within sucking distance of my cock I knew full well that I would be unable to resist her advances. However, the idea of a cup of tea did appeal to me, so I resolved not to disobey Doctor Elstree's advice again even as I agreed to Sally's suggestion and walked through to my room where I threw myself down on the bed and awaited her imminent arrival.

Ten minutes later she knocked on my door. As soon as she had closed it behind her, she brazenly began to undress until I held up my hand and said: 'No, don't do that, my dear, I really don't feel all that well myself. I'd prefer to fuck you tomorrow morning rather than now. Did you know that I'm going to the country on Friday. I just hope I'm not coming down with the malady which has laid poor Mister Teddy so low.'

To my great relief, Sally accepted this excuse although she was clearly disappointed whenever I refused her offer to suck me off. 'You could just lie there and rest while I give you a nice gobble,' she pleaded. But I was worried that this would over-tire my cock after the fine fuck with Mrs Robertson so, heaving myself up off the bed, I said: 'No, it's very kind of you, m'dear, but I think it would be best to wait till tomorrow. Now, what's this problem your friend has been having with her young man?

'Nothing too serious, I hope,' I added, concerned that the friend might be Sally herself, for using the cover of a non-existent chum was often the way a girl with a bun in the oven first broached her plight.

Sally must have sensed my anxiety for she gave a chuckle and said: 'No, no, don't worry, Mister Andrew, neither my friend Chrissie nor I are up the spout. Actually, the problem is to do with Peter, Chrissie's boy-friend. Not to put too fine a point to it, he's been having some trouble with his cock.'

For a moment or two I stared at Sally as she began coolly to button up her dress. This had to be a wild coincidence, for surely it was impossible that the girl should have any inkling that I was suffering from a possibly similar complaint which had led me to consult Doctor Elstree in Harley Street. Nevertheless, I gave her a long hard look as I remarked: 'Is he now, poor chap? What's the trouble with him? Can't he get it up?'

Sally shook her head. 'Not exactly, it's what happens afterwards which is causing all the trouble. As soon as he sticks his prick in Chrissie's cunt, he shoots his load.

'She said to me: "It's so terribly frustrating for both of us but I just don't know what can be done about it." Now, Chrissie is one of my closest friends so I wasn't offended at all when last week she asked me if I would let Peter fuck me and see whether a fresh pussey would help him.'

I couldn't help but give a chuckle as I remarked: 'Goodness me, I've heard of share and share alike but isn't that taking things a bit far?'

'Well, *I* don't think so,' she said defensively. 'If it was all right with Chrissie, it was all right with me. And I don't mind admitting to you that I quite liked the idea because Chrissie had told me that Peter had always been a sensitive lover till his prick started to play up.

'Anyhow, he too was keen on the idea when we suggested it to him, so last Friday night he took me out for a drink and then we went back to my place. My Mum and Dad were already asleep upstairs so we went into the sitting room where we quickly locked ourselves in a passionate embrace on the sofa. Chrissie was right about Peter being a sensitive lover: a lovely warm glow ran through me as we exchanged tender searching kisses whilst his hands strayed to my breasts which he gently caressed whilst I ran my fingers through his shiny brown hair. I was soon so aroused that, when his hand dropped down to rub my pussey, I responded by squeezing the bulge in Peter's lap, whispering to him that he should help me undress as I prefer to make love in the nude.

'He didn't have to be asked twice! After he had unbuttoned my blouse and unhooked my skirt, he tore off his shirt and trousers. Whilst he whipped off my knickers, I could see the tip of his uncapped helmet sticking up under the waistband of his underpants. I could feel my pussey getting wetter and wetter as I sank to my knees and tugged down Peter's pants. His thick cock sprang free and I leaned forward to kiss his knob as I took hold of his hot, throbbing shaft in my hands.'

Sally paused for breath and gratefully accepted my offer of a sip of tea whilst I took the opportunity to observe that so far she had said nothing about Peter that would given any cause for concern.

'Ah, but wait a moment, Mister Andrew,' she exclaimed warmly. 'By now I could hardly wait to feel Peter's prick slide between my pussey lips and pound its way into my cunt. So I lay on my back and opened my legs as Peter climbed on top of me. I closed my eyes in blissful anticipation of a delicious fuck – but then I heard Peter choke out a strangled cry of distress. I opened my eyes and saw the poor dear furiously rubbing his previously rampant rod which was now dangling uselessly between his thighs.

' "Relax, Peter, you're just too eager," I said soothingly and grasped hold of his soft shaft. I slid it up and down inside the cleft between my breasts, thickening up his tool again almost immediately. It looked as if all now would be well, but as soon as I released his prick, it began to deflate back into limpness.'

'Dear, oh dear,' I sympathized as my own cock, which had begun to swell up whilst Sally was recounting her story, now also began to lose some of its stiffness. 'Presumably you tried again to keep Peter's prick hard.'

'Yes, of course I did,' sighed Sally, 'although at first he couldn't even raise a smile. But after I sucked his cock and stuck my little finger up his bum, Peter finally succeeded in maintaining a stand and he fucked me as best as he could. I did enjoy the feel of his thick stiffie sliding in and out of my juicy quim, but I don't think his prick was inside me more than half a minute before he spent. I had to finish myself off by diddling my pussey with my fingers.

'Peter apologized to me as we dressed ourselves. I could see how ashamed he was about cumming so quickly so I tried to put him at ease. However, he could not be consoled. When he left to go home, I watched him walk down the path with his head bowed and looking very miserable indeed.

'So there we are, Mister Andrew – Chrissie and I just hope that you can suggest something that Peter can do about his upsetting condition.'

I stroked my chin thoughtfully as I considered this unfortunate young man's problem. He couldn't afford a visit to Doctor Elstree and whilst I am normally loath to proffer advice on such delicate subjects, I ventured: 'Well, let's get one thing clear, Sally. Neither you nor Chrissie should take this apparent rebuff to your pussies personally. From what you say, Peter is genuinely distressed by his condition and I do know that it is not uncommon and almost always passes away very quickly.'

Then I repeated the gist of what I had heard Doctor Elstree say to his partner when we had played a foursome on the course at his golf club. This gentleman had complained to him that his nephew was suffering from a problem similar to that which had afflicted Peter.

'Premature ejaculation is sometimes caused by over-anxiety,' I went on. 'A chap who is worried about his technique might shoot off too quickly because subconsciously he might believe that this will prevent him from revealing his lack of experience.'

'H'm, I see what you mean, but I doubt if that would apply to Peter,' Sally commented. 'He fucked his first girl when he was only fifteen.'

'Yes, you're probably right,' I nodded. 'And it's more likely that he has another common anxiety which dates back to when he was a boy and first began tossing off. He might have taught himself to come quickly to lessen the chances of being found out and now finds it difficult to change. If Chrissie wants to help him, tell her to try the girl-on-top position because that usually delays the man's climax. Then, when he is about to spend, she should roll off and wait till he gains control before impaling herself on his shaft again to complete the fuck.

'But whatever the reason, this kind of problem feeds upon itself. All Peter needs is time to rebuild his confidence. I'm certain that in due course his cock will make a complete recovery.'

'Thank you, Mister Andrew,' said Sally gratefully. 'I'll tell Chrissie what you say and let you know how she and Peter get on.'

'Please do,' I said. Then, hearing sounds coming from the direction of the kitchen, I said to Sally: 'Mrs Pelgram has arrived. Would you tell her to prepare some beef tea for Mister Teddy and I'll go into his room to see how he is getting on.'

Well, I am pleased to record that the intensive nursing combined with Professor Mulliken's aspirin tablets helped Teddy shake off his feverish chill by the next morning. By Friday morning he was fighting fit again, straining on the leash to accompany me to Oxfordshire where Katie Judson and her friends were eagerly awaiting our arrival.

CHAPTER THREE

Country Matters

Katie Judson had sent back a telegram to me, stating that she would meet Teddy and myself at Woodstock Station. Sally woke the pair of us up in good time to catch the mid-morning train from Marylebone Station, Mrs Pelgram served an excellent breakfast and, his appetite now fully restored, Teddy joined me in wolfing down a large plate of bacon, eggs and sauté potatoes and lashings of hot buttered toast, all washed down with cups of hot, strong tea.

Since New Year's Day when I had sworn to give up the noxious weed, I found the smell of tobacco offensive and, being only a light smoker, Teddy had no objection to travelling in a no-smoking compartment. It looked as though we might have it to ourselves until just before our departure when a young, well-dressed couple came in. From the way they squeezed themselves tightly together and burbled sweet nothings in each other's ears, I speculated that they might be honeymooners, a conjecture which was soon proved valid in an astonishing manner.

More of this anon; meanwhile, as the train chugged out of Marylebone, I settled down and leafed through a copy of the *Daily News* whilst Teddy immersed himself in Mr Jason Kelvin's latest mystery thriller *21b Lyttelton Road* which he had purchased at the station bookstall. We gathered speed as we passed through the suburban stations. I was thoroughly enjoying the trip and actually finished reading the newspaper which for some odd reason I never find time to do at home.

Then I rose to my feet. Teddy put down his book, followed me out into the corridor and said: 'Andrew, would you like to join me for tea and biscuits in the restaurant?'

'No thanks, old boy, I only got up to wash my hands,' I answered. Then, before my chum could say anything more, an elderly gentleman wearing a clerical collar walking towards us stopped, peered at Teddy and cried out: 'Bless my soul, unless I'm much mistaken it's young Teddy Carmichael. My dear chap, what a happy coincidence to meet you on the Oxford train.'

Teddy gave him a glassy smile and said: 'Indeed it is, sir. I don't think we've seen each other since you retired down to Winchelsea. How are you and Mrs Ball keeping?'

'Capital, thank you, dear boy,' he beamed. 'Do come and say hallo to her yourself, she'll be delighted to see you. She's in the next carriage having a cup of tea in the restaurant.'

Teddy looked at me in despair as he attempted to find a way out. 'Padre, I don't think you know my chum, Andrew Scott. Andrew, this gentleman is Canon Gabriel Ball who for many years was the vicar of St Peter's in Wisborough.'

'And who happened to be the temporary choirmaster when Teddy sang in the Church choir,' said the Man of the Cloth with a surprisingly roguish twinkle in his eyes.

Canon Ball: how appropriate a name, I thought to myself as I shook hands with the Man of God. 'How do you do, sir? How interesting to know that Teddy sang in the Church choir. He has never mentioned this to me. Has he been hiding his light under a bushel?'

'Well, he was one of our finest boy sopranos but, alas, his career did come to, ah, a rather dramatic end,' chuckled the cleric as he elbowed Teddy gently in the ribs. 'However, I think it best that Teddy himself gives you chapter and verse about the events which led to his expulsion. Now, Mr Scott, I am going to haul this young rascal off to take tea with my wife and you are, of course, very welcome to join us.'

'Thank you, sir, but if you will excuse me, I have some important papers to read before we arrive in Woodstock,' I said, grinning to myself as I turned my head to watch Canon Ball lead my resigned chum to the restaurant car whilst I walked along the corridor to wash the newsprint from my hands.

I must note how impressed I was by the gleaming white pristine towels, the roll of soft crêpe toilet paper and the high standard of cleanliness in the washroom. I returned in good spirits to the compartment where I saw that the shutter had been pulled down over the glass in the door. I guessed that this had been done by the young couple opposite. This was confirmed when I slid open the door to find the pair already spooning, although they immediately broke off the embrace as I passed to take my seat in the corner by the window. Not wishing to embarrass them, I said nothing but gave them a friendly smile to show that I was in no way offended by their kissing and cuddling.

The regular rhythm of the wheels clattering along the rails soon made me drowsy so I put down the newspaper and closed my eyes. However, to the later discomfiture of the lovers opposite, I was merely dozing and not, as they fondly imagined, deep in the arms of Morpheus. I distinctly heard the young chap whisper: 'Look at him, Ellen, he's fast asleep. I'll lock the door, though: the other fellow's probably gone off for a cigarette and a coffee so there's no need to wait any longer.'

'Are you sure he's asleep, Cyril?' enquired the girl softly and Cyril happily assured his beloved that I had indeed nodded off.

Looking back on what followed, I dare say that at this preliminary stage I could have prevented matters from getting out of hand simply by yawning and letting my eyes flutter open. But I readily confess that I was wondering why they were

133

so happy to see me take forty winks, although, from the flushed excitement on Cyril's face, I hardly needed to be Sherlock Holmes to have a pretty good idea of what was in his mind!

So I continued to feign sleep. But about two minutes later, I opened my eyes just enough to see the honeymooners locked into a passionate clinch with Cyril's hands roaming across Ellen's breasts whilst her fingers were fumbling with the buttons of his flies. *Omnia vincit amor*, I said to myself, even to the extent of making these lovers disregard the very real danger of landing up in the police court charged with indecent behaviour – not, of course, that I would have ever pressed charges or given evidence against them.

Nevertheless, I was still startled when I saw Ellen's hand dive into Cyril's trousers and pull out his quivering stiff cock. Cyril writhed in delicious agony as she rubbed his twitching tool vigorously before leaning forward and brushing her lips against his uncapped knob.

'Aaaah! Aaaah!' he gasped wildly as Ellen sucked his prick in between her lips. She bobbed her head up and down until Cyril's hips jerked upwards and he spunked into her warm wet mouth. Then she raised her head slightly and giggled as she licked his cock clean before stuffing his now limp shaft back into his trousers.

'Gosh, that was wonderful, darling!' enthused Cyril as he swiftly buttoned himself up. 'Isn't it marvellous to be able to enjoy ourselves without listening out in case your parents come downstairs to see what we are up to in the sitting room?'

'Yes, dear, but as we're now married, couldn't you have waited until we reached the hotel?' smiled Ellen as she wiped her lips with a pretty lace handkerchief. 'Let's face it, if that gentleman opposite had woken up we wouldn't have known where to put our faces.'

'Very true, my darling, and I promise I'll be a good boy till we're safely in our bedroom at the Randolph Hotel,' answered

Cyril as he planted a huge wet kiss on her cheek.

Then I actually did fall asleep and was woken up by the sound of a knock on the door. Cyril sprang up to release the bolt and Teddy stumbled in and let out a long sigh of relief as he sat down beside me.

'Didn't you enjoy yourself with the Balls?' I asked and he looked sharply at me as I added: 'Oh very well, Canon and Mrs Ball, if you prefer. Teddy, you sly dog, you never told me that you were ever in a church choir, let alone expelled from one! Did Canon Ball catch you playing conkers during evensong? Or did the curate find a copy of *The Oyster* underneath your cassock?'

'Certainly not,' he replied indignantly. Then, lowering his voice, he said: 'If you really want to know the sordid details, I'll tell you all about what happened when we're alone.'

He picked up his book and I stared out of the window, watching the countryside roll by as the Stratford-Upon-Avon express raced on at great speed though the Chiltern Hills towards Oxford which we reached almost ten minutes ahead of schedule. There the honeymooners alighted and we had the compartment to ourselves whilst the engine driver waited for the signal to proceed on to Woodstock.

'Come on, old boy, now you can spill the beans about your excommunication from St Peter's Church,' I chortled. Teddy frowned and said heavily: 'Andrew, I was *not* excommunicated from the Church and I resigned from the bloody choir. I wasn't even fourteen years old at the time and was very much the innocent party who happened to be in the wrong place at the wrong time – or right time, according to how one views the incident which led to my departure.

'It all began after a rumour began around the village that the new curate, a Mr Longford, had been seen shagging the village postmistress on top of a haystack in one of Farmer Gower's fields. "It's probably just idle gossip, Albert," I heard one of the male choristers remark after our Thursday night practice, but Albert replied: "Oh, I wouldn't be so sure about that, Fred. You know what they say, there's no smoke without fire."

'I was dying to know whether or not the story was true and I agreed to take part in a lookout rota organized by George Pearce, the oldest choirboy, to spy on the haystack because like the others, I would have given anything to watch the couple having a fuck. Only a few days before, George had brought the copy of the Reverend Jeffrey Burton's *A Young Person's Guide to Human Procreation* which he had been given by his father for his fourteenth birthday to show us.'

'My Uncle Humphrey gave me a copy of that book when I was at school,' I said reflectively. 'We all called it *Fucking For Fun* as it didn't have all those stupid warnings about wanking.'

Teddy nodded his head and continued: 'Yes, I sent a copy to my nephew only last week. Anyhow, I didn't have to spend any time in Farmer Gower's field because that very night Canon Ball asked me to finish setting up the seats in the Church Hall which was going to be used for a performance of Mr Hutchinson's farce *Lord Bresslaw and the Missing Postal Order* by the village Amateur Dramatic Society. "It should only take you about twenty minutes at most, but I'd be most grateful as they are having a rehearsal there later tonight and it would be useful practice for the actors to pretend there is an audience watching them," he said. As I had nothing special to do, I agreed to help him.

'However, the Canon was called away on some errand and I was left alone in the hall where the stage had been erected and the spotlights set up. It didn't take long for me to arrange the remaining seats and I was about the leave when suddenly the door opened. Who should walk in but Mr Longford and Miss Blake, the village postmistress, an attractive full-figured lady of about thirty years of age.

'I ducked behind the back row of seats and saw Miss Blake extinguish all the gas lights except for one which lit up the front of the stage. "Ruth, I can't help worrying that we might be discovered?" asked the curate. But she shook her head and answered: "No, no, Cecil, we'll be quite safe from any prying eyes here and it will be much more comfortable than the haystack."

'My eyes were out on stalks and my cock stood up as stiff as a little poker as the couple fell into a fierce amatory clinch, tumbling back onto the *chaise longue* which had been placed at the front of the stage.

The curate's hands roved around the postmistress's curvy body, dextrously unbuttoning and unhooking so that she was able to wriggle out of her clothes. I was quite transfixed as I watched him yank down her knickers. When Miss Blake was stark naked, the Reverend Cecil Longford stood up and feverishly started to tear off his own clothes. I immediately noticed the matted bush of hair at the base of his belly from which rose a massive prick that stood majestically up against his tummy, the tip level with his navel.

'Miss Blake smacked her lips as she snaked her fingers around this gigantic shaft and lustily fisted it up and down in her hand. Surely the curate's enormous cock could never fit inside her cunt, I thought to myself as, to my surprise, she now slid down on her knees to lick his knob, swirling her tongue over the wide uncapped helmet to his obvious delight.

'My own little cock was now bursting for relief. Ripping open my flies, I moved forward towards the stage, pulling my throbbing tool out of my trousers and starting to rub it as Miss Blake scrambled up and laid herself face down on the *chaise longue* so that her generous bottom was sticking high up in the air.

'This puzzled me somewhat because, at this early stage, I was totally ignorant about fucking doggie style. But I was soon to be enlightened as, without further ado, Reverend Longford climbed onto the long low chair behind the postmistress. Parting her creamy soft bum cheeks, he thrust his rampant chopper deep into her cunney from behind. I could see his balls jiggling against her beautifully rounded thighs.

'Not only was this sight tremendously exciting to watch but

137

it also made clear to me that any worries about how Miss Blake would be able to accommodate the curate's thick cock were totally unfounded. Of course, her slippery quim naturally stretched itself to welcome his surging shaft and the aroused lady threw back her head to let out yowls of delight as he slicked his rod in and out of her juicy love funnel.

'I was so enraptured by this erotic scene that, still furiously frigging myself, I moved even closer. Then waves of ecstatic pleasure engulfed me as a jet of frothy spunk shout out of my cock and arced through the air to splash on Reverend Longford's heaving bottom. Luckily both he and Miss Blake were oblivious to my presence for they were both jerking and panting away as they gloried in the joys of a mutual spend so I was able to scramble back undetected to my previous hiding place.'

I nodded sagely then enquired: 'But if the couple never saw you, why did this lead to your expulsion – oh, awfully sorry, old boy, *resignation* – from the choir?'

'Ah, well, whilst nowadays it would be easy to keep what I had seen to myself, at that early age I found it impossible to resist spreading the news among all the other boys in the choir. In time, of course, Canon Ball heard about how I had been telling anyone who would listen how his curate had been fucking Miss Blake in the Church Hall.

'Now, unlike many of his fellow clerics, the Canon was not one to thunder in the pulpit against worldly pleasures. As he said to me sternly, there were many worse sins than fornicating, especially as neither Miss Blake nor Reverend Longford were married. Whilst he could not condone their behaviour, it was reprehensible of me to blacken their characters by telling tales out of school. I felt truly remorseful when the Cannon added: "Think on the text I talked about in my sermon last week, *Let he who is without sin cast the first stone*."

'I hung my head in shame and, to cut short the story, I was so ashamed about what I had done that I resigned from the choir the next day. Much to my mother's chagrin, I also refused point-blank to accompany her to church for at least a month afterwards,' he concluded while the train slowed down as we approached our destination.

'What happened to the curate and the postmistress?' I asked and Teddy gave a weak smile. 'Oh, about a year later they married and the last I heard of Reverend Longford was of his appointment as the Dean of St Albans.'

'Well, at least your conscience is clear, for the scandal did nothing to hinder his career,' I remarked as I stood up and pulled down my travelling bag from the overhead shelf. With a great hiss of steam, we glided slowly into Woodstock station.

As promised, Katie Judson was waiting for us on the platform. What a truly delightful girl she was, with her round, heart-shaped face which boasted large, wistful blue eyes, a demure little Grecian nose and a soft, tremulous mouth. Katie was wearing her shiny light brown hair in a prim oval-shaped bun at the back of her head with a tiny fringe of curls at the top of her smooth forehead. She looked quite adorable as she walked towards us with a sparkling smile on her face.

'Hallo, boys! I'm so glad you could both come up to join our party,' she cried as she gave us both a tiny hug and a chaste peck on the cheek. 'It's so good of you to drop everything and rush up here at such short notice. Now, I've brought Hobart with me to look after your cases. There he is, standing by the luggage van. Will you show him which bags belong to you?'

Teddy and I pointed out our valises to the burly footman who wheeled them out on a trolley and loaded them into a small Riley motor car whilst Katie directed us to a gleaming black Austin York Landaulette which was attracting admiring glances from passers-by in the station forecourt. A smartly dressed chauffeur jumped out and opened the door for us to enter the car – *[this 40-horse-power car was a favourite with Edwardian ladies as it had a vast amount of headroom for passengers, a feature insisted on by Herbert Austin who always travelled everywhere with his bowler hat jammed firmly on his head – Editor}* – and Katie said: 'Thank you, Gresham. We'll go straight back to the house but don't drive too quickly as Hobart is following you in the Riley with these gentlemen's luggage.'

As Teddy had never visited Woodstock before, Katie explained that the town derived its name from the Anglo-Saxon *Wudestoc*, 'the woody place', and that there were many rich historical associations. She said: 'Henry II used to come here to visit Fair Rosamund, the sister of Walter, Lord Clifford, and it was at Woodstock that Becket first broke with the King. Richard I came to Woodstock after his experiences in an Austrian prison and John to recover from the effects of signing Magna Charta, whilst Edward the Black Prince was born here and Mary temporarily imprisoned Elizabeth here after the death of their father, Henry VIII.'

Then, as we passed by the Palace of Blenheim which was built by the grateful nation for the Duke of Marlborough, she added lightly: 'The Palace is open to the public and we must take you round it before you leave.'

Gresham drove slowly through the winding country lane to Upper Chagford, then turned into the narrow driveway of Judson Manor which ran for a good half-mile through splendidly kept gardens. These were first laid out by Owen Harrowby, one of the assistants of the famous 'Capability' Brown who designed the gardens at Blenheim Palace.

We skidded to a halt on the loosely laid gravel in front of the impressive front steps of the imposing mansion built some sixty years ago by Sir Michael Bailey, a local merchant banker who had made a fortune in the railway building mania of the 1840s.

The Riley chugged up alongside us while a grave-looking old butler opened the front door and descended the half-dozen steps to welcome us as Gresham jumped out to help Katie out of the car.

'Good afternoon, Miss Katie,' intoned the butler. The sweet girl returned his greeting and went on: 'Fielding, these are the two gentlemen, Mr Scott and Mr Carmichael, who will be staying with us over the weekend. Mr Scott will have the Blue Room and Mr Carmichael the room opposite.'

The old retainer gave us a slight bow and said: 'Welcome to Judson Manor, gentlemen: let me take you upstairs. Hobart will take your cases up to your room and Janet will lay out your clothes.'

Then he turned back to Katie and said: 'Mrs Matlock says that luncheon will be at two o'clock as you instructed.'

Katie nodded her approval. 'Very good, Fielding. Now, where are all the others? I suppose the Hansen twins are playing tennis, Miss Susie is still busy catching up on her correspondence while Mr Pethick is out somewhere with his camera and Mr Dennison is sitting in the drawing-room nursing a whisky and soda!'

Fielding allowed himself a tiny solemn smile. 'Yes, Miss Katie, the Danish ladies are indeed playing tennis. However, the two gentlemen went out together for a walk about half-past twelve but have yet to return.'

'H'm, knowing those two I would surmise they walked only as far as the Dog and Duck,' she commented as she led us into the house. After we had washed off the dust of our journey, Teddy and I went down into the sitting-room to join Katie in a glass of sherry.

'Ah, here are Andrew and Teddy, Susie, let me introduce them to you,' said our hostess to a most attractive girl who was sitting with her on a brown Chesterfield *[a large, tightly-stuffed leather sofa with straight upholstered arms of the same height as the back – Editor]*.

Susie could have been no more than eighteen with long tresses of light gold dusted hair, a cheeky little face with a flawless complexion and luscious red lips that glowed with promise. She was wearing a white close-fitting blouse through which her small but perfectly formed breasts jutted out like two firm apples ripe for the mouth. From the way his jaw dropped as Katie made the introductions, it was crystal clear

141

that Teddy was bowled over by her pretty cousin. I wondered fleetingly whether any pairing-off had already occurred before our arrival. Then two identical slim flaxen-haired girls dressed in tennis shirts and short white skirts came into the room.

'Alexa, Erika, did you enjoy your game?' asked Katie. 'Come in and meet our two new arrivals, Andrew Scott and Teddy Carmichael. Gentlemen, I am sure you cannot wait to meet these ravishing blonde beauties who are my lovely Danish chums, the misses Alexa and Erika Hansen from Copenhagen.'

I rose to my feet, overwhelmed by the vivacious twins who, I was shortly to discover, had been blessed with sunny natures as appealing as their pretty faces with their laughing blue eyes, delicate little noses and rosebud mouths which were simply made to be kissed.

'Good afternoon, ladies,' I stammered. Alexa, whose eyes were perhaps a touch larger and of a slightly lighter blue than those of her sister, answered in an impeccable if slightly accented English: 'Good afternoon, Mr Scott. Would you and everyone excuse us for fifteen minutes? We just need to wash and change after our game.'

Moments later Ian Pethick and Jack Dennison, the other two male members of the party, arrived back from (as Katie had correctly surmised) the Dog and Duck. Ian was a handsome wiry fellow of about my age with a rather serious disposition, whose main hobby was stamp-collecting although later, at the luncheon table, Katie whispered to me that Ian had the reputation of being a superb cunnilinguist. Anyhow, his family had been friendly with the Judsons for many years. Jack was slightly older, having just celebrated his twentieth birthday, and was more broadly built, with a bronzed complexion and twinkling grey eyes.

Both these gentlemen appeared amiable enough. During the course of conversation I discovered that Jack Dennison had palled up during his time at University with Bentleigh Barnes-Williams, an old school chum of mine who was number three in the winning Cambridge team in the Boat Race four years ago.

'I rowed a little myself at Cambridge and stroked my college team,' remarked Jack. 'But I wasn't in the same class as Tony even though he tried to coach me and the rest of the chaps from the river bank. He would always hammer home to us that long slides coupled with a long swing, leg work, steadiness and a firm grip would secure victory.'

'How very true, Jack,' murmured Katie with a wicked grin. 'And this would be very good advice for other sports besides rowing. I would like to meet this gentleman, he is clearly a man who knows what he is talking about.'

'Ah, but it's actions not words that are important,' Jack murmured as Fielding opened the door and announced that luncheon was ready to be served. I was delighted that Katie took my arm and we led the others into the dining-room where we enjoyed a splendid repast of vichyssoise soup, poached salmon, wild roast duck with chestnuts and orange sauce served with a variety of vegetables and potatoes. This was rounded off with ices and fresh fruits, including some early peaches from the greenhouse, all washed down with an excellent Haut Barsac white wine.

'We really should now take a constitutional after that delicious meal,' remarked Ian Pethick. But the two Danish girls pleaded exhaustion after their strenuous game of tennis, whilst Teddy and I demurred on the somewhat spurious grounds that we were tired after our journey from London. Katie suddenly remembered that she had some household chores to perform.

However, Susie said that she would be pleased to stroll round the gardens with Ian and they left us shortly afterwards. Then Alexa and Erika announced that they planned to go upstairs to rest in their room. Teddy made his way to the library where he planned to sit down and finish the novel he had been reading on the train, although he added that he would probably fall asleep inside ten minutes.

'Oh, poor Andrew! It looks as if you're going to be left all on your own,' exclaimed Katie. I hastened to say that this did not trouble me and that I would take the opportunity of writing a short letter to my parents. 'Then, perhaps, we could take a short walk together,' I added hopefully and was delighted when Katie readily assented to this proposal, saying that she would meet me in the hall at half-past three.

On this note the party broke up. I sauntered into the drawing-room and was about to sink down into a comfortable armchair when I noticed a copy of *The Sporting Life* lying on a small table. I remembered that I had quite forgotten all about the wager I had made a couple of days before after bumping into Sid Cohen, the Jim Jam Club's bookmaker. I picked up the paper and scanned the results from Kempton Park race meeting. I let out a triumphant burst of laughter and punched the air in glee as I read that I was now twenty-five pounds to the good because What a Cracker had won the Headline Stakes by a short head from Fletcher's Folly, the horse on which Teddy Carmichael had laid five pounds to win with Sid. I was sorry for my pal although he enjoyed a generous enough allowance from his father and would scarcely miss the fiver. Still, I made a mental note to buy him a slap-up dinner at the Jim Jam when we returned to London.

However, as I was about the throw *The Sporting Life* back onto the table, I saw that the newspaper had been covering three sheets of notepaper which had also been left lying there. Now, I would be the first to agree that only cads read other people's correspondence but in my defence I had at least to scan part of the letter to find out who had written it. And furthermore, in this case I can state in all honesty that, once I had ascertained the identity of the scribe and gathered the gist of his raunchy essay, it really didn't matter a jot whether or not I read the uninhibited epistle through to the bitter end.

I glanced underneath the final paragraph and discovered that the author was none other than Ian Pethick and that he was writing to a close friend named Cuthbert about the jolly time he was having at Judson Manor. In fact, as will later be recorded, this letter was never sent but I reproduce it here as it forms a minor but important part of this story. After enquiring about the health of Cuthbert's family, Ian's letter continued as follows:

I must tell you, old chap, that I am having a spiffing time at Judson Manor. Katie is a marvellous hostess and her entrancing young cousin Susie is an equally delightful companion. Sadly, though, neither Jack (the other fellow who had already arrived for the weekend) nor myself have found them responsive to any suggestions of hanky-panky. This is true of the other girls here, Alexa and Erika from Denmark, two extremely pretty twin sisters with whom Katie chummed up during her year at a finishing school in Switzerland. They are also pleasant enough and speak excellent English, but I don't have too much in common with them as their prime interest seems to be in outdoor sporting activities.

Nevertheless, I had a jolly time yesterday afternoon when I decided to walk down to the village. Upper Chagford is not a particularly exciting place although the Church is well worth a visit, being a quite interesting study in the development of Norman architecture from Early English and Decorated to Perpendicular.

I had taken my pocket camera with me and, after taking some photographs of the Church, I began to amble back to Judson Manor. However, when I reached the outskirts of the village I noticed a small shop all on its own with a selection of cameras in the front window. I stopped and looked again in surprise because it was strange to find a specialist establishment in such a quiet rural setting as distinct from an urban High Street.

Perhaps the place is run purely as a hobby by an enthusiast, I said to myself and, curious to know more, I decided to go in and buy a roll of film for my new Kodak

Brownie. There were no sales staff inside the shop and, strangely, there were no goods of any description on the empty shelves nor on the counter behind which the back wall was covered by a huge blown-up photograph of the Eiffel Tower.

Then my interest was aroused further when a girl cam through a red-curtained doorway at the back of the shop and said to me brightly: 'Good afternoon, sir, how can I help you?'

'May I have a roll of film for a Brownie camera, please?' I answered as I tried not to stare at this extremely pretty girl whose glossy tresses of ash-blonde hair fell down to her shoulders. She was dressed in a dark skirt and a white open-necked blouse which exposed enough cleavage to make my prick stir inside my trousers, especially when she leaned down to pick up a magazine which was lying on the floor.

'I'm sorry, sir, we don't sell photographic films,' she said politely. I scratched my head in bewilderment as I repeated blankly: 'You don't sell photographic films. That is very odd, if you don't mind me saying so, for I doubt there is any other camera shop in the entire country that doesn't stock any films.'

'Ah, but you see we don't sell cameras either,' she informed me. 'If that's what you were looking for, then I am sorry to have wasted your time. Really, the door should have been closed as we don't usually open for business until seven o'clock in the evenings unless a regular customer make a prior appointment beforehand.'

Now, of course, I was totally intrigued and I asked: 'Well, if you don't sell cameras here, what on earth do you sell?'

This question clearly amused the girl for a smile played about her lips as she replied: 'Are you just passing through Upper Chagford, Mister, ah—'

'Pethick, Ian Pethick, and no, I'm not just passing

146

through the village. I'm staying at Judson Manor for a few days,' I said. She revealed a set of dazzling white teeth as she laughed out loud and said: 'I'm delighted to make your acquaintance, Mr Pethick, my name is Kitty Campbell. Now, in answer to your question, this domicile is not really a shop, it is a house of pleasure run by Madame Antionette Defarge of Paris.'

I was utterly flabbergasted by her answer, for in my wildest dreams I could never have envisaged the existence of a house of pleasure run by a Frenchwoman in the heart of the English countryside. However, when Kitty saw the expression of disbelief on my face, she said: 'We don't advertise ourselves to all and sundry, Mr Pethick, but only to discerning gentlemen like yourself. You do like girls, I take it? I can't imagine that such a masculine-looking fellow as yourself could be a nancy boy.'

'No, that's true enough, I've been called a few names in my time but never that,' I chuckled. Kitty moved round the counter and took hold of my arm as she enquired: 'Have you any film left in your camera, Ian?'

'Yes, I can take three more photographs,' I nodded. She winked at me and said: 'Well, whilst you're here why don't you take a snap of me? Don't worry, we never charge for the first visit.'

And before I could say yea or nay she pulled down a blind over the front door and locked it before turning back to me and saying: 'Now you just take off your coat and make yourself comfortable whilst I change into something more suitable.'

She disappeared behind the red curtain whilst, as if in a trance, I slipped off my coat and jacket and clicked open the shutter of my Brownie. Within a couple of minutes, Kitty came back clad in only a negligée of such fine silk that it was almost transparent. It was evident that she was wearing nothing underneath the flimsy

147

garment because I could make out the outline of the rounded globes of her bottom as she executed a graceful pirouette in front of me. My cock now tented out my trousers as I observed her large nipples push out provocatively from their translucent covering.

Kitty glanced down at the bulge between my thighs as she smoothed her hands over her breasts and said softly: 'Ian, does your girlfriend have sensitive titties?' Unable to answer, I simply stood stock still as she moved closer towards me and whispered: 'I wonder if they are as sensitive as mine. Wouldn't you like to find out for yourself?'

She giggled while she pulled me over to a chair and pushed me down upon it. Then she unbuttoned the negligée and let it slip from her shoulders as I threw my left arm around her waist. With my right hand I fondled Kitty's jutting bare breasts which were topped by nut-brown nipples which I tweaked between my fingers.

'Suck my titties, Ian,' she moaned and I eagerly complied, nibbling gently on one nipple and then the other as the luscious wench squirmed in delicious agony. Now, in my experience, rubbing a girl's titties is a prelude to the main event but Kitty needed no further stimulation as, shaking all over, she spent with a happy yelp of ecstasy.

'Now it's your turn, my dear,' breathed Kitty as she slid off my lap and knelt down in front of me. She quickly unbuttoned me and pulled out my prick which she held in both hands. She proceeded to wash her talented tongue all over my knob before closing her lips over my purple bell-end and sliding my thick shaft down her throat in one fluid gulp. Then she eased back, licking the underside of my shaft until she reached my balls which she sucked into her mouth, swishing them around before releasing them to lick all the way back up to my knob.

This was a sucking-off par excellence for Kitty now

eased her lips over my helmet and slowly took my shaft between her lips whilst her hands busily circled themselves around my balls, gently caressing the wrinkly pink sack as her head began to bob up and down over my throbbing tool. My own hand automatically shot out to the back of her head as she gobbled more of my quivering cock into her mouth. Her tongue darted along the sensitive underside and I jerked my hips upwards as she sensually sucked on my chopper. Thrilling spasms of pure delight swirled through my body until I croaked out that I was about to cum.

With her mouth still filled with my hot, wet cock, Kitty nodded. She carefully squeezed my balls as I shot a stream of creamy jism down her throat. A wonderful orgasmic wave of release swept through me as she swallowed every drop of my gushing emission, draining my shaft of its salty essence. Then Kitty pulled my fast-deflating shaft out of her mouth and, raising her head, she smacked her lips and said: 'Wasn't that nice, Ian? Now how would you like to fuck my little wet cunney? I've a free afternoon tomorrow and it won't cost very much, only six guineas for two whole hours.'

Frankly, I was tempted to take up Kitty's offer. But I'm sure that Katie had made arrangements for her guests so I reluctantly declined, although I paid her a sovereign to let me take some naughty photographs of her which I promise to show you, although I will have to develop the film myself: I certainly cannot take it to Boots!

I must close now as Jack Dennison and I are off to the Dog and Duck for a drink before luncheon and the other two gentlemen who are making up the numbers for the weekend festivities have just arrived. I could be wrong but I have a sneaking feeling that Katie is carrying a torch for one of them, a chap named Andrew Scott.

Give my best regards to your parents and—

Here the manuscript ended, no doubt when the aforementioned Jack Dennison had called Ian away to the public house. With a chuckle, I placed the sheets of the letter back on the table where they had been so carelessly left by its author.

Well, the old saying might observe that eavesdroppers will never hear good of themselves but I was buoyed up to read that in Ian's opinion Katie was keen on me. Teddy, too, would be very happy to know that Susie had not succumbed to the charms of either Ian or Jack. I heaved myself out of my chair and strolled towards the door which I opened to find none other than Ian Pethick standing in front of me.

I gave a short cry and stepped back a pace as I gasped: 'Hallo there, Ian. Goodness, you startled me! I thought that you were taking a stroll in the garden with Susie.'

He gave a thin smile and replied: 'That was indeed the plan. But I have a slight headache and when your chum Teddy Carmichael rolled up to join us I made my excuses and walked back to the house.'

'Oh dear, I am sorry to hear that, headaches can be an awful drag,' I said sympathetically. 'Let me go upstairs and get you a pain-relieving pill from my bathroom. I have a bottle of Professor Mulliken's Aspirins which had been specially recommended to me.'

'Thank you, Andrew, but I think I'll just sit in the drawing room and sleep it off,' he sighed. 'Anyhow, Teddy and Susie won't miss me. Two's company and three's a crowd, you know, and I think those two are already very attracted to each other. I've no wish to play gooseberry.'

'That's very considerate of you,' I remarked but Ian shrugged: 'Not really, old boy. Susie's a scrumptious girl but Jack and I both fancy those gorgeous Danish twins.'

'They *are* quite enchanting,' I agreed and was about to move away when Ian said: 'Ah, just before you go Andrew, did you come across a letter of mine in the drawing-room, by any chance? I really am getting absent-minded but I put it down somewhere and I'm damned if I can find it anywhere.'

150

'Well, I just went in here for a nap and haven't looked for any letter,' I said disingenuously. Deciding to take a short stroll in the bright sunshine, I walked away from him to the front door. Katie was standing in the driveway talking to Hobart and when she saw me she waved to me.

'Andrew, do come over here,' she called. She quickly finished giving her instructions to the driver who saluted her and made his way to the motor houses *[the word 'garage' was not in general use until after the First World War – Editor]* as I approached her and remarked that it must be quite a responsibility for her to run a big house like Judson Manor on her own.

'Yes, as far as that goes, I'll be pleased when Mama returns. But Fielding and Mrs Matlock have been here for many years and they've been very helpful,' replied Katie, wiping her brow as she added: 'Gosh, isn't it warm?'

Then her face lit up and she said eagerly: 'Andrew, I have a super idea. Let's cool off by having a swim in the stream which runs behind the woods about half a mile over there on your right.'

'I would love to go for a swim with you, Katie,' I answered with genuine enthusiasm. But then I grimaced and went on: 'So long as you can lend me a bathing costume, that is, because I foolishly did not bring one with me.'

'I might be able to find one of my father's but I doubt if it will fit you, he's much broader round the waist – though I suppose you could tie a belt around the costume,' she said with a twinkle in her eyes. 'But there's no reason why we can't swim in the nude because there's a bathing hut on the bank of the stream and the area around it is fenced off on both sides of the water as well as being hidden by the trees.

'Of course, I'll understand if you're too shy,' she continued teasingly.

I grinned at her and answered: 'Just lead on, Katie, just lead on.'

'Why don't you go on by yourself? I'll join you in about ten minutes as I need to have a final word about dinner with Mrs Matlock. I'll bring down some towels for us.'

'Very well,' I said. Katie escorted me round the side of the house to a small path and pointed me in the right direction. The route was simple enough to follow and the sun was shining so fiercely now that I was glad of the shade afforded by the trees. When I reached the fence which Katie's Papa had erected to ensure privacy for bathers, I noticed that there was a wire-mesh gate in the fence which, surprisingly, had been left open. But I decided not to shut it as Katie would soon be following me down to the bathing hut which I could see about fifty yards ahead of me.

As I approached the stream I heard a girlish cry coming from behind a copse of bushes – which solved the mystery of why the gate had been left open. Perhaps Susie had come down here for a swim but had slipped and was lying on the ground in distress, so I hurried towards the bushes to see if I could be of assistance.

However, there I discovered that Susie was not in the slightest distress and needed no help from me nor anyone else! For that nubile young lady was lying naked on a pair of pink bath towels, engaged in a sensual embrace with an equally naked Teddy Carmichael whose right hand was jammed firmly between her sculptured thighs. It was abundantly clear that he was finger-fucking Susie's pussey, thus causing the squeals of ecstasy to escape from the luscious girl's lips.

Now, if I had not known that Katie would shortly be arriving on the scene, I might have simply walked away. But thinking it best that she did not view this erotic exhibition, I thought it advisable to warn the naughty couple of impending danger so I made my presence known by a discreet cough.

'My God! Somebody's spying on us!' gasped Teddy. The pair of them scrambled hastily to their feet and covered themselves with the towels as I stepped out and confronted them.

'What the blazes—' my pal began but I held up my hand

152

and said quietly: 'I must apologize for the interruption, but I think you should know that Katie will be down here in about five minutes.'

'Will she? Oh, thank you for letting us know, Andrew,' said Susie as she gathered up her clothes which she had left strewn across a deckchair. 'Are you and Katie going to have a swim? We've been in for a dip and the water's lovely and warm.'

'Yes, I'm looking forward to cooling off,' I said as I watched her and Teddy throw on their clothes. Then I waved goodbye to them and went inside the bathing hut to undress. I took a large bath towel from the pile on the beach and wrapped it around my waist as I stepped back out into the blazing sunshine. There was still no sign of Katie so I wandered down to the edge of the stream and stepped gingerly into the water which felt so refreshing that I peeled off the towel and threw it back onto the grass. Then I waded into the water until it reached my navel and splashed around by myself until Katie made her appearance.

'Sorry to have been so long, I can't wait to join you,' she called out. Then she disappeared inside the hut from which she emerged a few minutes later stark naked with a towel across her arm.

I shuddered with excitement as my eyes roved over the full glory of Katie's beautiful nude body as she stood on the bank of the stream. Her finely formed features were framed by shiny loose tresses of silky brown hair that fell down across her rounded snowy white breasts. These breasts were tipped with rosebud-red nipples set in dark pink circles. My eyes travelled down to her flat, smooth belly, so cunningly dimpled in the centre with its sweet little button. My cock was already standing thickly upright in the water as I gazed at the rich triangular growth of curly pussey hair between her thighs.

'Is the water warm, Andrew?' Katie called out. I gave the adorable girl the thumbs-up sign, and with a happy squeal, she ran straight into the stream. We frolicked about happily whilst

153

I sang to Katie a verse of Mr Godfrey Hendon's old music hall song:

'Isn't the water wet?
Isn't the sky ber-lue?
Nobody here but us
And nothing but things to do.
Don't the girls look grand,
Shapes you'll never forget,
Ain't the winkles wonderful
And isn't the water wet?'

After ten minutes or so I led Katie out of the water by her hand and we lay on our towels, drying ourselves in the bright sunshine. Katie made us pillows from Teddy and Susie's towels and she breathed: 'There's no great rush to get back to the house. We can stay here undisturbed for at least another half an hour.'

'That will be lovely but I do hope that we will be undisturbed,' I said. Then I explained how I had inadvertently stumbled across Susie and Teddy and interrupted their love-making.

'Oooh, tell me all the juicy details,' she laughed. Not surprisingly, my cock began to thicken up again whilst I recounted what I had seen, especially when I saw Katie's hand slide downwards to let her fingertips play along the edges of her pink-lipped pussey.

My voice trailed off as our eyes locked together. Then Katie rolled over towards me and kissed me passionately on the lips. I had time only to choke out: 'Darling Katie,' before our mouths melded together and my arms were wrapped about the gorgeous girl. It was as if her soft trembling body had been especially fashioned for my touch. She arched to it, sighing and gasping as I responded with my fingertips, my lips and my tongue.

Caught up in an exquisite whirl of sensation, I found myself

154

lying on top of the delectable creature, my cock pressing insistently between her thighs. But she whispered: 'Andrew, don't make love to me here, wait till later and we can spend the whole night together. But if you would like to bring me off with your fingers like Teddy did with Susie . . .'

'I have an even better idea, my sweet girl,' I murmured whilst I slid down Katie's beautiful curves, caressing her firm breasts and kissing her horned-up wine-red nipples which hardened so sensually under my nibbling. Down and down I went until my face was buried between her legs and my lips were only inches away from her thick fleece of curly chestnut pussey hair.

'Are you going to kiss my cunney, darling? No boy has ever done that before,' she said softly as she pushed my head deeper into her crotch, opening her legs and then clamping her thighs around my head with a long contented purr as I began to lick her swollen pussey lips. My tongue swished around her quim, delving, probing and sliding from the top of her long crack to the base of her juicy slit, lapping up the fragrant love juice which was already trickling out of her honeypot.

As Mark Twain once remarked, cunnilingus, like artichokes and whisky, is an acquired taste, but from my very first experience (at the age of sixteen with a scullery maid) I have always thoroughly enjoyed muff-diving and, without wishing to boast, I quickly acquired some skill at this noble art. Katie moaned with joy and shivered all over when I stopped licking her quim to pay homage to her clitty which had hardened up like a tiny nut.

I took her love bud between my lips and nibbled its fat, unsheathed base with my teeth. When I began lashing her clitty with my tongue her throbbings grew into twitches, the twitches into tremors and the tremors into convulsions until she shrieked out her delight as the delicious sensations of a shattering cum swept through her. Fleetingly, it struck me that even anyone walking outside the perimeter of the fence would hear Katie's cries of passion. But I could not have cared if the

155

entire domestic staff of Judson Manor had suddenly appeared in front of us when I hauled myself up and Katie clutched my pulsating erection in her hands.

With a salacious giggle, she wound strands of her silky hair to make a web around the base of my shaft whilst stroking it slowly and feeling my tool throb under her gentle touch. Then Katie moved her head forward and licked my wiry pubic bush, moving her face slowly from side to side, enjoying to the full the voluptuous grazing of my rock-hard stiffie against her soft cheek.

Katie looked up at me and smiled as she moved her lips across the smooth wide dome of my knob and kissed the minute 'eye' out of which some drops of pre-cum moisture had already started to ooze. I let out a tiny gasp as her tongue circled my helmet, savouring the taste of cock as she drew my shaft between her generous lips.

'H-a-a-r!' I gasped as Katie's warm fingers fondled my balls whilst she sucked my shaft with an intense verve. I instinctively began to slew my prick in and out of her willing wet mouth. She slurped happily on her fleshy lollipop until I felt the sweet surge of seed was about to burst out of my cock and I panted: 'Katie, I can't hold back, I'm going to cum!'

But the dear girl did not attempt to pull away. She continued to suck my cock until, with a rasping growl, I shot my load and spurted a potent fountain of hot sticky jism down Katie's throat. She greedily gulped it down and licked and lapped my trembling tool until she had milked it dry.

'My word, what an abundant spend, Andrew!' she commented after pulling back her head and releasing my now flaccid todger from its succulent prison. 'Oh, I do love sucking off a nice thick prick like yours. I'm sure I could happily gobble it for a full hour but of course this will never happen because all you men squirt off too quickly.'

'I read somewhere that the Marquis de Soveral *[the Portuguese ambassador during the first decade of the twentieth century and a great favourite of fashionable London Society —*

Editor] can keep going for at least half an hour, though that could just be a rumour.'

'Very probably,' agreed Katie as she planted a farewell kiss on my shrivelled shaft. 'No girl I know has ever met any man who can last longer than ten minutes once their pricks are being sucked.'

She snuggled herself into the crook of my shoulder and we lay silent for a while until I said: 'Dearest, did I hear you say that till this afternoon, no man had ever tongued your divine little pussey?'

'That's quite correct,' concurred Katie. 'Does this surprise you? Don't worry, though, you brought me off beautifully, Andrew, just as well if not better than Alexa and Erika or indeed any of the girls who have ever lapped up my cunney juice.'

I looked down at her and said with interest: 'So both the Danish girls have licked out your honeypot, have they?'

'M'm, on several occasions,' she answered brightly. 'And the best time was when they did it together when I visited them in Denmark last year. If you like, I'll tell you what happened, although it's rather a rude story.'

'I'd love to hear all about it,' I said eagerly.

Katie laughed as she replied: 'Well, all right then, but you must promise not to mention it to anyone this weekend. Now, Alexa and Erika live with their parents near the port of Odense on Fyn Island and on my first visit there two years ago, the girls took me for a long walk around the town one afternoon to show me the cathedral which was founded by King Canute – you know, the man who tried to command the waves – in the eleventh century.

'Anyhow, when we arrived back at their house, they suggested that we refresh ourselves with a sauna. Now, I had no idea what a sauna was and they explained that it was a Scandinavian style of bath which I would find very invigorating – and this turned out to be true, although not in a manner I could have expected!

157

'So, on their instruction, I went upstairs to my room and undressed. Then I slipped on a dressing gown and a pair of slippers and walked down with Alexa and Erika (who had also undressed) to the bottom of their garden where there were two large log cabins. They ushered me into the first which was furnished only with a single bench, with a wooden stove in the middle of the floor which generated a considerable amount of steamy heat.

' "Take off your dressing gown and lie down on the bench, Katie," said Alexa as she whipped of her robe and walked naked to the stove onto which she ladled a pannikin of cold water. "This will make the room even steamier but the heat opens the pores and lets all the grime of the city seep out of the skin."

'Obediently, I sat naked alongside an equally nude Erika. Alexa came across and laid herself down on the wide bench with her head in my lap. "You don't mind if I use your lap as a pillow, do you, Katie?"

' "No, not at all," I stammered as she made herself comfortable with the back of her head lying on the tops of my thighs. Then she passed her hands over her high pointed breasts which were topped by enormous tawny nipples which soon swelled up even larger as Alexa played with them, twisting the rubbery bullets between her fingers. However, I pretended not to notice what she was doing and I must say that, despite the proximity of her face to my pussey, she made no move to interfere with me in any way.

'We sat chatting for some fifteen minutes and then, at Alexa's bidding, we put on our robes and slippers and padded across to the second, larger cabin some twenty feet away. Now, the floor of this cabin had been partially scooped out and a miniature tiled swimming pool had been built.

' "Brr, it'll be freezing!" I remarked, but without any hesitation, the girls slipped off their robes and plunged straight into the pool. Erika shook her blonde tresses away from her pretty face and called out: "Do join us, Katie, you'll find the experience most invigorating."

'Gingerly I stepped into the pool but Erika was right – for once I braved the cool water I felt wonderfully clean and fit and I didn't notice the cold as we splashed around for about five minutes. Then we climbed out and dried ourselves with lovely soft bath towels which were hanging on pegs in a small open-doored area at the back of the cabin where there were two beds, one double and one single. The girls told me to lie down and rest on the smaller mattress while they shared the larger one.

'Swathed in my towel, I was now so totally relaxed that I was soon dozing peacefully. But after a while I thought I felt a soft palm rubbing against my crotch. I must be imagining it, I said to myself, but the rubbing became more insistent. I opened my eyes to find that both the girls had removed their towels and were kneeling naked at the side of my bed and it was Erika's long fingers that were tracing their way through my curly bush of pussey hair. Perhaps I should have stopped them but, frankly, the sensations were delicious and I made only a token attempt – which was easily repulsed – to prevent Alexa pulling off my towel and leaving me lying there completely naked.

' "You naughty things, stop that at once," I murmured as Alexa caressed my breasts and tweaked my titties whilst Erika rubbed her palm against my moistening pussey and whispered how she would like to stick her tongue up my cunney and suck on my clitty till I came off and flooded her face with love juice.

'However, it was Alexa who climbed up on the mattress, positioned herself between my legs and began lapping on my pouting pussey lips. But little did I know what was being planned whilst Alexa licked up and down my quim and brought me up to a fever-pitch of unslaked desire – for the wicked little minx didn't put her tongue inside my crack and left me desperate to achieve a climax.

' "Aaaah! Aaaah! I want to cum!" I cried out as I twisted

and bucked under this teasing tongue. To my relief I heard Erika answer: "It's all right, Katie, I'll make sure you spend."

'Then I opened my eyes and saw to my amazement that Erika had strapped on around her waist a leather belt that at its front sported a shiny wooden affair painted in pink and shaped exactly like a thick stiff cock, complete with two carefully fashioned rubber-covered balls. I had never seen anything like it before and was a tiny bit frightened as Alexa gave way to her sister who pressed her soft curvaceous body on top of me as she kissed me passionately on the lips.

'Alexa must have seen that I looked scared for she said encouragingly: "Relax, Katie, this ladies' comforter has been modelled on the prick of none other than the Danish military attaché in London, Colonel Schmiechel, who fucked Erika after a party at the Embassy last year. She made a plaster cast of his cock and had her dildo fashioned to his measurements by Zwaig et Cie, the famous Parisian manufacturers of saucy novelties."

'For some reason, this reassured me. I parted my thighs to allow Erika to insert the knob of this imitation shaft between my pussey lips and I must say that this had the desired effect! I swung my legs around her waist and locked my ankles together behind her back. Then she leaned forward, the dildo started to slide right into my sopping slit and I gasped with delight as Erika fucked me with this smooth wooden cock. Every time she thrust forwards it rubbed against my clitty and at the end of each thrust, when the dildo was fully embedded inside me, it nudged itself into the deepest recesses of my dripping honeypot and sent electric sparks of ecstasy shooting through my body.

'At the same time I was shocked to see Alexa, who was now kneeling behind her sister, slide her hand between Erika's legs and work her finger under the dildo to begin frigging her sister's cunt. This lewd sight helped bring me to the boil very quickly and from the beaming smile on her flushed face, I think that Erika and I climaxed together.

'When we had regained our senses, Erika offered to strap the dildo around my waist so that I could fuck Alexa, but I declined because, although I won't say that I don't enjoy an occasional tribadic encounter, I definitely prefer good old-fashioned fucking!' Katie concluded firmly with a sensual smile on her pretty face as she looked down on my straining shaft which had recovered from its previous delicious exercise and was standing up stiffly between my thighs.

'Well, that was a most stimulating story,' I said hoarsely. Katie giggled as she gave my throbbing tool a loving squeeze before she scrambled to her feet and said: 'Come on, Andrew, I would love to have you slide that thick stiffie into my cunney but we had better get dressed and return to the house before Fielding sends out a search party for me.'

I sighed as I took hold of her proffered hand and hauled myself up. But Katie was right and it would have been extremely foolish to take the chance of being caught *in flagrante delicto*, especially when there would soon be an opportunity to romp the night away with the gorgeous girl in the comfort of a soft warm bed.

We arrived back at Judson Manor in time to join the other guests for tea. Despite the excellent luncheon, the swimming and other more intimate exercises had given me enough of an appetite to do justice to Mrs Matlock's slap-up repast of hot scones, fresh strawberry jam and cream, a fine choice of tomato, cucumber and cheese sandwiches and – the *pièce de resistance* – a still warm apple-and-plum cake straight from the over.

'My goodness, old boy, anyone would think you haven't eaten anything since breakfast,' remarked Teddy as I tucked into my second slice of cake while Susie sat down at the piano and entertained us with her dashing rendition of *Parthenia*, one of Smolask's best-loved waltzes. We applauded politely and then, as she played the opening bars of a familiar old music hall chorus, Jack Dennison frowned and said: 'Now what the devil is the name of that song? It's on the tip of my tongue but I can't quite recall it.'

'Isn't it *The Hound That Caught The Pubic Hair*?' said Ian Pethick innocently which made us all laugh heartily as he went on: 'No, actually it's Stan Satterthwaite's theme song, *Naughty Little Maudie*. Don't you remember seeing him sing it at the Holborn Empire a couple of months ago?'

'Of course it is!' Jack exclaimed and to prove that he did remember this popular ditty, he sang in a rich tenor voice:

'Oh you don't know Maudie like I do,'
Said the pretty little bird on Maudie's hat.
'I could tell you some stories about Maudie
About many strange places she's been at.
By the sea, by the shore,
There's lot's of fun in store,
But always wipe your feet upon the mat!'

'You have a splendid voice, Jack,' said Erika admiringly. 'But I do not understand the song. What is the connection between a girl being naughty and wiping feet? Perhaps you would please explain this to me?'

Jack could not help smiling at the puzzled expression on the pretty blonde's face as he answered: 'Don't fret, it isn't your command of English that is at fault. The fact is that there's no connection at all. You see, Stan Satterthwaite is one of those so-called "eccentric comedians" who rush on stage dressed in weird costumes and bawl out nonsensical songs.'

'I agree with you, but Stan Satterthwaite's songs have very catchy tunes even though the lyrics are no better than nursery rhymes,' remarked Susie as she thumped out a stirring introductory melody on the piano. 'Have you heard his latest, *You Can't Give Daisy Any Winkles*? No? Well, it goes something like this—

'You can't give Daisy any winkles.
You can't give Dora any shrimps,

162

Gertie's a sport
But don't give her port
You'll never know what she'll begin!'

The two Danish girls laughed as Susie sang the chorus. Then the rest of us roared out *Let's Go Down The Strand, Burlington Bertie* and my own particular favourite *The Girl I Love Is Up In The Gallery*. Whilst I sang the lilting sentimental melody I caught Katie's eye and looked meaningfully at her which caused a delightful reddish tinge of colour to appear on her so-kissable cheeks.

Not that Katie could ever be classified as one of those empty-headed girls who deliberately give the impression of helplessness to attract a man. In my opinion, one of the most remarkable evolutions of recent times has been the rebellion of women against remaining second-class citizens denied the same educational and political rights as men – and whilst I deplore violence as a method of argument *[the militant Suffragettes had begun their campaign of civil disobedience to demand the right to vote – Editor]*, the women's suffrage movement has my total support.

As I said warmly to a recalcitrant acquaintance in the bar at the Jim Jam Club only the other day – he was bemoaning the fact that women no longer seemed to know their place – it is precisely those women who take an interest in economic, political and social affairs outside their own narrow horizons who make the best wives and lovers.

'Such girls are capable of making fair judgements, of ceding a point as well as enforcing a demand, and unless they are very stupid chaps, their male friends will not sigh for the "foolish little things" of other days,' I concluded sternly. The fellow slunk away, unable to counter my reasoning.

Be that as it may, it is undeniable that I would have been smitten by Katie whatever her views on the matter! Certainly, I sprang to my feet like a shot when she asked if anyone would care to come to the art gallery on the mezzanine floor and see the new pictures the Judsons had bought on their recent visit to the Continent.

Frankly, I was far from unhappy that none of the other guests took up her invitation, which I suspected was not because of any lack of interest in art. But it was clear that Teddy and Susie wanted to slip away by themselves whilst Ian and Jack no doubt were keen to find out if any pairing off could be arranged with Alexa and Erika.

I said as much to Katie as we climbed the wide sweeping staircase and commented that it was a pity that these young men were heading for certain disappointment. But Katie looked at me with a smile on her face and said: 'Oh, I wouldn't be so sure about that, Andrew. Alexa and Erika do not confine themselves to tribadic encounters. Indeed, I am sure they would have grown out of these feelings long ago if they had only been given the opportunity to meet more young men by their parents who brought them up very strictly. So I don't think that Ian and Jack will be too disappointed because, as far as the girls are concerned, they want to make up for lost time!'

'I know just how they feel,' I murmured in Katie's ear as I slipped my arms around her and pressed my hands to her breasts as she opened the door to the gallery.

'You *are* an impatient boy, Andrew,' she scolded me with a giggle. But she responded by feeling behind her and rubbing her hand against my thickening prick. 'Don't work me up now, there's a dear, because somebody might come in. Besides, I'm looking forward to being fucked by you tonight and I'm sure you wouldn't want to spoil my appetite.'

'No, of course not, Katie,' I said humbly. 'Please forgive me. Now I promise I shall behave like a monk whilst you show me the most interesting pictures in your parents' collection.'

And I kept my word whilst we strolled through the gallery – which did not prove too difficult a task for I genuinely enjoyed looking at the wide variety of paintings hanging on the whitewashed walls. There were canvasses by contemporary

British artists of the calibre of Spencer Gore, D. S. McColl and William Nicholson. But my eye was most taken with two rich portraits, placed on either side of a window, which had been executed in the style of the Dutch Old Masters, one of a bright-eyed young girl and the other of a gentleman dressed in the fashion of an English Cavalier.

'These pictures are first class, Katie. Who it the artist? A pupil of Rembrandt or Rubens?' I remarked as I peered at the pictures. But Katie shook her head and said: 'No, the artist is a Dutchman named Anton Dourlein and he's not from the seventeenth century but is still very much alive. So are the models, even though he has painted them in historical costumes. The man is his cousin Henk who bears a strong resemblance to Prince Rupert of the Rhine, the nephew of King Charles I who fought for the King during the English Civil War.

'Since he learned about his feats at school, Anton has been fascinated by Prince Rupert who was a skilled engineer, chemist and artist. He developed the mezzotint process of engraving on copper by scraping and burnishing the roughened surface and devised a new method of painting colours on marble which, when polished, would be permanent, as well as inventing a new, more powerful gunpowder and a quadrant for measuring stellar altitudes at sea.'

'Really? Well, I've definitely learned something this after-noon,' I said and resisted the temptation to kiss Katie's perfectly shaped red lips. 'I never realised that Prince Rupert was such a polymath. And what about the girl? Is she also a relation of Mynheer Dourlein?'

Katie gave me a roguish smile. 'Not exactly. At the time she was only seventeen and the youngest daughter of a wealthy merchant who lived next door to Dourlein in his little home town of Maastricht,' she answered as we sat down on a small sofa in the centre of the sparsely furnished room.

'And now?' I queried and she shrugged: 'Well, Bernice is still the youngest daughter of the wealthy merchant but the last

I heard of her was that she now lives with Dourlein in Amsterdam!'

'There is certainly something to be said for taking up an artistic career, especially if one has the benefit of even a modest independent income, as there never appears to be a shortage of pretty girls who are ready, willing and able to be bedded either before or after their portraits have been painted,' I mused thoughtfully. I slid my arm around Katie's waist as she continued drily: 'Yes, Anton Dourlein has a jolly life because women are queuing up to sit for him and he gets well-paid for his portraits, however they might turn out.'

'So how did your father acquire these two pictures?' I asked. Katie shook her head. 'He didn't buy them, I did when we went to Amsterdam last April for the wedding of Princess Helena of the Netherlands to Sir Trewin Cheetham, a distant relative of my mother. Well, the day after the wedding my father returned to England. But my mother and I decided to stay on till the weekend to see more of the city and take a trip out into the country to see the tulip fields in full bloom.

'Like many other guests who had come to Amsterdam for the wedding, we were staying at the Kresnapolsky Hotel. The next day, whilst we were having breakfast, Mrs Flora Murdoch, the elegant and charming wife of the American textiles magnate whom we had met at the wedding reception, came across to our table and kindly invited us to accompany her to the Rijksmuseum to see Rembrandt's *The Night Watch* and all the other superb masterpieces which are on display there.

'In fact, it was whilst we were looking at a group of pictures by modern Dutch artists that Mrs Murdoch suddenly exclaimed: "Heavens alive! Just look at this picture of a picnic party, ladies, I've been put in it!"

'I studied the painting more closely and, sure enough, I could see that Mrs Murdoch *was* portrayed in a scene which showed a group of people sitting around a table that had been set up by the side of a small country road with two motor cars parked under the shade of a nearby tree.

166

' "So you have, Mrs Murdoch, and it seems you all spent a very pleasant afternoon," I observed and she chuckled: "Yes, I'm sure I would have had a jolly time, my dear, except that this gathering never took place. I've never met any of the other people in the picture and I doubt whether any of them are actually acquainted. However, the artist and I are old friends, I met him on my first visit to Europe about ten years ago when my husband commissioned him to paint my portrait. His name is Anton Dourlein and his work is very popular just now, but when we were first introduced, he was a struggling young artist who had yet to achieve recognition. Come to think of it, I remember now he told me that he would ask people if they would pay a small fee to be shown in his paintings – all he needed was a photograph from which to work – and clearly my husband must have agreed to his proposal."

' "What a clever idea," my mother remarked but Mrs Murdoch said: "Well, maybe so, although it's not original. Anton told me that Rembrandt used a similar scheme before he began work on *The Night Watch*. Almost all those men in the picture paid him to be in it and those who paid Rembrandt the most are shown at the front of the painting!"

'Anyhow, we stayed in the Rijkmuseum till one o'clock and then Mama insisted that Mrs Murdoch join us for luncheon. We took a horse-drawn cab back to the hotel and as the head waiter was about to show us to a table, Mrs Murdoch gasped: "My word, this is quite unbelievable! That gentleman sitting by himself by the window dressed in a grey suit with a flower in his buttonhole is none other then Anton Dourlein!"

'I looked across at the handsome broad-shouldered gentleman and said: "What a coincidence! Mama, why don't you ask him if he would care to take lunch with us? I presume that like most Dutchmen he speaks good English."

'Mrs Murdoch protested that this would be an imposition, but I take after my mother who enjoys the company of artistic folk like actors, painters and writers and we soon prevailed on Mrs Murdoch to invite Anton to sit at our table. Well, to cut short the story, he did indeed speak perfect English and his easy manner and good humour (despite having been 'stood up' for luncheon by a potential client) made an excellent impression on my mother and myself. So much so that when he suggested to my mother that I should sit for him, all she replied was that, unfortunately, there would be no time for me to do so as we were leaving for home in a few days' time.

' "But I would enjoy sitting for Mr Doulein this afternoon, Mama," I pleaded with her. "At least this would give him time to take some photographs and make some preliminary sketches for a portrait he could then paint after we have left Amsterdam."

'Mama still looked doubtful but Anton finally won her over by settling for what I thought was a ridiculously small fee of fifty sovereigns to paint my portrait. "I'll just go upstairs and pack a change of clothes," I said excitedly and less than half an hour later Anton was escorting me through the door of his studio just off Dam Square. I went upstairs into his bedroom to change and when I pulled off the last piece of underwear, I stood in front of the long wall mirror and wondered whether Anton would admire my firm breasts and the curly thatch of chestnut pussey hair between the tops of my snowy white thighs.

'Now I must confess that I had been very naughty because the clothes I had brought with me were hardly suitable for a portrait of a demure young lady! First I slipped on a camisole fashioned from the softest Irish linen, trimmed with lace, through which the generous swell of my breasts and long pointy nipples were plainly visible. To complement this flimsy garment, I put on a pair of close-fitting French knickers made from the same sheer fabric which accentuated the contours of my tight curvy bottom. I completed my wardrobe with the choice of my best white silk stocking held up by frilly baby-blue satin garters.

'As I checked my reflection in the mirror, I cupped the full roundness of my breasts in my hands and my nips swelled up to stand out like two tawny bullets. It occurred to me how silly it would be to hide these sexy underclothes under the frock which I had brought with me, even though I had deliberately chosen the dress because of it low-cut bodice which revealed a daring amount of cleavage. True, I had known Anton for only a very short time, but I guessed that he would make no complaint if I tripped down the stairs with my bare breasts bouncing up and down under my virtually transparent camisole and my bottom cheeks jiggling enticingly, covered only by my skin-tight knickers.'

'I'll *bet* he made no complaint,' I said thickly, pulling at my trousers in a vain attempt to make more room for my rock-hard cock which was pushing up uncomfortably in my lap.

Katie looked down at the bulge between my legs and patted my shaft gently with her hand. A smile began to play about her lips as she said: 'Andrew, I don't want you getting over stimulated because you'll need all your strength later tonight. Perhaps it would be best if I stopped here and continued the story another time.'

'No, please don't do that, darling,' I begged her and added hopefully: 'I find this tale extremely exciting but I won't spend unless you pull out my cock and bring me off with your hand.'

The sweet girl wagged her finger in mock reproof as she giggled: 'Don't work me up, you naughty boy! All right, I'll quickly finish telling you what happened with Anton and then I shall go upstairs and get ready for dinner. Now, where was I? Ah yes, I opened the bedroom door and called out to Anton that I was ready for him and, as I expected, he was far from upset when he watched me walk slowly down the stairs in a state of *déshabillé*.

' "You look truly magnificent, Katie," he said in a husky voice as he picked up a large stick of charcoal. "Now go and sit on that stool over there and we'll begin."

'For an hour or so I sat stock still as Anton worked assiduously. But then he threw down his pencil in disgust and groaned: "Katie, I am sorry but you will have to change into a less revealing set of clothes. I simply cannot carry on like this – it is absolutely impossible for me to concentrate on your face when my eyes keep wandering up and down your exquisite figure."

' "Do they?" I said in as innocent a voice as I could muster. "Well, in that case, it's my fault for wearing an outfit which has distracted you. But let's have a break now and I can decide which of my dresses to wear."

' "Very well," he agreed. I sat on an easy chair and watched as he brewed a pot of coffee and then produced a bottle of Schnapps from his sideboard. The fiery liquor blended so well with the coffee that I was soon feeling totally relaxed, and when Anton again brought up the subject of what I should wear whilst he sketched me I smiled him and said: "Would it really solve the problem if I covered myself up? Whatever dress I wear, I suspect you might still be thinking of how I might look *au naturel*."

'He did not reply but his dark eyes brightened as he slid his arm around my waist and murmured: "You know, some years ago when I first studied in Paris, the great Toulouse-Lautrec told me that even the most talented artist could never capture the essential spirit of a woman on canvas unless he first made love to her."

' "That sounds very much like Toulouse-Lautrec who, despite his other physical deformities, was reputedly exceedingly well-endowed," I rejoined with a giggle as a delicious tingling sensation spread out all over my body from my fast-moistening pussey. "I don't know how much truth there is in that maxim but I have a feeling that I am about to find out."

'Anton smiled and leaned forward to kiss me. I responded immediately, sliding my tongue between his teeth as his tongue probed inside my open mouth. My senses began to dance when his hands moved under my camisole to fondle my bare breasts and, tearing myself away from his passionate embrace, I gasped: "Wait a minute, I must be careful not to

170

crease these clothes or Mama might suspect something. So I had better take them off."

'It only took a few seconds for me to undress and in no time at all I was standing in front of Anton in the nude. With a cheeky grin on my face, I said: "There you are, Mynheer, all the goods have been unwrapped so you had better make a purchase before they are wrapped up again."

' "Oh, have no fear, I shall buy everything on offer! My only worry will be not to spend too much too quickly!" he retorted wittily as he pulled me down upon his lap and whispered in my ear: "Katie, I've been willing this moment from the very first instant I saw you."

'The randy artist slipped his hands back onto my breasts, pressing them together and showering them with noisy wet kisses. Then Anton buried his face in my soft rounded spheres and lunged at my quivering nipples which instantly hardened under his lips. An erotic shiver sped through me when he nipped each one lightly between his teeth. Then he squeezed my breasts together, taking both titties in his mouth simultaneously, flicking each engorged cherry with his tongue before sucking them in a strong, powerful rhythm which caused me to moan with delight.

'My blood was now up. Climbing from Anton's lap with my breasts smeared with a mix of perspiration and saliva, I slid to my knees in front of him and when I tugged open the buttons of his fly out sprang his thick, stiff cockshaft. I held the huge pulsing tool in my hands but, though Anton might well be disappointed, I was determined not to break my rule of never making love on meeting a man for the first time. However, it was with no little regret that I informed him that he could tit-fuck me although I would appreciate it if he too would undress so that I could enjoy the sight of his manly frame.

'Happily, Anton took this news in good part. To his credit, he did not sulk or attempt to persuade me to travel further than I wished to go – not that he could have persuaded me to do so – unlike some foolish young men I have had to deal with in the past who refuse to believe that when a girl says "no" she really means it.

'Anyhow, I must admit that, as he rapidly undressed, it took all my resolve to resist temptation when I gazed on his broad shoulders and deep chest which was lightly covered with curly hair – though it was his thick cock which most attracted me as it stood majestically upright between his muscular thighs.

'I dropped to my knees in front of him and, taking hold of his blue-veined boner, I fisted my hand at a great pace up and down his hot smooth shaft whilst I planted a big wet kiss on the wide ruby helmet. Then I pressed my breasts together and slid his throbbing love truncheon into the cleft between my firm, jutting titties.

' "Go on, Anton, cream my titties with your spermy jism," I urged him, wrapping my fingers even more tightly around his cock as I continued to frig his palpitating prick. Now, I don't wish to boast, but no man has managed to hold back for more than a minute of this bosomy massage. Sure enough, very soon Anton moaned as, in a tumultuous climax, he let fly a tremendous fountain of frothy seed and sprayed a white necklace of sticky spunk across my breasts.

'With one hand I jerked his quivering shaft from side to side and with the other I smeared his copious emission over my rubbery nipples. Then I pulled his prick upwards and sucked his knob whilst he spurted the final gush of seed into my mouth.'

My own cock was now aching for similar treatment and I observed acidly that at least Anton was given the chance to relieve his frustration. Katie peered down at the tenting protrusion in my trousers and wrinkled her brow as she said thoughtfully: 'Unlike someone else, you mean? Now, I wonder who you can have in mind?'

'There's no prize for getting the right answer,' I replied as Katie shook her head, repeating that patience was a virtue and my prick would only have to wait a little longer for relief.

'Now, where was I?' she continued. 'Oh yes, Anton slumped

back into a chair, exhausted from this thrilling little sexual exercise and his cock started to droop and hang limply downwards over his balls. But his eyes shone as he watched me massage my breasts with his cum until they gleamed wetly in the soft lambent sunlight and he let out a tine groan as I languorously licked each finger in turn, savouring the salty tang upon my lips and tongue.

' "I trust there will soon be an opportunity for us to continue where we left off," he sighed whilst we dressed ourselves. "Is there no chance of seeing you again before you leave Amsterdam?"

' "Probably not," I said sadly as I walked across to his easel and stared at the bold sketch of my face which Anton had drawn before we let our emotions interrupt his work. "I'm afraid you'll have to finish this portrait from memory."

Katie sighed and pointed to the picture which was hanging on the wall in front of us. 'About six weeks later Anton sent that painting of his young mistress to my mother with a letter saying that he hoped she would accept it in lieu of a portrait of her daughter. Actually, his note is tucked away behind the picture and you can read it for yourself.'

She led me across to the wall and pulled out from the back of the frame a sheet of paper which she passed over to me. As Katie had said, after apologizing for not producing the commissioned work, Anton went on: *You must forgive me, but I will not be able to portray Miss Judson in a manner which will reflect her radiant beauty and charm unless she is able to sit for me again in person.*

'It's terribly vain of me to keep this note,' she remarked as she folded it back in its hiding place. 'But who knows? A letter from Anton Dourlein might one day be almost as valuable as one of his pictures!'

[Alas, the paintings of Anton Dourlein [1869–1938] would not have proved to be good investments. His 'chocolate box' portraits quickly fell out of favour with the public sector after

173

*the rise of the post-Impressionists and the Cubists such as
Chagall, Picasso and Miro – Editor].*

'Now I am going to my room for a rest,' announced Katie as
she guided me towards the door. 'We'll dine at half-past seven
and if all goes according to plan, I don't see why we shouldn't
have an early night!'

She kissed me lightly on the cheek and made her way
upstairs. Being curious to know how Teddy had fared with
Susie, I descended the staircase to see if my pal had returned
from wherever he and his *amorata* had hidden themselves.
However, none of the other guests were to be found downstairs
so I trudged back up to my room where I contemplated a nice
long soak in a warm bath before I changed into my evening
clothes.

But this was not to be, because as I walked by the large
room shared by Alexa and Erika, the door was flung open. I
almost jumped out of my skin when one of the pretty blonde
Danish twins, dressed in a pink dressing gown, scurried out
and grabbed me by the arm as she exclaimed: 'Ah, I thought I
heard someone coming up the stairs. Andrew, have you a little
time to spare please? Erika and I need the services of a strong
young man.'

I was so startled (and flattered) that I allowed Alexa to pull
me into her room where I was stunned to see Jack Dennison
standing stark naked against the wall. Erika, who was wearing
only a pair of brief lace knickers, was kneeling down in front
of him with her hands holding his huge erect cock and her lips
just inches away from his purple mushroom bell-end.

'Hello, Jack, I'm sorry to interrupt but Alexa grabbed hold
of me on the landing just now and insisted on dragging me in
here,' I stammered. But he was so eager to have his cock
sucked that he cheerily waved away my embarrassment as he
gasped out: 'There's no need to apologize, old chap. I'm truly
delighted to see you because I can't pleasure more than one of
these frisky little fillies and Alexa will be left out in the cold

174

unless we can find her a juicy thick prick.'

'Well, I agree that would be grossly unfair,' I grinned as Alexa slipped her robe off her shoulders to reveal her lissome naked body to me. 'But what about Ian Pethick? Surely he—'

'Ah, poor Ian! He is too much of a gentleman – if such a thing is possible. Did you not hear the front door bell about half an hour ago? The vicar of Chagford came round to ask for a donation for the village summer fête. Ian gave him a half-sovereign and his kindness impressed the vicar so much that, when Ian told him of his interest in brass rubbings, he invited Ian to go with him straight away for a look at the seventeenth century plaques on the floor and walls of his church! We listened to all this from the landing and heard the reverend gentleman say how happy he was to meet a fellow enthusiast. To our amazement, Ian accepted his invitation, being too polite to disappoint him!'

'Good heavens! I can't say I would have taken that course of action,' I remarked whilst Jack nodded his agreement and declared: 'Neither would I. Really, if you look at the situation in another way, he was guilty of being impolite to Alexa's pussey!'

Alexa smiled at this light-hearted remark and rejoined: 'Maybe Ian is too polite for his own good, but I have not taken any offence. For, though I say so myself, I know that he would have far preferred to poke me rather than go traipsing down to the village with the vicar! Anyhow, there should be plenty of time for lots of rumpy-pumpy later this evening.'

Then she looked straight at me and added: 'However, I don't feel like waiting till then, Andrew. So unless you have any objection to fucking me, Ian's loss is your gain.'

I gulped nervously as she took my hand, sat me down on the bed and instructed me to undress. For what should I do? Notwithstanding the fact that Katie was expecting me to behave like a wild stallion after lights-out – so much so that she would not even bring me off even after telling me the exciting story of her encounter with Anton the artist – she might well take a dim view if she discovered that in her absence I had shagged one of her best friends.

But if the spirit was willing, the flesh was weak and there' cannot be many men who could have refused to fuck such a deliciously nubile girl as Alexa. And as if her voluptuous charms were not enough to turn my head, whilst I was pulling off my shirt I looked up to see Jack Dennison having his cock palated by Erika who was lustily working his knob in and out of her mouth, clearly determined not to lose contact with the rigid fleshy shaft.

'Please don't let me disturb you,' I called out to him as I fumbled with the buttons of my trousers.

'You're damned right I won't!' he retorted as he placed his hands on Erika's tousled blonde head and muttered: 'That's the way, you dear girl, suck out all my spunky cum!'

She replied to Jack by grasping hold of his thick prick in her hands, frigging the shaft as hard as she could whilst she teasingly titillated the smooth wide crown with the tip of her tongue. Then Erika ran her lips up and down his pulsating shaft before opening her mouth wide and gobbling in almost the full length of his tool, bobbing her head to and fro as she slid her hand underneath his scrotum to cradle his balls in her palm.

Meanwhile, Alexa had helped me undress and luxuriant strands of her flaxen hair fell over her shoulders as she bent down and rolled down my drawers. With a hoarse growl, I pulled her head towards mine and she grabbed my stiff shaft greedily in her fist as we kissed, our tongues entwining as our eager bodies pressed together.

We crashed together onto the bed and I grabbed a pillow which I stuffed under Alexa's bottom so that her thighs and cunney were positioned at a good angle for my bursting boner as I moved between her legs. Alexa squeezed my shaft, capping and uncapping the rounded domed knob as she guided my cock between her yielding pussey lips deep into her clingy wet crack. My hands moved to her breasts and covered her nipples whilst I slid my trembling tool in and out of her squelchy slit at a slow yet steady pace. The blonde beauty sighed with delight as she relished the sensations afforded by my throbbing truncheon inside her juicy honeypot.

I continued to fuck the gorgeous girl at this relatively gentle pace until she gasped: 'Oh, Andrew, how lovely! I've cum twice already! Now fuck me hard, you big-cocked rascal!'

Nothing loath, I increased the tempo until I was slamming my prick in and out of Alexa's squishy quim at a great rate of knots and my balls slapped against her bum-cheeks as she clamped her legs around my ribs.

'Ahhhh! Ahhhh! Ahhhh!' she panted as with one hand I rubbed her swollen nipples between my thumb and forefinger whilst the other snaked behind her. Alexa squealed wildly when I jammed the tip of my little finger into her bum-hole as we moved into the final lap of a wonderful poke. Her body writhed out of control as my cock drove home at an ever-increasing speed until I exploded into her and a stream of frothy jism poured out of my prick into her saturated cunt.

Exhausted from this delicious exercise, I rolled off the delectable damsel who swung round and gave me a big hug as she said: 'Oh, thank you so much, Andrew, Katie told me that she was sure you would be a first class lover.'

My jaw fell open as I looked at her in astonishment. 'Katie told you *what*?' I said incredulously.

'Well, Katie *is* a most conscientious hostess. She wanted to be sure her guests were all having a good time before she would think of enjoying herself,' Alexa replied defensively. 'So she was very pleased when, during tea, I told her that Erika and I were happy to be entertained by Ian and Jack tonight. "Splendid!" she said, "I don't have to worry about Susie because she has clearly fallen for Teddy Carmichael and I'm very much looking forward to being fucked by Andrew's lovely big cock."'

I was initially staggered by this uninhibited reply, although when I considered her explanation more carefully, I realized there was really no cause for me to be so shocked by her frankness. As I said to myself, if there had been a rôle reversal of the sexes I would have thought nothing of confiding such a complimentary description of Katie's pussey to Teddy – but even in this first decade of the twentieth century, gentlemen still find it difficult to accept that women have similar needs and desires to their own!

In the meantime, Erika had long since finished milking Jack's balls of their cargo of creamy jism. He was now leaning against the wall in a state of happy exhaustion with his limp shaft dangling over his thigh, whilst Erika was busying herself pouring out small glasses of a colourless liquid from a bottle with a black label on which was printed a silver coat of arms.

'What's this drink? Surely it's not a malt,' said Jack as she handed round the glasses. But one sniff was enough for me to be able to inform him that we were being given kummel, a liqueur based upon the humble caraway seed which was very popular in Central and Eastern Europe.

'I'm sure you'll like it,' I said to Jack who clinked glasses with me before downing his drink in one swallow.

'M'mm, it's a very pleasant tipple,' he commented as he held out his glass for a refill. 'I don't expect it's available round here but I must order a dozen bottles from Harrods when I go down to London next month.'

Rather unwisely, Erika poured Jack out second and third refills, after which he stood up, walked somewhat unsteadily to the door and announced that he was going back to his room for forty winks before dinner.

'Hadn't you better put on some clothes first?' I suggested. But he shook his head and said: 'Not worth the bother, old boy, I'll only have to take them all off again to have my snooze. Don't worry, my room is only across the landing and no one will see me. Anyhow, what matter if one of the maids does catch a glimpse of my todger? If she hasn't seen a cock before, then it's high time she did.'

'That's true enough,' I laughed as Jack staggered out and closed the door behind him. Then I looked at Erika in some surprise when she slithered across the bed to lie next to me. 'Why don't we follow his example and have a rest for half an hour before getting ready for dinner?' she murmured as she snuggled herself into the crook of my shoulder. 'There's plenty of room if we all cuddle up together.'

This is like a dream come true, I thought to myself, as I lay on my back with each of my arms wrapped around a ravishing young blonde. Yet there was a proverbial fly in the ointment – I could see from the glint in Erika's ice-blue eyes and the way her hand was edging nearer and nearer my groin that she wanted to do more than just relax for the next thirty minutes.

Of course, in other circumstances I would have not wasted more than a few seconds before mounting the luscious lass. But I had already succumbed to her twin sister's salacious charms and in only a few short hours Katie would rightly be furious if my cock failed to give full satisfaction. On the other hand, it would be churlish to humiliate Erika by rejecting her advances even if I were able to summon up enough will-power to resist the temptation to fuck this sweet girl.

So shiny beads of perspiration were already forming on my furrowed brow as her fingertips brushed against my shaft which automatically began to stir. I clenched my teeth as I desperately tried to think of a solution to this pressing problem. Dear reader, I am sure it will come as no surprise to you to learn that I was about to take the line of least resistance and fuck Erika when my reverie was shattered by a series of sharp knocks on the bedroom door.

'Come in,' called out Alexa as I dived beneath the eiderdown. I heard her exclaim: 'Hallo there, Susie! What can we do for you?'

'Not a great deal, I'm afraid,' replied out unexpected visitor. 'Unless you have brought some strong pain-killing pills with you. Poor Teddy has a frightful headache and I can't find the box of aspirin tablets which he brought with him.'

Reluctantly, I hauled myself up and my presence naturally surprised Susie who thought I was already neatly paired off with her cousin. I said to her sheepishly: 'Ah, you'll find a bottle of Professor Mulliken's aspirins in the drawer of my bedside table. If Teddy swallows two of these now he will hopefully be fit again by dinner time.'

'Thank you, Andrew,' she replied and I mumbled: 'I'd be grateful if you would say nothing to Katie about finding me here. There's no time now to explain but there is a good reason why—'

'Of course there is,' Susie cut in frostily. 'And it isn't very difficult to know precisely what that reason is – honestly, you men! Look, I'll just give those aspirins to Teddy and then I'll come back here and you can explain to me exactly why you are in bed with two naked girls – though I can't see why any further explanation is needed!'

She swept out of the room. I groaned: 'Oh God, that's torn it. Katie will have my guts for garters, if you understand this colloquial phrase.'

The puzzled twins were familiar with the idiom but they were curious to know why Katie should be so cross with me. 'She's not a jealous kind of girl and the three of us have often shared boyfriends,' said Erika. I smiled wanly as I confessed to her how I had promised Katie that I would save myself for a bedroom romp with her that night.

'Well, if that's all that's the matter, you should certainly beg her forgiveness for breaking your word,' Alexa declared roundly. 'But you can also inform her that your cock will have fully recovered from poking me this afternoon. As the English proverb puts it, practice makes perfect.'

'Yes, I suppose you're right,' I said slowly. 'Only I have my doubts as to whether we can persuade Susie to see things in the same light.'

'Let me speak to Susie,' advised Erika as she winked at her sister. 'I think I can persuade her not to tell Katie about your little indiscretion.'

'Can you?' I said hopefully. She chuckled: 'Don't worry, Andrew, you can safely leave it to me. I'm sure that she'll agree to keep our secret after I've finished with her.'

Perhaps I should have guessed what Erika's plan might be, but in all honesty I hadn't a clue as to what she had in mind when Susie returned and informed us that Teddy had taken his pills and was now sleeping peacefully. Then she perched herself on the foot of the bed and continued: 'Now then, Andrew, what do you have to say for yourself?'

I drew breath but Erika chipped in before I could speak and said brightly: 'Oh, never mind about him, Susie, did you know that Jack Dennison has a truly enormous cock? It isn't the longest I've ever seen but the shaft is so thick that I could hardly cram it into my mouth when I sucked him off.'

'Is that so?' said Susie with interest. 'Well, I can tell you that Teddy Carmichael is also very well-endowed although his prick isn't particularly thick. But he was poking me quite beautifully this afternoon until the poor boy suddenly contracted a blinding headache and neither of us even managed a single cum before we had to stop.'

Erika tsk-tsked sympathetically and said: 'What a dreadful shame! But then, even the best cocks can prove to be unreliable and I've always said it's just as well that we girls don't have to rely on men to bring us off or we would be permanently frustrated.'

'What do you mean by that?' demanded Susie. Erika lifted her arms to sweep some stray tresses of hair from her face, an action which lifted her breasts, and she stroked her prominent nipples as she replied: 'Take off your clothes, come here next to me and I'll show you exactly what I mean.'

'My dear, I think I already have a fair notion of what you have in mind,' said Susie drily. But nevertheless she kicked off her shoes and stood up as she started to unbutton her skirt.

Of course, my cock began to thicken up whilst I watched the pretty girl disrobe and this process was speeded along by Alexa who reached down to stroke my swelling shaft under the cover of the eiderdown. Susie undressed quickly, although even before she rolled down her knickers I had a throbbing hard-on as I feasted my eyes on her delectable naked figure. The Danish girls murmured their admiration of her slender, lithe body whilst she caressed her proud uplifted breasts before moving her hands down to the base of her flat dimpled belly and the thatch of brown curls which covered her Venus mound.

Alexa and I squeezed up to make room for her as she slipped into bed beside Erika who replaced Susie's hands with her own as she smoothed her palm over this inviting moist bush of cunney hair. Erika threw back the eiderdown and then moved one hand upwards to rub Susie's erect tawny nipples as she breathed: 'What a glorious little notch you have, darling! You must let me pay homage to its beauty.'

'Erika, stop it at once, that's extremely naughty of you,' Susie scolded her. But she made no attempt to move Erika's hand when the Danish girl placed it firmly on the fluffy fuzz of light brown cunney hair which shielded Susie's pouting pussey lips.

'Naughty but nice,' concurred Erika as she pulled open Susie's cunney lips and gently rubbed her knuckles back and forth across the entrance to her moistening slit. This insistent frigging of her sensitive quim soon made Susie change her tune. In no time she was purring with pleasure as she lay back on the pillow and let the tingling waves of ecstasy sweep through her trembling body.

'Oh yes, please bring me off, you wicked thing,' she sighed and began wriggling with delight when Erika eased first one and then a further two fingers into her cunt, sliding them in and out of Susie' sticky honeypot at an ever-quickening pace.

Erika moved herself up over the writhing girl, still keeping her busy fingers working relentlessly inside Susie's sopping pussey whilst they exchanged a passionate open-mouthed kiss. My cock shot up to bursting point when Susie rolled over onto her side and I saw her dimpled buttocks tense as Erika toyed with her clitty. I grasped hold of my shaft to position my knob in between her gorgeous little dimpled bum cheeks.

'Aaaaah! Aaaaah!' shrieked Susie in blissful agony as she was brought to the very brink of a cum by Erika's skilful finger-fucking. Her cries of delight were so loud that only Alexa could have heard the opening and closing of the bedroom door. She tapped me on the shoulder and giggled, 'Andrew, turn over and say hallo to our visitor.'

'Oh no,' I muttered softly, for my first thoughts were that the newcomer must be Katie who had come in and caught me threshing around in bed with her cousin and the twins. I groaned in despair as I heaved myself over to face the music. However, to my great and perhaps undeserved relief, it was not Katie standing beside us with a thunderous frown on her face but none other than Ian Pethick who must have managed to escape from his guided tour of the old church at Upper Chagford – and from his wide-eyed look at what he had missed, Ian was now desperate to make up for lost time!

'It took me half an hour to get away, but I hope I'm not too late to join in,' panted the missing guest. On receiving a chorus of approval, he began tearing off his clothes as Erika generously rolled off Susie to let him finish fucking the lovely girl who was trembling with lust. Ian yanked down his drawers and his quivering shaft stood sky-high, slamming up against his belly as he ran round the bed and jumped in next to Susie who sat up and took hold of the throbbing tool that stood up so eagerly before her.

'Give him a good suck to begin with,' advised Alexa. Susie nodded as she bent forward and began licking his hairy scrotum, flicking the tip of her tongue around the wrinkled pink-skinned sack. Ian gurgled his appreciation when Susie opened her lips wide and crammed both his balls inside her mouth, gently sucking them as he wordlessly gasped out his delighted excitement.

Susie was also clearly enjoying herself, although after a while she released him and held the uncapped dome crown of his cock in front of her face. She washed her tongue over the smooth surface of his bell-end before stuffing the rubicund helmet back between her lips. Then she gobbled about half of his thick blue-veined truncheon into her mouth and bobbed her head up and down his cock whilst Ian clutched her head in his hands as Susie slurped uninhibitedly on her fleshy lollipop.

The delectable little minx paused for a moment and with her mouth filled with Ian's pulsing prick, she looked up at him as if to enquire whether he was enjoying this delicious tonguing.

'Carry on, don't stop!' Ian croaked out. She smiled and wet her lips before resuming her work, running her tongue along Ian's shaft as her head dipped back and forth. When it became clear that he was about to cum, she gripped the base of his cock and sucked and swallowed even faster whilst she tickled him under his balls to speed the flow. Almost immediately, a stream of creamy jism erupted into Susie's mouth and Ian's prick bucked uncontrollably as she held his knob lightly between her teeth. Alexa, Erika and I looked on admiringly as she managed to gulp down every drop of his spunky ejaculation, lapping around the bulging knob and licking up the last salty drops from his shrinking shaft.

'Now you can fuck me,' Susie breathed. But Ian had spent so copiously that he was unable to achieve another hard-on despite the other two girls giving her a helping hand in kissing, rubbing and sucking his drooping prick.

However, *my* cock was in a state of avid, unbridled lust. I crawled behind Susie and parted her peachy bum cheeks with my hands to insert my bursting boner below them. As the tip of my bell-end touched her cunney lips, Susie turned her head and when our lips met in a burning kiss, she drew my tongue into her mouth and cleverly wiggled her bottom so that I was able to embed my knob deep inside her juicy cunt.

With a passionate jolt of our loins, my eight-and-a-half inch shaft was fully sheathed. She cried out with glee as I began to fuck her and our hips worked away in unison. How tightly her sopping slit clasped my cock! We gloried in each tremendous thrust while her love juices dripped upon my balls as they slapped against the backs of her thighs.

Our voluptuous fucking fired the other girls up so much that they tried again to stiffen Ian's flaccid shaft. Alas, his cock was *hors de combat* and so Erika rolled her sister onto her back and began to tongue Alexa's ear whilst she pressed her taut nipples between her fingers. Then she dipped her face quickly down to Alexa's soft nest of flaxen pussey hair and this excited the other girl almost beyond endurance.

Dipping her face close, Erika inhaled the heady aroma of an aroused cunney. Then she began to lick out her sister's snatch, forcing her tongue inside the quivering wet love tunnel, sliding it up and down the slit, pushing and probing as Alexa rubbed herself off against her lips.

Naturally, this stimulating sight affected us and Susie threw back her head in sheer ecstasy, tossing her mane of glossy hair over her shoulders as she urged me to drive my cock deeper and deeper. With her rounded bum cheeks cupped in my palms, she writhed savagely whilst my sinewy shaft rammed in and out of her dripping honeypot.

'Y-e-s-s-s! Y-e-s-s-s! Y-e-s-s-s!' she screamed and I could feel the throbbing of Susie's cunney muscles increase to spasm point. When she finally spent with shuddering cries of release, within seconds great gushes of jism spurted out of my twitching tool and creamed every nook and cranny of Susie's clingy quim. We collapsed down together in each other's arms and I grinned when I saw that Ian Pethick's todger had regained all of its former strength and was standing up to attention between his wiry thighs.

'Better late than never,' exclaimed Alexa when Ian moved round on his knees behind her. She felt him duplicate my actions with Susie and push his newly erect prick between her bum cheeks. 'You can smear some cold cream on your cock and go up my arse, if you like. Don't be shy, I really have a fancy to be bum-fucked.'

Erika passed him a jar from the side table next to the bed. Ian greased his tool and then directed his knob towards the tiny

185

starfish-shaped rosette of Alexa's rear dimple. At first she gave a little yelp of discomfort but the cold cream worked like a charm and she wriggled her arse until Ian's cock was safely inside her back passage. For a brief moment he rested and then, taking a deep breath, he threw his arms around Alexa's waist and frigged her cunney whilst he began to plunge his prick in and out of the now-widened rim of her puckered little arsehole.

This double stimulation made Alexa squeal as she squirmed under the surging strokes of his shaft and she cried out joyfully: 'A-h-r-e! A-h-r-e! I'm cumming, Ian. I'm cumming! Empty your balls in my backside, you randy rascal!'

Her love juices flowed freely as Ian flooded her bottom with a copious discharge of sticky seed and continued to work his prick to and fro until, with an audible 'pop', he unplugged his cock from her bum-hole.

The insatiable girls were ready to carry on with this orgy but I pleaded the absence of time for we all still had to bathe and change into our evening clothes. True as this was, masculine pride caused me to omit the other reason for finishing this glorious bout of fucking – which was that Ian and I were frankly exhausted from our labours!

So the pair of us slid out of the bed and started to dress ourselves whilst the girls continued to play with each other, with Erika and Susie rubbing their pussies together while Alexa climbed on top of Susie's back and brought herself off by frigging her clitty with her left thumb and forefinger and Susie's cunney with the fingers of her right hand.

'I've always maintained that the fellow who said that women were the weaker sex was a damned fool,' I whispered to Ian who gave a throaty chuckle as he pulled on his trousers and nodded: 'Yes, though I feel our pricks both performed with distinction.

'Come to my room for a drink and I'll explain why, old boy,' he added quietly. Frankly, I was rather surprised to hear Ian make this slightly self-satisfied comment for whilst I was

186

happy enough with my own efforts, he had been unable to fuck Susie after she had sucked him off – not that my own cock had been an unwilling substitute! On the other hand, he did manage to summon enough strength to cork Alexa's arse, so I dare say his prick deserved its accolade – although I thought than an assessment that gave it a 'very satisfactory' mark would have been more appropriate.

Therefore I accepted Ian's invitation as I was curious to hear the reason for his apparent complacency. 'I can't stay too long though, *tempus fugit*,' I added as I followed him up the stairs to his second-floor bedroom.

'Of course, it would be most rude to Katie if we were late after being specifically requested to come downstairs by half-past seven,' he concurred as he waved me to a chair and pointed to a small cluster of bottles on his sideboard. 'Now, will you join me in a whisky and soda or would you like a cognac or a glass of a fairly good claret?'

I said that I needed to keep a clear head for the evening's entertainment and that truthfully I would prefer a mineral water. 'Then that's what you shall have, my dear chap,' Ian said lightly as he waved me to a chair whilst he poured out a glass of fizzy Apollinaris which he handed to me before mixing himself a large whisky and ginger ale.

'Cheers!' he said as he sat down opposite me. He chuckled as he sipped his drink and said to me: 'You know, Andrew, I'm quite an avid reader. I must get through at least two novels a week and sometimes I get rather cross when the plot turns on what I consider to be unlikely coincidences.'

'Yes, indeed,' I agreed warmly. 'I ploughed through a daft detective story last week which hinged on the hero's girlfriend being able to remember a scar on the murderer's face when she saw him having breakfast with her uncle three years later in the dining room of the Hotel Crillon in Paris.'

Ian smiled: 'Precisely so – and yet strange coincidences *do* occur, as I can testify from what happened to me this afternoon. Now, I'm sure that Jack Dennison and the twins must have told you how I was dragged off by Reverence Ridout who wanted to show me some interesting features of his church. Quite honestly, I should have been more forceful with him because I would far rather have spent the time in a romp with those gorgeous Danish girls!

'But before I could think of an excuse to refuse him, I found myself walking to Upper Chagford with the vicar. He was burbling on about his seventeenth century pews and pulpit when we heard the pitter-patter of the approach of another traveller. We stopped and turned to see a pretty girl hurrying towards us. She was dressed for the heat of the afternoon in a linen blouse and a white tennis dress which barely reached more than an inch or two below the knees of her uncovered legs.'

He leaned forward and added emphatically: 'And when I say she was pretty, I really mean it. She was a lovely rosy-cheeked girl of about eighteen with a saucy little nose and pouting lips. When she came up to us my heart started to pound as I watched the clearly visible heaving of her proud young breasts while she recovered from her exertions.

'Obviously, this entrancing creature was known to Reverend Ridout for he said to her affably: "Heather, my dear! Is something wrong? I saw you only half an hour ago cycling along the track to General Goldstone's fields with your portable easel and a box of paints strapped to the back of the bicycle. Dear me, I trust this luggage did not affect your steering and cause a collision with the General and Mrs Goldstone who often take a short constitutional round their grounds after tea."

'Two delectable dimples appeared on either side of her sweet mouth when she replied: "No, the easel weighs very little as it is made out of bamboo and I reached my destination without any difficulty. But I do have a problem because Anthony Goldstone was supposed to meet me at half-past four sharp but he hasn't showed up."

'Reverend Ridout turned to me and quietly murmured: "Miss Colchester is referring to General Goldstone's eldest son who is studying to become a veterinary surgeon. Anthony is an extremely clever young chap but I'm afraid he's well-known for being rather absent-minded."

The dimples vanished as the girl said crossly: "I can certainly see how he acquired that reputation, vicar. He's let me down badly because I need to complete my portfolio which must be sent with my application to study art at Girton College and Anthony was supposed to sit for me this afternoon."

' "Well, can I be of any assistance?" I asked her. "I've an hour or so to spare and if all I have to do is sit still, I'll be happy to be of service."

'She looked across at me and her dimples reappeared as she answered: "How very kind of you, Mr, um—" and the vicar explained: "Oh, do forgive me, my dear, I should have introduced you – Mr Pethick, this is Miss Heather Colchester who lives at Hinckley Grange, just a mile up the road on the outskirts of Chagford. Heather, may I present Mr Ian Pethick who is staying at Judson Manor for a few days."

'We shook hands and I said to Reverend Ridout with as much regret as I could muster that I would have to look over the church at some other time.

' "By all means, Mr Pethick," he said kindly. "After all, one has a duty to help a damsel in distress."

'I was pleased that he did not feel too badly about my unexpected departure. Heather and I chatted in a friendly fashion as we walked back to where she was supposed to have met her missing model and a very nice spot it was too, a secluded glade surrounded by a forest of trees. Heather had brought a Thermos flask and whilst we refreshed ourselves with a cool drink of ginger beer, she explained to me why it was so important for her to complete her portfolio of sketches.

' "Is there still much prejudice against women artists?" I enquired. Heather gave a wry smile as she replied: "As much as there ever was, unfortunately. There is still a bar on women at several meeting places such as art clubs or, heaven forbid, becoming pupils for lectures on figure studies at many studios.

189

So I am especially grateful to you for offering to sit for me this afternoon. Gosh! I can hardly wait to begin! If you've finished your ginger beer, I'll get out the sheet from my saddle-bag which you can put your clothes on whilst you get undressed."

' "Get undressed?" I repeated blankly. "Why should I do that?"

' "Well, how else can I draw the undraped male figure?" she retorted. Seeing the shocked look on my face she sighed: "Oh, Ian, you're not going to let me down as well, are you? I'm sure that Anthony didn't simply forget to come but took fright at the last minute. Heaven knows why, he might not have such a strapping figure as you but I'm sure that there is no part of his body which he should want to hide."

'So this was why Heather had been so effusively grateful when I proffered my services as an artist's model! However, I decided it would be caddish to go back on my word and I said slowly: "Go and get the sheet for me, I shan't let you down."

' "Oh, thank you, Ian!" she cried excitedly as she ran over to the bicycle which was propped up against a nearby willow tree. Nevertheless, I still hesitated. Sensing my modesty, she spread out the sheet and then said encouragingly: "Come on, Ian, there's really nothing to it. Look, if it makes you feel less inhibited, I'll take off my blouse and skirt. It's so nice and warm that I'll feel more comfortable working in just a chemise."

'This ploy neatly closed off any avenues of retreat. I sat down on the stump of a felled oak and removed my shoes and socks. Then I shyly turned round and slipped off my jacket, shirt and vest before unhooking my belt and pulling down my trousers and underpants together and slowly stepping out of them. Stark naked, I turned back to see Heather had indeed taken off her top clothes and was clad only in a camisole over which the swell of her creamy breasts was all too visible. I had to begin a fierce concentration on the conjugation of an irregular Latin verb to prevent my prick from stiffening up there and then!

'Heather said nothing as she chose a charcoal pencil from her case before asking me to go over and lean against the willow tree and to keep as still as possible. I complied with this request and, surprisingly enough, the fact that I was standing in front of her in a state of complete nudity soon began to fade in importance. She chatted away gaily as she worked and complemented me by saying: "Your body is well suited to a figure study, Ian. You have the necessary striking physique and, more importantly, you exude the confident pose of a man who believes himself able to surmount any obstacles that might occur in the future – not just through brute physical strength but by the sheer force of your personality.

' "Now, please try to stay perfectly still as I want to capture a clear-cut profile of your face with that proud look of determination stamped upon your brow," she continued as she put the final touches to the sketch which she then tore off the large pad of paper set up on her easel. She placed it face down upon her case.

'When Heather had finished three further sketches, she thanked me again for my patience and said that she was very satisfied with what she had managed to do. Naturally, I could hardly wait to walk across and see what likenesses of me she had committed to posterity. But Heather stepped forward and, placing her hand on my chest, she said: "No, Ian, I would rather you didn't see these rough outlines. But if you write down your address, I'll gladly send a finished portrait to you."

'I must have looked very disappointed because she looked at me with a mischievous gleam in her eyes and added: "Never mind, Ian, you'll just have to wait for a week or two. Meanwhile, though, I would like to give you a little present for helping me. Perhaps something along these lines appeals to you?" '

Ian gulped down the rest of his whisky and exclaimed: 'Andrew, I could hardly believe what happened next, but I promise you that this lovely young girl then reached out with her hand and began stroking my cock! This instantly made my shaft swell up to a pulsing erection as she allowed her fingers to trace a path around and underneath my balls.

' "Oh, I say," I gasped as she closed her fist around my burgeoning boner, sliding her fingers along its length as she dropped to her knees. With an impudent grin on her face she looked up at me and said: "Say what, Ian? How nice it is to feel me frigging your big cock with my hand?"

'Trembling with joy, a wordless growl escaped from my throat as Heather licked her lips and went on: "Well, if you think *that* feels good, tell me what you make of *this*."

'With that, she leaned forward. Her pink tongue shot out and licked my shaft from tip to base and back again. I clung to Heather's tousled mop of curls as she planted a series of butterfly kisses on my rampant rammer. Then she opened her mouth wide and jammed my tool inside its delicious wetness. Her head bobbed up and down wildly and when she rolled her tongue cunningly around my knob I could feel the playful bite of her pearly teeth as she nipped the sensitive cockflesh.

'My prick began to twitch and Heather began swallowing in anticipation as she waited for the gush of creamy cum to come spurting out of my knob. "H-a-a-r-g-h!" I cried out as I filled her mouth with a fountain of hot sticky jism and she gulped down every last salty drop, licking my helmet until my cock softened under her tongue.

'Then she pulled back her head and, wiping her lips across the back of her hand, Heather hauled herself to her feet and said: "So what's the verdict, Ian? Which way do you prefer to be brought off?"

'I replied that, whilst having one's prick frigged in her clenched fist was most enjoyable, any man would tell her that being sucked off was a truly heavenly experience. She nodded her agreement and said with some slight pique in her voice: "Yes, I've often heard similar sentiments expressed by other boys, but for some reason they start to make all kinds of excuses when I suggest that they should return the compliment by kissing my pussey."

192

' "Well, you won't find *me* passing up such an opportunity," I replied with a gruff laugh. "I would be delighted to lick out your juicy little notch."

' "And I would be more than happy for you to do so," she rejoined as she stepped into her skirt. "But not here, even though it's lovely to fuck in the open air – but it would be too shaming if General Goldstone found us in a compromising position! Mind you, knowing the General, he would probably just drop his trousers and ask to join in the fun!"

'Anyhow, I've arranged to meet Heather tomorrow afternoon at her house,' concluded Ian triumphantly. 'Her parents will be out and she says that the servants can be relied on not to tell any tales.'

So it was now clear why the Pethrick prick deserved the praise heaped upon it by its owner! 'My word, you're a lucky chap. You had better not plan anything too strenuous tomorrow morning because I have a notion that none of us are going to get much sleep tonight,' I observed mildly. After finishing my glass of fizzy water I added that I had to be on my way. But as I walked to the doorway I suddenly turned back: 'Just one thing, Ian. Why did you bring me here and tell me this admittedly absorbing tale?'

He shrugged his shoulders and grinned: 'That's a good question, Andrew. Have you heard the story about old Mr Cohen who goes rushing into St Mary's Church and gasps out to his friend, Pete Murphy: "Brendan, Brendan, you won't credit it but a beautiful young girl walked into my workshop early this morning, stripped off all her clothes, bent over the table and I fucked her doggie-style. Then half an hour later her sister came in, pulled off my trousers and gave me a wonderful gobble!"

' "Abie! Abie!" the priest reproaches him. "Why are you telling me all this? You're not even a Catholic." And Mr Cohen replies: "I know, I know, but I just had to tell somebody!" '

I guffawed at this witty anecdote as I waved goodbye to Ian. I marched back to my room where I showered and shaved before donning my dinner jacket suit that I had recently sent to my tailor to be altered and that had been sent back to me only the previous week. Inside one of the pockets was a note from Mr Elbaum which read:

Dear Mr Scott,

Here's your dinner jacket suit back which I hope you will continue to wear in good health. The jacket's fine, all I had to do was give it a good press, but I've had to let out the waist of the trousers by a couple of inches. My wife Ada says that you should watch your weight, Mr Scott, you don't want to end up with a big belly like some of our other clients. Tell him to take more exercise, she says, but if the letter and photographs from a certain young lady which my son Maxie found in your trousers pocket is anything to go by, you would be better off taking it easy for a while.

Don't worry, I've thrown them all on the fire and you'll never hear a word about them again from me although Maxie wants me to tell you that should this young lady ever require a nice pair of knickerbockers, he will make them for her at below cost price.

Respectfully yours,
Sam Elbaum

P.S. I'm sure you will agree that one favour deserves another and I'd be much obliged if you would kindly settle your account by the end of the month.

Gritting my teeth, I carefully tore up Mr Elbaum's message into little pieces before dropping them into the waste-paper basket. How foolish it had been of me to keep such a personal letter, let alone those explicit photographs from Lady Cassandra Gossborough. She had sent them to me the day after we had made some private music together in her bedroom following a recital by the noted Russian violinist Herschel

194

Motkalevitch and the London Symphony Orchestra at the Royal Albert Hall.

I should explain that Lady Cassie is a keen and knowledgeable camerawoman. By the use of an ingenious delayed exposure mechanism, she had been able to take a series of excellent photographs of the pair of us entwined in a 'sixtynine' with her open mouth crammed with my cock and my tongue sliding across her pouting cunney lips.

And, to cap it all, if these prints were not damning enough, she had also sent me a detailed *billet doux* about how she would like to be fucked when I came round for tea in two weeks' time.

However, to be fair to Lady Cassie, it was hardly surprising that she was desperate for a good fuck because Sir Horatio Gossborough spent more time supervising his vast financial interests in South Africa than at home with his wife. As I remarked to Teddy Carmichael the morning after the concert, it was probably the first time that she had had a stiffie between her legs since Sir Horatio had left London on his latest voyage back in April. Teddy looked doubtful and said that it was an open secret in Society circles that the very next evening after her husband's departure, Lady Cassie dined with Count Gewirtz of Galicia at his house in Green Street, Mayfair and did not return home until the following afternoon.

Well, at least the letter and photographs had been consigned to the flames, I muttered to myself whilst I pulled out my fountain pen and chequebook from my case to settle Mr Elbaum's account. The tailor was an honourable man but I put my cheque without further delay into an envelope on which I scrawled his address because I reasoned that it would be stupid to try Sam's patience and keep him waiting for his three guineas.

It was seven twenty-five by the time I had finished dressing and I hurried down the staircase, pausing only to give Fielding instructions to post Mr Elbaum's letter as he opened the drawing-room door for me.

'Ah, there you are, Andrew!' called out Katie who looked adorable in a blue cashmere dress. The swell of her beautiful breasts was accentuated by the daringly low-cut gown. 'You've just time for a glass of Buck's Fizz before dinner.'

Hobart stepped forward with a tray from which I took a glass. Looking round at the assembled company, I raised it and toasted my fellow guests. 'Bottoms up, everybody,' I declared, a remark which left Ian and Jack the task of explaining that I was not being rather rude!

Fielding re-entered the room and announced in sonorous tones that dinner was served. I had time only to see that Susie was wearing a black gown with a similarly revealing *décolletage* as were the Danish twins who had decided to tease us by choosing identical emerald green dresses. This made it almost impossible for the rest of us to tell them apart as the girls rose to be escorted into the dining room.

Assuming I was talking to Alexa, who incidentally was the eldest by fifteen minutes of the stunning Scandinavian sisters, I said to the ravishing blonde who was standing next to me, 'Your sister and you both look lovely in you pretty dressed but please forgive me if I address you as Erika by mistake.'

However the gorgeous girl took the wind out of my sails by replying with a wide smile: 'Andrew, I would be more annoyed if you called me anything else but Erika because that is my name.'

'Oh dear, how foolish of me to make such a mistake,' I said in no little confusion, but the other girl wagged a reproving finger at her sister as she scolded her. 'Alexa, it's very naughty to tease poor Andrew like that, I shall have to punish you for being so naughty after dinner.'

'Is that a promise?' asked Alexa unblushingly as she took the arm of Ian Pethick to escort her into the dining room. Katie slipped her arm inside mine and we led the party into the dining room.

'Hurry up, Andrew, I'm feeling quite ravished,' she said to

me and I smiled: 'If that's so, how will you be feeling after dinner, my poppet?'

'Well fucked I hope,' she responded quietly and I almost choked with laughter as we strode out into the hall. By the time we reached the dining room I could hear the familiar sound of champagne corks popping and the eight of us – Katie and myself, Susie and Teddy, Alexa and Ian, Erika and Jack – enjoyed this superb repast prepared by Mrs Matlock:

Croutes de Caviare

***

Creme d'Asperges

***

Filets de Sole à la Toulouse

***

Selle D'Agneau

***

Jambon de York

***

Canetons aux Petits Pois

***

Baba au Rhum

***

Baverois aux Fruits et Glaces

[This might appear a huge feast to modern readers but the menu would have been considered relatively small by Edwardian standards when twelve courses was the norm for dinner at country house parties – and it was considered bad form to pick at your food or plead loss of appetite. No wonder that upper-class ladies were invariably stout and that a glutton like the Prince of Wales measured fifty inches around both waist and hips in 1901 when he ascended the throne – Editor]

Fielding and the retinue of footmen served champagne and fine wines throughout the meal and I must confess that Katie's parents would have considered our behaviour around the table more than a shade too boisterous for polite Society even before the footmen had cleared the table and retired to the servants' hall to gossip over a well-earned cup of tea.

For example, Katie had placed herself on my right and Erika was sitting on my left with Jack Dennison next to her. The glass of '02 Château d'Yquem dessert wine trembled in my hand when I glanced towards them and saw that the lissome girl had brazenly undone Jack's fly buttons and her fingers were now busy fumbling inside his trousers. With a flourish, she brought out his thick throbbing truncheon which stood stiffly to attention as Erika began to jerk her hand up and down his swollen shaft. Jack gurgled with delight as the touch of her artful fingers sent shivers of pleasure running through his entire frame.

Meanwhile, Teddy had risen to his feet and asked for quiet as he wished to recite a poem he had composed in honour of Susie, 'a fair English rose whose beauty is unparalleled in town or country', which he would now read aloud to the assembled noble company.

To a round of applause, he took a sheet of paper out of his pocket and declaimed:

Come Susie dear! now lay your body down
Upon my naked belly white,
Now rapture soon will embrace my crown:
This is the path to true delight.

Flowers bloom their brightest there,
Unknown fragrance fills the air.
Come, sweet Susie, grant my prayer
Kneeling I make to thee!

A pretty blush coloured Susie's cheeks whilst we gave Teddy a rousing standing ovation which was enlivened by the inevitable consequence of Erika's frigging Jack's gigantic cock. For she had not released his tool from her grasp when he rose to cheer Teddy's poetic prowess and had continued to rub her hand even more vigorously up and down his hot hard shaft. So, just as everyone else turned their attention to gape at this public tossing-off, a miniature fountain of white froth jetted out of the top of his bulbous knob in a looping arc directly into a bowl of fresh fruit salad that had been set on the table in front of him.

There was a stunned silence for a moment or two and then Katie said coolly: 'Jack, how kind of you to flavour the fruit with your tangy jism. I'm sure it now tastes quite delicious. Would you kindly ladle some out on a plate for me?'

Her remark was greeted by a roar of laughter. I turned round to him and said: 'I say, Jack, why don't you and Erika entertain us properly with a full show of *l'art de faire l'amour*?'

'Quite right, Andrew, what a splendid idea!' exclaimed Teddy heartily. 'But I'll wager a fiver that he hasn't the nerve to fuck Erika on that Turkish rug in front of the fireplace.'

'You're on, my friend, this will be the easiest fiver I've ever earned,' scoffed Jack as he stood up and began pulling off his clothes. But Susie said thoughtfully: 'Jack, don't count your chickens before they hatch. For are you certain that you can cum again so quickly?'

He grinned wickedly at her and answered: 'I don't see why not, so long as Erika is happy to give me a helping hand, so to speak.'

'Of course I will,' said the wanton girl. She bent forward and, peeling back his foreskin, licked up the remaining dribbles of spunk which glistened on Jack's knob. Then she took his shaft back into her fist while he continued to undress and in no time at all she had cajoled his cock back up to its former majestic height.

Erika now swiftly disrobed. My cock swelled up immediately at the sight of the blonde's naked charms as she and Jack walked across to the fireplace. No doubt Ian and Teddy were similarly experiencing the difficulty of finding space for their stiffstanders inside their trousers as I murmured to Katie about what exquisitely firm, uptilted breasts the lucky girl possessed! It was no wonder that Jack immediately placed his hands on her pointy red nipples and tweaked them up to a fine state of erection.

Jack took all the liberties he desired with the young Danish damsel, kissing and sucking her lovely lips and then her firm yet rubbery titties as they sank down onto the crimson-and-gold Turkish rug. He knelt between her legs and rubbed his knob along her puffy pussey lips whilst she moaned with erotic ecstasy and grappled for the uncapped helmet of his shaft which she wedged inside her juicy crack.

'Roll over, Jack, I want to be on top,' Erika panted as she grabbed hold of his arms and rolled him over onto his back. Then she climbed on top of his muscular frame and speared herself on his cock which stood as stiff as a flagpole as she rode up and down upon it.

As Erika's love channel opened up to receive Jack's thrusting tool, her juices began to flow. The slick squishing of their mating aroused not only myself but other members of the party. I looked around the table to see that Teddy and Susie were locked in each other's arms whilst Ian was caressing Alexa's breasts as their mouths jammed together in an uninhibited open-mouthed kiss.

I was about to wrap my arms around Katie when she pulled back her chair and, taking my hand, pulled me over to the sideboard from which she produced a large table cloth. She said: 'Andrew, will you please move Jack and Erika whilst I lay out this cloth on the rug? My father would be fearfully angry if he returned home to find it marked by love juices.'

'I'm afraid that we may be too late,' I replied with a grin as Jack jerked his hips upwards and Erika let out a cry of satisfaction as his thick prick reamed out her tingling cunney. 'But my old chum Lord Philip Pelham swears by Professor Goulthorp's All-Purpose Cleaning Cream for removing spunky stains. If necessary, we'll have to send the chauffeur to Oxford to buy a bottle from Boots tomorrow morning.'

'That sounds like a good idea, although I might ask you to run the errand rather than entrust a servant with such a delicate purchase,' remarked Katie as the obliging couple rolled over onto the carpet to allow us to spread out the white damask cloth over the rug.

'Now we'll have to drag them back onto the table cloth,' I muttered as I slid down on my knees. However, my services were not required because, as I placed my hands on Erika's soft and warm body, she dextrously gyrated herself and her lover towards the fireplace so that by the time they were back in their original place, she was now underneath Jack. Without breaking the rhythm of this lubricious fuck, he continued to slew his sturdy shaft in and out of her juicy snatch.

Teddy and Susie came over now to watch the fun. But before I could haul myself back to my feet, Erika's hand shot out and grabbed my own stiff cock which she could see bulging out of my trousers. 'I say, steady on,' I gasped as she tore open my fly buttons. Clamping her long fingers around my pulsing prick, the salacious young miss panted out to Jack that she wanted to revert to their previous position.

'Very well,' he croaked hoarsely, glad no doubt to have the chance of a breather whilst Erika took charge of the fuck. When she had regained her former position, Jack closed his eyes and relaxed whilst she bounced gaily up and down on his quivering cock.

Now, Jack must have been tired but Erika's blood was up. She fisted her hand up and down my shaft as she panted: 'Go and stand behind me, Andrew.'

No further explanation was required. When Erika let go of my twitching tool I looked enquiringly at Katie who immediately nodded her approval for me to fulfil Erika's lewd request. So I sidled round and undressed before I cupped her jiggling bum cheeks in my hands. At once I realized that it would be impossible to insert my cock in her cunt for that happy haven was engorged with Jack's thick chopper. But the

201

crinkled entrance to her arsehole caught my eye so I took a deep breath and prepared to bottom-fuck the lusty little vixen.

However, just as I was about to press home, Teddy came up with an open butter-dish in his hand. 'Hold on a moment, my dear chap, you should always first grease your cock before sliding it into the tradesmen's entrance.'

'Thanks, Teddy,' I mumbled as I released Erika's wiggling bum cheeks and smeared the butter over my throbbing boner, feeling ashamed at having to be reminded of a cardinal rule for this particular mode of coupling. He took the dish from me as I angled my uncapped helmet into the cleft of Erika's jouncy backside. Now I had little difficulty inserting it into the tiny entrance to the narrow sheath of her back passage.

'Aaaah! Aaaah! Aaaah!' the excited girl cried out as she gloried in the feeling of being fucked by two cocks at once. Then she asked us to stay still for a moment which we were happy to do. I must say how strangely enjoyable it was to feel my tool throbbing against Jack's shaft with only the thin membrane of Erika's anal canal between them.

But, as one would expect, once we resumed moving our cocks this exquisite sensation soon led to us spending. Erika let out a high-pitched yelp of delight as she received two libations of hot sticky jism simultaneously in her cunt and her arse.

The watching spectators (Teddy and Susie had now been joined by Ian and Alexa) broke into applause spontaneously as we disentangled ourselves. Erika took our pricks in her hands and shook out the last drainings of spunk from our glistening shafts.

'Gad, that was a magnificent poke,' puffed an exhausted Jack Dennison. 'You Danish girls certainly take the biscuit when it comes to fucking.'

'Hey, there's nothing the matter with home-grown pussey!' laughed Teddy as he caressed the creamy globes of Susie's pert tits which were barely covered by the low cut bodice of her gown. She responded by sliding my chum's jacket off his shoulders whilst she whispered some words which I could not quite catch into his ear. Teddy smiled broadly and replied: 'Well, why not darling? I'm game if you are!'

It quickly became clear that the erotic exhibition we had just witnessed had made Susie receptive to the idea of being threaded there and then by Teddy's thick tool. She adroitly undid the hooks and eyes at the side of her dress until she was able to pull it to the ground. The wanton girl was wearing only a skimpy pair of tight frilly knickers and everyone stared with unabashed lust at her superb bare breasts, each crowned by a tawny nipple set in a large rounded areola. Without further ado Teddy stepped forward and took her in his arms as she tore open his shirt.

Erika, Jack and I hastily moved ourselves off the table cloth to give Susie and Teddy some room as they sank down beside us, exchanging the most ardent of kisses as he unbuttoned his flies. Out popped his straining shaft, springing up like a miniature red-bereted guardsman between his thighs.

'Wooooh!' he gurgled wildly as Susie encircled his rigid rod with her long fingers as her tousled head plummeted down to Teddy's groin. She planted a wet kiss on his balls which she cradled in her hand. Her wet tongue fluttered out and tickled the tender crown of his cock before she opened her mouth and slowly drew his shaft into her mouth.

Teddy jabbed his todger to and fro in a frenzy of excitement. Susie's tongue slithering up and down the sensitive underside of his trembling shaft quickly brought him to the brink of an orgasm.

'I'm going to cum, I can't stop!' he cried out through clenched teeth as his cock slid in and out between her rich red lips. Susie bobbed her head up and down until, with a final juddering throb, he squirted his spunky tribute down her throat.

Susie joyfully swallowed his sticky emission and Alexa thoughtfully dipped her head to help lap up the final trickle of creamy jism which dribbled out of Teddy's knob.

Now Alexa stood up and started to unbutton her dress as she said to Ian Pethick: 'Come along, my dear, by now you should have already taken off your jacket and trousers! You do want to fuck me, don't you?'

'Of course I do,' said Ian with a flustered look on his face as he sat down on the floor to unlace his shoes. 'It's just that I thought you might feel embarrassed about, um—'

'Poking me in front of our friends?' Alexa said cheerfully as she lifted her skirt and peeled off her black stockings. 'I don't see why our chums shouldn't have some fun by watching us enjoy ourselves. Did you know that when he got older, there was a famous Danish playwright *[Thorvold Haagen (1698–1792) – Editor]* who regularly invited his friends to fuck his pretty wife, Beryl, who was twelve years younger than himself? She was happy enough with this arrangement for it excited her husband so much that after she had cum he fucked her with the energy of a sixteen-year-old boy.'

Ian still looked slightly doubtful but Teddy said encouragingly: 'Well, there you are, Ian, there's no need to feel shy. I've heard it said that Lord Nelson was another chap who liked a cosy threesome. He was supposed to be the author of an ode to Lady Hamilton which concludes:

'She opens her thighs without fear or dread,
And points to her sweet little crack,
Whose lips are so red and all overspread
With hair of the glossiest black.
Reclined on her breasts and clasped in her arms,
With her my best moments I spend;
And revel the more in her ravishing charms.
Because they are shared with a friend.'

As he finished the recital of this stirring verse, the nubile blonde girl pulled her chemise over her head to reveal her rounded milky-white breasts. She touched them lightly, her fingers brushing the perky nipples as she raised her arms to unloosen her hair.

This sensual movement lifted Alexa's breasts even higher, heightening the colour of the flushed pink circles which framed her erect little nipples.

The two lovely orbs of her ripe young breasts gently bumped together as she lowered her hands to wriggle out of her shiny silk knickers. Then Alexa ran her fingertips through her fluffy golden triangle of pussey hair and licked her lips as Ian yanked down his drawers to display his huge pulsating prick which stood up stiffly against his stomach.

We watched with growing interest as Alexa played with his chunky cock, sliding her hand up and down the throbbing blue-veined shaft as she sank to her knees and kissed the uncapped purple helmet. Then, with a downward lunge, she plunged it far into her mouth and started to suck it with all her might. Ian gurgled with delight and clutched her head in his hands as Alexa crammed more and more of his thick prick between her lips. She must have felt the tip of his knob touch the back of her throat, for she gagged for a moment and was forced to ease out an inch or so of Ian's throbbing tool from out of her mouth.

The rapturous feel of Alexa's wet lips slurping on his shaft swept aside any traces of Ian's previous inhibitions and he bucked to and fro as waves of ecstasy rippled through his body. He inhaled a series of deep breaths before growling a hoarse warning that he was about to spend. Alexa gently squeezed his balls as he shot his load into her mouth and – despite her frenzied attempts to swallow all his creamy jism – a trickle of spunk rolled down her chin and dripped down onto the table cloth.

However, even though the lascivious little vixen had milked his cock so well that it now hung flaccidly over his balls, Ian nevertheless now pushed the willing girl down on her back. He slid his hands under her thighs to fondle her chubby bum cheeks whilst he pressed his lips to her inviting cherry nipples which he kissed and sucked in fine style. Then he pulled his hands away to part Alexa's thighs and bent his head down to kiss the puffy pink lips which pouted out from her golden fluffy bush of pussey hair.

Although I could not actually see his tongue flash up and down her sopping slit, Ian Pethick clearly knew how to palate a pussey for Alexa was soon shuddering with pleasure. She gasped out: 'Enough! Enough! Please fuck me with your cock now!'

He answered this heartfelt plea instantly by clambering up on her sumptuous curves. I noted with a mix of admiration and surprise how in such a short space of time Ian's shaft had stiffened up again and was pulsing furiously in his hand as he guided it into Alexa's juicy cunt.

A loud moan from the lewd pair signalled that his lusty cock had slithered into her cunney. They kissed with an intense fervour as Alexa jerked her lovely bottom up and down to absorb as much of Ian's palpitating prick as possible.

He began by pumping in and out of her squishy furrow with long, slow strokes. When he changed the pace to one of swift, short jabs I distinctly heard his balls banging against Alexa's wiggling bum cheeks as they thrashed happily away.

'Oh my God! What a gorgeous fat cock you have!' she panted as she twisted from side to side under his fierce onslaught. 'Can you feel my cunney muscles gripping your prick as it slides in and out? Yes, yes, push it in deeper, that's the way!'

Ian readily obeyed her, slewing his sinewy shaft to and fro whilst Alexa clamped her feet together behind him to keep every inch of his rampant chopper inside her luscious quim.

'Wooooh!' Ian cried out as she sensually rotated her hips and answered his powerful plunges with upward thrusts of her own.

'I'm cumming, Ian, I'm cumming!' screamed Alexa. His body tensed as, with a savage shudder, he pumped the first gush of sticky seed into her squelchy honeypot. While she clawed at his back, he discharged spurt after spurt of spunky jism into her love funnel.

We applauded the exhausted couple who lay still for a few moments until Alexa sat up and said cheerfully: 'Thank you, Ian, that was a glorious fuck!'

'Thank *you*, Alexa,' he panted with a weak smile as he looked down on his limp shaft which had shrivelled up and lay limply on his thigh. 'I hope you will let me fuck you again a little later on if Mr Pego here can be persuaded to come out of hiding.'

A soft hand now slithered across my waist from behind to stroke my own pulsing erection. Katie's sweet voice whispered in my ear: 'Andrew, I think I can now leave my other guests to their own devices so let's retire upstairs to my bedroom.

'To be honest, I can hardly wait to be threaded by your lovely cock after watching everyone else screw themselves silly!'

The words were scarcely out of her sweet lips before I had taken hold of her hand. I guided her towards the door which I opened as I called out: 'Goodbye for now, everybody. Katie and I will see you later.'

'Where are you off to, as if I couldn't guess?' exclaimed Susie. Katie riposted: 'To be well fucked, for I have every hope of a grandstand performance by Andrew's beautiful prick. Apart from bum-fucking Erika, he has been saving himself for my cunney this evening.'

I hastily pulled her out of the room before the other girls could enlighten her on where my cock had been sheathed in the Danish twins' bedroom before dinner. So, despite the fact that I was stark naked and Fielding and the other servants were still on duty, I threw caution to the winds and rushed headlong up the stairs to her bedroom where I hugged the delicious girl tightly. Katie responded by raining eager kisses all over my face whilst I traced the circle of her mouth with my tongue which slid between her lips as she swiftly began to pull off her clothes.

207

I slowly stroked my throbbing tool whilst Katie deftly undressed herself. When she was also nude we staggered across to the bed where we exchanged a wildly passionate kiss. Then we fell upon the soft mattress and I let my hand move across her flat belly. My fingertips entangled themselves in the delicate tangle of chestnut curls which covered her delectable pussey mound.

With deliberate gentleness, I slid my hand all over Katie's hairy muff, enjoying the rub of her soft pussey hair on my skin. With my fingers pressed firmly on each side of her slit, I drew the yielding puffy love lips apart. She squirmed from side to side when I jabbed my thumb directly inside her juicy honeypot.

'O-h-h-h!' Katie moaned. She wriggled with delight when I now also piloted two fingers into her dripping wet cunt. But it was my thumb that she made her principal instrument of pleasure, rubbing her fleshy clitoris against it until her juicy cumbud protruded out of her pussey like a tiny cock.

Katie was clearly enjoying being finger-fucked in this fashion so much that I stretched her cunney lips a little wider apart. My fingers were instantly drawn deeper inside her quim as she drove me on to frig her with increasing urgency.

Now I moved my body downwards and she twisted her thighs around my head when I pressed my mouth to her luscious quim. I imprinted a long, clinging kiss on the moist chink and rubbed my nose back and forth against her clitty, inhaling the pungent cuntal aroma. Her body jerked in a frenzy of lust to meet my questing tongue as it probed her pussey, sending the sweet girl into paroxysms of delicious pleasure. With little difficulty, I soon sent Katie off into a series of heavenly spends by opening her velvet folds and playfully biting her clitty which sent fresh waves of ecstasy coursing throughout her body from the epicentre of erotic excitement between her thighs.

'H-a-a-g-h! H-a-a-g-h! H-a-a-g-h!' shrieked the glorious girl as she achieved an all-enveloping, shuddering cum which sent a deluge of cunney juice flooding into my mouth.

'Have you finished, darling?' I enquired, lifting my hips from her sopping crack. Katie's blissful sigh was answer enough so I hauled myself over her and spread her thighs with my knees as I whispered: 'Now I shall fuck you with my cock. Won't that be jolly?'

'Yes, yes, yes! I can hardly wait,' gasped Katie as she reached down to hold my pulsing prick, positioning the mushroom helmet at the entrance to her juicy honeypot. Then I pushed forward and penetrated her juicy love funnel, not stopping until my throbbing todger was fully ensconced inside Katie's slippery sheath.

'M'mm, that feels divine,' she murmured. I began fucking her in a carefully sinuous motion that ensured that my quivering cock caressed the slick walls of Katie's cunney with every luxurious stroke.

Then I reached underneath her trembling body, clasped her voluptuous cheeks with both hands and pressed the sublime young girl tightly against me as I embedded my shaft even deeper inside her sticky quim. I began to fuck her with long powerful thrusts. Now I shifted my hands up to her breasts, massaging the jiggling spheres whilst the tip of my tongue teased her nipples until they stood up in hard, pointy peaks. I pumped away until I was on the verge of orgasm.

But I quickly realized that Katie's heaving gasps indicated that she too had reached the brink. I pistoned my prick into her wet, clingy cunt just three more times before we spent together. I bucked and bounced upon the curvy contours of her soft body as I ejaculated my jism inside her.

'Did you enjoy the fuck, Andrew?' she smiled as I slumped down beside her. I panted: 'Darling, your delicious cunt has such delicate lips and gripped my cock so divinely that a couplet from Shakespeare's lost sonnet comes to mind:

'There is not in this wide world a valley so sweet
As the vale where the thighs of a pretty girl meet.'

'Thank you, my poppet, I'm most flattered – only I doubt if the Bard of Avon actually composed those lines,' giggled Katie as she gave my flaccid shaft a friendly rub. 'My own feeling is the words originated from the fertile pen of Andrew Scott or one of his friends, but let that pass. Now, if you don't mind, I would like to go downstairs and have a drink of seltzer water.'

I kissed the tip of her nose and replied: 'By all means. I'm also in need of liquid refreshment but a glass of champagne sounds far more exciting.'

She shook her tousled mop of glossy hazel hair and exclaimed in an anxious voice: 'Oh, please don't get inebriated, my angel. You will fall asleep and miss all the fun, for I have an intuition that this party will go on all night. Look, I'll slip on a robe and come with you to your room where you can put on a dressing gown before we rejoin the others. Of course, if I'm wrong, we can always come back here and continue with our own private party.'

Naturally, I concurred with this sensible suggestion. As soon as we reached the hallway it immediately became plain from the squeals of joy behind the dining-room door that the other guests had not been spending time playing ludo or snakes and ladders whilst Katie and I had been fucking ourselves silly.

Holding Katie's hand, I quietly opened the door to find that the lights had been lowered. But when Ian and one of the Danish twins (I could not see whether it was Alexa or Erika in the dim light) saw us they disentangled their naked bodies from a passionate embrace on the table cloth and Ian scrambled up on his knees. He said hoarsely: 'Oh, hallo there. Did you want us or are you looking for any of the others? Alexa and Jack went up to the billiards room and Teddy and Susie just left for his bedroom.'

I gave a little chuckle as I realized that Ian and Jack had changed partners, although our presence obviously did not bother Erika. She smiled a welcome to us as she lazily stretched out her arm and pulled a cushion off a nearby chair.

210

Next she ran her tongue lasciviously over her lips and kissed the domed bell-end of Ian's erect cock which stood majestically up against his lean belly with the tip pressed against his navel.

Then, using the cushion as a pillow for her head, the lissome blonde laid herself down on the carpet. In a flash Ian was on his knees in front of her, his head buried between her thighs and his hands running over her jutting breasts, tweaking the engorged tawny nipples between his fingers.

Ian showed us his skill at muff-diving. Erika was soon purring with pleasure as he kissed and sucked her pussey until the raunchy girl called out, 'Ooooh! Ooooh! Stop it, Ian, my cunney is all juiced up and ready for action. Now I want every inch of that beefy big cock of yours inside it!'

He did not reply but wordlessly hauled himself over Erika's trembling body with his stiff prick waggling in the air as he lowered himself down upon her. Their lips met in a burning kiss as he slid his shaft inside her squelchy cunt. Katie and I grinned at each other as we heard Ian's balls slap against Erika's bum-cheeks. Once his cock was fully embedded, Erika rotated her hips to absorb his throbbing tool and Ian's dimpled buttocks jerked up and down as he fucked the nubile young wench at a faster and faster pace.

'H-a-r-r! H-a-r-r! Keep pumping, Ian, I'm going to cum!' she shrieked and he gasped out breathlessly: 'Just as well, because I'm cumming too!'

A giant shudder ran through his wiry frame when the first frothy jet of jism cascaded out of his cock. Desperate to prolong the frenzied fire of fulfilment, Erika tightened the grip of her legs across his ribs as the electric orgasmic sensations crackled through every fibre of her body.

'I'm cumming, Ian, do more, do more!' she panted. Ian drew a deep breath and slewed his shaft to and fro at a great pace, creaming her cunney with spurt after spurt of spunky seed as he pistoned his prick in and out with all his might before collapsing down into her outstretched arms.

211

'My word, I had no idea that Ian Pethick could fuck so powerfully,' murmured Katie as we padded our way back outside into the hallway. 'I'm surprised that Alexa swopped partners with her sister – although I suppose that's being rather unfair to Jack Dennison who, I'm told, also wields a mighty member.'

'Not to worry, Katie. At this moment of time, Jack will be more concerned with how best to fuck Alexa,' I advised her as we climbed the stairs up to Teddy Carmichael's bedroom to see for ourselves what her cousin Susie and my old chum had been up to during our absence.

There we came across an erotic *tableau vivant*, but not the lascivious scene we had expected to find. For it was not Susie and Teddy who were locked together on the bed in the throes of a nude embrace, but Susie and Alexa!

Perhaps this should not have come as such a great shock because I had, after all, been in the Danish twins' bed whilst Erika had skilfully creamed Susie's cunney with her lips and tongue. Fortunately, there was no need to mention this to Katie who looked on with fascination at the uninhibited tribadic behaviour which was taking place in front of her.

It must be said that the girls were clearly having a fine old time without the benefit of their male partners – their mouths were glued together as they kissed long and hard whilst the blonde girl cupped Susie's perky breasts in her hands. After a while, Alexa released them to brush some stray wisps of flaxen hair from her face and began sensually caressing Susie's slender thighs, letting her hands stray into the mossy chestnut thatch of curls whilst Susie rubbed her own rosy nipples up to hardness between her fingers.

Then Susie gave a knowing smile as she stretched herself out. She parted her thighs to allow Alexa to dive down and nuzzle her lips against the inviting fluffy-brown bush of cunney hair. Susie lay perfectly still, enjoying to the full the thrilling sensation of the tip of Alexa's busy tongue twirling inside her cunt. She let out an ecstatic sigh as Alexa reamed out her sopping slit, teasing the puffy pussey lips, licking and lapping until the naughty pair had both worked themselves up into a perfect frenzy of lesbian lust.

'Woooh!' panted Susie when Alexa slid her mouth away from the English girl's juicy honeypot and substituted long, tapering fingers for lips. The salacious Scandinavian minx found the aroused Susie's swollen clitty straightaway and a wicked smile spread across her face as she tugged at it vigorously. Susie's lissome body threshed from side to side and when Alexa cunningly slid her hand beneath her bottom to slip a fingertip inside her bum-hole, Susie's back arched upwards as spasms of sensual excitement coursed through her cunt. She shrieked out her joy when her body exploded into a tremendous orgasm.

When the force of this delicious climax had finally melted away, Alexa fell upon her trembling female partner and they melted into a further passionate cuddle, their soft breasts sliding against each other and their tawny nipples rubbing together as they feverishly exchanged deep, open-mouthed kisses. Susie laid herself back once more, no doubt expecting her partner to suck her off again. But Katie pulled on my erect cock and whispered: 'Why don't you poke my pretty cousin, Andrew? Susie might like having a lovely girl like Alexa play with her pussey but I know that, if given a choice, she would definitely plump for a nice thick cock.'

'Well, I *would* love to fuck Susie,' I murmured. Katie chuckled: 'Well, don't stand around like a spare prick at a wedding, dear. England expects every man to do his duty!'

She pushed me forward. I stumbled towards the bed where, sure enough, Susie grabbed my cock and slid her clenched fist up and down the warm velvet shaft. Alexa generously moved over to let me take her place and make love to the ravishing girl.

'M'mmm,' purred Susie as I settled myself down on top of her soft, curvy body. My hands were instinctively drawn to her firm, creamy breasts and their taut crimson nipples and I squeezed the succulent globes whilst I moved my face towards her. Our lips and tongues brushed together in a gentle, loving kiss.

But the gentleness soon gave way to a sensual frenzy when I smoothed my hand over the flat expanse of Susie's belly and into the curly locks of silky chestnut hair which formed such an inviting hirsute triangle around her pussey. She parted her legs to allow me a view of the delectable red chink of her cunt before she sat up and kissed my twitching todger which was now pulsating furiously in expectation of the delights to come.

'What a splendid prick!' said Susie admiringly as she held my eager truncheon. 'I like this kind of well-proportioned cock which isn't too small for me to feel inside my quim or too big to take without making my pussey sore afterwards.'

I said nothing but smiled and pulled her closer to me. She responded at once to my embrace and playfully rubbed her delicious body against mine. Her mouth was at my shoulder and the tip of her head was level with my chin whilst her nipples traced tiny circles against my chest as she ground herself lustfully against me.

'H-a-r-g-h!' I growled out as I gloried in the erotic warmth emanating from this saucy little wench. My prick found its way unerringly between her legs and her pouting pussey lips brushed the tip of my knob, frigging my cock up to bursting point.

'May I ride you?' Susie enquired. When I nodded my assent she wriggled herself between my legs and, rising to her knees, she took hold of my rock-hard rod and placed it to the mark.

Then Susie pressed herself down and, effortlessly, her cunt ensheathed the entire length of my swollen shaft. She moved sideways a little before settling herself down upon me so that her bottom cheeks sat comfortably upon my thighs. When she moved her shoulders I watched in awe as her jutting breasts jiggled above me.

The gorgeous girl leaned forward and I reached up to cup

214

her breasts in my palms, squeezing and fondling the soft fleshy globes whilst she bounced up and down on my twitching todger. Her large nipples rose up like twin projectiles as I sucked them into my mouth. Susie sighed and leaned further forward, sticking out her tongue and thrusting it deep inside my mouth whilst I moved my cock upwards in time with the downward pistoning of her hips.

'Just a second, darling,' she gasped and adjusted her position slightly so that I could now feel her silky pussey hair and erect clitty rubbing along my shaft. We matched thrust with counter-thrust until I suddenly had a great fancy to fuck Susie doggie-style. Gently ungluing my lips from hers I asked if she had any objections to being taken from behind.

'Not in the slightest,' replied the submissive young miss. Obediently she turned herself over onto her elbows and knees, raising the glorious globes of her backside high into the air. Cradling her head on her arm, she looked backwards at me through the tunnel of her parted thighs with a cheerful smile and added encouragingly: 'Go on, then, Andrew: you can stick your wicked prick up my bottom, if you like.'

This was a tempting proposal for, like her breasts, Susie's bum was beautifully divided and I did indeed briefly contemplate corking my cock into the winking little eye of her rear dimple. But below it the glistening damp hair of her pussey hung down like an inviting tropical forest so I slid my shaft beneath the cleft between her jouncy bum cheeks which I clutched in my hands as I began to fuck her juicy cunney with great relish.

Susie purred with delight as I pushed in and pulled out at a steady pace while I looked down with equal pleasure at my throbbing shaft disappearing into the crevice beneath Susie's buttocks like the glistening piston of a river steamer.

I held her firmly just below her breasts as they swayed from side to side, the pointed nipples brushing against the sheet as she lowered herself even further. Still at a deliberate steady speed, I continued to fuck the trembling girl who squealed

215

with joy every time my cock plunged deeper and deeper into her squishy cunney.

'Faster! Faster! Faster!' she pleaded. I instantly raised the tempo – though not by too much because I was determined to make these marvellous moments last as long as possible and I wanted to savour every second of this magnificent poke. Also, I realized that, in all probability, Katie would shortly require my services as might one or indeed both of the luscious blonde Danish twins.

So I closed my eyes and tried to keep a tight control over my balls which were already threatening to send a gush of spunky cream hurtling out through my cock. However, try as I might, the divine sensations of reaming Susie's slippery love channel soon finished me off: a strangled cry escaped from my lips as I was forced to surrender to the delicious familiar feeling of an approaching spend. My balls tightened as, swollen with seed, they slapped against the back of Susie's thighs. I took a deep breath and began what I imagined would be the final series of powerful thrusts inside her juicy cunt.

However, Susie had sensed that the end was near for she suddenly lay down flat. Without pausing, I sank my cock deep inside her but the clever little miss did not clamp her legs together. Instead, she opened her legs even wider which allowed me to move my knob around inside her quim, plumbing any hidden nook or cranny that I had not previously touched with my straining shaft.

Her love juices were now pouring out of her pussey as the first unstoppable surge of spunk coursed its way through my cock and burst out into her welcoming love funnel. This set Susie off and the lithe girl twisted in exquisite torment as her body was racked by huge shudders when the force of her own cum rippled out of her sated pussey.

She rose to meet me as I rammed home my spurting shaft again and again. My balls banged against the back of her thighs as a tide of blissful relief slowly ebbed through me.

216

Gradually I slowed the pace of the fuck and, as the last irregular spasms shook my body, Susie gave a shriek of triumph and with one final convulsive heave lay very still in a dead faint, her arms and legs splayed out, only her breasts still jiggling from the experience of our exhausting mutual climax.

In sudden terror I rolled off her limp body. But her eyes quickly opened and Susie stared over her shoulder up at my face as her tongue snaked out and licked up a drop of moisture at the corner of her mouth. Then she rolled over and lay back again. As her hand roamed over her pussey to investigate the wetness there, she said softly: 'Oh darling, that was simply stupendous. You must promise to fuck me again before dawn.'

Now I have yet to meet the man who is not delighted to hear a woman praise his prowess between the sheets. I replied that it would be my pleasure to ram Susie's cunt again when my cock had recovered from this previous frantic spend.

To my shame, I have to admit that I had forgotten all about poor Katie who had been standing patiently by the bed whilst I ravished her cousin. She immediately protested: 'Hey, that's not very fair on me, Andrew! Surely I have first call upon your cock.'

At once I realized how I had inadvertently slighted Katie by offering my next stiffie to Susie and apologized to her for my unthinking remark. I swung my legs off the bed and said to her: 'Of course you do, Katie, please forgive me. I assure you that no offence was intended.'

'And none has been taken,' she answered with a smile as she passed me my dressing-down. 'After all, I did encourage you to fuck Susie since I believe in fair shares for all. Anyhow, why don't we go up to the games room and see what Jack and Teddy have been getting up to during the last half-hour – frankly, I'm most surprised that they would rather play billiards than fuck these two pretty girls.'

Alexa had been very quiet while she watched me fuck Susie. But now she cleared her throat as she slid her arm around Susie's waist and said: 'Of course, it's up to the boys, but as you saw when you came in, we don't need their cocks to enjoy ourselves.'

'We'll pass on that message,' I promised as we made our way out. After Katie had closed the door behind us she grinned: 'Well, I wonder whether we shall discover Jack and Teddy kissing and hugging each other in the same way as we found Alexa and Susie.'

'I very much doubt it,' I said drily. 'Teddy Carmichael has been called many names in the heat of the moment by friends and tradesmen alike but I can't recall anyone ever accusing him of being a nancy boy.'

'The same applies to Jack,' Katie agreed with an amused grin. 'I've heard all sorts of gossip about him but never anything remotely like that!'

Be that as it might, we scampered up the stairs to the games room and when I opened the door Katie and I were treated to an extraordinary sight. Jack Dennison was sitting on his haunches in the nude in the centre of the billiards table while the equally naked Erika knelt between his muscular thighs, lustily sucking his erect swollen shaft which she held in her hand. When she saw us enter, she gave us a friendly wave with her other hand but continued to bob her head up and down on Jack's thick rigid rod.

'Don't let us interrupt anything,' said Katie politely. Jack (who was clearly fast nearing his climax) looked up sharply. Placing his hands on Erika's tousled mop of golden blonde hair, he grunted hoarsely: 'With all due respect, Katie, I wouldn't let Erika stop sucking my cock for twenty thousand pounds and a baronetcy!'

I gave a tiny chuckle and looked around the room but Ian Pethick, Erika's former partner, was nowhere to be seen. However, Teddy Carmichael was standing in a corner stripped for action with his beefy cock standing high up in the air and he also acknowledged our presence with a wave of his hand. But before I could respond to his greeting, there was a low growl from Jack. I turned my attention back to the table to watch Erika clasp the base of his cock in both hands as she eased her lips back and swirled her tongue sensually over the purple uncapped dome of his knob.

There was no way that Jack could dam the tide of seed which was rising inexorably up from his tightening scrotum. With a harsh cry he ejaculated his sticky spunk-flood deep into her throat, almost choking the girl with the fierce gush of his jism. Nevertheless, Erika managed to gulp down most of his copious emission. Then she pulled his prick from her mouth so that the last dribble of creamy cum trickled down her chin. She rubbed her face into his crisp black bush of pubic curls before running the tip of her tongue around the ridge of his helmet, capturing the final drainings of his spend as it oozed out of his prick – which quickly diminished in size to dangle over his balls.

'Now fuck me, Jack,' she breathed. But her sweet sucking-off had left the poor chap *hors de combat* and, despite his frantic attempts to achieve a further cockstand by sliding his fist up and down his slick shaft, it was clear that Jack's veiny truncheon needed some time to build up its strength for a further joust.

Erika looked down in disappointment at Jack's flaccid cock but, ne'er one to leave a lady in distress, Teddy climbed up on the table and, giving his twitching tool a quick rub to bring it up to its fullest height, in a trice he pulled the blonde girl away from Jack and into his arms. With practised ease he caressed her thrilling young breasts and tweaked the tawny nipples between his fingers, making them flesh up into two rubbery stalks.

Then he laid Erika down on the smooth green baize and began to kiss her trembling body, starting from her forehead and moving down until he arrived at her moist open pussey. She was so aroused that Katie and I could smell the spicy tang of her love juices. My own cock began to thicken as I inhaled the pungent cuntal aroma and watched her guide Teddy's majestic shaft between her yielding cunney lips.

'Hard and fast, Teddy – that's how I like it,' Erika muttered fiercely as she wrapped her arms and legs around him.

'As you wish,' my chum answered as he plunged his prick into her sopping little nookie. In seconds they were locked into a hard pounding rhythm with his thick todger sliding in and out of her squelchy slit as together they rode the wind. Teddy let out an excited growl as the lascivious lass drove her lissome body upwards with undiminished delight to meet his downward thrusts, bouncing up to meet him at every fresh onslaught. Erika crossed her legs behind his back to trap his quivering cock inside her tingling love funnel. She cried out with joy as Teddy searched out every tiny wrinkle of her cunt, pistoning his prick in and out of her dripping quim with all the strength he could muster.

At this point I heard the door open behind me. I turned to see Ian Pethick silhouetted in the doorway in a blue silk dressing gown, holding a tray on which stood a bottle of champagne and four glasses. 'I've just been down to the kitchen for some refreshments,' he exclaimed as he looked across to where his erstwhile partner was being well fucked and added: 'I should have brought a dildo for that girl, she's truly insatiable.'

I'm not sure whether Erika heard this comment for, when she saw that Ian had returned, she cried out to him: 'Well, don't just stand there, come and join in!'

Nothing loath, he put down the tray and shucked off his dressing gown before jumping athletically onto the table (which was full size with eight solid mahogany legs) where he knelt down beside Erika and Teddy. Ian grabbed hold of his swollen shaft and fisted it up and down in his clenched hand.

'Oh! Oh! Oh! I'm cumming, Teddy! Fill my snatch with spunk!' Erika gasped, bucking wildly beneath him as he slammed his shaft home and shot a copious emission of jism into her sated crack. Erika arched her back to receive the creamy squirts of seed which surged out of his cock. This mutual climax rocketed through the lusty lovers with such

force that Katie and I could actually see the convulsive
running through their bodies. Ian tried to thrust his
Erika's mouth but she was flinging her head from si
in the throes of orgasm and he was unable to prevent ____
pumping spurt after spurt of creamy jism over the entwined
lovers. Oblivious to their coating of sticky seed, they
shuddered away until their movements slowed and they lay
panting and heaving together in an exhausted tangle of limbs
on the fine green baize – which I guessed was now in urgent
need of a dab or two of Professor Goulthorp's All-Purpose
Cleaning Cream.

I murmured some words to this effect to Katie who nodded
her head and said: 'Yes, we'll definitely need a bottle of that
elixir tomorrow. I'll ask Fielding to look at the cloth in the
morning after he has cleaned the rug in the dining-room.'

She grabbed hold of my stiffie as she continued: 'M'mm,
I'm glad to see that my little friend is ready for action. We can
go down to my bedroom and have a lovely fuck – but there's
no hurry, the night is young. Why don't we have a drink first
with our friends?'

'Why not, indeed. I'll open the bottle,' I replied. While I
carefully untwisted the wire around the cork, Jack reached out
a hand to assist Katie as she climbed up onto the table. I
popped the cork and poured out the sparkling wine into the
glasses which I handed round before joining the party myself.

'Cheers, everybody, Let's drink to Katie for organizing such
a wonderful evening,' I said. After we had toasted our hostess
Susie said brightly: 'Good gracious, do you know it has
occurred to me that tomorrow it will be four years to the very
night since my first fuck.'

'My word, what a wonderful memory you have,' I said
admiringly. 'Please allow me to offer my congratulations.'

'Thank you, Andrew,' she continued blithely, 'and come to
think of it, I will also be celebrating the anniversary of my
second and third fucks as well.'

'It must have been a very exciting evening,' commented

221

Ian. Susie nodded: 'It certainly was, my dear. One evening and three fucks one after the other, though naturally there was an extended interval between the second and third couplings.'

'You certainly started with a bang,' chuckled Katie and we all laughed whilst Susie wagged a reproving finger at her cousin. 'Don't be coarse or I shan't tell you about it.'

'Oh, but you must, my sweetheart,' said Alexa warmly as she took hold of Susie's hand. 'You know how we love to hear all about such naughty things. See, the boys' cocks are already stirring whilst as for me . . .' Her voice trailed off as she placed Susie's hand between her legs and squeezed her thighs together.

'You wicked girl, your pussey is all wet,' scolded Susie although she made no attempt to pull her hand away. From the satisfied look on Alexa's face, I am sure that Susie started then and there to slide a finger into the blonde girl's juicy honeypot as she began her fascinating confession: 'It happened only a month after I had celebrated my sixteenth birthday. I was still a virgin, although my hymen had long since gone due not only to horseriding at home during the school holidays but also to the attentions my cunette had received from other girls at Miss Godfrey's Academy for the Daughters of Gentlefolk. For, as one might imagine, many of the older girls, deprived of any contact with the opposite sex, naturally developed close inter-feminine friendships of an intimate nature.

'My own favourite bedmate was Claudia Kyle, a beautiful half-Italian girl with shiny jet-black hair. We often used to sleep together after the duty mistress had made her nightly round to switch off the lights.

'Well, on this particular summer night I had arranged to slip out and go to the guest room which was occupied by Colin, Miss Godfrey's nephew, who was staying with his aunt for the first fortnight of the University vacation. We had fallen for each other after meeting at the school's Spring Ball and we had corresponded ever since. Without wishing to sound immodest, I think that it was my presence rather than the obligation of a

222

family duty visit to his aunt that made Colin come straight down to Hampshire from Trinity College Cambridge where he was reading for a degree in mathematics.

'Anyhow, I was already tingling with anticipation when Claudia swept into our bedroom (it was a small school and most senior pupils shared with just one or two other girls). Pulling off her nightdress, she jumped straight into my bed.

' "Susie, I'm feeling very sensual tonight," she said as we hugged each other. "So off with your nightdress, I'm going to frig your pussey till your cunt is all nice and juicy."

'Without further ado she covered my face in kisses whilst she caressed my breasts and toyed with my nipples before inserting her finger into my moistening quim. She whispered: "There, isn't that nice?"

' "Oh yes!" I panted. Then, begging Claudia to shove her fingers further up my cunt, I squeezed my thighs together whilst the lovely girl eagerly finger-fucked me faster and faster until she brought me off and I covered her fingers with my warm, creamy spend. She wanted me to repay the compliment but I was keen to see Colin so I told Claudia that I would lick her pussey out in the morning. Luckily, this promise satisfied her and she slipped across to her own bed. In no time at all she fell fast asleep.

'Quietly, I threw on a robe, tip-toed out and made my way to Colin's room. I gently pushed open the door – but there was no sign of the good-looking young man so I closed the door behind me and laid down on his bed to wait for his arrival. I laid my head on the pillow and closed my eyes as I recalled what had happened the last time Colin and I had been together in this room some three months before. We had sneaked in here after the school danced and kissed amorously on this very bed. I had allowed Colin to cup my breasts in his hands whilst I had somewhat nervously stroked the enormous bulge between his thighs. However, I had resisted his attempts to put his hand up my skirt even though I did enjoy the sensation of his palm pressing down upon my

223

pussey through the fine silk material of my dress.

'My hand snaked down and slid inside my robe as I gently frigged myself while I waited for the dear lad, dipping my fingers slowly in and out between my puffy pussey lips. Then I suddenly heard a stifled cough and, opening my eyes in a flash, I saw him standing at the foot of the bed with a book in his hand and an amused smile playing about his lips.

' "Colin, you're very naughty to frighten me so!" I scolded the handsome young scoundrel as I pulled my hand away from my pussey and covered myself with my robe.

' "Oh Susie, I'm sorry for startling you," he apologized. He sat himself down next to me and went on: "I went down to the store room to get out this book from the suitcase in which I had hidden it because I thought the contents would be of interest to you."

'I stretched out my hand and, taking the slim leather-bound volume from him, I opened it and read out the title page: "*Human Procreation Explained for Boys and Girls* by Doctor Jeffrey Burton, Emeritus Professor of Psychological Medicine, Edinburgh University."

'As it happens, I could have told Colin that I was already acquainted with Doctor Burton's excellent work but instead I said teasingly: "Now I wonder why you wanted me to read such a book? Maybe you thought it would help the progress of our physical relationship and—"

'My voice trailed off as I looked down at the bulge that had formed between his thighs. Colin took hold of my hand and placed it on his throbbing shaft as he blurted out: "Yes, you're absolutely right and I'm not ashamed to admit it. May I show you what a glimpse of your sweet little pussey is doing to me?"

' "Of course you may, Colin." I answered without hesitation. "After all, as you've already had a peek at my naked charms it's only fitting that I should see yours."

'The handsome scamp needed no further bidding and he swiftly shucked off his clothes to stand naked before me. Now, I must say that Colin was a real young Adonis with a broad hairless chest, narrow waist and fine long legs, but naturally my eyes were chiefly riveted to his beautiful big cock which was standing up stiffly with the tip of the knob pressed against the dimple of his belly button. As if in a dream, I reached for this pink-headed monster and, though I had never taken a prick in my mouth before, my lips were drawn as if by an invisible magnet to its mushroom dome. I kissed the uncapped helmet and, when I swirled my tongue over the smooth skin, a tiny blob of pre-cum came out of the tiny "eye". I licked this up and swallowed it. Ah, it tasted so masculine with its delicious salty tang that I closed my lips tightly over his knob and circled the base of his thick boner with my fingers. Then I eased my face downwards to take in more of his throbbing tool inside my mouth and Colin sighed with delight as he gently pushed my head further down his shaft – but then I choked on this fleshy lollipop and was forced to release his cock as I came up for air, gasping and spluttering for breath.

' "Don't worry, Susie," he whispered reassuringly. "Why don't you just rub my cock instead whilst I play with your gorgeous titties?"

'He slid into the bed beside me and reached for the tie at the neck of my nightdress, tugging on the ribbon which opened the garment, and I signalled my assent to his suggestion. Our mouths met in a burning kiss and Colin began to flick at my hard little nipples, exciting me even more as my hands slid over his erect cock and the wrinkled ballsack underneath it. I cupped his hairy balls and gently massaged them, then I grabbed his shaft in both hands, one on top of the other, and slid them up and down his hot truncheon. I already possessed some experience of tossing boys off and I pumped his glistening shaft so well that in no time at all Colin's cock was jerking uncontrollably between my fingers. A low sigh escaped from his lips as he squirted out jets of frothy white seed over my hands.

'I was fascinated at the sight of his spending but, being a young man in prime condition, Colin did not have to rest before carrying on with our sensual adventure. He gave his cock a quick rub and instantly it shot up back to its full height whilst he pulled me to him and kissed me deeply, his tongue parting my lips and twisting inside my mouth. His strong hands were now on my bum cheeks which he pulled apart. I gave a yelp of surprise when he pushed the tip of his little finger into my arsehole.

'At the same time I could feel his cock beating stiffly against my tummy. I twisted and writhed in Colin's embrace as his free hand slid back from my bottom to his shaft which he rubbed sensually against my fast moistening crack.

'For just a moment he drew back. "Are you sure, Susie?" he asked, his voice husky with desire. "We don't have to carry on further so if you want me to stop . . ."

' "Hush, Colin!" I murmured in his ear. "Action, not words, if you please."

'He smiled and began my first fuck by moving his head down and parting my legs before kissing my sopping slit. I shall never forget how the tip of his tongue tickled my clitty and how I twisted my thighs around his head as he sucked the pungent love juice which was now pouring out of my juicy cunt.

'Then Colin raised himself over my trembling body and pressed his cock against my yielding pussey lips. The dear lad jiggled his knob between them, just inserting an inch or so, and when he realized his cock would meet little resistance, he slid fully home. He was a very considerate boy and let his cock rest still inside my love channel for a few moments to give me time to feel how I liked having his hot, hard prick inside me and how well suited my cunney was to hold and keep it there.

' "I'm not hurting you, am I?" he asked anxiously. But I shook my head, for in truth there was only a moment of slight discomfort which quickly changed to a delicious sensation as his shaft slicked into my sticky wet honeypot, in and out, in and out. Colin thoughtfully pulled my love lips apart with his hand to ease the passage of his thick prick.

' "Oooh, this is wonderful," I panted as I felt his ballsack slapping against my bum cheeks. "Are you really poking me, Colin?"

' "I certainly am," he assured me. "I'm fucking your tight little cunt with my cock. Have you had enough or shall I carry on?"

' "Don't stop! Don't stop!" I beseeched him and now he raised the pace, thrusting faster and faster into my ripe young pussey with all the energy he could muster. I was now well past the point of no return but I had enough sense to croak out that he should be careful not to shoot his spunk inside me.

' "I won't," he promised and sure enough, when he was about to spend, Colin pulled his quivering cock out of my cunt and, with a loud groan, spurted a fountain of creamy jism all over my belly. I rolled my fingers in the sticky pool and licked them clean, enjoying the tangy flavour of his cum, and then Colin collapsed down on me. We lay happily in each other's arms until we heard the church clock strike eleven and I hauled myself out of the bed and slipped on my nightdress.

' "Oh Susie, why must you go? I would love you to stay the night," he said lovingly. But I told Colin that I had to get back to my bed in case his aunt made one of her nightly inspections of the bedrooms and dormitories which she was often wont to do before she herself retired for the night.

'Anyhow, I must confess that the next morning I told Claudia all about how I had crossed the Rubicon into womanhood and – well, I should have known better than to have confided in her because within twenty-four hours, news of my escapade had reached the ears of Miss Godfrey. Luckily, she was unaware that it was her nephew who had fucked me but I was given a severe warning as to my future behaviour and Colin was sent packing the very next day, presumably because of the risk to his chastity that my sinful presence posed.'

She gave a little chuckle and concluded: 'Colin and I keep in touch but I haven't seen him for at least three months. However, we have both been invited with our families to Sir

227

Rodney Burbeck's annual ball at the Savoy Hotel, London in aid of the East End Milk Funds next month and I dare say we may well sneak away to some quiet place before the last waltz!'

There was a brief moment of silence as Susie finished her raunchy story. Then, whilst we congratulated her on regaling us with such a fascinating tale, Katie whispered urgently in my ear: 'Quickly now, Andrew, come with me.'

Hand in hand we raced across the landing to her bedroom. There we flung ourselves on the bed and fell into a wildly passionate embrace. We helped each other out of our dressing gowns and lay naked as we kissed rapturously, sliding our tongues into each other's mouths as I clasped Katie to me with my left arm whilst I frigged her dripping wet quim with my right hand. She opened her legs wider and I gloried in the view of the luscious red chink of Katie's cunt and of her stiff fleshy clitty which protruded out from between her pussey lips.

With a twinkle in her eye, she gazed up at me and said: 'Well, I hope your cock is raring to go because after watching and hearing about all my guests' sensual escapades, I'm dying to be fucked!'

'And so you shall be, my angel,' I said tenderly as I hauled myself up onto my knees between her shapely thighs and hooked her legs over my shoulders so that her delectable backside was lifted high into the air. Katie gurgled with anticipation as I slid my hands under her jiggling bum-cheeks while she took hold of my throbbing boner and guided my knob into her sopping cunt.

'H-a-r!' she gasped as I slid my rod inside her welcoming honeypot. But, remembering how Susie had told us how much she had enjoyed the feel of a motionless cock in her cunney, I stayed still so that Katie too could enjoy to the full the delicious sensation of having her love funnel filled with my swollen shaft.

Then, slowly and surely, I pumped in and out of her soaking slit. As I pumped my pulsating prick to and fro, her love juice dripped down onto my balls as they slapped against her jouncy bum-cheeks. Cupped now in my palms, these same dimpled arse-globes rotated savagely as I pounded away and her kisses rained upon my neck as a series of electrifying climaxes crackled through her body.

'Oh Andrew, I can't take much more, you lovely big-cocked boy,' she gasped breathlessly. 'Just spunk into me as soon as you can!'

So I plunged down hard upon her in one final energetic burst and drenched the depths of her cunt with a fierce gush of creamy white seed.

When we had recovered we rejoined the others. They had all gathered in Teddy Carmichael's bedroom and we finished the evening's entertainment with a glorious 'daisy chain' in which I fucked Katie doggie-style whilst she sucked Erika's titties. At the same time, Erika's bottom was filled by Teddy's noble tool whilst Alexa lay on the carpet with her head between his legs sucking at his balls as she held Ian Pethick's cock in one hand and Jack Dennison's in the other whilst Susie crouched over her face to let her lick out her dripping pussey as she bent down to nibble on the Danish girl's pointy nipples.

In the end, after we had collapsed into a sweaty heap of naked bodies, I wiped the perspiration off my brow and remarked to Teddy that perhaps we had overdone things somewhat. But he shrugged his shoulders and grinned: 'I wouldn't say that, my dear chap. As the Italians say, *quando viene il desiderio, non e mai troppo!**'

* When desire comes, it is never excessive.

229